Understanding
Women

Books by C. W. Smith

Novels

Thin Men of Haddam

Country Music

The Vestal Virgin Room

Buffalo Nickel

Hunter's Trap

Short Fiction

Letters from the Horse Latitudes

Nonfiction

Uncle Dad

UNDERSTANDING WOMEN

a novel by

C. W. SMITH

TCU Press

Fort Worth, Texas

Library of Congress Cataloging-in-Publication Data
Smith, C. W. (Charles William), 1940-
Understanding women : a novel / by C. W. Smith
p.   cm.
ISBN 0-87565-189-5 (alk. paper)
I. Title.
PS3569.M516U53   1998
813'.54-dc21   98-14563
CIP

The passages quoted on pages 108-109 are from
On the Road by Jack Kerouac. Copyright © 1955, 1957 by Jack Kerouac;
renewed © 1983 Stella Kerouac; renewed © 1985 by Stella Kerouac and Jan
Kerouac. Used by permission of Viking Penguin. a division of Penguin
Putnam Inc.

Book design and cover illustration by
Barbara M. Whitehead

To Marcia

ONE

The year I turned sixteen, my parents let me spend the summer with my Uncle Waylan and Aunt Vicky, but had they known more about the lives of my host and hostess, they'd have nixed the plan for sure.

On Easter eve Uncle Waylan and Aunt Vicky stopped in Dallas on their way home to New Mexico. They'd visited her folks in Baltimore, where they had motored (that quaint verb!) in Uncle Waylan's new '56 Mercury. They'd also toured Washington because Aunt Vicky thought it important for him to see the nation's capital. Though they'd been married three years, my family had not met her. From knowing Uncle Waylan's first wife, Aunt Noreen, and subsequent girlfriends, I'd expected a dolled-up lounge lizard, a cow-gal, a barmaid or waitress wearing tight slacks and sporting large costume jewelry in the shapes of, say, fruits or vegetables. Uncle Waylan's usual formers wore bright lipstick and flung their outsized personalities about with the huzzah of circus barkers. It didn't bother them to tickle-wrestle with Uncle Waylan before an audience of adults or trade licks bicep-to-bicep. Once one offered to share the gum from her large moist mouth. They were as awesome as Amazons.

My new Aunt Vicky wore black-rimmed glasses and a blue calf-length dress; she said she believed the Rosenbergs were innocent and that the cherry blossoms in Washington had made her think of *haiku*. We were seated in our living room on Amherst that distant Saturday afternoon, my father drawing on his pipe and my mother quietly blinking while Uncle Waylan and Aunt

1

Vicky chain-smoked Phillip Morrises from a pack on the table between the matching brocade wing chairs in which visiting couples were customarily enthroned, though it wasn't usual for the male to sling a booted leg over one chair arm. Beyond the bay window behind them, my sisters Alise and Diedre were playing hopscotch on the front walk.

My mother didn't know a *haiku* from a "Heil, Hitler!" Neither did I, so I asked.

"Oh, I'm sorry," my new aunt said. "It's Japanese poetry. It has only seventeen syllables." She closed her eyes—not dreamily or theatrically, but as if reading off the backs of her eyelids—and recited, quietly, while ticking off the numbered syllables on her digits. *"Si-lent cher-ry bloom/With your old el-o-quence/Speak to my in-ner ear."* She opened her eyes and smiled.

"Why that's lovely," said my mother.

My father harrumphed, "I used to know *The Charge of the Light Brigade* by heart, and some Chaucer, but I guess kids don't memorize poetry these days."

"Yes, they do," I piped up. They waited, expectantly, so I added, "Something something something fired the shot heard 'round the world,'" and they laughed.

"I make my students learn it," my new aunt said.

Uncle Waylan beamed. "Schoolteacher," he bragged. "How about that? Me, only poem I know is 'There once was a man from Nantucket—'"

"That's enough, Waylan Kneu!" snapped my mother, though you could tell he hadn't planned to go on. My new Aunt Vicky cocked a brow at him as if cautioning a child to save his charming antics for later.

My father was a Vanderbilt alumnus, but my mother had been the only one of three children to finish high school. Years later, I understood that the Depression had given her a ferocious desire to better her station in life. I think her younger brother was a disappointment, if not an embarrassment. She said he had "done well for himself"—he owned and operated an oil field roustabout service—but he should have cultivated an interest in finer things. "What would those be, exactly?" my father asked her. "Church and charity, for two," she said. "More education, for another. Why should you have to ask?" My father said, "Well, May, because I thought maybe you meant symphony orchestras or art

2

museums, and I doubt there's either one within 300 miles of Hedorville, New Mexico."

According to his sister, Uncle Waylan belonged to no church, drank unapologetically, drove too fast, blew money on quarter-horses in Ruidoso, owned no footwear other than cowboy boots, played poker and bingo and listened to Bob Wills and the Texas Playboys or Ernest Tubb, read only the newspaper and *True* mag-azine, and wasn't fastidious enough about his grammar and swearing before women and children. His freely chosen partners were guilty of drinking beer straight from the cans, smoking cig-arettes on the street, owning no white gloves, and not knowing any better than to put a jar of pickles or a bottle of catsup on the dining table.

I liked him though. He called me "Sport" and over the years had given me presents that my parents invariably said I was too young for: a big-league ball glove when I was six, a pocket knife at seven, a BB gun when I was nine. Once he let me fondle a loaded revolver he kept in his glove compartment and browse through playing cards whose backs were adorned with bare-breasted women. So far as I knew, my father didn't know such things existed, and I sometimes envied the son Uncle Waylan might have one day "if he ever settles down with the right woman," as my mother always put it.

I admired his looks. His hair was very black—he looked vague-ly "Indian"—and with his ever-present boots he frequently wore a black leather vest over a pearl-button shirt. You thought of old West poker sharks. His face was a little pocked from old acne, but he was cowboy-handsome, and he grinned when he teased me or his wife or my mother in his droll, whiskey-and-cigarette baritone. He had a laugh like a shotgun's pop, and he punctuated it by slap-ping whatever was close by with the fingers of one hand.

They were "having drinks" on this Saturday afternoon—mixing Coca-Cola and whiskey from a flat pint bottle Uncle Waylan brought in. He and my new Aunt Vicky were, that is. My mother sipped daintily from a six-ounce bottle of Coke that had a paper napkin saronging its green hips like the wrap of a genteel lady leav-ing a swimming pool. My father had poured about a teaspoon of whiskey into his tumbler and filled it to the brim with water.

"How about you, Sport?" Uncle Waylan grinned, holding up the bottle.

"You do and I'll skin you alive."

"Aw, hell, May, it won't kill him. I started drinking this stuff when I was still on the tit. I remember Daddy used to—"

"I'd just as soon not hear about what used to happen when people overindulged!"

Uncle Waylan laughed. "Remember when Daddy passed out on the front porch and Mama sewed him up in a sheet while he was sleeping it off?"

My mother shot up from the sofa. "Well, I better see about dinner. You will stay, won't you?" She aimed this at Uncle Waylan. I didn't know if he understood his sister the way I understood my mother. The subtext I heard but couldn't have fully articulated at sixteen—it was like a deep but very soft pedal tone from a church organ vibrating up through your soles, up your spine and into your brain, by-passing your ears--was this: *It would have been nice if you'd called ahead and told us you were coming so I could've fixed a proper dinner; now you've caused a ruckus in the kitchen, but you are going to stay whether you want to or not, because since you made me endure the anxiety of this makeshift arrangement I get to pay you back by complaining during the meal about how each and every item might have been better if I'd had time to fix it right.*

Aunt Vicky said, "Waylan, since we dropped in unexpectedly, the least we can do is take everyone out to dinner."

"Aw, hell, Vicky, May don't mind. She's gonna feed five, anyway. What's another two?"

Aunt Vicky favored my mother with the sorrowful gaze of martyred sisterhood. "I'm sorry, I tried to get him to stop so we could call—"

"It's no problem," chirped my mother. "So long as y'all don't mind taking pot luck."

"At least let me give you a hand." As Aunt Vicky rose to chase after my mother into the kitchen, she plucked up her green Coke bottle and empty tumbler and held out her hand for his. He gave her the Coke bottle, and she cradled it against her breast with her own. Then he looked perplexed as she put out her hand again. She wanted his glass.

"I ain't through."

She poked him with a look. "Bottom's up, sailor."

He tossed back the drink and gave up the glass. When she'd

4

gone, he crossed his legs and lit a cigarette. Standing alone atop the burnished walnut smoking stand, the pint bottle looked as out of place as a dog turd. Uncle Waylan eyed it as if wanting a swig but couldn't bring himself to take one.

"That Olds treating you okay?"

"Well, it has a few miles on it now." My father smiled at me. "Since Jimbo got his license, he's been hounding me to buy something new."

"What you want, Sport?"

"Ford or maybe a Merc, like yours."

"You want to drive it?"

"Sure!"

"It's a nice automobile," Uncle Waylan said to my father. "Heated up a little between here and Memphis but you figure that's going to happen to a new one." He turned to me. "You probably been thinking about your own car."

"Oh, yeah. Yeah." I grinned at my father, hoping my joshing Jimmy Cagney diction would disarm him. "Skinflint here won't cough up the dough, though."

"A boy ought to earn his car. Nobody ever gave me one."

"Me either," harmonized Uncle Waylan. They stared me down, these two popes of the Protestant work ethic.

"I never said I wasn't willing!" I protested. "It's just I can't make enough mowing yards or bagging groceries."

"You mean you can't make it fast enough to suit you."

Uncle Waylan laughed. "Oh, I do remember that! Tell you what, why don't you come out to the oil patch this summer and work for me? I pay my hands $1.75 an hour, and you could board with us for nothing, of course."

"Oh, wow! Uncle Waylan! Man, that would be, man, that would be—Jesus!" (Whoops, forgot myself!) "Well, that would really be great. What would I do?"

"Lots of lifting, lots of digging. It's hot and dirty and there's long hours and you'll use every muscle in your body, and there'd be days you'd wish you was back here lounging at the pool."

"Oh, man, I don't care!" I yelped. "Bring it on!" My brain was racing—$1.75 x 50 hrs.? a week x 12 weeks in the summer = man, over $1000! I could buy Bill Howard's '49 Hudson Hornet and repaint it MG green and tool cool as you please down Forest

Lane with one arm hanging out the window, and girls would think *that's such a swell car, wish he'd ask me out!*

"Daddy?"

"Sounds like a pretty good idea to me," my father ventured cautiously. "Might make a man out of you. Hard work never hurt anybody. Of course, you'd have to do every bit as much as any hand and not expect special favors."

"Oh, no! I wouldn't expect any—I'd carry my weight, I promise!"

"Well, we'll see," my father said. "I'm sure your Aunt Vicky needs to be consulted about this."

"Don't worry"—Uncle Waylan slipped this to me, then, earnestly, he appealed to my father: "I've got a good one this go-round. She's an understanding woman." The same phrase had praised my Aunt Noreen and his later girlfriends, but this time, though, he added, "She's got real class."

"I can see that."

Uncle Waylan used to have a steering knob he transferred from the wheel of one car to another as he traded them, a knob featuring a cheesecake pinup under the Lucite cap. But the one on his new Merc encased a yellow rose, instead. I cupped the knob with my palm and wheeled the Merc up Preston and down Lover's Lane with its stately old homes and bois d'arc trees that dropped softballs of green-clad pitch onto the walks. Then I cruised up to Forest Lane hoping to be seen by someone I knew. I tried to will away the presence of the two grown men, tuned the radio to catch "My Prayer" by The Platters, and imagined this was my very own Merc, and I, we, were parked on a summer night by White Rock Lake. I and who? Louise Bowen? No, some-one . . . *sexier* (this thought shocked me, it was so unexpected), groping and wallowing in the back seat, her kneecaps showing white like snowy mountain peaks above the seat back.

I was overwhelmed with riches, and I longed to be alone in my room to relish this shower of good fortune, be a Scrooge McDuck diving in and out of all these possibilities. Aside from buying my own car, my blood was likewise stirred by the delicious prospect of getting away from home for a summer—going west, escaping family, the burdens of tradition such as the one that required allegedly idle boys to awaken each day to a mother's list of chores.

6

Instead of baby-sitting my sisters or mowing the grass or delivering papers or wheeling around on my bicycle like a ten-year-old looking for odd jobs, I'd be working like a man at *manly work*. I'd be using muscles, handling big steel things, wearing steel-toed boots, doffing a roughneck's hard hat, chowing down from a tin box, smoking, cussing, and rolling my shirt sleeves up to show my muscles when I came back after a summer as an *oilfield worker*. Good as a Charles Atlas course!

Louise had told me she would be working at Camp Longhorn as a counselor. That scotched my long-term goal to feel her up (if only through her panties) by our fifteenth date. Now I could go away too and not be the one abandoned.

Also, there was the prospect of hanging around with Uncle Waylan—the varieties of poker he might teach me, what he knew about guns, car engines, etc., and he was relaxed and cool and probably wouldn't be strict about a curfew.

Aunt Vicky interested me, too. She didn't fit my picture of an Uncle Waylan wife, and she was a teacher. Teachers were the category of adults I'd had the most exposure to, following my parents, but I didn't know much about them. Sometimes when I passed by the teacher's lounge and the door was cracked open, I'd see one smoking and drinking coffee and talking to another, and that was always a tantalizing cameo. I'd caught them at being ordinary mortals. A teacher's private life—what did it consist of? Already in my own living room, I had seen one play the Wife and Visiting In-law. She was cool. Cherry blossoms? Well, you might expect that, but Bottom's up, sailor?

I hoped she'd agree to Uncle Waylan's invitation. He'd told me not to worry. And though all his partners had been "understanding women," he'd assured my father that he'd "gotten a good one this go-round." What "good" implied (at least to that laughably green sixteen-year-old male coming of age in a world long since gone) was that she could be counted on to approve his ideas.

TWO

My going to New Mexico soon became as compelling to me as gravity and the tides. During dinner, I drifted away from the adult conversation. What should I take? What would I need? I inventoried my room and was shocked to realize that a stranger walking into it would presume I was twelve: model airplanes on my bookshelves, three volumes of my old stamp collection—my bedspread was decorated with cuddly cowboy and Indian tikes, for God's sake!

I'd need my Boy Scout camp gear—knapsack, axe, knife, hatchet, compass, sleeping bag, waterproof match case, canteen and mess kit—and my portable radio. A few hand tools. Ball glove, football. . . .

As I was debating whether my BB gun was too childish to make the cut, raised voices jerked me back.

"You out there in New Mexico might be happy to encourage criminal behavior, but believe you me, I'm not about to let crooks and gamblers ruin my state legislature! You let gambling in and it's the nose of the camel under the tent, Waylan! How do you think crime syndicates get rich?"

My heart sank. They were arguing about pari-mutuel betting again. Uncle Waylan brayed, "God-a-mighty, May, what skin is it off your nose how other people spend their time and money? You wanna know why I never joined one of your dad-blasted Baptist churches? Because there's too dad-blasted many hypocrites who don't want anybody else to have a lick of fun but they sure as hell don't mind getting on a bus for the race track in Louisiana! They won't vote their own precinct wet but they'll drive over to the next one for a drink! Why do you think half the bars in New Mexico are on the state line?"

My new Aunt Vicky said, "Waylan, nobody in here needs a hearing aid."

Uncle Waylan fumed for a moment. "I'm sorry for shouting, May." He waited a beat but couldn't resist adding, "But there's nothing wrong with betting on a horse race."

"I'm sure it's fine for those with nothing better to do with their money," said my mother, and my father, with one eye on my awestruck sisters, abruptly passed his plate to my mother and said, firmly, "May, dish me out some more rice, please?"

They dropped the subject and paired off by gender—the men talking SMU and UT football, my mother and Aunt Vicky discussing the ingredients of the casserole we were eating.

But my heart had fallen like a bag of BBs to the pit of my stomach. I had completely forgotten the person whose opinion about my plans mattered the most. Why did Uncle Waylan have to bait my mother? Didn't he know that if you wanted to keep her in good humor, you didn't poke at her with "wrong" opinions about things that truly mattered to her? She was an earnest, moody person, and to get along with her it was best not to irritate her. With her, nothing was simple, though. She was Baptist but didn't mind my father taking a drink now and then—we kept a bar stocked, if you'd call a dusty-shouldered bottle of Jim Beam that had stretched over three Christmases "stocked"—and she'd take a glass of wine at holiday meals. But the family's alcoholics had cast a shadow that made her feel that *any drinking done beyond the purview of her personal control was dangerous.* I guess Uncle Waylan would call that hypocrisy, but I thought I understood it, even if I couldn't have explained it then.

She was not about to let me live for three months with a man whose *philosophy* defined drinking and gambling as harmless recreation. I slumped in my chair and studied with sour relish her saggy chin, her crow's feet, her thin straight lips. I hated her smallness.

I hated Uncle Waylan's redneck stupidity, too. Obviously he wanted my parents to be proud of his marrying somebody with "class," so why would he undermine his own efforts to win their approval?

I hated them both for ruining the greatest opportunity that a young man had ever had.

After dinner my mother asked Uncle Waylan, "Would you like to spend the night?" which to my ear sounded more like a request for information than an invitation.

Uncle Waylan took his cue and said, "Well, thanks, May, we appreciate the offer, but we'd best get on the road. I left Iddybit with Wally, and that Merc's been heating up a little, so I'd just as soon make this last leg at night."

While my mother cleaned up the kitchen, my father went to the garage to finish taking apart the hand-pushed mower for cleaning, a job this visit had interrupted. I helped him like a surgeon's nurse for a bit, then I said, "Daddy, what's mother going to say about my spending the summer with Uncle Waylan and Aunt Vicky?"

"Hard to say, really. You want me to find out?"

"Please."

He grinned. "You want me to put in a good word for you?"

"Or for Uncle Waylan."

He laughed. "Oh, deep down she knows he's a pretty good fellow."

Having so much at stake, I couldn't resist stalking them the rest of the evening. I knew nothing crucial would be said with me there, but I didn't want to be too far to eavesdrop, so I lurked just out of sight.

Eventually they settled into the wing chairs, my father with his pipe and the *Dallas Morning News,* and my mother with Diedre on the hassock in front of her so that her hair could be combed and braided. In the foyer I pressed my back against the wall hoping Alise wouldn't come bounding down the stairs and flush me. The adults ping-ponged boring single sentences back and forth like people in a doctor's waiting room; now and then my father inserted snippets from the paper into the silences and my mother passed quick condemnation on the events or the persons mentioned. He: *"Elvis the Pelvis may appear on the Steve Allen Show, says here."* She: *"Humpf! I sure won't be watching!"*

It took a while, but eventually he said, as if stumbling upon Uncle Waylan's picture in his newspaper, "Well, it was good to see old Waylan. He always does liven things up."

No comment.

"You know, that Vicky is sure an improvement over Noreen."

"Yes, she's quite nice. At least she seems so. You might wonder what a lady like that sees in Waylan, though."

"Oh, May!" He sounded genuinely shocked. "Now that sounds like prejudice to me. I wish to heck I could enjoy life half as much as he does."

"Thank goodness you don't!"

"Well, I mean he's witty and good-spirited, always on the upbeat, you have to admit that! I'm sure he knows how to show a gal a good time—now, I know what you're going to say, but he's also a darned hard worker and a good provider. He's generous and good-hearted. I'd say almost any woman would think he's quite a catch."

"Oh, I suppose so. He is handsome, I admit, and he's not poor. And he can be fun."

Then I heard her chuckle.

"What's so funny?"

"Oh, I was just remembering something."

"What?"

She chuckled again. "Some other time."

The memory was not fit to be described before my six-year-old sister, and I cursed her presence, but that was nothing new. My sisters were like household pets, likeable nuisances who had to be fed and watered and groomed and walked.

"You could tell he's darned proud of her and wanted to show her off. I wouldn't be surprised if that wasn't the whole point of the visit. Maybe she'll be a good influence on him," my father said.

"It's possible, but I sure didn't see much evidence of it yet."

"May, there's something you have to understand about men—especially one like Waylan. I'd bet he told himself he wasn't going to get lassoed into a squabble with you. I bet he might have even promised Vicky not to. He knows how you want him to behave, but he can't cave in to you completely. He brought her to show to you that he means to behave better than he has before, you see? And that made him feel like he was losing himself, so he had to put his back up and prove to himself he didn't have to change. And you put yours up. You two bring out the worst in each other. Give him a little credit for trying."

And now, my fellow citizens, I give you the Smartest Man on Earth—my father, Frank Proctor!

Though I waited longer before Diedre came out and rousted me from my listening post, my father didn't then mention the summer job. Maybe the discussion took place when they were in bed, but he'd laid the groundwork, and soon my mother said yes.

Letters exchanged with Aunt Vicky reassured my mother that I wouldn't be imposing on them, and two days after school let out I boarded the Greyhound for New Mexico. I so itched to leave my youth behind that in my notion of myself, essence preceded existence: my life in the burly, wide-open West could not make a man of me—I was one already—but it would allow me to live as I now defined myself.

To my embarrassment, as the other passengers inched by and I stood fidgeting wretchedly beside the open door, my sisters hugged and kissed me. My mother wept and slobbered on my cheek, but my father purged me of the taint by giving me a grin and a firm handshake.

THREE

A half hour out of breakfast I broke into Mother's prodigious lunch, inhaled three fried chicken legs and two slices of bread and butter while Fort Worth slid by and the true West began with huge, cloud-struck vistas showing four kinds of weather at once; I sniffed the dusty air and smelled cattle and campfires, cocked my ear for tom-toms and rebel yells. I was a gigantic pulsing antenna sucking up signals from the farthest reaches; inside me was the hollow carved from leaving a life much loved behind, and I was eager to fill it with my future.

Weatherford, Breckenridge, Anson . . . as the hours rolled on, last night's fitful sleep proved a quick-burning fuel and I napped, head bumping against the window. When the bus stopped in Snyder I finished off the lunch and bought and ate an ancient Zero bar because I'd never had one. Then on across the ruddy sandswept cotton fields of far West Texas I murmured Platters hits, peering through the windshield as the black, ruled road slipped mile by mile under the wheels. At the New Mexico line stood a clump of roadhouse honky-tonks, and I remembered Uncle Waylan's telling my mother why they were there. The state line marked the entry into the Mountain Time zone, so I turned my watch back an hour from five to four (another "first" for me), holding my wrist high above my head as if to read the face better but mostly to let people see I was keen as a pilot to keep the time exact.

The bus pulled up to the station on Hedorville's main drag, and when I stepped off carrying my father's old army duffle, Uncle Waylan was standing at the curb.

"Say, Sport! Welcome! Have a good trip?"

He clapped my back then took my duffle. We retrieved my trunk from the belly of the bus, then I followed him to an old green Chevy pickup, where we heaved my gear into the bed. When I mounted up into the passenger side, an ancient, gray-chinned Chihuahua with one eye clouded by a cataract curled its upper lip in a show of menace and disdain.

"This here's Iddybit," crowed Uncle Waylan. He'd slid under the wheel and now he leaned over to kiss this repulsive canine on its bare and boney little head. That astonished me. "We weren't too long, were we darlin'?"

I vaguely remembered this dog from a previous visit, but I thought it belonged to a girlfriend.

"We've met." I smiled at the dog to be civil but it swiveled its snout away with lordly contempt. I couldn't believe Uncle Waylan would claim this bug-eyed overgrown wood rat as a pet.

"Well! You hungry?"

"Yeah, pretty much." I grinned. It was manly to have a good appetite; I pictured Aunt Vicky rustling up the grub.

"What say we mosey on to where the kids hang out? You might be interested in that. Couple burgers and some fries and a shake suit you?"

"Sure!" Nice of him to presume I'd be eager to see where others of my kind could be found. Was he worried I'd be bored here? Pleased though I was by his consideration, I preferred to go straight home so I could take a leak, wash my face and comb my hair, claim my room and unpack, then rest for a minute before sitting down to a big hot meal such as my family would soon be eating.

As we passed through town, Uncle Waylan ran an inventory: the Western Auto run by a poker buddy, Billy Sample; Anthony's Department Store, a couple of jewelry stores, one movie theatre currently showing *The Searchers,* a drugstore owned and operated "by the stingiest sonofabitch in town," a dress shop whose proprietress was a big-hearted divorcée (wink and a grin), the offices of *The Hedorville Herald,* a dozen other small establishments offering plumbing or pecan pies or pliers. Then we cruised past the oil-well supply warehouses with their pipe yards. The repugnant reptile lay on its back alongside Uncle Waylan's long thigh, splay-limbed, indolent, and while he scritch-scratched its hairless pink belly, it let its head loll my way so that I could read the look on its pointed little face: *He's all mine!*

The drive-in called The Dairy King stood on the highway leading west out of town. That the town's teen hot spot was but another imitation of a true Texas-born and bred Dairy Queen made me unaccountably uneasy, but I chastized myself for snobbery. At this hour of day only two cars were parked under the awning, both containing elderly couples. Uncle Waylan pulled into a stall and turned on his headlights. "Later on tonight, this place'll be hopping. You can't hardly find a place to park."

"That sounds great." I wondered for the fiftieth time whether Uncle Waylan would lend me his Mercury. I'd even settle for this old truck, I thought. Surely he wouldn't dangle the possibility of an exotic night-life before my eyes without a way to get there.

A carhop strolled out wearing red shorts and a white blouse with the tails tied just above her navel. A little paper hat shaped like a sailboat hull was pinned to her hair.

"Hey, Waylan," she said. "Hi, Iddybit. What's your pleasure?" Her lipstick was like Lucy Ricardo's—a tad bigger than her mouth.

"Vera, this boy needs nourishment—he's my best nephew. Hell, he's my only nephew, so he's a little like a son to me and I wanna keep him hale and hearty. Bring Iddybit the usual"–(this turned out to be a cut-up weiner the dog ate off a paper napkin on the seat beside me, making wet clicking noises deep in its gullet)–"and us humans'll have about four deluxe burgers and a couple orders of fries and a chocolate?"—eye cocked at me, I nodded —"shake, and I'll have a Jax or three."

Grinning, Uncle Waylan pressed back against the seat. Vera and I understood that Uncle Waylan's order had also served as an introduction. She looked straight at me and said, "Well, he's cute, ain't he?" leaving me to wonder whether she was speaking to me of him or to him of me. I murmured, "Howdy, ma'm." When she walked our order back, Uncle Waylan gazed at her rear and sighed theatrically.

Later, when she took our littered tray, Uncle Waylan tipped her a dollar and said, "When are you going to leave your old man and marry me?"

She said, "Quit talking trash, Waylan," but I thought she liked it. Uncle Waylan winked at me. "I mean it," he said to her. "You're the woman of my dreams. You're a heartbreaker."

"That's me," she said. "It's my onliest ambition."

We drove back up Broadway and hooked a left and two blocks farther Uncle Waylan pulled onto the rocky apron before the hanger-like tin building that housed his roustabout service.

He turned off the motor. "Home."

I thought he must really love this business to think of it as "home" and that he must have a chore before we joined Aunt Vicky.

"Need some help?" I asked as he got out of the truck.

He didn't answer; he reached into the bed and heaved out my trunk, so I hoisted my duffle and followed him and the dog through the barn-like doors and onto the concrete floor of the shop. Two winch trucks were parked there, and some men were talking and laughing in a corner. The open ceiling was criss-crossed with steel I-beams from which hoists suspended their chains like lax spider webs, and the walls were lined with work-benches, tools, the clutter of valves and fittings. I could smell gasoline, crude oil, paint. Merely standing in this bracingly mas-culine environment made me two inches taller.

I followed Uncle Waylan into an office where a stunning blonde in her twenties wearing black toreador pants and a white blouse embroidered with flowers was standing expectantly as if on a train platform. Soon as we came through the door, she skipped forward, beaming, grabbed my biceps with her surpris-ingly strong hands (her nails pinched my flesh) and said, "Gosh! Hello! You must be Jimbo! I can see the family resemblance!"

"Hi! Yes!" No one had ever said this and to hear it from her lips sent me sailing toward the ceiling like a helium balloon.

"I'm Sharon!" she announced, as if I'd already heard about her elsewhere.

Uncle Waylan was hovering impatiently at the mouth of a dim hallway holding my trunk in his arms, so I said, "Pleased to meet 'cha," and shrugged sheepishly to apologize for rushing off.

We went down the hall, through another door and into what looked like a summer camp bunkhouse. The large room had a concrete floor, an old woodburning stove, a set of army-issue metal bunk beds and one single, also military surplus. Poking out of the darkness under it were two bug eyes watching me. (Maybe this dog was dreaming of being an alligator?) A standing rack on rollers held clothes I might have recognized had I more presence of mind. An opened door off this room showed a bath with toilet and shower. An alcove held a stove, a refrigerator; before them stood an aluminum-rimmed table and chairs with red vinyl pads repaired with gray duct tape. On the table was a milk bottle serving as a vase for three large yellow roses. The walls were tin and their only decoration was a tool-company calendar featuring a smiling, huge-breasted Varga woman with legs six feet long.

"Who's Sharon?"

"She works here. She brought those in for you." He dipped his head toward the yellow roses. "She figured you're from Texas, you'd like them. Stuffy, you think?" Uncle Waylan turned on the swamp cooler stationed in a window.

"Sit down, Sport, make yourself at home. Bathroom's right yonder."

He'd set my trunk on the floor next to the bunk bed. A blanket and sheets were folded atop the stained bottom mattress. The single bed across the room had been slept in and hadn't been made.

I went into the bathroom and closed the door. I took a leak, washed my hands and face and dried them on a sour blue towel hanging from a nail, though a clean one lying folded on the toilet tank was probably meant for me. I combed my hair. The unpainted sheetrock walls were laced with pencilled scrawls: *Here I sit all broken-hearted. . . .Tried to shit but only farted.* I'd seen that before. *This may not be the police station but it's where all the dicks hang out.* The usual cock and balls and a double-lined M with a nest at the bottom of the v. Phone numbers and insults: *Aggies eat shit.*

When I came out, Uncle Waylan was rooting about in the refrigerator. He pulled out a can of Coor's, punched a hole in the top, and offered it to me with a raised eyebrow. Dumbfounded, I took it. He got another for himself, sat at the table, and I did likewise. He took a drink. I took one. I'd drunk beer before but never with an adult.

"Well, Sport, here's the deal. Vicky and me have had a little disagreement, so it's probably best that we bunk here for a bit. That okay?"

I said, "Sure," as if this were perfectly normal, though I had a dozen questions and felt cheated or tricked. Had they argued about me? It must have been truly serious—my parents had "disagreements," but they only lasted a few hours and were worked out behind closed doors. Never in my memory had my father slept elsewhere.

We could hear each other's Adam's apple galooping as we swigged the beer. "It's just a little spat, that's all, Sport. Nothing to worry about. Be over before you know it."

This sounded a little plaintive, so I nodded quickly and grinned. *Women! Sure! I know, believe me, pal!*

"We'll do fine batching it. I learned to sling a little hash in the Navy, and I reckon you're smart enough to boil an egg. We won't starve."

"Fine. I reckon we could always eat that dog."

"Aw now!" He twisted around and made kissing noises toward the repellent popeyed cur lurking under his bed, but it wouldn't respond. "Naw, hell, I'd feed Iddybit my own arm and leg before I'd eat one of hers. She's my darlin', ain't you darlin'?"

I got the feeling that he'd feed the dog my arm and leg before he'd let it go hungry, and I said so.

He laughed. "Well, don't neither of us has to worry about it yet. Your Aunt Vicky's invited us to dinner tomorrow night, so you can look forward to some home cooking." He looked at his watch. "Well, my working day ain't quite slipped over the yard-arm, so tag along and I'll show you what we're here for."

Eager to plunge into whatever lay ahead, I dogged his heels into the barny machine shop. He operated four crews, each with a truck, and when we came out, the last truck had returned from the field. The men stood about smoking and cleaning their hands with a pungent, lard-like substance that they dug from a bucket with their fingers, worked it in like soap, then wiped themselves clean with red shop-rags stacked like Kleenex on the workbench. They wore battered tin hats. They stunk of a wonderfully heady aroma of crude oil and sweat, and they needed to shave; some chewed tobacco and spat on the concrete floor then wiped the smudge with their boot soles. Some had tattoos—anchors like Uncle Waylan's, hearts, daggers and snakes. Every damn one cussed like a sailor, and it was my deepest desire to be exactly like them.

Uncle Waylan introduced me; they all vise-gripped my hand as if determined to make me yell, but I grinned and bore it. They were named Rabbit and Slim and Lefty and Red and Louis and Mex, then there was also a Pete, a Willie, and Jake. Pete had lost his left hand in a drilling rig accident and wore a white cotton glove pinned to his sleeve.

Uncle Waylan told him, "I want you to take this worthless squirt tomorrow, and if he don't come back in with his ass dragging behind his heels, then you didn't really work him."

"Where we going?"

"Lay a flow line down in Diamondback Draw."

"How long?"

"Couple hunnerd yards, but you gotta piss-ant the stuff half a mile first."

Somebody snorted, somebody groaned. "Hellfire, Waylan, why don't yew just put a gun to the lad's head and be done with it?"

They laughed. I laughed too, but I wished I knew if they were teasing. I desperately wanted to ease into the circle, so I sucked in a breath, went for broke and said, "Well, I'm here to do a job of work even if it is for a no-count Ess-Oh-Bee like him—" thumb hooked toward Uncle Waylan—"who tries to take advantage of his own kin."

I flushed red with the dicey bravado of my own bold joke and couldn't look directly at Uncle Waylan, but he roared and punched me on the arm, knocking me atilt, and everybody laughed again.

"Waylan?" The blonde was standing in the office doorway. "There's a fellow—a pumper for Shell?—on the phone who wants to know when you're coming about that leak at that tank battery down at Jal."

We all looked at her. Her black toreador pants left her shins and calves exposed, and her ankles were trim and white, and she had on black ballet slippers. The collar of her blouse was standing up and the tips were curled back from her lovely throat, and you could see a little flash of gold—maybe a cross—there in the white hollow, that I hadn't noticed before. She looked very clean compared to everything here. The mens' stillness had an air of awe—you'd have thought she was a movie star.

I swallowed. Shoes creaked as men shifted weight and cleared their throats. Someone murmured "Whew!" Her blonde hair glimmered in a sunbeam choked with dustmotes that shot down from a window high on the wall.

"Tell him tomorrow," Uncle Waylan said. She turned to go, then stopped and said, "Oh, hey, do any of y'all know how to change a ribbon on a Smith-Corona?"

"Yo!" said Red.

"I do!" yelled Lefty.

"Me, I can!" hollered Rabbit.

"Oh, for God's sake!" said Uncle Waylan. "You turds wouldn't know a typewriter from a turnbuckle." He waved her off and said, "I'll take a look at it in a minute."

I wanted to say I'd changed the ribbon on my mother's Smith-Corona and I'd be happy to show her how it's done. But I kept my trap shut. Much as I wanted a closer look, I was afraid I'd stutter.

Uncle Waylan discussed the next day's work with his four crew bosses and everyone left. It was 6:30. Uncle Waylan led me into the office. Sharon was sitting with her arms crossed in the swivel chair, whistling through her front teeth.

"Did he get you settled okay?" Her question had a faintly maternal air. "Is there anything you need?"

"Yeah, sure. Fine. No, I'm okay. Thanks for the flowers."

"Give him one of them forms—you know, for new employees —and have him fill it out."

Sharon said, "Which form is that?"

"Bottom drawer, the yellow ones."

I sat in a hard wooden chair beside the desk. Sharon hooked the bottom drawer handle with her big toe and pulled it open. She bent to rummage in it and I tried not to look down her blouse. Uncle Waylan dropped to his knees before the typing table.

"Vicky usually does this."

Sharon stopped riffling through papers. "I usually can, Waylan. We worked on Royals in school. I tried to do it myself before I—ah hah!" She tugged a folder out of the drawer by its shoulders and held it up as if it were a shirt she was inspecting. "Yellow? It says 'Personnel Information Form'?"

"Atta girl!" Uncle Waylan caught us both up in his gaze. "She's new but she's mighty sharp, this kid."

"It wouldn't take an Einstein, Waylan." Her smile invited me to share her joke at Uncle Waylan's expense, and I chuckled much too loud. She handed me the yellow form, and as I filled the blanks, she bent closer like a helpful grade-school teacher supervising a kid learning cursive. The little gold cross swung into the space below her chin as she leaned, and if I peered up under my brows I could probably see down her blouse, but I vowed not to try.

"He don't need much help," said Uncle Waylan, and she leaned back away from me. "He's a straight A student. Hell with this. I'll get it later." He rose, knees popping. "Let's mosey."

Sharon lifted her purse from the desk. It was a tan wooden box with a red plastic handle and a red rooster painted on the sides.

"I'm gonna run Sharon home, Sport. Look under my bunk for a pair of steel-toed boots that'll fit you. Insurance won't let nobody work without them."

When they went out the door, I skipped around the desk and watched through the window as they walked to his truck. They were side by side but not especially close. He opened the passenger door for her. When he got behind the wheel, they talked for maybe three minutes before he turned on the engine and pulled away.

I went back to the form. When I reached the blank for the name(s) to be contacted in an emergency, I remembered I was supposed to call home to report I had arrived. This panicked me. If I told my mother that my aunt and uncle were "sort of separated" and that he and I were "batching it" in the shop, she would order me home on the next bus.

I could "forget" to call, but if I hadn't called before their bedtime, my mother would probably ring Uncle Waylan's house to check on me. I had to buy time. I picked up the desk phone and called home collect. I caught a faint floral fragrance from the receiver and realized Sharon's lips had maybe brushed the mouthpiece, and I squelched an irrational urge to lick it.

I told my mother her lunch was great and that I'd gotten here fine and that Uncle Waylan was fine. Everything was fine. Everybody was fine.

"Let me speak to your Aunt Vicky." My mother obviously wanted to express appreciation to the hostess for allowing the intrusion. Then I remembered she'd put a gift-wrapped package in my trunk. She wanted to give Aunt Vicky an opportunity to thank her for it.

"Well, she's not here. I'm not there, I mean. I'm at the shop. We're getting ready for tomorrow. I'm going out with one of Uncle Waylan's crews, Mom. My boss is this guy Pete, and he's only got one hand. He lost the other in a drilling rig accident," I babbled on, realizing too late that I'd inadvertently raised the spectre of her only son being maimed by machinery. "A long time ago, though, so don't worry. We're going to do something about a pipeline tomorrow."

"That's fine, dear."

She told me she loved me and handed the phone to my father. I repeated the same spiel. "Great!" he bellowed. "Starting right in!"

When I hung up, I could picture my mother and father seated in the livingroom, my sisters probably still playing outside in the long summer twilight—that seemingly endless twilight of childhood I had abruptly ended in my hasty rush into maturity. My eyes stung. No other human was present in the office, the shop, the bunkhouse. Maybe I should've have told my parents the truth. Then they might make me return and I wouldn't be trapped in my decision.

I shook off my homesickness by installing the new typewriter ribbon. It was simple and doing it made me feel better. I wanted to type a note to the blonde so she'd know who fixed it, but everything I imagined saying to her sounded stupid. So I rolled paper into the platen, typed "Now is the time for all good men to come to the aid of their party," then whacked out my name five times as if I was only testing the machine.

I went back to the bunkhouse. Without anyone there—even the dog had vanished—it seemed forlorn and squalid. The three yellow roses were already shedding petals onto the table. I pretended not to be disheartened; I told myself that this was how cowboys and roughnecks and such lived and that only a limp-dick sissy would bemoan the absence of carpets, curtains, easy chairs and needlework samplers, all those signs of "a woman's touch." After all, it was to escape a woman's touch that I'd come west to be a man. This was like camping out, and I'd always loved that. I'd only been surprised to be living in such quarters.

I opened my trunk. My mother's present to Aunt Vicky lay cocooned inside my clothing, so I eased it out and set it on the table. I was only mildly curious about the contents. The box was a nagging reminder, though, of my lie of omission on the phone. I hung my wrinkled suit and a few shirts and jeans on the rolling wardrobe rack next to Uncle Waylan's things, then I used the upper bunk like a table to lay out the rest of my gear. I wished I had a shelf or a stand beside my bunk to put my watch and a glass of water on at night. Uncle Waylan said we'd be here "a bit," but was that a day or a week? I didn't know how much effort to put into making myself comfortable, but it cheered me up to think of it as a campsite for the next couple of days.

So after I'd made my bed, I went exploring in the equipment yard behind the shop—three acres full of giant rusting cogs and tubes, skeletal rig foundations, dismantled motors, valves, and gear boxes. I browsed happily until I came upon an empty wooden cable spool and—Da-dah!—my nightstand! I rolled it back toward the bunkhouse but stopped for a while midway to watch the sun set over the plains beyond the yard. It was your fabulous western sunset as loud with color as a paperback cover. I breathed in the dry evening air and grinned.

I set up my table beside my bunk, tuned my portable radio to a local station playing Carl Perkins' "Blue Suede Shoes," got a beer out of the refrigerator and helped myself to one of Uncle Waylan's cigarettes. I lay back on my bunk, the cowpoke relaxin' after a hard day on the range. My gaze soon landed upon the Varga girl. I thought of Sharon. Too old for me but no harm dreaming. Now the cowpoke's thinkin' about his lady love. He comes, hat in hand, to woo her. She takes off her blouse. He takes his whangus expertly in his hand. . . .

I kept waiting for Uncle Waylan, but at nine, worn out from the eventful day and the ragged sleep from last night, I undressed and got into my bunk. I started worrying about how I'd do tomorrow. I wouldn't want Lefty and Slim and Rabbit and Red or Cotton to think that Uncle Waylan was going light on me. But could I measure up?

Then I remembered the boots, so at 9:30 I turned on the light, rooted around under Uncle Waylan's bunk, half expecting to find that dog there, and dragged out a jumble of work boots and selected the closest fit, a half size too big at 10 1/2. I put on two pairs of socks then tried on the boots. They'd do, though when I walked my feet slipped a little along the inner sole. I liked their heavy anchoring feel. I set them neatly side by side and upright by my bunk.

When Uncle Waylan came in at 10:30, I was still awake. I'd left the bathroom light on so he could find his way, but he hit the switch to the overhead fixture. That dog came trotting in behind him, its little nails going tik tik tik on the concrete.

"You hit the rack already, huh, Sport? That seems like a good idea to me, too. We get up at 5:30 here."

"Okay with me."

He got a bottle of milk from the refrigerator, took a long drink, sighed, poured some into the dog's red ceramic bowl under the stove. The dog stuck its muzzle into the milk up to its marble-sized eyeballs.

"Ulcer's acting up."

Didn't ulcers come from worry? What was he worrying about? "I see you made yourself at home—that spool's a damn good idea, Sport. Don't know why I didn't think of it myself. Radio, too. Hell, you're gonna make a damn sight better roommate than what I'm used to. You don't snore, do you?"

"Not that I know of."

"That's good. Vicky does. Like a steam engine, bless her heart."

He laughed. He picked up the gift-wrapped box from the table. "What's this?"

"It's from mother to Aunt Vicky. Oh, hope you don't mind—I called home from the office. I was supposed to tell them I got here okay."

"Oh, no, that's fine. Everything all right at home?"

"Oh sure."

"You didn't mention. . . ." He gestured to the room.

"No. I guess I didn't think to."

"Just as well, Sport. Your mama don't always understand things the same way I do." He set the box down and tapped it absently with his fingers. "Sorry I took so long getting back."

"It's okay. I went out back and looked around, saw the sunset."

As if he didn't hear me, he went on. "The trouble is, you see, I got myself in a pretty sorry mess." His fingertips went pitter-pat on the silvered paper. "Comes from thinking with my pecker, I guess." He sighed and looked at the ceiling. "I wish to God someday I'd learn to look before I leap."

I waited, frozen in expectation and raging curiosity, for more to come. But he stood glumly mute, staring at the box or toward it as if it held an answer to the riddle of womanhood, then he put the milk back in the refrigator, and inside of three minutes he was undressed, in bed, and snoring like a steam engine.

Ten million thoughts buzz-bombed my brain. The more I worried about getting enough sleep, the more awake I felt. Finally my mind unknotted and my thoughts broke into strands wafting on the fitful breeze of consciousness. I saw in my mind's eye his hand on the silver box and thought how odd that neither of us knows what's inside it; then just before I fell asleep I was wondering why my mother had sent it, anyway? What made that necessary? After all, my father hadn't wrapped up a trinket for me to bring for Uncle Waylan. That would've been really strange, wouldn't it?

This little silver box with its unknown contents had something to do with both women; they were passing an *object of understanding* between them, though they were virtual strangers, and the contents constituted a message in code from one to the other, a code to which they had the key because they were women.

FOUR

S omeone shook me hard, I smelled smoke and popped upright in my bunk shaking with alarm. Uncle Waylan was rousting me from sleep.

"Let's go, son! Drop your cock and grab your socks."

Heart pounding, I leapt from my bed. While dressing in a t-shirt and jeans and the work boots, I was astonished by the barnyard symphony struck up by my roommate: it was as if he had to grab himself and jump-start every organ to get under way. He pissed and farted, he groaned, he coughed while inhaling his cigarette, hocked up a wad and spat it in the toilet, he sneezed and blew his nose—"Lord! Morning is the curse of the working class!"—stretched and popped his knees, his knuckles, his neck, rubbed the grit out of his eyes and his fist went squick-squick against the sockets, gulped down more milk, sighed, yawned and hollered "Youch!" when he got scalded by hot water in the bathroom basin.

We drove down to Runt and Dot's Cafe at a cave-dark 5:45 A.M. Though we were too groggy to talk, you'd have thought his yawns were a form of speech: first a great rushing sigh of wind was sucked down the tunnel of his throat and into his ballooning lungs, then he sang a gray whale's moaning, tuneless, quavering song as the exhaled air spumed into the crisp predawn air. There were rhetorical interjections, too, such as, "Lord!" or "Aiii, caramba!" and "What a life!"

On the main drag several vehicles with lights on proved we weren't the only humans up this early, but I was surprised when we pulled up to the cafe: pickups and utility trucks and company cars with logos on their doors and stinger-like antennae were parked along both curbs, choking the street down to one lane.

At the door we stood aside so four men in hard hats and overalls could exit, then when we stepped inside we were hit with a cacaphony of loud talk and laughter; bacon grease and cigarette smoke formed a toxic light-grey cloud a yard below the ceiling. Every table and booth was filled with men dressed for work. Vibrations from their talk, their scraped-back chairs, their laughter, hummed up into the soles of my boots. Uncle Waylan shouted in my ear and pointed at two men vacating counter stools, so we squeezed through the clutter of chair backs and claimed them. Uncle Waylan hailed several men from where we sat, then I met 6'3" 300-lb. Runt and his average-sized spouse, Dot, a woman my grandmother's age who wore a hearing aid and kitty-kat glasses on a chain. I looked for a menu but never saw one.

Uncle Waylan told Dot, "Double the usual there, Sugar."

She wrote on her pad and talked around the filtered butt in her mouth. "That's cheese grits, three fried eggs and a short-stack, both links and patty sausage—"

He halted her, palm out, and asked me, "You want a pork chop, too?"

I said no, even though I did.

Dot continued: "—hash browns, biscuits and gravy. And two sack lunches?"

"Right."

"You want three or four sandwiches in them lunches?"

"What the hey, Sport, let's live it up."

I said, "Fine."

"What kind?"

"Hell, Dot, you ain't got but four kinds: baloney, fried egg, peanut butter and jelly, and cheese."

"You want to double one of your usual to get a fourth or you want the peanut butter?"

"Double my baloney. Don't know about Jimbo here."

"That's fine," I said.

"You want the peach pie or the apple?"

Uncle Waylan winked at me but spoke to her. "They're the same except for the color. You use the same goo for all them pies."

She laughed. "We don't make 'em and you know it, Waylan."

She cocked her head and squinted at him. "You looking for home cookin', you oughta go home."

"This town's too damn small," he muttered.

"It's just friendly, that's all. People care about one another."

"And I'm just trying to be a good Samaritan."

When Dot didn't respond, Uncle Waylan said, "Speaking of that, how's she working out?"

Someone across the room whistled for Dot. She signaled "hold it" with her index finger and said to Uncle Waylan, "Girl's got a good disposition and she's willing to work but you can tell she ain't done a lot of it. We all like her, and when we put her to waiting tables, she gets along with the customers, even if people don't always understand what she's saying."

Dot scooted off to lift three platters from the serving ledge, and Uncle Waylan called to her back, "Ask her when she gets a minute to come out, if you don't mind."

While we waited for the food, I wondered who "she" was, and Uncle Waylan shouted to several men seated at nearby tables to introduce me. I tried to live up to his pleasure in showing me off by grinning and waving at them in what I hoped was the blasé, offhand manner of a full-grown man in complete control of himself. He might as well have used a bull-horn: *Hey everrrryyybooody! Here's a green one, not a scratch on him, not a callus, not a scab! I know he looks a little pale and puny now and his grammar's too good, but take it from me he's got some promise!*

Dot set our heaping platters before us. I was bear-hungry, and it seemed like just the right amount of food. I was going to need extra fuel for my imminent test of strength. Toiling away at this lumberjack breakfast was like calesthenics or manual labor—so much cutting and chewing and swallowing, spreading the materials, selecting and handling the tools, lifting, heaving, shovelling. It was a very satisfying miniature day's work in itself, and somewhere around quitting time, a young woman emerged from the archway into the kitchen and came over to us. She was wearing farmer's overalls with a white t-shirt underneath; she had wild red hair and huge brown eyes and a pretty little Cupid's baby-mouth. She was freckled and sweating; she seemed large but not exactly chubby, and I thought maybe her breasts were big but when girls wear overalls it's hard to tell. A package of Kools stuck out of her overall pocket. Her bare arms seemed a little hefty but that might

31

have been because her hands were tiny and very red from, it turned out, being dunked in hot dishwater. I thought she might be close to my age but wasn't sure.

"Hey, Waylan." She grinned. "How's it hangin'?"

"Trudy, I wanted you to meet my nephew, Jimbo."

"Copasetic," said Trudy. She held out a child-like hand that felt, when I shook it, very damp and warm.

"Proctor," I said.

She gave me a bemused look that widened the gap between our ages.

"You getting along okay down here?" Uncle Waylan asked.

"Oh, yeah, it's cool, you know? These people are really a gas. They're real, they're honest. No bullshit about them. And I kinda dig this pearl-diving, like down and out in London and Paris." She looked about the room. "The human brotherhood," she sighed over our heads.

"Well, I'm glad. You need anything you let me know, hear?"

"Oh, sure. Thanks!"

I was sorry when she went back to the kitchen but I couldn't have said why. She was cute but a little strange-looking—you might have called her "statuesque" or even "regal," maybe, but in those Big Smith overalls, she just looked larger and more lumpy than maybe she really was. Maybe that's how girls dressed on the planet this girl called home, I thought.

"She's something of a character," I said to Uncle Waylan, then cringed to realize my mother would have said that, in the same dry, faintly disapproving tone.

Uncle Waylan chuckled. "Sharon says Trudy's writing a book about her travels."

Her travels? Sharon? She knows Sharon the blonde goddess?

No time for a follow-up, though: Uncle Waylan rose, left a dollar tip for a $3.50 tab, and we went out the door into cool fresh air tinted a pale violet. Day was dawning. 6:25 A.M.

Going back to the shop, Uncle Waylan flicked on the radio and did top-of-the-lungs duets on "Crazy Arms" and "Honky-Tonk Man." He hollered "Wooo-wooo whoa!" and beat the wheel with the heels of his hands. He honked the horn in time with the music. He slapped his door panel with his palm. He waved, whistled and shouted at people he knew in passing cars.

He was up and at 'em!

He was ready to do a job of work.

Hours later: a vast, semi-arid plain under the blazing sun. If this were a cartoon there'd be a bleached cow skull in the foreground and a thirst-crazed cowpoke prostrate upon the sand, arm outstretched, eyes whirling as he imagines an oasis on the horizon. You've got hillocks of sand topped by knee-high scrub-oak, dry-wash arroyos, a klatch of gulches, yucca in bloom. On the horizon an oil refinery oozes a spume of black exhaust like a ship burning at sea.

Two pairs of men enter the frame. Each pair carries a length of pipe on their right shoulders, one man at each end. They tramp, tramp, tramp over the sand hills, breathing hard. . . .

Well, the pipe was heavy and hot and a very large stack awaited us when we arrived where the truck had dumped it. I had on gloves and a hard hat borrowed from my boss, Pete, who surprised me by sitting in the truck doing a crossword puzzle while the other four of us carried joints of pipe from the stack and strung it along the ground from a wellhead a hundred yards or so to a temporary holding tank. Each round trip took maybe fifteen minutes; each time we returned to the stack, we'd drink water from the galvanized cooler set in a rack on the truck. My partner was Slim, an older fellow who didn't look particularly underweight to me, but he was missing a front tooth, and he had those long, unkempt sideburns that I associated with Ozark inbreeding. When we had carried our first joint of pipe together, he'd taken the front end; I'd been so eager to prove myself that I felt frustrated by his poky, plodding lead up and over the sandhills, by his pausing at the foot of an incline to catch his breath. *I can work this sucker into the ground!* I thought. Maybe he'd felt me pushing from behind, because when we reached our unloading point near the wellhead, he nimbly stepped out from under his end without warning me, and since it hit the ground first, my end popped up then slammed back down on my shoulder. When we came back to the truck that first time, the other three all stopped for a drink, but I refused one and instead stood at the rack of pipe with my fists on my hip. *Pour it on—I can take it.* From inside the truck, Pete said, "Come here, Jimbo." I went over to receive the praise due me, but he asked, "What's a six-letter word for a mile-high place?"

"Denver?"

"All right!"

Slim and the others—Red and Cotton—laughed. Red said, "Y'all better be nice to Jimbo. He's gonna wind up riding shotgun."

With each successive trip, the pipe had grown hotter and heavier. After two hours, my calves trembled, I was gasping for breath, sweat drenched me to my underwear and stung my eyes, and Uncle Waylan's boots were just big enough to blister my heels. Now when we stopped for water, I malingered in the shade of the truck until the last possible second. My arms quivered when I lifted the pipe, and though I'd padded the end of the joint with a rag, the weight and the constant bouncing had made my shoulder ache deep in the joint. I thought, My God! Six more hours of this? Every weekday of the summer?

And each trek then became an object lesson:

The day is long and men are weak.

Working slow and steady gets the job done best.

Don't try to look better than others who work beside you.

Make work easier instead of proving you can do it the hardest way.

Make sure your shoes fit.

By lunch time, we'd strung the pipe. Pete ate in the cab and listened to the radio, while Slim, Red, Cotton and I sat on the hot sand in the slim margin of shade made by the truck. Red and Slim had black metal lunch boxes packed by their wives. Cotton was an almost-albino with golden eyebrows and lashes. He couldn't have been but a year older than me, and he hadn't brought a lunch.

"Aren't you gonna eat?" I asked.

He shrugged. He was drinking cold water from an empty Pepsi bottle. "Ain't hungry."

How could he work all morning and not be ravenous? It was a mystery, but I chalked it up to a personal whim. I buzz-sawed my own four soggy white-bread sandwiches, the bag of chips, the goo pie, and the mushy apple, then felt better. Cotton, in the meantime, had walked off a few yards from the truck to piss.

Slim and Red were smoking. I belched. "I'm gonna live now," I said. They laughed. "I can't imagine doing this and not gettin' hungry."

Slim shrugged. Red said, "Payday's still two days off."

This gave me a lot to think about, though not at the moment, because Pete climbed down from the cab to take advantage of a captive audience. I said Pete had "surprised" me by staying in the truck while we worked. My romantic image of "the working man" had led me to presume that a one-handed fellow would take pride in carrying his weight (Movie line: *I don't need your charity!*) But Pete had apparently decided that a foreman didn't have to break a sweat. He was, though, proud of the dexterity he had achieved. He sat Indian-style on the ground with us and rolled a cigarette with his one good hand. Nobody else who worked for Uncle Waylan smoked roll-your-owns. Slim and Red ignored this demonstration, as it was chiefly for my benefit, but I couldn't help watching. He used his teeth as an extra pair of fingers and a crease in his jeans as a mold for the paper, and after a hundred tiny, tedious motions, had made something close enough to a cigarette to be lighted by a kitchen match struck under his thumbnail.

He took a long drag, grinned at me. "I met this gal last night at Al's? Man, she like to have bucked me out of bed. She was somethin'."

"She good lookin'?" asked Slim.

"Believe you me!" said Pete. "Good lookin'? Stacked like a brick shithouse."

After working on it a moment, I knew he'd meant her breasts were large. But try as I might, I couldn't reconcile the soft curves of flesh with the square angles in a building of hard brick.

Red asked, "You take her home or go to her place?"

Pete laughed. "Don't think her old man would've cared to see us at theirs."

Red and Slim laughed, so I laughed, too.

"She told me I gave her the best lovin' she'd ever had."

"No shit?" said Slim. "I swear, you take the cake, Pete."

Cotton had come up and now stood listening. "You must have done something real nasty then, Pete."

"You know me."

Red said, "What'd you do to make her say that, Pete?"

"I can't give away my trade secrets."

"Aw come on, Pete," whined Slim. "Me and Red, we're married, it won't hurt nothing. We ain't gonna give you no competition."

"Yeah," said Red. "And it ain't like we could ever get to practice nothing."

They all laughed. Pete winked at me. He was a long-faced fellow with a cocky grin, and I'd have thought most women would call him homely and think that the white glove was spooky, but what did I know?

"It might give this here youngster wrong ideas."

"I bet Pete's been eatin' hair pie," said Cotton.

Hair pie?

"I ain't no *pervert!*" snorted Pete. "No, fellows, what I did, what I do, is just talk sweet and gentle."

They all guffawed. Pete was smiling.

"You trying to tell us it's the size of your wang?" asked Cotton.

"No, it's the cute way I crawl on and off. And I never take no for an answer because a woman only says it to make sure you think she's respectable and to see just how much you want it."

He grinned at me. As the rookie, I was supposed to benefit from this wisdom. I was grateful, as most of the adult men I'd known—fathers, teachers, preachers, and Boy Scout leaders—would never in a hundred years share something like this with me.

"She good as that redhead who had the Caddy convertible with the white leather seats?" asked Slim.

"Or that gal Suzy who knew that Japanese stuff?" asked Red.

"Naw, she wadden that good. But she was good, I tell you. Tight as a new pair of shoes."

This simile also sent my mind askitter—didn't tight new shoes hurt your feet?

"You gonna see her again?" Slim wanted to know.

"Aw, you know, if I run into her." He looked at me and winked. Or was it a tic? "Meantime, maybe we can get young Jimbo here to tell us about that gal in the office."

They all laughed, but I caught a nervous edge to it.

"Yeah, Jimbo," said Red. "Is old Waylan dipping his wick in that?"

"I sure as hell wouldn't mind," said Slim.

"I wouldn't kick her out of bed," said Red. "'Less she wanted to do it on the floor."

"I think she's got a yen for yours truly," said Pete.

"No shit, Pete?" Cotton looked wide-eyed. "How come you think so?"

Pete shot me a darting glance, then looked away. I got the feeling he was sorry he'd mentioned Sharon in front of me now. "Aw, hell, you know. Just the way she twitches her ass when she knows I'm looking."

"You do something, you'll tell us about it, won't you, Pete?" Cotton's eager face was the very picture of the brown-nosing student.

Pete chuckled. "Why, sure. It's the least I can do for you pore fellows."

A half hour later, as we were tramping across the sand hills loaded down with huge pipe wrenches and a bucket of sealer to make the connections on the strung-out line, Slim laughed suddenly and said, "Damn, Red, you're the biggest suck-ass I ever met."

"Me?" laughed Red. "'She as good as that redhead in the Caddy convertible?' Hellfire, Slim, you oughta crawl in a hole and die of shame!"

"Well, then you mentioned that girl with the oriental stuff."

"How about Cotton and that 'will you tell us all about it, Pete?'"

Cotton said, "God, ain't he full of shit!"

"Y'all think he's lying?" I asked.

This was far and away the funniest thing said all day.

FIVE

W ell, Sport, you still among the living?" Uncle Waylan whacked my back when I crawled off the truck. I grinned. I was stiff, sore, and blistered, but I also felt the buoyant lightness of going to the showers after a hard-played win.

After I'd cleaned up and dressed, I lay on my bunk and let my body be dissolved by gravity. Uncle Waylan showered, shaved again, slapped on Old Spice; he Brylcreamed his palm and passed his hands through his hair; then, whistling as he stood at the mirror, he carefully sculpted the cresting wave in front with his pocket comb. I watched but not as an idle spectator; I was taking notes on his musculature like an engineer planning to make such a body for himself one day. His tan was a V on his breastbone and a line on his arms below the elbow, and the vine-like veins on his arms and hands conveyed strength. His rippled stomach was pale and striped with fine black furrows. A long, slightly raised scar arched across his left ribcage. Slim had a scar on his chin. I wanted a scar. I also wanted a nickname like "Slim" or "Cotton" or "Lefty" or "Rabbit" or "Red" or "Buck," but I didn't know how to get one. I had the idea that other men had to bestow it. Maybe it wasn't a badge of merit, exactly, but a sign of tribal acceptance.

I catalogued and coveted his "going-out" wardrobe: gabardine slacks and western belt with his name tooled across the back, a plaid western shirt with pearl buttons, a bola tie, and tall black Tony Llama boots whisked to a sheen with a few brisk brush strokes.

Sharon sat between us when we left the shop in Uncle

Waylan's pickup. She was wearing a sundress but she'd covered her bare shoulders with a red cardigan sweater. Her skirt spread wide over all three sets of knees, and now and then her warm bare arm brushed mine. She smelled of Wind Song.

"Where you boys going so dressed up?" She looked at the gift-wrapped silver box in my lap. "Somebody having a birthday?"

When Uncle Waylan didn't answer, I said, "Over to Aunt Vicky's to eat."

"My."

"Don't make no federal case here."

"I didn't say word one, Waylan."

Actually, she had said one word, but I didn't think it wise to crack wise about it.

Uncle Waylan said, "I know what you're thinking, though."

"What?" She turned to me. "Waylan thinks he can read people's minds."

"Can yours."

They were too silent after that, and I regretted having provoked Sharon with this news. Was this jealousy? Of whom? It wouldn't make sense for her to be jealous of Uncle Waylan's wife. We drove several more blocks and pulled into the courtyard of The Round-Up Motel. She turned her wooden purse upright and held it between her hands, so I knew she was getting out.

Uncle Waylan said, "I'll call you later."

"Maybe I'll be here."

I stood holding the door open the way my father does—you stay alert in case the lady dismounting from the carriage should stumble—and Sharon stepped nimbly off the running board with a mysterious sneer and a glitter in her eyes. These were not aimed at me—she was looking into a distance that was somebody else's future.

When we were back on the main drag, I decided to be nosy —he could always tell me to mind my own business. "Does Sharon live there at that motel?"

"Uh, yeah. Well, she's staying there for the time being. She and Trudy—the girl at Runt and Dot's?"

The time being? Where were they scheduled to be after that? Did Uncle Waylan have a plan? What was the connection between Sharon and Trudy and Aunt Vicky? He'd told Dot he was trying to be "a Good Samaritan." Exactly what did that mean?

"I guess Sharon's about the prettiest girl I've seen in a long time," I offered as bait.

"Yeah, she's easy on the eyes, all right. And she can be an understanding woman when the green-eyed monster don't get a hold of her."

"She seems real nice."

Uncle Waylan chuckled. "I'd say feisty and I'd say tricky and I'd say sexy and I'd say contrary. But I don't know if *nice* would've come to mind, Jimbo."

"How'd you meet her?"

"She's from Dumas. She and Trudy both. They're cousins. We were moving a rig up that way a few years ago. I needed some paperwork done and I figured I'd get somebody over at the business college in Amarillo. There she was. There I was. Then a couple weeks back she came to town and I hired her." He shrugged as if to say the *rest is history.* "I wasn't married when I met her. Vicky wasn't even in sight. I know everybody in the family thinks I'm the kind of fellow who goes out tomcatting even when he's got a wife at home, but I ain't. I just ain't. I generally took my vows of marriage serious—well, except for during the war and when we docked in a port you never knew if you'd live to see another liberty—anyway, I guess if Noreen had been a settle-down woman who wanted a home and kids as much as I did, I'd still be married to her and I'd be as true as any man can be."

"Is that why you and Aunt Noreen got divorced?" I couldn't believe I was asking this, but I wasn't about to let this opportunity slide by. Nobody in my family discussed such things with kids. The closest I came was "Can This Marriage Be Saved?" in my mother's *Ladies Home Journal.*

"Oh, I guess you could say it was the war," Uncle Waylan offered after a moment.

"Korea?"

He laughed. "Naw, the war, the war! My God!" He shook his head. "We grew up together, me and Noreen. Childhood sweethearts. Your mama knew her oldest sister, Eileen. She called them white trash. Probably were, I guess, but Noreen and me, we were both hot to get out of the house and start living like grown-ups, so we got married soon as I quit school. Then the war came, I went off to the Navy, and when I got back, she was different, I was different."

"How was she different?"

He smiled. "You sound like Vicky—I never have understood why my life with Noreen should be her favorite hobby. I don't pretend to know a hell of a lot about women, but I have noticed they take a keen interest in your past connections."

"I'm sorry. I don't mean to pry."

"Oh, no, it's okay. Talking to you about it won't get me into any trouble."

He lit a Phillip Morris with the lighter in the dash of the truck. "Noreen always was a wild child, see. That's what I liked about her from the start. I mean, you get a hair up your hiney to do something crazy and she'd be all for it quick as a wink. She was fun, I tell you. Fish, dance, drink, play cards all night—you name it. When I came back from overseas she'd gotten more that way— I always had a suspicion that she didn't let the war cramp her style. But I'd seen a lot of the world and way too many people dying, and for me it was time to raise a family. We stuck it out for a good while, but I couldn't never please her." He laughed, rue-fully. "She wanted to have a party all the time and she wanted me to turn myself into a millionaire in a big hurry, and I couldn't fig-ure out how to do both things at once." He paused, smiled. "One time she told me that a man only needs three things to keep a woman happy—a big heart, a big dick, and a big wallet."

I engraved those criteria on my memory. They seemed a pret-ty tall order.

"Where is she now?"

"Last I heard she was married to a real-estate king out in Riverside, California. I guess she did all right for herself in the big wallet department. Only thing gripes me is I heard she has kids now. She never wanted them when we were together. I guess she finally grew up enough." He sighed a plume of smoke at the windshield, like a blue cloud of regret. "Sometimes, you know, the trouble between a man and a woman is a matter of timing."

"Timing?" Was he referring to that thing called premature ejaculation?

"Well, yeah, people want different things at different times in their lives, and sometimes a man and a woman just aren't syn-chronized."

Was that the trouble now? "Aunt Vicky seems like a very dif-ferent kind of person from Aunt Noreen."

Uncle Waylan slapped his thigh with his free hand. "That's a good one, Sport! Yes and no, yes and no! I could write you a book on that particular subject."

I wanted to say I'd settle for a few paragraphs right now, but I hesitated to push. Still, no harm in asking. . . .

"It's hard to see how they're alike."

"Well, as wives, you see? No, you don't. It's hard to explain. It's how women expect things and what they expect from you, no matter if they're ignoramuses like Noreen or Pee H Dees. They're going to do certain things alike, every damn one of them. Mainly it's wanting me to be more of something or less of something than I am. They're always wanting to change me, dammit all!" He was talking louder. "Noreen, she wanted me to be dancing with her until past midnight every night. Then come morning she'd be nagging about money for a new this or that. I can't say Vicky cares much about money, but she does want to hang around a crowd I ain't used to. Bingo at the VFW or dancing out at Al's ain't good enough for her, oh hell no! She wants us to join the goddamned country club, and the very last thing I want to do when I ain't working is go hiking around in the pasture wearing white shoes and a stupid Ike cap in the company of this town's biggest turds and liars and outright crooks who'd gyp their granny out of her last thin dime, or spend a Saturday night in a suit and a necktie—well, that's another thing, I could go on for a week about how little by little she's been picking on me about my clothes and buying things behind my back for me to wear—so she'd have me looking like an undertaker on Saturday nights and sitting around a table listening to Guy Lombardo music while some banker like Jackie Redfearn bullshits some realtor like Raymond Eigor about how big a wad he's got, and they're all slapping each other on the back feeling like they're one big happy family running the whole damn deal around here, and to top it all off they're all going to show up Sunday morning down at the Episcopal—*Episcopal!*—church because Baptist ain't good enough for them no more, no, too many people there still ordering their clothes through the Sears or the Monkey-Ward catalogue and if your old lady ain't burning up the road between here and Lubbock or Midland twice a week to buy something to show off at church, then your dick ain't big enough—anyway, at the Baptist church all of a sudden there ain't near enough colored glass windows and mumbo-jumbo and jumping up and down on your knees, and she, I mean Vicky, of course, starts whining and nagging about going there at the Episcopal, too! So you ask me how are they alike? They're both wives! And the first thing a wife sets out to do is turn a husband into some other man! And the second thing she does is stop being who she was before you married her!" He was shouting. I had pushed a button. I felt in awe of my power, as if I were riding a riled-up stallion and didn't know whether to spur him on or calm him. As he might put it, what the hey, let's go for broke.

"I thought maybe y'all were disagreeing about, uh, other things."

"It's a long list, that's for sure."

He gave me a sidelong glance—he was having second thoughts about being so frank with his teen-age nephew. So I changed the subject and repeated Pete's story about his adventures and how others had reacted to it.

"Aw, he's famous for his bullshit." Uncle Waylan chuckled. "His old lady left him after he lost his hand, and I think the only women he'll touch are the whores in Juarez. But he's a good crew boss, Sport—steady, dependable, knows his business. It may not seem like much, but he can read and write, too. Between me and you, there's plenty of fellows you'll work beside who can't." I guessed he meant Cotton, who'd gone without lunch because he couldn't buy it. The connection between his being poor and being illiterate seemed logical, maybe even fitting—then, as a child of the Eisenhower '50s, I believed that one condition caused the other, and going without supper was Cotton's just punishment for not learning to read and write.

SIX

Uncle Waylan parked behind the new black Mercury nosed up under the protective roof of the carport. His yard was bare except for a sapling no thicker than a baseball bat. Up and down the street were other brick ranch-style homes just like his except for the color of the trim or the personalized touches in the spare landscaping. When he got out of the pickup, he slowly circumnavigated the Merc, brushing the flanks with his fingertips, stopping to rub a spot, frowning, pressing the tires with his boot toe, then, as a parting gesture, he jumped onto and off the rear bumper to check the shocks.

Aunt Vicky met us at the door in shorts and a blouse, and she hugged me like she'd known me for years. Her body was lean and firm, and we were about the same height so her thighs pressed mine. She wasn't wearing her glasses. A big round white earclip went cold against my cheek; she'd dabbed her neck with a cologne I'd never smelled, and when it hit my brain it seemed we were clinching even tighter, and I got a little scared.

"From my mom," I said.

"How sweet!" She set the present on the foyer table. She said, "Hello, hon," to Uncle Waylan, pecked his cheek while he stood by uncertainly, as if finding himself hat in hand in the parlor of the preacher.

"Hi, babe."

We went through the kitchen and onto a patio surrounded by a wooden windbreak. There were large pots of geraniums and a flowering vine draped over the fence. On a picnic table stood a bowl of potato salad covered with waxed paper, another bowl with pork and beans, a platter of sliced tomatoes, onion, and pickles, a large bag of chips, a standing row of jars: mustard, mayonaisse, and ketchup. A black drum barbeque was boiling out blue smoke. I was a little disappointed—I'd been thinking nice big baked ham, scalloped potatoes, black-eyed peas, cooked cabbage, Parker rolls, pecan pie with ice cream.

"I've got everything ready but the burgers. You boys want anything to drink?"

"The usual," said Uncle Waylan.

"How about a Coke, James?"

"Fine."

We sat in metal lawn chairs while Aunt Vicky got the drinks. Then she laid the patties on the grill and sat with us, drinking a Jax and smoking a Pall Mall.

Uncle Waylan said, "Any trouble with the Merc?"

"Well, it seems different. The motor."

"Different how?"

He got up and disappeared into the house. The instant he was out of earshot, Aunt Vicky said, "James, I'm so *very* sorry that you had to get caught in our sordid squabbling. I'm very very ashamed and I feel terrible about it. I hope Waylan told you to feel free to stay here instead of down at that filthy shop."

Her legs were long and tan and I could smell the coconut oil that sheened them. Her toenails were painted red. She crossed her legs and the heel of one sandal dangled loosely in the air. Her foot seesawed slowly, and my eyes moved with it as though connected by an invisible tether. I blushed. Surprise—my new aunt was sexy.

"Oh, I appreciate the offer, ma'am. But actually I like it there."

"Well, if you change your mind, come here, you understand? I'd be mortified to think that you're uncomfortable because two adults are acting like children."

I noticed she portioned out the blame fifty-fifty. "Yes, ma'am. I will."

"I shudder to imagine what your parents must think."

I took a slow swig of Coke. "Well, I think they'd understand, you know."

"So you haven't mentioned it yet?"

She was smiling with one corner of her mouth. I'd temporarily forgotten that she was a teacher and so was used to tricking the truth from people. But I was also a wary student accustomed to hiding it. "No, not yet. I only talked to them a minute last night to let them know I'd gotten here okay. I guess I didn't think to mention it."

"Well, James, under ordinary circumstances it would probably be the right thing to let them know what your living arrangements are."

I watched her face; the key word was *ordinary*. "Yes ma'am."

"I'm hoping this won't last too long, though."

"Yes ma'am."

"You can call me Aunt Vicky or just Vicky."

"Okay. Thanks."

"So I'd hate to think that by doing the right thing we might do the wrong thing."

"Pardon?"

She sighed, stubbed out her cigarette. "Well, if we were to speak too soon about it, you see, and have your mother think that you were plunk in the middle of a trashy domestic fracas, and then it blew over. . . " She shrugged.

"Yes, ma'am."

She winked at me. "So if you won't tell, I won't."

I laughed nervously. "Okay." The plan suited my needs, but conspiring with Aunt Vicky against my mother nagged at my conscience. Aunt Vicky wanted to protect her reputation. She wanted Uncle Waylan to join a country club; she was that person maybe most detested by my mother—a social climber. The disdain this aroused in me bumped against the desire those long sleek legs inspired.

Uncle Waylan returned, wiping his hands with a red rag and I could smell that pungent hand cleaner we used at the shop.

"Seems okay to me, Vicky."

"Fine, hon. Thanks." She smiled at him and flicked her eyes at me and I knew she'd sent him out to the car so we could make this pact.

Over the burgers, I gave dutiful answers to Aunt Vicky's perfunctory questions about my school, my favorite subjects (English and mechanical drawing), and my love life ("Do you have a steady girl yet, James?" asked with an amused twinkle in her eye and that crooked smile). Between snippets of our one-on-one she and Uncle Waylan had single-sentence exchanges on trivial subjects that petered out after a raft of, say, three or four. It was like watching two children play tennis for the second time. Uncle Waylan kept looking wishfully at his empty Jax bottle as if trying to will it full again. I didn't know whether he was going to wait politely for his hostess to offer him another or whether he didn't want to appear to be drinking too much. Several times he got up to inspect something within our field of vision—a crack in the patio cement, a tear in a window screen, paint flaking from the eaves—and she would turn her face toward me while I answered a question, but her gaze would follow him about the yard, then she'd look back at me with that enigmatic smile and mockingly raise her brow, making a tacit aside to our conversation. Once when he went to fetch her a Coke (but not another beer), she smiled, bobbed her head as if tagging the places he'd marked like a tomcat with his worry, and said, "He has to let me think I need him." I laughed, even though her tone implied he was a fool.

Later, returning from the bathroom, I saw them kissing. Uncle Waylan was seated and Aunt Vicky was standing beside his chair with an empty platter in one hand; her other hand was laid across his cheek as she bent down to his upturned face. One large brown hand of his was curled about the back of her upper thigh. She broke the kiss by straightening, patted his cheek and smiled at him. He looked sorrowful as a hound. When she came into the kitchen to set the platter down, I went out to the patio. His eyes looked faintly red. His leg was jittering up and down. He said, "Well, Sport, I reckon we ought to mosey. Been a long day for you, I'd say."

Aunt Vicky had me follow her to a dim room with a double bed in it. I wondered if this was where I would have stayed. The large doors on the closet slid open with a muted rumble. She took out a stack of towels, wash cloths, and folded sheets.

"James, I want you to take these. When they get dirty, you bring them back, hear? and I'll give you clean ones."

"Oh, well, thanks, that's really not necess—"

"James! I insist! I've seen that place you boys are staying in. Your Uncle Waylan is like everybody else in the world—he prefers clean sheets and towels. But he's not about to ask me for them—he's much too proud. It's the one thing you can count on in a man."

"Okay. Thanks."

"The thing is, I wouldn't want somebody else getting it in mind to do this sort of thing for you. Not when it's rightfully my place."

"Ma'am?"

She looked exasperated. "Do your laundry. Or his."

"That's really nice of you, Aunt Vicky."

"Nice has nothing to do with it. It's my job. I'm his wife, your aunt." Hands free, she danced between me and the door and leaned with a palm against the knob as if she would open it any second. But she didn't.

"And when you want a home-cooked meal, you let me know, okay? I wouldn't want somebody else to think you boys were being neglected. Your Uncle Waylan and I are only having a little spat—" she grinned ruefully—"unless of course my worst suspicions are eventually confirmed and he simply doesn't love me any more—but I certainly don't want it to be misconstrued by anybody you might meet here."

"Don't worry," I said, helplessly.

"Well, I can't help but worry." Tears welled along the lower rims of her eyes and she looked away. "I can't help it. This is my first time for being married. And I waited a while for it to happen. I hope I haven't made a terrible mistake." She turned back to me, smiled feebly, and dabbed at her eyes with the back of her wrist. "I'm sorry, I know this must make you very uncomfortable."

"Aw, don't worry, please. Maybe he's just being a Good Samaritan."

Her laugh was "hollow" and "mocking"—a B-movie laugh. "Oh, mercy, James! Excuse me! A Good Samaritan." Her eyes were gleaming. "Do you suppose it's just coincidental that the object of his charity is such a curvy young blonde? Maybe she has a case of leprosy I don't know about?"

I grinned nervously and shrugged. I could have answered that he was helping Trudy, too, but Aunt Vicky'd obviously aced the course required of teachers that hones their skill for sarcasm. I'd relished my ringside seat on a marital dispute only to find myself being splashed with the contestants' blood.

She leaned forward and stroked my forearm. "Oh, I'm sorry to drag you into this. It's not about her, believe me. It's about how he and I are going to spend our lives during the precious little time we have on earth."

That was sure a lofty way to say you wanted to belong to a country club, I thought, but held my tongue.

As we went out the door, Aunt Vicky picked up the gift-wrapped box from the foyer table. "I'll drop your mother a note right away." She caught my alarm and added, "I'll tell her you're getting along just fine."

I said thanks and went out the door as quickly as I could so they could be alone.

On the way home he kept yawning conspicuously as if to discourage me from talking. When we stepped out of the truck, we heard the phone ringing. Uncle Waylan said "Damnation!" and stomped off to the office. Instead of going to the bunk room, I pretended to look for something in the shop and cocked my ears to eavesdrop. My guess was that Sharon had called to grill him about his evening and to complain of being neglected. This was the idea I'd formed: Sharon was an old girlfriend who had never gotten over Uncle Waylan, and she'd come to town to wreck his marriage out of spite. As my mother would say, *Hell hath no fury* . . . . My opinion of Sharon's character was in inverse proportion to her beauty. (I was too young to know that's how men often steel themselves against a woman's attractiveness.)

In this battle of the sexes, Sharon had potent assets that I believed put my poor aunt at a disadvantage. In one corner was the bespectacled teacher and wife; in the other was Sharon, younger, more beautiful, and. . . what? What was the element left undefined? Something lay just beyond the grip of my boy's shapeless understanding, something as elusive as Sharon's own elusiveness: she was not married, could come and go as she pleased, could toss over her shoulder a "maybe I'll be here" that might send a suitor into a panic of uncertainty. And what I couldn't have explained at sixteen was that Sharon's essential advantage lay in what she inspired in men by her *provocative* freedom.

Uncle Waylan's "damnation!" struck off a complicated chain of consideration in me. I remembered Sharon's bare arm brushing mine in the pickup; I remembered how her skirt spread over my knees and created the sensation that I was in it with her; I remembered the way her flesh gave off the heady fragrance of a woman who'd been marinating in her cologne all day; I remembered the pale pink hollow of her throat flushed and damp from the heat and the tiny gold cross on a chain caught in it. If she'd been hounding me via the phone I'd have felt as if I'd won the Kentucky Derby. For my uncle to consider this call a nuisance was an awesome measure of his manhood.

"Kneu Well Service," he said, though I would've bet he knew it would be Sharon. "Hey there, kiddo. Huh? No, we just got back, just came in the door . . . . Yeah? Was it good? Did Trudy like it? Oh. Didn't go. I see. Just you and Cotton. Sharon, I'm glad, I really am." He laughed and listened for a minute. "I know you're an awful tease—you're not telling me anything I don't already know." He fell quiet and I could hear his boot heel thumping against the desk he'd hiked one haunch up on. "It's too late, Sharon, good golly—it's ten-thirty already, and we got work . . . . Oh, hell, I know I'm the boss. That's why I've got to be fresh as a daisy, you see?" After a moment, he lowered his voice. "Of course, I do, baby, you know I do," he murmured. He made kissing noises against the mouthpiece. Pete would call him *pussy-whipped*, but that seemed to me a condition to aspire to.

I scurried off to my bunk only a half minute ahead of Uncle Waylan, and shortly we were both lying in the dark. I thought we'd go right to sleep, but he after a minute he said, "Sweetie."

For a second I thought he was talking to me, or to Sharon or even Aunt Vicky, then I heard the *tik* of canine toenails. Then a rustle and a doggy grunt and I guessed he'd hoisted that baloney-with-a-butthole into his bed.

"Darlin' will you please tell me what it is with women?"

I said, "Can't live with them, can't live without them?"

He laughed. "You don't know the half of it, Jimbo. That was Sharon on the phone."

"What'd she want?"

"She wanted to punish me for spending the evening with my own wife."

"Why should she be jealous?"

"She thinks she and I should be, uh, together."

"Even though you're married to Aunt Vicky?"

"I know it doesn't sound reasonable."

"Is it because she knew you before you met Aunt Vicky?"

"Well, yeah, partly." He let out a long breath that fluttered his lips like a horse's. "I'm afraid I'm guilty of muddying the waters. I should have left well enough alone."

I heard the note of self-reproach. "What do you mean?"

"I should've told her to turn around and go home." He yawned. "Aw, God, let's get some shut-eye, whata you say?"

Uncle Waylan was snoring within seconds, but my head was too full of new ideas and sensations to let me rest. What had looked to be a minor dispute between husband and wife now shaped up as a love triangle. I'd never seen an adult version up close. As the impartial observer, I felt duty-bound to understand and to resolve it. I had a clear grasp of the problem at this point: Sharon was a homewrecker. Uncle Waylan was too generous for his own good. Aunt Vicky was a social climber. "Can This Marriage Be Saved?" The solution seemed obvious—all I had to do was wedge out Sharon and then get Aunt Vicky to accept Uncle Waylan as he was.

SEVEN

When I rang the bell I heard a cha-cha seeping through the door. "Cherry Pink and Apple Blossom White." I leaned closer—vacuum cleaner whine. My heart pounded. My Aunt Vicky was vacuuming! In the nude? Uncle Waylan had said that she had peculiar habits such as this. "She says nothing's more boring than running a Hoover. So she figures to make it more interesting." He'd seen this? "Naw, heck no!" he snorted. "She won't do it when somebody's around."

I doubted she could hear the bell over the Prez Prado brass, but I rang again with a trembly hand. Maybe I could innocently peek through the curtains to see if anyone's at home? Before I could work up the guts, the Hoover died down like a jet turbine. I rang again. The music sank as if dashed with cold water.

"Just a minute!" she called.

I imagined her striding nude down the hall. After a bit, she opened the door. Her white sleeveless blouse was tucked into wide-legged shorts. She was wearing her glasses.

"James!" she said brightly. She poked her head out and surveyed the sky as if expecting something to sail out of it. Then she held the screen door back so I could enter. She was barefoot, and her toenails had a fresh coat of red. That scent of coconut oil made my stomach growl.

"Sorry I didn't hear you—I was running the sweeper."

"It's okay. I wasn't here long."

"Want a Coke?"

"Sure, that'd be good."

Ostensibly I was here on this first Saturday morning to mow

the lawn. I was also supposed to call home from here to shore up our conspiracy and to give my aunt an opportunity to speak to my mother. Also, Uncle Waylan had urged me to spend the day "so y'all can get to know each other better," a hopeful sign that they had a future.

But my most compelling motive was to write the next chapter of *The Hardy Boy and the Mystery of the Marital Estrangement.* "Estrangement" was the word Trudy had used to describe my aunt and uncle's relationship. "Well, they're separated," I told her. Trudy said, "It's more than that—or at least that's what Waylan's telling us. Separated can mean one of you is out of town; you're 'estranged' when you don't want to be together. Besides, they're not legally separated. Are they?" I couldn't answer that.

Aunt Vicky lifted newspapers from a chair and gestured me into it. Then she handed me a napkin, a glass, and a cold six-ounce bottle of Coke. I thanked her, but I wondered, as always, why women believed the napkin and glass to be necessary. She rounded up the same trio of objects for herself then sat east to my south. Under the base of my green bottle I felt the grit of spilled sugar or salt.

"I thought maybe you should do the yard first before it gets too hot, then we could have lunch here." She smiled. "Then if the fallout's not too bad, I'll give you a little tour."

"The fallout?"

"We've been experimenting this week to see if we can vaporize an entire Pacific Island—the H-bomb tests at Bikini?"

"Oh, I didn't know."

"Where do you stand on that?"

"On H-bombs?" My heart was sinking—would I have to go to school today? "They're better than A-bombs. If the Russians or the Red Chinese are going to have them, I guess we better." This opinion was a consensus in my barbershop, so I thought it safe to adopt.

"Oh. *Do* the Russians or the Chinese have them? Or will they be getting them quick as they can because we have them?"

I was wearing the face version of nervous shoe-shuffling, so she laughed. "Never mind. How was your week? What'd you do?"

With relief I told her I'd laid a flow line, dug out a cattle guard, hooked up a well, learned to cut and thread pipe, and painted a meter run. I said I had a sunburned neck and sore muscles, but my tin hat now had a few dents in it and an oil stain, and my initiation was over. When I started in about Pete, she said, "Oh, I know Pete! I used to be the office gal now and then." She looked into her glass and grinned. "I never imagined growing up in Baltimore that I'd ever be in the same room with men who had such names as 'Red' and 'Buck.' How's Cotton?"

"Fine." Actually, Cotton was the one coworker who'd resisted my efforts to be friendly. I wondered why she would single him out.

"Waylan kind of looks out for him. I did, too. He's young, you know. Doesn't have any family we know of. We put him up in the bunkhouse for a while."

I wondered if my coming had displaced Cotton, but there was room for three. "They're all really great guys."

"What do you like about them?"

"Well, they know how to do things. And they tell funny stories and horse around. And they'll accept you if you do your share of the work and don't whine."

"It helps if you're the boss's nephew, too."

That stung. "If anything, Aunt Vicky, it makes me work a little harder."

"Oh certainly!" she gushed. "I didn't mean that you would take advantage of it. And believe me, Waylan's been singing your praises to me."

"He has? No kidding?"

"Yes. He's very proud of how well you've fit in."

I sought to cap my virtues with a becoming modesty. "Well, how has your week been?" I asked thoughtlessly, and as the echo of my question bounced about, Aunt Vicky appraised me with a narrow look, then apparently decided she wasn't ready to confide in me.

"Pretty well, apart from the government's attempt to atomize a lovely Pacific atoll and the Dixiecrat efforts in the Senate to squelch Ike's civil rights bill, and what with Kefauver and Stevenson both turning into reactionaries, it's been okay, I guess. Business as usual. Helen and I—you'll meet her later, she's my best friend—we've been trying to get up a Harriman committee here in town, and we're also working to head off a couple of Baptist preachers who want to ban about a dozen books from the library shelves because the authors are supposed to be Reds or because the contents are too shocking for decent, upright people, etcetera. You know, I didn't know much about Southern Baptists until I came here—they're about the sole source of public mischief to my mind. Ignorance and bigotry: boy, they've got the corner on the market! You should have heard them carry on when the Brown decision came through! You'd have thought the Apocalypse was here!" She laughed caustically. "Oh, my God, I just remembered—your family's Baptist!"

"My mom. Dad's Methodist. That's the church we go to."

"Oh, well, I'm sure not all Baptists are morons!"

"My mom's smart but she is pretty straight-laced."

"I'll bear that in mind." Aunt Vicky grinned. "Anyway, Helen and I have been organizing resistance to this nonsense. We're trying to get appointed to the library board and we had a meeting this week with Harold Jackson—he's the publisher of this rag"—she held up the *Hedorville Herald* and flapped it at me—"though I'm afraid that trying to get him to do anything but worry about his advertisers is a lost cause. You know what he said? 'Ladies, if half the books in that library were taken off the shelves, there'd still be more reading matter than there are readers in this town.' Can you believe that? I said, 'What about the First Amendment? What if somebody wants to take your newspaper out of the library? What then?' And he said, 'Why I can't imagine such a thing! I'm very careful about what goes in it.'"

She'd sung to a bird's-eye pause. I piped in with "Huh!" I'd imagined that she'd spent her week playing bridge and tennis at the country club, even though Uncle Waylan refused to belong.

"You know what happened last night?"

Well, *I'd* played miniature golf with Trudy and Sharon and Uncle Waylan. "No—what?"

"I went over to Helen's to watch 'Medic.' Have you seen that show?"

"Yes, back home. I've missed TV here." The one channel Hedorville received from Odessa required a tall roof-top antenna. The Round-Up Motel had the only TV set I'd seen, and the reception was wretched.

"The episode that they'd planned on 'Medic' last night was canceled because General Electric had gotten protests. It was supposed to show a Cesarean section."

"A what?"

Aunt Vicky sighed. "That's what makes me so furious! Don't you think you need to know about such a thing?"

"I guess."

"It's an operation that's done when a baby can't be delivered vaginally. They make an incision in the mother's abdomen and the child is removed from the womb through that."

Vaginally. Vaginally. Reflexively, I saw the graffiti vagina from countless gas station restrooms. "Huh," I said. I had known, vaguely, what the operation was.

"For God's sake! What's to be gained from keeping people from learning something like that? Sometimes I think the whole country's been taken over by retardates from the Planet Ignoramus."

She smiled to show she was kidding. I got the idea that she might be a very entertaining English teacher, the sort who'd make Shakespeare fun.

"Waylan tells me you've got a girl here already. She works at Runt and Dot's?"

I almost choked on my Coke. "I don't have no—any—girl-friend yet, Aunt Vicky." It was sly of Uncle Waylan to identify her that way rather than say she was Sharon's cousin. How much did Aunt Vicky know about this situation?

She smirked. "If you say so."

My ears burned. When your mom insists that you take her bridge partner's daughter to a church social—that's how Trudy and I were a couple. We were both juniors, but she was one in college, and, boy, did she lord that over me! But we were good cover for Sharon and Uncle Waylan, I guess.

"Didn't you tell me you have a girl back in Dallas?"

"Yeah. Her name's Louise Bowen. She's a counselor at Camp Longhorn this summer. We're not going steady or anything." I squirmed not only from the embarrassment of talking about my "love life," but because it implied that like my Uncle Waylan I could be a bigamist, you might say. I'd promised to write to Louise but hadn't. She wore saddle oxfords and ribbons in her hair, still had braces and blushed frequently and clammed up when we were alone together; once when were slow-dancing I slid my thigh deep between her legs, but she kept backing away. "She's only a sopho-more," I added. "I better get to that mowing."

Like my father, Uncle Waylan had not yet bought a gas-powered mower—a new invention at the time—so his Bermuda grass had to be cut by pushing a wheeled cylinder of blades to and fro, two steps up, one step back. The thing weighed a couple hundred pounds, it seemed, but it had a distinctive sound as it churned—a soft, rising and falling *ruh-duh-duh-duh-duh* that is among the many aural cultural artifacts lost to us now, like the playing card *slap-slap-slap* on a bicycle's spokes, and Lamont Cranston's laugh. To cut the grass, you set up a rhythm like that of a woman working on a sewing machine, pulse and rest, pulse and rest, a pattern that mimics our larger, circadian cycle.

I took off my shirt to embellish my tan and covered the front lawn in compulsively aligned furrows like a farmer planting with a tractor. Not hard work for a guy who spent all week heaving big steel stuff around. The sun was blazing in summer glory, and I could hear other mowers inhaling and exhaling as they moved over neighboring lawns. Across the street a man was washing a '54 two-tone Chevy Bel-Aire V-8 four-door using a galvanized bucket and a red towel. The car had white sidewalls.

After forty minutes of mowing, I rolled the machine into the carport and wiped the sweat off my face and arms and torso with my dry shirt. I went through the gate into the back yard where a brick walk led around a windbreak and onto the patio, where, unexpectedly, I came upon Aunt Vicky lying limbs askew in the lowered deck chair, her limp form cupped aloft from the flagstones by the awning-striped sling of canvas. Thinking she was dozing, I glided toward the patio quietly. She lay with one bare leg cocked ankle-to-knee over the other; the hem of her shorts yawned open and the dark secret space within snatched up my gaze like a sudden start might have taken my breath, and before I could catch myself I glimpsed: It. Not directly, of course—that would have blinded me—but in my mind's eye, behind the scrim of her white cotton panties, a slice of which, elasticized, pressed diagonally across her loins and was embroidered by errant black cilia. My heart stopped.

Shocked, I snapped my gaze to her face. Her eyes were opening or had already been open and she'd shut them again to give me room to think she hadn't caught me looking.

"Oh!" She raised up, shot me a *tsk! tsk!* look that might have been a self-reproach for napping, pressed the shorts hem down with her palms, picked up her glasses, then stood awkwardly from the low-slung chair. "I must have dozed. All done?"

I cleared my throat. I was aware of being shirtless and compulsively flexed everything I could without making an obvious show. "I reckon."

She smiled. "Reckoning is for navigators."

"I'm through, I mean."

She ruffled my hair the way you would a ten-year-old's. "What a nice smart boy you are!" She had a jocular glitter in her eyes and the barest suggestion of a mocking smile, as if to goad me with this compliment. A sarcastic allusion to my peeking? "I bet your sisters adore you! Let's have lunch, shall we?"

I let her see me comb back my hair with my fingers. In the kitchen, I asked if I could help. She had me slice a cucumber, and when I finished, she said, smiling, "That's good! You know, James, you'll make somebody a nice husband someday," leaving me to wonder if I shouldn't have objected to doing woman's work. Was being a "nice husband" something a boy should desire?

She'd made tuna salad with dill pickles (my mother used sweet) and tomatoes with cottage cheese—it was a "lady's lunch," and I'd yearned for meat and potatoes. My mother's voice instructed me to put on my shirt before I sat down, and, even had I not heard it, an indefinable fear of attracting Aunt Vicky's notice would have inspired me to do it. Every exchange we'd had rattled me. All the categories I'd placed her in—teacher, grown-up, aunt, easterner—were occupied by females I customarily regarded as void of "sex appeal," we called it then. I didn't know how to cope with what she aroused in me.

Struck dumb, I didn't make much of a lunch partner, but I did listen as she talked about her school year. "You're so very different from most of my kids," she said.

"I am?" I was horrified to hear this.

"Yes. Most of the boys are destined to be gas-pump jockeys and the girls will be brood mares. I'm afraid they have a dismal future. I've got a feeling about you, James, and I'd guess you've got college plans already. What do you want to be?"

"Maybe a lawyer like my dad. Or a civil engineer. But I'm not so good at math. Sometimes I think I'd like to be an architect, too."

"You said lawyer 'like my dad,' as if you were more interested in being like him than in studying law? Is that the case?"

"I don't know. My dad's a pretty great guy."

"That's wonderful that you can say that. Waylan—" She stopped herself, and, of course, I had a terrible curiosity as to what she held back.

"Mom says Grandpop was a worthless drunk."

"I don't know about that. I was about to say that Waylan hopes to have a son someday." Before I could nudge the conversation along, she got up from the table. "Speaking of parents and kids, we'd better call your folks and be on our way."

I didn't offer to help wash the dishes, as I foresaw it might inspire a maverick remark from her about my masculinity. As it turned out, she merely stacked the dirty dishes in the sink, a mildly shocking act of procrastination judged against my mother's habits.

As was usual in those days, the Kneus had but one phone, and it was in the first room off the hallway, which might have been a bedroom but had the appearance of a cluttered office. The phone sat on a roll-top desk amongst stacks of pamphlets and issues of *The New York Times,* delivered, I learned, by mail one week late. As I waited for the phone to be answered in Dallas, I saw on the front page of the top issue that the famous scientist, Robert Oppenheimer, was warning against "nuclear Apocalypse." But hadn't he helped make the bomb!? (It was my second Apocalypse of the day.) A supporter of Adlai Stevenson in Florida was calling Kefauver "a sycophant of the Negro vote." Sycophant? My exchange with Aunt Vicky about the H-bomb made me alert to these headlines, and the A student in me automatically took notes in case she tested me later. Though I knew this paper by reputation, I'd never known anyone who actually read it, and seeing the real thing on that desk right at hand was still another curiously electrifying fact of this day.

The room was dim, the drapes shut against the noon-day heat and light; Aunt Vicky came in and hovered behind me, passing back and forth, stirring up currents of coconut oil that eased up my nostrils. She made me nervous; she seemed unpredictable.

I was relieved to hear my dad answer; I knew that he'd merely keep booming "Good! Good!" to whatever I reported and wouldn't ask about anything other than work. I pumped him full of information to keep him on the line so that when my mother got her turn she'd worry about the long-distance charges and not feel free to ask penetrating questions. Finally, he relinquished the phone to her, and, quickly as I could, I asked about Deidre and Alise (wondering, as I did, do they "adore" me?) then told her Aunt Vicky wanted to talk to her.

Aunt Vicky stood at the phone and I sat in the desk chair, but that put my face too close to one sleek leg, so I moved across the room to a love seat.

"I wanted to thank you for that lovely book of *haiku*, May. It was so thoughtful. What an adorable cover!"

She listened for a moment. "Oh, he's been no trouble at all." She whirled suddenly and grinned at me over the receiver. "He's a sweetheart. He's very helpful and eats about anything put before him."

I thought—these are my virtues as a man?

"Oh, well, no, I haven't tried Brussels sprouts on him! Thanks for the warning!"

She smirked at me as if this were uproarious, but I wanted her to get the hell off the line: it was one thing for a kid to be a weasel, it was another to conspire with an adult against your mother.

"Oh, no. It's been a real pleasure. You're very welcome! Well, I hope so, too! My best to Frank, too. Good-bye, dear!"

Good Lord, my Aunt Vicky talked to my mom as if they'd been friends for decades—and lied, to boot! What a hypocrite!

As if sensing my disapproval, Aunt Vicky said, "We can't keep up this charade forever, James. It's not fair to your folks."

Was she blaming me? Irritated, I asked, "Do you think you and Uncle Waylan will get back together soon?"

She sighed. "I honestly don't know. It depends."

I waited, but she wasn't forthcoming. Having witnessed her lies, I felt licensed to ask, "What's the fight about, anyway?"

"I'm not sure."

I had her on the run, I thought. "Is it the country club?"

"What? The country club?" She scowled at me.

"The, uh . . . " Now I'd jumped into waters way over my head.

"What in the world has he told you, anyway?"

I wanted to crawl under the love seat.

"Whatever it was, I can assure you our problems are not related in any way, shape or form to the Hedorville Country Club, James!

If he—oh, gosh, I'm sorry, I'm not going to make you a party to all this unpleasantness! And I wish he wouldn't! If he won't go to a marriage counselor, then the least he can do is keep his mouth shut so other people won't go around with half-baked ideas about our problems! Really!"

"I'm sorry. I—"

"It's not your fault, for God's sake! You're sixteen years old! I'm really furious with him!"

She fumed in silence. I stared at the beige carpet. The result of my first effort to unlock the mystery and find a satisfactory solution for everyone was this: they were now even more estranged, thanks to me.

"You think there's hope?"

"Yes. Yes, I do! If I didn't I certainly wouldn't hang around here! I'm a fighter, James, and my greatest failing is I keep gnawing at something even when everybody else sees a lost cause. Maybe I'm stupid that way. Well, I know I've been stupid that way before. *But I do not like to give up on anything!"*

EIGHT

She let me drive the Merc. First stop—a new, tan brick building beside a requisite one-bleacher stadium. The high school sat smack in the middle of vast acres of prodigally luxuriant grass empty but for parallel ranks of portable aluminum tubing that fueled the sprinklers. We drove up a horseshoe drive past an old cannon painted yellow and black and to a bank of glass doors. The sprinklers rotated on their stanchions with a metronomic clatter and hiss and flung arcs of glittering water high overhead. We stopped to peer through the car windows at the entrance. Aunt Vicky waved to a black man trimming hedges with wooden-handled clippers, and he waved back.

"That's Henry Mahew—he's head custodian. His son's one of my students."

"I guess Negroes go here now?"

"They used to have their own ha-ha 'separate but equal' facilities in an old army-surplus Quonset hut. I'll say one thing for this town—when the Brown decision was announced, nobody but the Baptists raised a stink, and a lot of them saw the light—ah, yes, saw the light, once the football team had its first winning season in ten years." She laughed. "How about your school?"

"There's one girl, Wynetta Drake," I said with pride. "She's on the student council and everything."

"A credit to her race, no doubt." The target of her sarcasm was invisible to me—it's not okay to be a credit to your race?

"Education's the key, I guess." Another piece of conventional wisdom obtained at the barbershop.

"Key to what? Turn left." She pointed back toward the center of town.

"Well, the key to the race problem, I guess. That's what people say."

"What in the world do you suppose they mean?"

"Gosh, Aunt Vicky, are you going to make me go to summer school the whole time I'm here?" I grinned.

"I hope you plan to be in school all your life, James. I'm just making conversation. I want to know what your ideas are."

Of course, my ideas were unformed, vague suppositions, easy generalizations. "Maybe people mean that if Negroes become educated, then they—"

"—they'll get all dressed up and go to nice Baptist churches and stop playing bebop jazz and talking in dialect and eating watermelon and they'll start getting interested in banning books and television programs, maybe? Then the race problem will go away because there'll be no more Negroes. I think that's what people have in mind." She chuckled. "Tell you what I think. I think white people are badly in need of education, too."

She let me off the hook by asking me what I liked to read; I answered that I liked science fiction some, and also westerns.

"Did you bring any books with you?"

"Aw, no. I didn't think I'd have time."

"That's fine—we're going to the library today, anyway. We'll load you up. Maybe I'll check out the novels Reverend Wright is so eager to ban—have you heard of *Catcher in the Rye* or *Tobacco Road*? Or *The Naked and the Dead*? I'll bet you'd like those."

I'd heard of *Tobacco Road*. Reading it would be something to keep from my mother.

"What's *The Naked and the Dead*?"

"Not as racy as it sounds. It's a war novel by Norman Mailer. I checked it out for Waylan thinking he might read it and kept it around for weeks, but . . . ." She laughed again. "He seemed afraid of it! Isn't that something—he's not afraid to go to war, but reading a little ole bitty book? Oh, my!"

"Why do they want to ban it?"

"The F word. I figure it won't harm you to see it between hard covers since you've read it a thousand times on restroom walls and probably heard it in as many dirty jokes."

I smiled. One lesson I'd learned this week was the florid variations on standard curses, the most astounding to my ear being *"mother-goddamn-fucker"* and *"son-of-a-mother-goddamn-fucking-bitch."*

Cruising the main drag, we passed a three-story building of red brick.

"That's the Harding Hotel—it's where I lived for a year when I first came here, in one tiny room and a bath down the hall."

"With Uncle Waylan?"

"Oh, no! I didn't know him then. When I showed up here I knew absolutely no one. My clan is the rootbound type. That was one reason I came out here. Because . . . . " She looked out the window at the hotel. Aunt Vicky was full of words, but the gaps between were significant, as if she was so used to speaking her mind that she sometimes began talking before she'd given herself permission. Naturally, these ghost predicates were of great interest to me, but I didn't yet know how to make them manifest.

Finally, she chuckled. "Well, why have people always come west, anyway?"

"To be fur trappers and gold-miners and cattlemen and farmers?"

"Oh, sure. Some, of course. I'm not any of those. You're forgetting the outlaws."

She winked in an officially "mysterious" fashion, grinned playfully at me, showing a line of strong-looking teeth.

"You're Aunty Oakley?"

She guffawed. "Good, James! No, I guess you'd have to call me Calamity Jane these days!"

When we stepped inside Buford Pharmacy I saw a soda fountain along one mirrored wall where you might order a grilled cheese or club sandwich and chocolate shake (you'd get the frosted cannister along with the glass tulip). In addition to the long counter of mottled gray marble and its chrome-ringed stools of burgundy vinyl, a small service area of six booths stood between the end of the fountain and the back of the store, partitioned from Ralph Buford's pharmaceuticals antechamber by a frosted glass divider. Here, I was told, the merchants and councilmen and lawyers and salesmen met mornings for coffee and tobacco and talk. If you wanted to give someone a message, you left it on a corkboard fastened to the wall or you told Evelyn Buford at the register to pass it on. The front windows displayed posters advertising bake sales and dances at the American Legion and the Yellowjacket football schedule, and for most things people needed—shoelaces, EverReady flashlight batteries, a gift box of Prince Machiabelli bath powder—Buford's was the first place they thought of: not only was Buford's likely to have it, but while getting it they could run into someone to chat with over coffee.

On Saturday afternoon, the store boiled over with talk and smoke, the sizzle of the grill and whir of the mixer, clatter of crockery and laughter.

Aunt Vicky said, in an aside as we were entering, "I've got to pick up a prescription, but we'll have to run the gauntlet to get it."

Aunt Vicky had to stop, greet, and introduce me to two glad-handing councilmen, her high school principal, the counter gal Gladys, the mother of a student, and a Baptist deacon, who cracked a grin as he shook her hand then mine, and said to me, "Watch out, son, she's a pistol!"

"Don't go building any bonfires yet, mister!"

They laughed in each other's faces like two dogs barking through a fence. At the drug counter, Aunt Vicky discussed her medicine for "nervousness" with Ralph Buford (eavesdropping was as irresistible as snooping in a medicine cabinet), and while we waited for her prescription for Thalidomide to be filled, a matronly woman in a Mamie-Eisenhower hat sidled up, pressed Aunt Vicky's hand between her own white-gloved digits, and crooned, "Oh, dear, I'm so sorry about your trouble. You know things usually work out for the best!"

"Thank you, Miz Beasley," murmured Aunt Vicky, but I could tell that she wanted to throttle the woman.

"Miz Beastly we call her at school," cracked Aunt Vicky when we were outside. "She's teaches home economics. I hate how you can't blow your nose here without somebody handing you a hanky. Worst is when you have your hair done at the Cut 'N Curl and soon as you get your head in a dryer bubble, you can almost see people talking about you. So long as they all seem to know so dadgum much I wish they'd tell me, too."

I twitched inside. I'd bet I knew more about Uncle Waylan's relationship with Sharon than she did, but I sorely wished I didn't.

Back in the car she directed me west on the main drag and said, "That's where I met Waylan, you know. I was campaigning for Stevenson in '52. I was going down the line of people sitting at the counter introducing myself and handing out pamphlets. Helen was with me. Waylan wouldn't let go of my hand. He said he wasn't going to turn loose until he'd heard a compelling reason not to vote Republican for the first time in his life. He was a terrible flirt. He is a terrible flirt! I thought he was good-looking in a rugged way, and really full of bullstuff, but he made me laugh, and he had a step-right-up directness and a kind of, well, animal magnetism I wasn't used to in a man."

I asked, cautiously, "He wasn't like other men you'd dated?"

"That's an understatement! The fellow I was most used to, back home, was slow-moving, veeerrrry slooooow-moving. Sometimes it took half an hour to decide on a restaurant, and then there'd be still another thirty to pick a movie." She laughed to herself. "An ounce of prevention kind of person, you could say. Always wanted to be fair, you know. Let you endlessly debate the *little* things with him because he was never going to . . . . Well, what I saw in Waylan was how he'd get an idea to do something and zip! right there he'd go. I liked being with a person who had no second thoughts. I was in a frame of mind to be exactly likewise. He didn't debate, cogitate, masticate or ruminate, James. *Vini, vidi, vici!* Another thing was Waylan is so physical! Since we've been together, I've learned how to square-dance, ride a motorcycle, and water-ski, and once he talked me into jumping off that thirty-five-foot tower in the Pecos River over at Carlsbad." She grinned and shook her head. "I'd never done anything in my life like that. That water about snatched me bald-headed! Waylan was supposed to hold my hand all the way down, but soon as we both jumped, he turned loose." She turned to me and cackled. "Doesn't that sound just like him?

"Anyway, that day he said he'd seen me before in Buford's and had asked a couple of hundred people all about me." She smiled. "I said I hoped they all had good reports, and he said they all told him that there wasn't anything wrong with me that a night of two-stepping out at Al's with him wouldn't cure. That's where we went. I'd never been in a honky-tonk, let alone dance with a cowboy—that's what I thought of him, then—and I guess what surprised me most was how he could waltz better than any man I'd been with, even in those boots. Better than all those Annapolis cadets who've had lessons all their lives. Women really like that, you know."

I could feel her gaze on me. "They do?" I'd have to take her word for it. I thought of how clumsy I felt herding Louise around on the cornmeal-salted floor of our gym.

"You bet. It's romantic, you get up close and hold each other and move. Don't tell me you don't dance."

"Not very well. I can do a box step okay."

"Well, maybe you and Waylan and your girlfriend can come over and we'll give you lessons. Take the next right." She was quiet for a moment, then she said, ruefully, "I drank more than I meant to that night."

"Really?" It was astounding that she'd confess this to me, a student.

"Yeah, he kept calling me his 'schoolmarm' and that really irritated me. Sometimes I'm a contrarian. Well, I'm often a contrarian! He wasn't too sober, either, though. He told a lot of funny stories, and he told me a lot—way too much—about Noreen, too . . . . Talk about ironic—if I could get him to talk that much to me about us . . . "

"I've heard stories about Aunt Noreen."

"Who's to blame for their break-up in the ones you heard? Oh, never mind, I'm sorry, James, I seem to keep drawing you into this."

"That's all right. It's interesting."

"It's better as a spectator sport, believe me." She fell silent again, and then, as if succumbing, said, "But I do want to tell you why I wanted a second date with him. I mean, I had a good time dancing and joking that night and, well, fencing with him I guess you could call it, but I was suspicious that he was too glib and was used to having women get crushes on him. I found him enormously attractive, but his charm was too ready, like a tool he knew he was good at using. Kind of the opposite of sincerity, you see? It's fun to be charmed, but you don't trust it."

I made a note not to be too charming to girls I wanted to impress, but given how tongue-tied I usually felt, there wasn't much danger.

"So we were having a good time, really, and it was the first date I'd been on for months and for sure the first I'd enjoyed—you know what I just realized? I guess I'm talking so much because it was just about this time four years ago that all this happened—but anyway I was thinking I wouldn't mind going out with him again but wouldn't expect much to come from it except a good time, which was okay, but there was that resistance I had to his quickness because I thought it could mean he was shallow, too. Am I boring you?"

"No ma'm. No."

"I find it hard to believe a teenage boy would want to hear such stuff. Not that something's wrong with you if you do, of course."

"No, really," I protested. True, I had started this day doubtful that I'd enjoy spending hours alone with a grown female relative, but now I saw I'd been completely wrapped up in her talk.

"What happened was Waylan almost got into a fist fight. We stayed until closing time and came out into the parking lot and got into his car and we were laughing and talking and he'd just turned the engine on when we heard somebody scream. On the other side of the lot there was a man, a really big man! and a woman standing by a car, and this galoot was slapping this poor girl—oh, gosh!" Aunt Vicky cringed and shivered. "Just slapping her and cuffing her on the face and ears, and she was crying and yelling and trying to cover up and was kind of doubled over by the car door. Waylan jumped out and I got out and stood by our car and looked around hoping to see somebody else. He started calling out to the guy, 'Say there, fella! That's not a good idea! Knock it off! She's not your size!' He was talking loud but didn't sound worked up or angry, just, you know, insisting on being heard and getting the man's attention. Well, of course, this big bruiser did stop hitting the woman and he turned to Waylan and said, 'Go eff yourself,' and then he grabbed the woman's arm and wrenched her away from the car and started dragging her off like he wanted to get her out of the light so he could whale the dickens out of her again." Aunt Vicky pressed her palm to her chest. "My God, I'm shaking just to remember it now! I was so so scared! For the woman, and for Waylan, too! For a second, I thought about running to get help, but I didn't want to leave—I mean, at least I'd be a witness, and I kept feeling that maybe I'd help, some way.

"Well, Waylan scrambled around and got in front of the fellow again. 'Damn if I don't find I'm having to repeat myself to you!' he said. What he said is crystal clear in my head. 'I just hate that. You seem like a reasonable sort of hombre—I'm asking you, let go that woman. Leave her be! She ain't big enough to fight back.' The fellow let go of the woman, but he squared off against Waylan. He said something like 'Shut your hole or I'm gonna shut it for you!' Waylan took off his hat and set it on the hood of a car. He was still acting calm. He told this palooka, 'I'd just as soon not have to do this, but if you're gonna be a horse's ass instead of cooling off, well, then I reckon that's that.' And just when Waylan was taking off his watch, the woman called out to the fellow, 'Lloyd, I'm goin' home! You coming or not?' I looked at her—she was really young, probably not much older than my students—and she looked at me, and I knew that she was trying to save Waylan from a terrible beating. This yahoo said, 'I'm coming soon's I whup this nosy so-and-so's ass.' The woman started for the bar. She said, 'I'm sure the sheriff's gonna appreciate having to have another talk with you.' The fellow cussed for a minute, then he trotted after her into the building. But he yelled back that he better not catch Waylan out here by himself or he'd—you know, some impossible vulgarity."

Aunt Vicky laid the nape of her neck against the back of the seat and closed her eyes, her hand still over her heart. "I'm haunted by what happened to that girl later."

"Something happened to her?"

"No doubt."

"Oh, you meant probably."

She opened her eyes and squinted at me. "Would it hurt any less?"

When I didn't answer, she said, "When Waylan got back into the car, I was shaking all over. He was trying to be calm for me, you know, solid and steady. He said, kind of joking, 'Boy, am I glad she talked him out of that! I had better plans for my body tonight than getting it beat to a bloody pulp.' I said, 'Waylan, that was really really brave of you!' He said, 'Too bad it won't make any difference in the long run.'"

This story suited my conventional idea of what made men attractive to women—in the Charles Atlas ads bullies kicked sand in the faces of ninety-five-pound weaklings, but once the weaklings had the body-building course, girls were fairly trampling one another in a race to hang onto his meaty biceps.

I said, "So his being willing to fight this big guy made you want to have a second date?"

"Not exactly. He could have have a dozen fights with bigger men and it wouldn't have moved me. It was trying to save the girl."

NINE

I came out here because it was as far away from home as I could get," said Aunt Vicky. "But it sure looked wicked ugly at first, and I got pretty depressed. It was so flat and bare and the wind blew sand in my eyes and ears, and all I could see were tin buildings and tumbleweeds and every nook and cranny full of trash the wind had blown. And I know it sounds snobbish, but there didn't seem to be a soul at that high school worth talking to. I thought I'd come to the end of the world. But I had a one-year contract, and I was determined to see it through."

She pointed ahead to a large, Santa-Fe-style adobe structure standing under huge old cottonwood trees in a park-like lot.

"This place saved my sanity."

I carried a shopping bag of books taken from the back seat. Along the walk leading to the doors were cactus gardens and shrubs in bloom. A flock of boys was playing football along one side of the grounds, and on benches scattered here and there women with strollers sat chatting.

Aunt Vicky said she'd found the library soon after her arrival. It was once an old ranch homestead, so, unlike other buildings in Hedorville erected since the '30s oil boom, it had been here over fifty years. The surviving widow had willed it to the city. It had a dozen beam-ceilinged rooms with polished tile floors. The thick earthen walls held in the coolness of the night in the summer and the day's heat during winter. She said she claimed a spot near the fireplace in a secondary reading room; after school on open evenings, she did her homework here and enjoyed a respite from the hotel. Seated in the quiet, dim room, surrounded by the old heavy Spanish furniture, admiring the Navajo rugs, she could picture herself as a woman of the older West, the Spanish Conquest West (well, all these years later I can imagine her imagining this, at least), not this West of oil-patch trash and honky-tonks and men in hard hats who whistle at you on the street.

Behind a check-out desk stood a young man in a white shirt and red bow-tie.

"Truman, Hi! You home for the summer now?"

"Yes ma'am. Boy, I had no idea I'd be in the middle of a hornet's nest!"

Aunt Vicky laughed. She introduced us, and we shook, I of course giving him a bone-crusher—the working man's response to meeting a white-collar counterpart. I judged him to be a college man who wouldn't last five minutes laying pipeline.

I heaved the shopping bag onto the counter. The fellow drew the books from the bag with a slim, clean hand.

"Wish you'd have been here earlier. Some Christian citizens have taken a sudden interest in fiction."

"They check out all the dirty books?"

"The ones they could find. They're not used to the card catalog." He grinned. "I wasn't much help."

"That's good! Who was it?"

"Thelma Wiggins was one, then Eddie Bickley came in about ten minutes later. He wanted to know if we had *Peyton Place* or *Lady Chatterley's Lover*. He made sure I didn't think he was actually going to read them."

"Skim for the good parts, huh? Well, I wanted to treat James to something they might object to." She thought a moment. "I don't imagine that they've discovered *Lolita*, yet. Maybe that?" She looked at me as if I could judge, but of course I couldn't. "Yes, that might do."

Even this fellow Truman looked unsure of the wisdom of this. "Are you a Nabokov fan?" he asked doubtfully.

"He will be," said Aunt Vicky.

"What's it about, anyway?" I asked when he stepped away to retrieve the book. I dreaded having to read something recommended by a teacher, knowing I'd have to give a report.

Aunt Vicky peered at me over her glasses. "A middle-aged professor comes to America and becomes, umm, infatuated with an adolescent girl. Believe me, the literary merit far outweighs whatever

72

prurient interest people think it has. Nabokov will be good for your vocabulary."

I shrugged. When the fellow handed me the book, Aunt Vicky said, "I'm trusting you to be mature about this. Not everybody's going to approve—they could accuse me of corrupting your morals, and I'm not joking! I wouldn't recommend it to one of my own students, James."

My mother was they. "Fine, sure, I understand." Now I was dying to read it. While Truman logged Aunt Vicky's returns, I thumbed through the book eagerly, as if expecting to see Varga girls.

"What'd you think?" Truman held up *Witness for the Prosecution.*

"Actually, I'm not much of a mystery buff," said Aunt Vicky.

"Somebody else in your family?"

"No, I did check them out for me. I had a friend, have a friend, who's an ardent fan of hers. He met her once in London."

"Really?"

"Not met, exactly. Stood in a theater line two people back from her. At least he thinks it was she. He said he stood for a long time trying to decide if the woman was actually Agatha Christie, and if he ever made up his mind, then he was going to go up and tell her how much he appreciated her work. He said he hesitated until the very last moment before the woman was about to pass through the door to her seat—hers was downstairs, and his was up—and when he finally got the nerve to tap her on the shoulder, he got nervous and said, 'Aren't you Miss Jane Marple?'"

Truman laughed. I didn't get it. He said, "I couldn't do that. John Ciardi came to read this spring and I couldn't make myself shake his hand!"

"My friend's an Anglophile. Being in London always brought out the worst in him. His idea of a good honeymoon would be travelling through Dorset tracing the paths of Hardy characters."

"That does sound interesting."

"Okay, but not for a *honeymoon,* Truman! I'd rather lie with my groom on sunny hillside terraces in Tuscany and drink local vino."

⨳

"Helen told us to meet her by the pool at the club," Aunt Vicky said when I'd cranked up the Merc, and I thought—aha! saved the best for last, huh?

"I expect there might be other kids you could meet. I bump into my students now and then."

Her earlier outburst about the country club discouraged me from commenting, so I drove in silence and considered the possibility of meeting other kids of the sort who'd be swimming at a country club pool. They'd probably view me as "the teacher's kid," a category of Other almost as contemptible as the child of a clergyman. I dreaded it. I also felt disloyal to Uncle Waylan to be going there.

We headed out the Carlsbad highway, passed oil-well supply pipe yards and caliche lots where pulling units were parked, drove until the industrial effluvia thinned to a sea of mesquite and Johnson grass and a vista that curved on the horizon. Barbed-wire fences along the road had snared prickly gray-green tumbleweeds in their strands like big wads of spinach caught in a kid's braces.

About three miles out of town, we turned left and passed under a too-fancy beige-brick gateway that looked out of place on a barren prairie. Far ahead lay a cluster of low brick buildings; along the entrance road were flagged holes and greens that were a lurid kelly green against the arid terra surrounding them, like emerald flying carpets that had run out of fuel and May-Dayed onto the dry brown prairie. Groups of men in Bermuda shorts and long white socks were standing in the lunar landscape like mannequins. Then we passed courts where sets of women in all-white outfits were playing tennis, and soon we arrived at a pool with a high chain-link fence corralling it.

"You know, I forgot to ask you if you want to swim," said Aunt Vicky as I pulled into a parking lot. "I don't swim here because of the chlorine. I'm sure we could rustle up some trunks for you in the clubhouse."

"It's okay for somebody who's not a member?"

"Of course. We're guests of Helen's. There's no reason for you to feel uncomfortable."

When I turned off the engine, she said, "I've been considering your question earlier about this place, and Waylan and me."

I looked off toward the shallow end of the pool where hordes of screaming children were churning the aquamarine waters into a froth.

"I want to give you a better answer. It caught me off-guard,

74

and I snapped at you. When I came to this town I was really lonely at first, and most of the women I've come to know here at the club are involved in things I'm interested in. We don't just sit and knit and eat bon-bons, James, and raise our noses at women whose husbands make less money. There's a book club, and the League of Women Voters, and we get together and drive over to Odessa for concert—we saw Andres Segovia this spring—and we have art exhibits and a lecture series. There's a garden club and a chamber music appreciation society. Okay, I do know that the same forty women belong to all these and not all are really devoted —some are bored and some are followers. But for better or worse, if I come here I can find somebody who will talk to me about something besides Yellowjacket football and oil and hunting and fishing, or real estate or automobiles and cows. Or furniture and recipes. You have no idea how starved intellectually and spiritually you can become in a town like this."

She poked me in the arm, and I turned. She was grinning. "Besides, it's the only place to eat out in a radius of fifty miles where you get a linen napkin."

I laughed.

"Or if I want to have a drink with Helen in the bar, we won't be pestered by yahoos. If you want to play in a tennis tournament, this is where you do it. I know it's full of shallow people who are here only because they think it makes them better. But I ignore that and take what I can."

"Does Uncle Waylan know how you feel?"

"Well, I've sure tried to *explain* it. He thinks I want to join. But I don't."

"You don't? Why not?"

She hesitated, leaned forward, and, for the first time that day, she took a pack of Pall Malls from the glove box and lit one with the car lighter. I wanted one too, but I didn't want her to know I was smoking.

"I'm a little ashamed to admit this, James." She blew smoke out of the passenger window then turned her frank gaze at me. "Thing is, I doubt the club would ever take in members who were Negroes or Jews or Mexicans." She sighed. "So I come out here and use the facilities as a guest and pretend to be blind to that, and by not joining, I imagine that I stay clean. I'm not proud of it. It's hypocritical."

"So in a way, you and Uncle Waylan actually kind of agree about it?"

She gave me a long, long look. "You're really a sweet kid, you know that?"

When we came through the gate, Aunt Vicky's friend Helen was standing three paces back from the end of the high board, poised to dive, palms pressed to chunky thighs. She was wearing a black tank suit and a white bathing cap. Aunt Vicky waved and yelled, distracting her, and she found us and waved back. "Don't watch!" she pleaded, but of course we did. She took two short-legged bounding steps, gave a pretty hefty boost off the end of the board, arched into a passable swan dive (though her large breasts and short limbs made it look more like a hen dive), and she hit the water with her torso and sent up a cartoonish mushroom spume.

We sat in webbed lounge chairs under an umbrella waiting for her to come out of the pool. Teenage girls sunbathed on the opposite side near the deep end, as far off to themselves as I suppose they could manage to get. A gaggle of boys in bathing trunks stood over them, posing and flexing and jostling one another. I hoped Aunt Vicky didn't notice them. They were all Coppertone tan, as if they'd spent weeks on end here. I'd considered swimming, but now I thought about my working man's tan—below the waist I was potato white—and felt superior and inferior at the same time.

Helen padded up, dripping, her bathing cap in one hand and the other forking out the damp strands of her short red hair. The edge of one front tooth was rimmed in gold, and her eyes were yellowish brown; a spray of large heavy freckles lay across her cheeks and nose like a handful of dull sequins that had been sown there and stuck.

Aunt Vicky introduced us; she leaned over to shake my hand, murmuring my name, smiling—shyly, I thought—then sat upright and astraddle on a chaise lounge with Aunt Vicky between us. To my suprise, she didn't immediately bombard me with questions about how I'm liking it here, etc., as I would've expected from my mother's friends. I couldn't have said whether this pleased me or not.

"You're looking like a pro, darling," said Aunt Vicky. "I'm really envious."

"It's nice of you to say so." Helen shaded her eyes and swept the pool with her gaze. "I hope Jack agrees—God knows my coach doesn't come cheap."

"Oh, don't be silly, Helen. If it makes you happy . . . . "

"Well, it's not buying a mink coat, that's true. He gets on these tears, though. Starts metering the shower water and lecturing the kids about turning out the lights." Helen leaned forward to catch my eye past Aunt Vicky's torso. She grinned. "Your Aunt Vicky is always talking me into things."

"Learning to dive was your idea!"

"Yes, that's true. But it was only an idea."

They laughed. Then Helen jumped up suddenly, startling me. "Jackie!" she yelled. "Gladys! I'm over here!"

She semaphored until she got a returning wave from two children among a throng thrashing in the shallow end.

I watched the teens across the way; I guess you could say they were cavorting and gamboling; they were standing up, sitting down, standing up again, up and down like Jacks and Jills in boxes, rubbing oil on one another's shoulders, now and then a boy picking up a girl and tossing her into the pool amidst a symphony of delighted squeals, and now and then one boy wrestling another to the edge to try to push the other in. I thought I could hear "Heartbreak Hotel" coming from there—a portable radio? Lying back on my chaise lounge in sneakers, Levis, and a white shirt, I felt overdressed and odd, the kid who can't go in the water because he's got polio. It struck me with unexpected force that if Wynetta Drake were here, she wouldn't be welcome to take a plunge, and I felt a curious (but probably false) kinship with her. I couldn't imagine changing into trunks and either being introduced to them *(please, please, please, do not do this, Aunt Vicky!)* or working my way slyly over to their area and hanging around pathetically waiting for a "chance" encounter.

Aunt Vicky was telling Helen about Thelma Wiggins and Eddie Bickley asking Truman for the dirty books, so I got up and walked out to the car to retrieve *Lolita*. If I were lying about fully clothed reading such a book and a girl happened by, I might be a great intriguing mystery to her, someone very different from (and therefore much more appealing than) the yowling apes rattling the bars on the cages of their libidos over there.

When I got back, Aunt Vicky and Helen were laying out plans

to see the superintendent of schools on Monday, seeking his support to keep the library shelves free to all patrons and to head off efforts by the Baptist book-burners to get started on the Hedorville school libraries.

I opened *Lolita* and immediately found that it was a lot more interesting to imagine getting to read such a book than it was to work from word to word in it. Nabokov's style was dense, a linguistic jungle thick with unfamiliar vegetation—and me without a machete or even the energy to raise my arm to hack away.

I laid the book across my chest, spine displayed, and closed my eyes. I dozed, but for only a moment, then continued to play possum when I heard Helen ask, "Did he ever say why he took off that night and never came back?"

"No. He keeps saying he doesn't know why himself."

"Do you have any idea?"

Aunt Vicky sighed. "No, he seemed to be in a pretty good mood while we were having dinner, and then when I asked if we could go dancing at Al's like we used to in the old days—ha! the old days, there's a good one!—he started clouding up. He said he'd been hoping we could stay home and be together. But he'd been sitting in that goddamn recliner for thirty minutes reading the paper, so I said, 'If you're so eager just to be with me, why didn't you come in the kitchen while I was washing dishes?' What really got my goat was that we hadn't been out of the house together at night since, well, you remember when we all came out here for your birthday? And here it was three weeks later. I was starting to get pretty scared."

"Scared?"

"Well, that we'd settled down to being another boring married couple. We used to do lots of things, all the time. But once we got settled, when he wanted to go out, he'd go with his buddies to play poker or to a bar or hunting or fishing. He stopped thinking of me as somebody to take with him somewhere. I guess that's why I made an issue of it that night."

"What'd he say then?"

"He said he didn't know why a woman couldn't be satisfied just to be a wife. Then he jumped up and left and hasn't been back since. Only thing he says when I ask him about our future is he needs time to think."

"What about this girl?" Helen lowered her voice, and even

with my eyes closed, I could feel their attention sweep over my form and probe for vital signs.

"I don't know for sure," murmured Aunt Vicky. "He says she's from out of town and she's the daughter of an old friend he owes a favor to, so he gave her a job. But I'd be a fool to believe there's no more to it than that."

My ears tingled. I had personal knowledge that Uncle Waylan and Sharon were intimate: I'd seen them making out. Whether more happened or not, I didn't know. Was it possible Sharon didn't let him go all the way? Should I say something now?

Before I could make up my mind, I heard a rustling and the scrape of aluminum across concrete, and I "came awake" to see Aunt Vicky standing with the chaise lounge between her calves while she smoothed out the seat of her shorts.

"I'm going to get a Coke. Anybody?"

She turned to me. I stretched and yawned and tried to look dopey. "Huh!" I said. "I must have dozed! A Coke? Yeah, sure."

When she'd gone, Helen said, "How do you like working for your Uncle Waylan, James?"

"Fine, ma'am."

"You know, your Aunt Vicky is a very special person to me. She's a breath of fresh air in this town. You hate to see someone that fine being hurt."

I snuck a glance at Helen. She was lying back now, her face to the sky, eyes closed. Her right shoulder had a nasty-looking bruise the size of a half dollar.

"Yes'm," I mumbled.

"Do you know this girl?"

"What girl is that?"

Helen was staring right into me with those yellow lion eyes. She was wise to me. "The girl your uncle hired."

"Sharon? Sure, I know her. I mean, when I see her."

"So, what's the deal between her and Waylan?"

"The deal?"

Helen's gaze made me feel very small: *what a pitiful liar, what a mere child!*

"I admire my friend Vicky very much, James. And I'd do about anything to help her. She's worth it."

"I like her, too. She's really great."

"So if she were my aunt and I knew something important I'd

sure as hell tell her about it," she went on, ignoring my homage as if it were so much hot air.

"Yes'm." She continued to bore into me with her yellow-eyed gargoyle stare. Absolutely unnerving. Apparently, unlike Aunt Vicky, she had no qualms about dragging me into this.

To get her off my back, I said, "They're just friends."

I felt wretched. Now I'd committed to The Big Lie, had become a co-conspirator!

"Just friends?" Helen snorted.

Her sarcasm smarted. I wanted to say "This is none of your business" but couldn't, of course.

"Yes ma'am," I said evenly. "Her daddy left her and her mother when she was just a kid, and her mother died a year and half ago of cancer. She didn't have anywhere else to turn. She used to work for Uncle Waylan a couple years ago, before he and Aunt Vicky got married. They were friends way back then."

This story had several sizeable holes, but I guessed it would serve for the moment, and it did.

TEN

O kay, Jimbo," said Trudy, "You think he's such a big hero, tell me why he wanted to kill Natalie Wood."

"Put her out of her misery, I guess."

"What misery?" asked Sharon. Both were picking on me; Cotton was riding in the bed, and I wished for the first time today we had room in the cab for him. I could use a male ally. I was driving—Uncle Waylan's truck was the sole source of transportation between us—and we'd just left the Corral Theatre after seeing *The Searchers* again. It wasn't that we liked the movie so much: with only one indoor theatre, the current picture was what you got, and it changed only monthly.

This was the first time I'd seen it with Sharon and Trudy, though, and no sooner had we hit daylight on this Sunday afternoon than they started in on me because I said that I admired how John Wayne was always a hero. It wasn't that they took a feminist's stance against what I could now, decades later, easily recognize to be a misogynistic "text." The movie bewildered them. Or, rather, the anger and bitterness that seemed chronic to the character of Ethan (Wayne) was inexplicable, unmotivated. His long search to find the niece, Debbie (Natalie Wood) who was kidnapped by the Comanches as a child, turns back upon itself when Ethan discovers that she's now a grown young woman "living with a buck," living as an Indian—and he sees this as a reason to kill her rather steal her away from the Comanche warrior, Scar.

I said, "I guess he thinks it's like she's been poisoned, and he believes she'd be better off dead than red."

Trudy laughed. I thought it was a good joke, myself, and she said, "Who would you rather have—Debbie or Laurie?" Laurie (Vera Miles) was the saucy blonde who played Earl Holliman off against Jeffrey Hunter.

"You mean who do I think's better looking?"

"If that's your measure."

I wasn't sure what she meant by "have." I steered the pickup past Buford Pharmacy and went left to take us out to the Dairy King. Sharon was sitting in the middle, firmed up next to my right arm and hip, wearing black pedal-pushers and a pink cotton blouse with the collar turned up smartly at the nape. Without turning my head I could see her fragile white forearm angled across her thighs, its silky blonde hair, the man's gold ID bracelet that, I'm sad to say, had my uncle's name inscribed upon it. It was all she had of him today—after our excursions yesterday Aunt Vicky called him last night and, to my surprise, coaxed him into counseling with a minister this afternoon. Naturally, when I arrived at The Round-Up with Uncle Waylan's truck, Sharon asked where he was. When I told her, she looked stricken. She crept off to her room. Trudy said, contemptuously, "It's sooo sad, Jimbo—after all, this is the third-week anniversary of our coming to town, and she had something 'really special' planned." Sharon marked each mutual motion made by her and Waylan as a "special date"—the first anniversary that she saw him at the business college in Amarillo, their first date, first kiss, second date, second kiss, third date, third kiss, etc.

Sharon later perked up, due in part to the attention Cotton had lavished on her all afternoon. And if my own thoughts about her were transmitted in any way to the pleasure centers of her brain, they were also a balm. Would I rather "have" Debbie or Laurie? How about Sharon lying nude on the white leather seat of a red Caddy convertible?

To the question, I finally said, "Laurie, I think." Sharon bore a faint resemblance to Vera Miles, and I hoped the ricochet compliment might flatter her.

"Aha! You like the good girls, then!" pounced Trudy. She was smoking a Kool, and the menthol nearly gagged me. She was wearing ragged cut-off jean shorts, sandals, and a large t-shirt with bold, vertical red and blue stripes. "Are you going to marry a virgin?" One arm was sunburnt.

"None of your bees-wax."

"Lame, James."

"Whoever, she won't be wearing overalls."

"Junior Leaguer, no doubt. We hear you went to the country club yesterday. Maybe you met your future bride? La Dee Dah. Hoo, boy, I bet you had yourself one hell of a debutante ball last night! John Thomas, may I present Miss Rosy Palm?"

My face glowed. Before meeting Trudy, I wasn't used to hearing girls refer to any sexual practice, let alone accuse me personally of masturbating, which of course I did with a frequency that distressingly corresponded with her accusations; at any given time when she accused me, I was probably guilty of a recent transgression, and often with Sharon as the object. I wouldn't say I'd grown used to Trudy's ribbing, but I was no longer shocked.

"You're as funny as a rubber crutch, Trudy."

"Interesting imagery, Jimbo! The detumescent phallus! Is that an autobiographical statement?"

"Okay, you're as funny as a fart in a phone booth, then."

"Least I don't imagine I look like a movie star."

"I didn't say I think I look like James Dean, Trudy! You said you thought I did, and I said, 'Really?' I knew you didn't mean it—you think I'm stupid?"

"You should have seen the look on your face."

"At least my butt doesn't look like a tractor seat."

"Y'all shut up," said Sharon. "I'm sick of hearing you bicker."

"Tractor seat, huh?" Trudy spat a spume of medicinal-tainted smoke across Sharon's lap and toward me. I got her!

"I'm sorry you took up smoking," said Sharon. She looked at me. "Her mama's going to blame that on me, sure as the dickens."

"It's the price you pay for being such a wonderful role model, cuz. Take Little Waylan, there—"

"Up your hole with a totem pole, Bucket Butt!"

"Don't you wish!"

"Hush!" said Sharon. We were nearing the curve beyond which lay the Dairy King, and she said, "Let's don't eat here. Let's go somewhere else."

I said, "Okay, but the chairs'll have to be extra big. Where?"

Sharon said, "Any place Cotton can sit with us."

We went to a Mexican restaurant where I had my first chile relleno and also my first beer in a public place. Sharon was of legal age; she ordered them, and Cotton and I drank from the bottles at her place setting when the waitress wasn't looking. It made me nervous, but if Cotton was doing it, I wasn't about to back down from a *mano-a-mano*. I was annoyed to have him along, anyway, since he was fairly slobbering all over Sharon, opening all the doors within sight whether she wanted to pass through them or not and acting the part of the bashful cowboy. He wasn't a talkative sort in the first place, and all he did at the table was sit and moon, and if he said anything, it was to crack wise at me. When, for instance, I said I liked my chile relleno, he said, "Hell, it ain't nothing but a damned old stuffed pepper." I could've written an essay describing all the *fundamental* ways the two dishes were *obviously different* and made his "ain't nothing but" characterization sound like the idiotic utterance of a redneck moron, but no—I held my tongue.

Trudy said she didn't like beer. "I like rum and Coke best. And there's this wine, I've got some back at the room—it's cool. We all drink it at school. Called Paisano. Two bucks a gallon."

"That's something else your mama is not going to be pleased to learn about."

"Why would she learn it? I know you're not going to tell her—you hate her guts."

"No I don't hate her guts, Trudy. I just get tired of always being compared to you."

I wondered how Trudy's mother would have found Trudy to be superior, since, to my mind, the contrast ran strongly in the other direction. Trudy cut her glance my way and read my mind, I guess.

"My mom thinks I'm an angel." She grinned impishly, as if proud of how deluded her mother was. "My parents are the kind of people for whom a decent report card is as good as a blindfold."

"And I'm the Devil. I lead the sheep astray. She never respected my mother, and she thinks I'll wind up just like her. She thinks I am just like her when it comes to men."

"I bet you could be about anything you'd want to be," purred Cotton. Quick—pass me the puke pan!

"Well, believe me, dead of cancer at forty-two isn't my ambition. Or married to a drunk who stays gone months at a time

84

God knows where. If I'd had a perfect childhood things might be different."

"Quit beating me over the head with that, Sharon. It's not my fault. You could have made good grades, and you could have gone to the senior prom with Billy Pettibone."

Sharon's glance touched my face and then Cotton's, though you could tell she meant mostly for Trudy to hear. "Trudy's mom had a hissy fit because I broke up with the only 'decent' boy that ever asked me out."

"You were crazy about him. You'd of married him if he'd asked, and you know it."

"He's a dope, even if his daddy does own the Chevy dealership. Maybe he did ask. And shut up about it."

Trudy grinned at me. "Touchy, touchy."

Cotton said to Trudy, "Maybe it ain't none of our business, maybe it's personal."

I took this as an attack on Trudy, or at least a declaration of allegiance to Sharon, and I blurted, "Friends tell each other personal stuff."

"Maybe where you come from," said Cotton.

Having bit my tongue about the *chile rellenos*, I had to take a stand. "Where I come from? Where do you think I come from?"

Cotton gave me a steely look. The difference between bantering with Trudy and with Cotton was that I had to act as if I were willing to stroll to Fist City with him. Was I? It always looked easy in the movies. In *The Searchers*, Laurie loves Martin Pauley, an orphan Ethan saved after the Comanches had slaughtered the boy's family, and he was raised by Laurie's parents. Laurie wants to marry Martin, but he keeps running off with his would-be Uncle Ethan to hunt for Debbie, and so, to get back at him, Laurie agrees to marry Charlie McCrory, a cornball hick who's always sniffing around her (like Cotton). The wedding is about to happen when Ethan and Martin return from a Debbie-hunting trip. Naturally, now that Laurie is marrying Charlie, Martin pitches a jealous fit, and he and Charlie feed each other economy-sized portions of fist pie in front of the assembled wedding guests. As the fight rages, the camera keeps coming back to Laurie's face—she relishes this. Before the conflict is resolved, though, Ward Bond runs in to say the Comanches are on the warpath.

Real fights are very different from movie fights. The past year, I'd had one with Rodney Turley. I think he picked it because our civics teacher, Miss Hill, had selected me to be the mayor in our class mock-government, so he called me a "pussy" and shoved my head into my locker. He told me to meet him behind the gym after school because he wanted to whip my ass. Stupidly, I asked "Why?" thinking I had done something I could apologize for, but, really, I knew that this was about personal chemistry: he didn't like my looks, he said. He was taller but I guessed I outweighed him and hoped I could hold my own.

I met him with my then-best friend, David O'Dell, as my second, and Rodney had several pals from auto shop. We squared off. He tried a right cross but I blocked it, then he feinted a kick to my nuts, and when I fell for it and covered, he punched me in the jaw. I jabbed left twice then went for a haymaker that whacked his eye and staggered him backward but also felt as if it shattered the bones of my right hand. Then he came back diving for me and bowled me over. We wrestled in the dirt until I got him into a headlock with his eye bleeding all over my shirt, and he had me scissored with his legs around my waist. It was very intimate. By this time, unlike movie fighters, we were panting and gasping and trembling from having used up every ounce of our considerable energy in probably less than thirty seconds, and were grunting and shoving and wrenching each other's parts with futile fury; I was more than ready to quit but wasn't going to say so first. Then he upchucked a sizable lunch all over me. It was chili dog and creamed corn day in the cafeteria. I doubt he knew vomiting was in his arsenal, but it sure made me turn loose and jump up.

What the movies never show is how your hands sweat all day while you're thinking about what's coming, or how your heart is a double-time hammer for hours on end and your nerves are sparking like a shorted light switch and if somebody gooses you, you could slam the ceiling with your head. You can't imagine anything else but the fight. You don't want to get the crap beat out of you—it hurts to get hit—but you don't want anybody to think you're gutless, either. You have to stand up. Be a man. It's not fun, but it's required. And if the movies never show the fear, they also miss the ferocious anger you feel toward the world after your school has lost the big game, after the girl has dumped you, after a Rodney Turley has called you a "pussy" and shoved your head into your locker. You want to smash his fucking face in! In your sweaty, jangly-nerved previews of the fight, you rip his fucking balls off, you pound his nose back into his brain! You're a jujitsu-karate world-class champ and your flying heels shatter his chin and cheekbones and send him sailing into a wall like a scarecrow. Take that, dogshit!

It's a terrible thing being a sixteen-year-old boy. Life is an agony of unending potential violence. Every male you meet, you automatically assess height and weight and reach and conformation of muscles; the mind of a sixteen-year-old boy constantly divides the world into males who could whip him and whose who couldn't. Deference goes to the former and contempt to the latter. You check your muscles in the mirror. My sisters snickered when they saw me doing this because they believed I was admiring myself, but they were oh so wrong: I was measuring, wondering (hoping) I had enough to hold back the tide of guys who might want to stomp my ass, call me a pussy; looking in the mirror I'm wondering if the mere appearance of muscles will deter them. *What're you looking at? Don't step on my blue suede shoes. I heard you called me a dipshit.* (No, of course I didn't, you dipshit!)

All week long I'd worked to prove I was as good a man as any on the crew. I'd not only kept up but had endured with good grace the usual new-guy pranks (go get the skyhook, the left-handed monkey wrench, the space adjuster, etc.). I believed I'd won them over.

Except for Cotton. I could feel this thing building between us and had no idea how to disarm it. If I checked my cultural handbook on the proper way a young man should cope with such persistent resistance, it would advise me to be tougher than he. Don't roll over and show your belly. Go nose to nose and do not blink. Do not waste time trying to "understand" him (who gives a shit if he's an orphan?) or attempt to reason or see his point of view: be *ready*.

I didn't know when or what might be the catalyst, but I would've bet five bucks Cotton would wind up calling me a pussy and shoving my head into my locker. Naturally, I was always updating my stats on him. He was so blonde he kept his shirt on for work because, I suppose, he burned too badly. I'd seen him shirtless at the shop after we came in, when he'd change out of work clothes, and his skin was almost transparent, like pale parchment, thin, and you could see ropes of blue veins on his arms and the backs of his hands. The nape of his neck was always raw, burnished red. The paleness of his skin and his solid muscularity made me think of marble statues. His biceps weren't long and ropey like my own but enviably orb-shaped, like softballs. He had no tattoos. I was heartened by this.

Cotton was a year older, about an inch shorter than my 5'10" but was compact, probably already five to ten pounds heavier, and he had more solid muscle because he'd been working longer. His reflexes seemed lax, though, and sometimes he was clumsy when he moved. I believed I was faster, so my plan was to stay on my feet and not let him take me to the ground where his weight and strength would help him. Then with my longer reach and quicker reflexes I could land a flurry of blows to his head and gut that might take the fight out of him before I punked out because I wasn't as conditioned as he.

So, there I sat at the table having met his challenge—"Where I come from? Where do you think I come from?"—and waited for him to back down or up the ante. This time he knew I was ready *to take offense*. That Sharon and Trudy were present put pressure on us. It'd be hard to save face.

"Some place they wear them Bermuda short pants," he said finally.

"Oh, man, that really hurts, Cotton!" I mocked being stabbed in the gut. "Oh, you *really killed me* with that one!"

Sharon got up from the table. She looked at us both and scoffed with disgust. "Y'all need to learn to be gentlemen."

"That means shut up and pick up the check," said Trudy.

I snatched it first. "It's on me!" I crowed with triumph.

ELEVEN

In the "lobby" of The Round-Up Sharon and Cotton and I sat waiting for "The Steve Allen Show" to begin while the motel's owner, Wally Ransom, fretted because Marilyn Monroe was marrying a playwright named Arthur Miller.

"Just look at this, will you?" He showed us an AP wire photo in the *Hedorville Herald* of Marilyn with a baldy wearing glasses.

"I don't believe it," said Cotton. "You sure?"

"Yeah! Guy looks like an owl, a book worm! How do you figure he got Marilyn Monroe? I mean Joe DiMaggio—that made sense, but this guy?"

He was asking us all. To tell the truth, I was suprised, too. It was a mystery, all right, and if Sharon were absent and my work crew here, the news would inspire speculation about the size of Miller's dick or his tastes in unconventional practices.

"Maybe he's rich and old," said Cotton.

"Nope, he ain't but forty-one. He won't die soon."

"Unless it's from the strain," I cracked.

Sharon snickered. "It means there's hope for all of you."

"Tell me, what have I got to do?" asked Wally. He was only half-joking.

Sharon grinned at me and Cotton. "Wally, you know what you have to do."

Wally had been a Marine in Korea and lost two toes from frostbite during the fight at "Frozen Chosin" and maybe part of his brain as well, to judge by his behavior. He was a bachelor in his thirties; his glasses had a snapped bridge-piece he repaired every other day with adhesive tape, like a wound you change the Band-Aid on. His cuffs regularly rode several inches above his ankles, and he wore see-through nylon short-sleeved shirts over tank-top undershirts. He had a "Devil Dogs" tattoo on his right forearm, but his Gomer-Pyle demeanor undercut whatever menace that might have conveyed. He'd been left The Round-Up by an aunt. In addition to the office and Wally's quarters and the eight tiny cabins arranged in a quadrangle behind it—your old-fashioned "tourist courts" common before the advent of chain motels—the aunt's legacy had included an ancient philodendron of mammoth proportions.

The plant was rooted in an old blue teapot that sat atop the television console, and from there it snaked to the window and climbed the dusty venetian blinds, swung across the window top, then wove itself in and out of items on a wall shelf—an ancient bowling trophy of Wally's and several Hummel figurines his aunt had brought back from Germany, volumes of the Reader's Digest Condensed Books, a couple of "snow-shake" globes, and the handle of an old iron that served to keep the books from falling over—then the wily philo had fingered itself up the door jamb and over the header and down the other side, stretched itself across the counter where the black rotary phone and ledger sat, dipped down to the dusty desk and around Wally's old crank-arm calculator and his cigar box full of dried-out ballpoint pens, dropped to the floor and started up a hall tree holding two broken umbrellas and a useless winter cap with fur earflaps, up the wall to the other window and across the backs of the vinyl-cushioned sofa and love seat and easy chair (all in blonde wood with wagonwheels and lariats etched in their visible arms). Then the sly greenery had worked its way in and out of the interstices of the wire postcard rack, zipped up the hollow center of it—and had then, years ago, started over on the same route, piggy-backing itself, so that now when you came into the office for the first time what you noticed were plaited ropes of green winding around the room like a big boa constrictor.

It was one for Ripley's. We called it Swamp Thing. I don't know why Wally hadn't ripped it off the walls when he took over, but when you hung around long enough you realized that it was a pet. Sharon and Trudy had told me he spent many hours wiping down the leaves with an old sock dipped in mayonnaise; he was obsessive, working a few feet a day, so that by the time he'd

90

gone one round, it was time to start anew. Trudy told him that it was going to crawl into his room some night, hog-tie and tickle him to death.

To Sharon's comment that he knew what he would have to do, Wally said, "Aw, I always heard a woman liked a man to have a green thumb."

"Grow roses, then. This thing's creepy."

During Steve Allen, Wally wiped down Swamp Thing with an idle, pleasureable absorption that suggested humming. I didn't have much interest in the show, but we'd heard that Steve Allen might put Elvis on soon, whereas Ed Sullivan had vowed "never!" so we were at least grateful to Steve Allen. Cotton sat with Sharon on the love seat and I took the easy chair on the other side of her. I liked her profile; her nose was pert, her teeth were curiously small like a child's but white and very even, like Chiclets seen through the cellophane window on the box, and her lower lip from this angle had a slight pout. When she leaned forward to tap an ash I could see down her blouse, but not far. The little gold cross didn't deter me in the least, and I hoarded whatever glimpse I could get of her brassiere and the swelling that disappeared too soon under the white material.

When the show was over, Cotton hoodwinked Sharon into going to his room "to sew up some pants." She made a point of inviting me, but I wasn't going to play tag-a-long, and instead I gave him a look that said he better behave himself.

Cotton lived in #4; Trudy and Sharon lived across the gravelled lot in #7, and that's where I headed. I worked on the riddle of Arthur Miller and Marilyn Monroe. Shouldn't the world's sexiest woman belong to the world's most manly man? Okay, so she and Joe DiMaggio hadn't hit it off, but if she was going for a writer next, shouldn't it be Ernest Hemingway, he of the beard, the guns, the bullfights? Obviously Marilyn knew something I didn't.

I knocked at #7, heard "Come in." Trudy was sitting at the desk writing in a Big Chief tablet. A jelly glass of wine sat near her elbow, and a smoking Kool was lying crosswise on the ashtray. On the desk a large book lay open, from which she seemed to be taking notes. I stepped closer and saw an icky cross-section of a woman's abdomen—it was like the illustration in the Tampax box only in lurid detail and thirteen colors. I remembered my conversation yesterday with Aunt Vicky about the Cesarean section.

"What're you doing?"

"What's it look like?"

"What's that book?"

"Who are you, the FBI?"

"I just wondered."

"It's a medical textbook."

"Are you going to be a doctor?"

"Not unless I have to."

She shut the book, picked up the burning butt and took a drag, squinting against the smoke. "How was Steve Allen?"

I shrugged. Without asking, I sat on the bed and lit a Pall Mall. "Cotton and Sharon went to his place to sew up his pants."

"So you expect me to entertain you?"

"Why not? It's pretty funny just looking at you."

She snickered and shook her head. "Want some wine?"

"Yeah. Sure."

She got a glass from the top of their chest of drawers. A red slash from sitting on the chair cut across the backs of her thighs. She poured me a glass, took her own, and we drank in unison, as if toasting.

"Well?"

"It's good," I lied. It was hot and had a sour, acidic twang. I wondered how it'd sit on the two beers and the *chile rellenos*. Having never been drunk, I had no idea what it took to get me that way or how to recognize the condition.

"Beatniks drink it."

"Beatniks?"

"Cool cats, hip cats. In Greenwich Village and San Francisco."

She sat sidesaddle at the desk chair, one arm thrown over the shoulder. Under her other arm were stacked several tablets.

"How come you're always writing? Do you keep a diary?"

"This one's my journal." She picked up the one she'd been writing in. "But I'm working on a novel in the others."

"A novel? Really?" I was very impressed but alarmed at how readily I revealed it. "A real one?"

"How could I write a fake one?"

There was a long silence; she was frowning at her bare feet. "I didn't mean to interrupt," I said. "Go ahead and write if you want to." It struck me that it might be interesting to watch her write a novel.

"Not with somebody in the room."

"How about Sharon?"

"Sharon's oblivious to anything I do."

"What do you write in your journal?"

"Mmm, just notes about things that happen."

I grinned. "Anything in there about me?"

She squinched her eyes and grinned evilly. "Of course."

I wasn't about to give her the satisfaction of hearing me ask what she'd written, so I said, "Did you know Marilyn Monroe's getting married again?"

"No."

"Yeah. To this old guy, a playwright who looks like an owl. Bald as an 8-ball. Can you believe it?"

"Why not?"

"Well, she's like a sex symbol, and he's an intellectual." It popped into my mind that Aunt Vicky might be a more suitable spouse for Miller.

"You think beauty should always mate a beast?"

"It just seems weird, that's all," I declared. I usually grew tired of Trudy's contrariness after five minutes of conversation. If I said black, she'd say white, she'd go up to my down, Mutt to my Jeff, etc. It had grown predictable, actually. "Never mind."

"No, this is really interesting to speculate about." She looked off into space.

"One for the old journal, huh?" I took my wine in one gulp. My palate had been numbed by that first hot and stinging swallow, so this second lug I chugged tasted less like Listerine and more like grape juice. I licked my lips. I got up and poured myself another glass.

"Yeah, maybe," Trudy went on. "I mean you think her choice implies there's something wrong with her judgment. There could be. But maybe to you 'Marilyn Monroe'"—she made airborne quotation marks with her fingers, like pairs of rabbit ears—"is only something to look at. From the outside, you know, hips, boobs, legs, blonde hair, and so on. But if you're her, you're *inside* her head, and that's the part that makes up her mind who to marry, not her cup size."

"Okay, sure, I get it. So you're telling me women always know inside exactly who they should be with and they're always right, right?"

Trudy laughed. "Gosh no, Jimbo! Sharon's a good example."

"You mean Uncle Waylan," I said tightly.

"Oh, not just him."

Trudy stubbed out her cigarette.

"Who is Billy Pettibone?"

"A guy back in Dumas she went steady with. They were really nuts about each other. Then she broke up with him."

"Why? Did he cheat on her?" I lapped at my wine.

"Because she got scared, I think. His family's pretty well-off and he was about the most popular guy in his class, but not like a Pat Boone type or anything. He could drink like a fish and could act goofy like anybody else, even though he always made the honor roll. But he was going off to A&M, and I think Sharon was afraid that she would lose him when he left. I also think my mom made too big a deal about the interest he took in her. She was always breathing down Sharon's neck all the time she lived with us, always checking every minute to make sure Sharon didn't do something to embarrass us, always trying to coach her, like she thought Billy Pettibone was Sharon's one chance at the big time. She was always afraid Sharon was going to blow it. I think Sharon was too, so she dumped him. It was a self-fulfilling prophecy. She's a very insecure person."

"She is?" That a beautiful woman could feel insecure was inconceivable to me.

"Yeah." She smiled. "Maybe that explains Marilyn and her new groom."

The wine was making me warm inside. "Trudy," I said earnestly, "you're really smart!"

She cracked a grin. "Good thing, since my butt looks like a tractor seat. Now there was one for the journal."

I hadn't realized I could cut so deep; I felt sorry but also strangely reassured. She was a college woman, after all. I'd presumed my jibes were too flimsy to penetrate. Truth was, even though Trudy was a trifle stocky, her flesh was compact and solid looking, and her butt was firm and nicely curved, and it was very easy to imagine that the same redhead's creamy freckled skin on her cheek would be found down there, too. If she'd given me permission, I'd have gladly stroked and kissed it and laid my head upon it for a nice long dreamy nap.

"Aw, I was kidding. I'm sorry."

"You're sure?"

"Heck, yes."

She heaved the jug up from the floor and poured us another glass of Paisano. It was getting better by the minute.

"So it's acceptable?"

She was making me blush. I nodded.

"I was hoping you'd come talk to me."

"You were?"

Trudy sat back down at the desk. "I'm worried about Sharon. This is a really sticky situation she's in. I didn't know much about it when I let her talk me into coming here, and I don't think even she knew the full story."

"What is the story?"

"I was hoping you could tell me. Trade notes. All I know is that Sharon knew Waylan a few years ago when he came up to Dumas to work, and they had a hot-and-heavy deal for a couple months. She was . . . ."

"You think they do it?"

Trudy laughed scornfully. "Of course! What'd you think?"

"Well . . . ." I shrugged, helpless. "Maybe just heavy petting. Above the waist."

Trudy fairly hooted at me and nearly choked on her wine. "Man, you sound like you've been reading Ann Landers or something! Heavy petting? I'll say!"

God I hated it when she did this to me! "Well, I didn't automatically figure she was a slut just because she's friends with you. I figured maybe I owed her the benefit of the doubt, at least. Even if she does run around with somebody with a draggy old butt that looks like two watermelons in a gunny sack."

"Oh, ha ha, James. I've already taken the fuse out of that one. Where was I?"

"When Sharon and Uncle—"

"Yeah. She'd just broken up with Billy and had moved to Amarillo so she wouldn't have to hear my mother going on about it. She had her own apartment. Anyway, so they met and—ha ha—had some very heavy petting, Jimbo. Then he just disappeared. I guess that's when he met your Aunt Vicky. Sharon didn't hear a word from him for three years until about a month ago, when all of a sudden he comes up out of the blue crying on her shoulder about his bad marriage, and Sharon fell for it. They had a hot weekend, then he came back here. Then he called her and told her she could work for him.

"I didn't know all this, then. I was looking for a summer situation, and soon as school was out, she told me about the job here and she wanted me to come with her. I sure as hell didn't want to stick around my house, so I said yes, let's hit the road, see the world! Getting stuck in the middle of a triangle wasn't in my plans."

"You didn't know about her and Uncle Waylan?"

"No. Not until I saw them together. Then I figured what the hell. If his marriage is really defunct and his wife's out of the picture and he's getting a divorce . . . ."

"You think they are?"

She saw my surprise. "That's what I wanted to know from you."

"I don't know. They went to marriage counseling this afternoon, you know."

"Yeah, we *all* know. Is he only going through the motions to appease his wife or does he really want to patch things up?"

"Oh, man. Trudy! That's the sixty-four thousand dollar question!" I was excited to get to talk about this with a third party. I told her what I'd learned yesterday at the pool about the fight that had apparently precipitated his moving out of the house. We conjectured that the same fight had immediately preceded his reappearance in Sharon's life and the summons to Hedorville to "work."

"Your Aunt Vicky doesn't know what that fight was about?"

Trudy didn't seem to believe this, but whether she doubted my powers of perception or believed Aunt Vicky was denying the truth, I don't know.

"She didn't seem to."

"Sharon says their sex life wasn't too hot."

"Yeah?" This was not my business! But it was also irresistible. "What'd Sharon say?"

"Only what Waylan told her, I imagine."

"What'd he say?"

"He told Sharon Vicky made it seem like a chore."

I was very uneasy knowing this. When I had no reply, Trudy said, "What's she like, anyway?"

Because I was chewing on the information about their sex life, against my better judgment I said, "Well, one thing is when she runs the vacuum cleaner she takes off all her clothes and plays cha-cha records."

Trudy howled. I chuckled along with her for a while, pleased to have provided some rollicking amusement, but the more she laughed, the more I saw I'd been indiscreet and felt downright disloyal. I was ninety percent certain she'd repeat this to Sharon.

Before we could continue, Sharon and Cotton barged into the room carrying a carton of Cokes and a fifth of rum.

TWELVE

C ut to a few rum and Cokes later and I had my answer to how much it took to get me tight and how it felt: turned out I was a dancing fool, a be-bop-a-lula dingdong daddy aching for a chance to bust out of the cocoon!

We shoved back the beds to leave a space between, and Sharon taught Cotton and me to do the dirty bop; we played "You Ain't Nothing But a Hound Dog" umpteen times on Sharon's little portable and bopped ourselves dizzy. Sharon swayed so cool, so smooth, and ogling her pelvis swinging in that naughty way made me want to howl. She danced between me and Cotton and revolved slowly as if on a Lazy Susan as she did her dirty steps, her head cocked back, eyes half closed, mouth a little open.

Disgusted, Trudy went off to check out the constellations. When she came back, I was wearing the shade from the desk lamp—I'd seen cartoons where the drunk guy wore one as a hat, so, realizing that I was drunk, I thought I'd size one.

"Trudy!" I screamed over the music. "Hey, Bucket Butt! Dig this, hep cat! Come do the dirty bop!"

"You better not puke on my bed," Trudy warned. She bent over the desk and riffled through her Big Chief tablets.

"Come on, party-pooper! Have a drink! You said you loved rum and Coke!"

I slung off the lamp shade; she caught it before it rolled off the bed and crowned the desk lamp with it.

"Oh, baby!" moaned Cotton. His version of the dirty bop made him look like an arthritic crab with a pickle up his ass.

"Hey, Cotton! You look like a crab with a pickle up its ass!"

99

This seemed so hilarious that I collapsed onto the bed and hee-hawed for minutes, when I caught my breath, I saw that Cotton's riposte had been to jitter-bug with Sharon. That allowed him to touch her in several places.

"Teach me how to do that, Sharon!" I scrambled from the bed, almost keeled over from the flood of blood into my brain.

Cotton danced his back into me and blocked my entry. They were doing a step where they inched toward each other, swaying in unison, palm to palm, fingers intertwined.

"Trudy, can you do this one?" I lurched backward, grabbed her arm, and tried to tug her up from the desk.

"Paws off me, ape-man!"

"Aw, come on! Drag your old butt up and let's do this dance."

I started dirty bopping in front of her, hunching and shimmying like a burlesque queen, and she sneered. She picked up a tablet, a pen, and the medical book, tried to duck under my outstretched arm, but I caught her wrist.

"Where're you going? Come on, don't leave! Let's have another rum and Coke."

"Yeah, that's what you need."

She yanked free and strode out the door. I floated to the threshold and watched her cross the gravelled courtyard in the moonlight. It wounded my pride to have her treat my new adult experience as if it were contemptibly juvenile. I had hoped to impress her by getting drunk, wanted her to consider me an equal, even if I wasn't as old as her peers. I was always struggling to hold my own with her. With a falling heart I saw that my guzzling her favorite drink only disgusted her.

I didn't know what else to do but to push onward and to hope I'd stumble out on the other side.

"Chicken!" I yelled. I stiff-armed the screen door ajar and stood on the stoop. "Buuuuccckkkett BUTT!"

Trudy halted, then she whirled and came striding back to me. Her face was drawn up like a prune.

"Don't call me that again!"

Then she twirled and was off again.

"Oh yeah?" I staggered a few steps into the courtyard after her, but she was fast and not drunk. "Yeah, what'll you do about it? Huh? Yeah, you can dish it out all right! But, noooo, you can't take it! Bucket Butt!"

She kept walking. I clawed at my shirt pocket for a cigarette and lit it. Bucket Butt. Sounded like an Indian name. I plopped onto the gravel and sat cross-legged. White light from the moon was so stark her head made a shadow over her back and I could see only one white calf and then the other when it flashed into the light as she moved away.

"Hey, Truuuudy! Listen!" I sang, "*The eyes of Texas are upon your bucket butt/All the live-long dayyyyy. . . . The eyes of Texas are upon your bucket butt/ You cannot get awayyyy. . . .*" This was uproariously funny. I wanted her to get so mad she'd turn around and carry out her threat. I was too old to be her patsy any more.

She went into the office and let the screen door slam behind her. The lights were on but dim in there, and I supposed Wally was stroking Swamp Thing by the glow of the television. I laughed. Wouldn't they make a pair! First chance I'd really go at her about that: she could be Swamp Thing's stepmother!

"Truuuudy!"

I chain-lit another Pall Mall, flicked the first burning butt off and watched it arc, a tiny rocket orange and white against the bony moonlight. I had so much nicotine zapping my synapses that my hands broke out in a sweat and the nape of my neck prickled. I had no idea of the time, but of the four cabins visible, only Cotton's and the one next to it were lit up. Wally had a hooded light over the office door, and it made a wedge of yellow, a light pie, laid up against the siding and the door. Moths flitted from shadow to light, and June bugs cart-wheeled drunkenly out of the dark to thunk themselves against the screen. Under the fake abobe archway to the courts, I could see cars glide past on the street, and I realized that if one turned in fast, there I'd be plonk in the thoroughfare like a big dumb boulder. I could get run over. It was against the law for somebody my age to be drunk, too. I could see these dangers, but they were distant, like dim low buildings way across a lake.

Ohh-oh yes, I'm the Great Pretender . . . Sharon had switched the record to a slow song, and I twisted about to look. The venetian blinds were not completely shut, so parallel slits of yellow light gave me an achingly indefinite glimpse of moving forms. *Pretending that I'm doing well . . . .*

I bent until my ear was almost to the gravel so I could see through the partly open door. Her black legs, his blue legs, a flicker, a confusion of intertwined limbs, whirling. . . . Then back into sight for a second, then gone again. Blue/black, blue/black.

They were slow-dancing. Louise had kept backing away. Looks like Sharon scootched right up to the plate. I got up on my elbow with the gravel digging into my funny bone and craned my head farther. Cotton's palm at the small of her back, fingers splayed so that his thumb and first finger were above the waist but the other three were slipping sliding down the slope. He spun her about in the tiny space, dipped her, and that made a fork of her thighs and her crotch mashed into his leg, then they rose and spun. I couldn't see her face because it was buried in his neck.

I got up. It was my responsibility to make sure Uncle Waylan's interests were protected. She'd better quit acting like a slut! Cotton better mind his goddamn manners!

I careened toward the door and tried to keep my eye on them, but they were bobbing in and out of sight, and if I made too big a detour in my flight path, I was afraid I'd topple over. They vanished from view too long for comfort, so I veered left and caught them swaying close but not whirling, and he had both arms around her in a bear hug with one hand planted right on her ass. He was working his lips against her face, and she was. . . trying to push him away? her hand clapping over his mouth the way you try to make somebody stay quiet.

In three steps I'd bounded onto the stoop and yanked the door open.

"Hey, ape man! Get your paws off her!"

They both jumped back. I lunged, head-butted his chest, and we went crashing against the wall. Then we wrestled on top of the night stand, and a corner of it impaled me in the gut and hurt like hell; I tried to tear free of his headlock so I could swing, and he kept thrusting his knee up at my face. He whacked me solid twice in the nose, and it gushed blood; I clawed at his face, and he bit my fingers, but I slammed him in the balls with one free hand; Sharon was screaming and yanking at us; she heaved us off-balance, and we tumbled off the night stand and onto the floor. Cotton heaved himself on top and banged my skull against the floor over and over until I cried, "You fucker! You fucker! You fucker!" because if I didn't say that I was going to beg him to stop. Sharon yanked him off, and I wriggled under the bed and blacked out.

A bit later, she was tugging me out from under it. I sat up with my back against the box spring. She made me drink a glass of cold water, but as soon as it hit my stomach, I had to lean to the wastebasket by the desk and puke. I puked all the rum and Cokes. Then I puked the wine. Then the beer. Then the *chile rellenos.* Then my lunch, then my breakfast. Then the lining of my stomach peeled away in swatches and my retching hauled them up one by one.

Exhausted, I sat stretched out on the floor with my back to the bed. An ice pick was boring into my forehead through my left eye, and my nose was big as a beet. I was empty and trembling, more sober, but my ears still rang.

"Where's Cotton?"

"I told him to go."

She sat beside me on the floor and dabbed at my face using a damp white towel with large red blobs on it I mistook for flowers. I felt immensely proud that no matter who the judges might award the bout to, I was the one Sharon stayed to nurse. If not the winner, the hero. The soldier recuperates, attended by an adoring Red Cross angel.

"It just got to me that he was trying something with you," I said with what I thought was becoming modesty. Not content with her presence as a testament to my heroism, I wanted to gild this lily by extorting a thank you.

"He only wanted to kiss me."

I opened my eyes. Her face was only about a foot from mine, and her green eyes looked sad. The cross and its threadlike gold chain were sweat-stuck in the hollow of her collarbone. Her mouth was set in a firm thin line, and this wasn't a tender regard. It was the look of a harried teacher silently counting to ten.

"Yeah, I'll bet!" It stung that she didn't acknowledge I'd prevented her from being ravaged.

"He drank too much, that's all, Jimbo. Me too. You too. I was too friendly, and he took it the wrong way."

"He won't do it again!"

"No. And I won't either. I was mad at Waylan and that's why I let things get out of hand."

"This wasn't your fault, Sharon! The guy's a butthole! He knows you and Uncle Waylan are . . . " I couldn't locate the word. My gaze automatically sought out the ID bracelet as if it might identify their relationship, but her wrist was bare now.

Sharon looked away. She shrugged. "I'd appreciate it if you wouldn't tell him about this."

"I don't think he'd blame you."

"I'm not worried about that." She got up slowly, her knees creaking, and I watched her trim legs unhinge and straighten, wanted to bury my aching face in the crevice between her thighs; she stepped away, went into the bathroom, turned on the water. "Thing is," she said when she'd turned off the tap, "it's Cotton. Waylan might not understand."

Here I'd had the crap beat out of me defending her honor, and she had the gall to ask me to protect him?!

"I'll say he won't!"

She moved to the bathroom door with the rope of wet towel wrapped about her knuckles, as if her hand had been injured and she was applying a complicated compress.

"I know Cotton won't bother me again, Jimbo. He's a very sensitive person. I'm sure this was humiliating for him. I wouldn't want Waylan to feel he has to be the high sheriff. He might fire Cotton. Cotton's very poor. It's not possible for him to walk out the door and find a relative willing to hire him."

Hey, I'm the one with the bloody goddamn nose! Her sympathy for Cotton had an edge turned against me.

"He's a throw-back person," she said.

"What?"

She sat beside me to dab at my face with the towel.

"Uncle Weldon, Trudy's Dad, he always goes fishing but never eats what he catches. If he gets something big, he'll give it away to somebody. Most times he just rips their lips yanking the hook out and throws them back. When we'd go out with him, I always pictured those poor throw-back fish swimming around with ripped lips that kept them from eating. Some people seem like that to me. Life has kind of snagged them and reeled them in and ripped their lips getting the hook out and then thrown them back in the water. For nothing."

"If his lip is ripped, I hope it's because I got a good lick in."

Sharon sighed and handed me the towel. She got two cigarettes and held them together in her red mouth while she lit them. I savored the dampness on the end of the one she gave me when I put it to my own lips, and the extraordinary intimacy made me shiver with pleasure.

"I don't want you fighting with him again, Jimbo. It makes me sick to my stomach. It makes me pee-oohed at both of you. It doesn't stir me in the slightest, believe me. I don't care what they show in the movies."

"Okay."

She bent close and murmured in my ear. "Will you promise not to tell Waylan?"

I pretended to mull it over merely to have a sliver of advantage, however momentarily. Really, though, I was already plump with luxuriant pleaures: the pleasure of forming a weeny two-person cabal with her, to say nothing of the pleasure of having an intimate bond that would permit me to sidle up, put my lips close to those delicate pink ears, and whisper hotly into them. What better could be gained from telling?

"Okay."

She hugged my head far too briefly to her breasts then released me to drag off her butt. She was smoking a lot faster than I. My cigarette was after sex, hers the one you have before your driver's test. In that small difference lay a world of contrast I was then much too blissful to recognize. It never occurred to me at the time that she stayed to nurse me not because I'd done something noble but to keep me from doing something stupid; it never occurred to me then to ask whether it was wise to model your behavior on movies or ancedotes about your uncle's standing up to bullies in another time and place; it never occurred to me to ask whether it was true that women enjoyed having men fight for their attention; it never occurred to me to ask why, really, I'd lit into Cotton, or to thank my lucky stars that he'd bloodied my nose and not shot me.

All I had room to consider was the rosy truth of how she'd cleaned my wounds, gave me that lighted cigarette with the lipstick on it, rubbed my face with her breasts because I'd tried to save her. I thought, Too bad we've sworn ourselves to secrecy!

"What about Trudy?" I asked, half hoping for permission to tell her.

"I won't say anything if you won't."

THIR-
TEEN

On the way to Ruidoso, the birthday girl was reading. I felt jealous of the book because I yearned for an audience: we were tooling along atop the Caprock in a sea of grassland spiked by spindly shafts of blooming Spanish dagger, and I wanted her to look up, enjoy the ride, appreciate my manly chauffeuring of the Mercury. In the back seat, Uncle Waylan and Sharon were metaphasing along their mutual flank, smoking the same cigarette.

"What's this book?"

"Kerouac," said Trudy.

"Who's Kerouac?" I flexed my right bicep. I was proud of what work had done to my body in three weeks and took every opportunity to display myself.

"Oh, only the hippest writer in America."

Trudy was full of herself today. Earlier she'd knuckled a Charlie horse into my shoulder—this was "good morning"—and eaten off my plate without asking at Runt and Dot's. She sneered and said "typical" when I told her Elvis was "cool." When we stopped for gas in Artesia I bought a postcard that featured a subterranean stone formation in Carlsbad Caverns called "The Hippo," and when I told Trudy I meant to send it to a girl, she said, grinning, "Hope she doesn't have a weight problem!" This got my goat, so I said, "Nope, not at all!" Then she taunted me in a sing-song, "Jimbo's got a girrl-friend!"

You'd think a person would summon more dignity than usual on the birthday that boosted her out of her teens. You might expect her to be even a tad too earnest and expect to be taken more seriously than she might deserve. But apart from whatever gravity reading gave to her demeanor, Trudy was otherwise bantering, barbed, and prickly. When she ignored me I wanted to flag down her attention, but no sooner would I get it than I became the butt of her jokes.

I couldn't get a fix on her today. She looked very different. Instead of wearing her overalls or shorts or her jeans and denim jacket, she'd worn a new blue cotton sundress. Her honeyed lashes looked thicker, and I was very aware of her Hershey-colored eyes. (Chocolate and honey: did she seem *edible?*) I'd always been a sucker for the Cinderella makeover in the movies, and I'd been giving Trudy furtive glances all day long as if I wasn't sure who she was. Her glorious, copper-colored hair was pulled back in a pony-tail clasped by a silver barette, leaving humidity-frizzed tendrils dangling at her temples. The spaghetti-strapped sundress showed her arms, shoulders, her throat and the swells of breasts below, all flecked with mica on a base of milk: she brought Ireland to mind, the earthy women with strong thighs and hearts of hummingbirds I'd seen in *The Quiet Man*. The more aware I became of her heretofore hidden beauty, the more I longed to have her look up, not down, at me.

Since she'd returned to the book, I had to rehook her attention.

"Is Kerouac somebody you study at school?"

Trudy went *puh!* "God, I wish! My English prof'd hemorrhage if she read this stuff!"

"Really? How come?"

She smiled as if at a preschooler who'd asked if storks bring babies. "It's American to the core. Jazz. Dope. Sex."

That Trudy was reading a dirty book while sitting beside me aroused my prurient interest. I wished I could tell her about *Lolita*, but I hadn't made much headway with it. "Read me some."

"Cool," she said happily. She flipped back through the pages to select a passage. "Okay, the protagonist is this guy Sal Paradise, and here he's walking around San Francisco feeling blue because he thinks his girlfriend has turned out to be a whore? But then he has a revelation about sin and life and forgiveness, and here's what he says: *And for just a moment I had reached the point of ecstasy that I always wanted to reach, which was the complete step*

108

across chronological time into timeless shadows, and wonderment in the bleakness of the mortal realm, and the sensation of death kicking at my heels to move on, with a phantom dogging its own heels, and myself hurrying to a plank where all the angels dove off and flew into the holy void of uncreated emptiness, the potent and inconceivable radiancies shining in bright Mind Essence, innumberable lotuslands falling open in the magic mothswarm of heaven." Trudy stopped and looked at me expectantly. What could I say? It wasn't The Hardy Boys, but it didn't seem smutty, either.

Sharon giggled behind us. "Groovy."

"Oh, now, don't be a smart-ass," said Uncle Waylan.

"He's talking about death and feeling connected with everybody who has gone before," Trudy directed at me, bending forward, brows crinkled. It seemed important to her that I understand, so, lacking a pad on which to record a note, I nodded to show I'd registered this. Her eyes flicked back to the book. *"I realized that I had died and been reborn numberless times but just didn't remember especially because the transitions from life to death and back to life are so ghostly easy, a magical action for naught, like falling asleep and waking up again a million times, the utter casualness and deep ignorance of it. I realized it was only because of the stability of the intrinsic Mind that these ripples of birth and death took place, like the action of wind on a sheet of pure, serene, mirrorlike water. I felt sweet, swinging bliss, like a big shot of heroin in the mainline vein; like a gulp of wine late in the afternoon and it makes you shudder; my feet tingled. I thought I was going to die that very next moment. But I didn't die, and walked four miles and picked up ten long butts and took them back to Marylou's hotel room and poured their tobacco in my old pipe and lit up."*

"He's smoking butts people have thrown away?" I blurted out.

Trudy looked exasperated. "He's poor. They're poor. It's a point of pride. That's not the idea, anyway, for God's sake."

I'd hurt her feelings. I wasn't so dense I couldn't see that the protagonist was having a profound spiritual experience and that was what she wanted us to know. I could even connect with his ideas about reincarnation. But I resisted talking about spiritual experiences; it seemed unmanly and made me wince with embarrassment. And I felt jealous of Trudy's regard for the author and his hero. The way her rich alto coiled so cozily around those peculiar words "Lotuslands" and "mothswarm" as if he'd written

109

her a love letter whanged a chord of sorrow deep in my heart. I'd wanted to belittle him so I'd called attention to his dubious hygiene. In truth, I'd never heard of an author mixing up whores and heroin and religion. And the idea of taking pride in being poor was novel to me. I'd heard of poor but proud but never proud to be poor. I'd always presumed all poor people wanted to get rich. Clearly, this Kerouac Trudy admired had a lot to teach me. Upshot was, I now felt ashamed of my ignorance.

"That stuff's going to warp your mind," said Sharon.

"At least I've got one to warp."

"We don't all have your opportunities, you know."

"You have what you want." Trudy raised the book to her face. "Right?"

They'd been at each other's throats all morning. I didn't know why. Since this trip was supposed to be in honor of Trudy's birthday, it didn't seem fair for Sharon to pick on her, and I was about to defend her when Uncle Waylan spoke up.

"I tell you what—if they'd had something that interesting when I was in school I'd of liked it twice as much."

Sharon playfully slapped his thigh. "Oh, you just like the part about his girl being a whore."

"Naw, I'm serious," said Waylan, but my rearview mirror showed that he was grinning at her. His bare tanned arm was draped over her shoulder and his dark veiny hand was a muscular silhouette on the backdrop of her white blouse. His thumb was hooked under the lapel. His gallantry and his authority came so easily that he could pacify Trudy and Sharon at the same time, each in a different way, and I found that masterful. I envied how he could say something conciliatory to Trudy at Sharon's expense and simultaneously pet Sharon's breast. Did confidence like that come automatically with age? I hoped so. In the past few weeks, I'd made a mental list of qualities Uncle Waylan had that I aspired to cultivate as fast as I could. Working hard every day under the burning sun had turned my skin a workman's leathery tan and trimmed my flesh back to wirey muscle. I'd learned to a dozen Byzantine variations on draw and stud poker with Uncle Waylan and others. I bought some western-style shirts with pearl buttons and a pair of cowboy boots. I smoked Uncle Waylan's brand now, Phillip Morris. Talking to my mother on the phone, I said, "We're fixing to go to chow," and she said, "I hope you realize you sound like a hick." Naturally, Cotton had caught Trudy's nickname for me and passed it on at work, so the guys on my crew now called me "Little Waylan." That smarted. I didn't want anyone to see that I modelled myself on him, least of all me, but a sneaky secret pleasure lay in knowing I'd done it well enough to show.

We stopped for lunch at a Furr's cafeteria in Roswell. Uncle Waylan and I both took the sliced roast beef and mashed potatoes with gravy, with yams and green beans and dinner rolls, salad, and pecan pie—he had pecan, that is, and I had chocolate meringue and a square of cherry Jell-O with peaches in it. As we sidled along the serving line, Trudy took fried chicken, mashed potatoes with cream gravy, black-eyed peas and yams and macaroni and cheese, three cloverleaf rolls, three pats of butter, a large chunk of German chocolate cake, and a glass of milk. Sharon's tray held a bowl of vegetable soup and a green salad. They were ahead of me in the line, and Uncle Waylan was the caboose with the wallet.

"Trudy." Sharon was squinting critically at Trudy's tray.

"What?"

"You know what."

"It's my birthday."

"I know, sweetie, but golly!" She made a show to Trudy of glancing back at us.

"What? Is this unladylike? God, Sharon, why don't you say what you mean?" Trudy burned red and moved the bowls of macaroni and yams to Sharon's tray.

"But I don't want them," Sharon said.

"Sure you do!" Trudy hissed. "Take this too while you're at it!" She put the three rolls and butter on Sharon's tray.

"I don't need these."

"I know you don't."

When Trudy tried to transfer the chocolate cake, Sharon protested feebly, then said, "Well, we'll split it, okay?"

"You can take two-thirds for all I care!"

By the time they'd reached the cashier, most of the food that Trudy had selected was on Sharon's tray. Neither seemed happy about it.

Uncle Waylan finished eating first and studied a racing form. Trudy and I chewed in a tense silence; Sharon bowed her head over her tray as if in prayer, and soon she was lost in a serene, rhapsodic cudding as she went through the many plates and bowls with an inch-worm's dedicated absorption in the task. She ate the cake oblivious to the Kool smoke a glowering Trudy blew in her face. Trudy put out her butt in Sharon's soup.

Uncle Waylan looked from the form to watch Sharon studiously mash cake crumbs with the back of her fork and slip the tines upside down past her wet red lips and small white teeth.

"Didn't you have breakfast?" He grinned. "I was there. I'd swear you ate flapjacks and bacon."

Sharon looked up at us as if emerging from sleep.

"She's eating for two, for both of us, I mean," said Trudy. "I'm not hungry."

"Trudy's *supposed* to be on a diet."

"I really don't think you want to discuss what people are supposed to be doing."

When we left Roswell, Trudy and I sat in the back, and Uncle Waylan drove. Sharon was curled around his arm like a honeysuckle vine about a porch post, and I wondered what her right hand was up to. There's something about sitting behind someone on a plane or a bus or in a car that makes you think about them, and the minute I did, confusion clouded my mind. I had a notion that Uncle Waylan was going to use this trip as an chance to "let Sharon down easy," but I'd seen no sign of it yet.

Since the night two weeks ago when I'd gotten drunk at The Round-Up, Uncle Waylan and I'd been to Aunt Vicky's house at least four times for dinner, and he and Aunt Vicky had grown more friendly with each meeting. Last Sunday night Aunt Vicky had fixed us a special Father's Day dinner, and, after I'd called my dad, she gave Uncle Waylan a cupcake with a candle on it in honor of the son she hoped he might have some day. Uncle Waylan almost broke into tears and they hugged like two old pals who hadn't laid eyes on one another in a decade. A few days later, I asked him how the counseling was going. (I actually said, "I've always wondered how marriage counselors work—do you lie on a couch?") He said theirs let them argue and played referee when one tried to climb out of the ring, so to speak, or hit below the belt or hide a horseshoe in their glove. He also kept nagging them to turn their lives over to the Lord Jesus Christ. I wasn't about to ask Uncle Waylan if he'd complained to the counselor about their sex life, but I wondered about it.

Then he had sighed and said, "I'm hoping he'll tell me real soon how I can let Sharon down easy."

Whoa! I thought. That's big news! But two hours later, he and

I were double-dating with Sharon and Trudy at the drive-in. I thought if Trudy and I wandered away off, maybe he would spring his news on Sharon. I wanted to get a chance to tell Trudy what Uncle Waylan had said, but when he sent us to the concession stand I couldn't get a word in edgewise. Trudy was yammering about how *The Forbidden Planet* was really an allegory of Freud's division of the mind into the id, the ego, and the super-go, with characters representing each, and she wouldn't shut up long enough for me to tell her that Uncle Waylan might be using our absence to dump Sharon.

Trudy read her Kerouac until we entered the mountains, when, eyes rolling with nausea, she dropped the book to her lap. Uncle Waylan kept the wheel constantly cocked one way or the other as the Merc charged up the hairpin turns, and Trudy and I gripped our respective armrests to keep from being flung into one another's arms.

Which, when I imagined it, gave me ideas. *Oops! 'scuse me!* I'd say while she and I unknotted our tangled limbs and I extracted my nose from her damp and freckled cleavage. Sitting behind the loving couple, now, and involuntarily observing them silhouetted against the bright road ahead, Trudy and I both felt distinctly uneasy, aware of our difference from them, intensely curious as to what adjustments might be made. I didn't know if I were truly on a date nor did I know if Trudy imagined she were having one. Whatever we'd been before now had lost its footing, and her new emergence as a female dressed for a male's attention put us somewhere new and unknown.

Before today my conscious sexual thoughts about Trudy were usually shunted to the side in favor of other partners. In my daydreams I'd had Sharon a thousand times in a thousand ways. She was, in my fantasies, wholly pliable. It was easy to leave off thinking about the who of Sharon and take up thinking about the what of her anatomy: her never-freshly painted toenails and the fine blonde hair on her forearm and the damp wisps at her neck's nape and the crescent of brassiere visible when she made certain movements, the fine blue lines on her pale, paperthin temples, the vulnerable backs of her knees, the way her tight red bathing suit clutched her gloved, faintly cloven mound like a narrow hand: all this usually absorbed most of my lustful attention when she was present. She was like a movie star in this respect: it hardly mattered what the actual Sharon thought or felt because her role was to perform lewdly and boldly in my imagination, where, as a silent goddess, she did unasked what I wanted done, without objection. My every secret wish was her silent command.

I confess to diddling my aunt, too. But her personality was formidable, intimidating. Her vocabulary of moods and aspects was enormous, changeable as weather, and her apparent self-possession and confidence were irritating and stirring. She handled me. Ever the teacher, she ordered me to do this and that to her. I secretly enjoyed being handled, but I also worried that it robbed me of my masculine dignity. My fantasies of her were far more troubling, fraught with nameless anxieties. Because of her age and her outsized personality, she seemed a tall and bountiful Athena and Sharon a wood nymph.

We came to a long straight stretch of mountain plateau, then to a valley between two wooded ridges, and the road ran parallel to a glittering icy stream foaming like a skirt about clustered boulders. Trudy went back to her book. I settled in to consider her, sneaking sidelong looks. One hand held the book like a handled mirror to her face. Did she need glasses, was she near-sighted? Her free hand dipped into the darkened floor well to scratch her calf, and her nails scraped pale parallel furrows into her skin. She batted at a gnat before her nose. She huffed a breath upward to blow hair out of her eyes. Her pupils and their surrounding mahogany irises flicked across the lines with electric intelligence, quivering in a warm and liquid sheen; an index finger probed, briefly, the entrance to her visible pink ear; the crest of her breasts above the sundress rose and fell, and she smelled faintly of bubble gum.

I smiled the smile of the sly seducer and leaned over to ease those straps off her lovely shoulders, then I snailed my mouth down to her rubbery nipples. Her arms wrapped about my head and she squeezed. *Take me!* she whispered hotly into my ear. *I'm ready, oh, I'm so so ready!*

Should I admit her to my imaginary harem? Stranded on a desert island, I have these three women for my concubines. When would I desire Trudy and under what conditions? I felt drawn to her in a way I hadn't yet defined, because the idea of her as a desireable female creature was new. She was neither slave nor master. If she neither serviced me nor demanded to be serviced, I hardly knew what to do.

This was an interesting problem, well worth working on. But I couldn't make much headway on it. I was nagged by an uneasiness that might have been guilt. Trudy's human dimension bristled up between us to discourage my taking even daydream liberties. It was easy to imagine her humiliation in the cafeteria line when Sharon had called attention to her tray; easy to know how she must have felt when Sharon said she was supposed to be on a diet; easy to realize that she desired to share her passion for this Kerouac fellow and that we'd rejected him, and so her, leaving her to feel alone.

It was her birthday, and yet she didn't seem happy. Maybe I wasn't such a nice boy, after all.

"So what's Sal doing now?"

She turned to look at me but didn't lower her book. Wary. "Stuff."

For me to know and for you to find out! Did she think I was trapping her?

"Is it more of that reincarnation sort of thing?"

"What 'reincarnation sort of thing'?"

I heard my description being mocked. I felt betrayed, since I'd meant well. "Like the one you read before."

"Nooo," she said slowly after a moment's hesitation. "They're back on the road now, and he's talking about Charlie Parker and Dizzy Gillespie."

"Who are they?"

"Jazz cats. Bebop stars."

"I've never heard that."

"There's a radio show out of New Orleans on WWL every night at midnight—well, it's eleven out here. It's called 'Moonglow With Martin.' He plays their records." There was a beat, and she added, "I listen to it almost every night."

"I'd like to hear it sometime."

"It's on every weeknight."

I'd actually meant "I'd like to listen to it with you," but she ignored or hadn't gotten the hint.

"Could I borrow that book when you're through with it?"

"You really want to read it?"

She left several "or's" hanging in the air: or are you only making fun of me? Or are you only trying to mollify me? Or are you only making polite conversation?

I rolled my eyes and dipped my head toward the front seat, meaning *Sure I do! I'm not like them, you're not like them, we're not like them!* It occurred to me that she and Aunt Vicky might enjoy each other's company.

"Yeah, I really would," I said. "I'm reading *Lolita* right now, but soon as I'm through with it, I'll loan it to you."

"Okay." Then she faced me full on and gave me a heartfelt, entirely uncomplicated smile that was like nothing so much as sunshine shooting all at once through a break in the clouds. I'd said the password. "It'd be really be cool to have somebody to talk to about it."

FOUR-
TEEN

It was a clear, fine day in the mountains. The sun tingled hotly on your skin, but when you stepped into shade or a cloud glided by, a delicious chill in the rarefied air feathered your cheeks. We drove along Ruidoso's main street in tourist traffic, bunched in a caravan of pickups towing horse trailers, cruising past stores with wood-plank fronts and boardwalks protected by an overhang like those on the set of a western. On the street every rich man from Texas wore a Stetson and boots and their women shiny tight Dale Evans slacks and scarves and more turquoise and silver than all the Pueblo peoples put together. Mescalero-Apache families from the nearby reservation galumped slowly along the shoulder on horseback, their mounts leaving olive-hued apples steaming in clumps about the potholes.

At the edge of town were The Old Corral Cabins, several log-cabin cottages strung along a gravel road that meandered up a slope back from the highway. They were cute (they reminded me of my old Lincoln Logs); their roofs were shingled with green asphalt sheeting and each had a small screened porch.

Uncle Waylan pulled up to the office, left the car running, came back carrying two keys. "We got Six and Seven. I'm glad I called ahead, so we can be next door to one another. Big crowd in town this weekend."

We rolled slowly up the winding path, our tires popping pine cones, and stopped in a cleared space before #6. We got out and stood stretching in the dazzling sunlight as we inhaled pinon-scented air. Beyond the last cabin the slope reared up steeply into a ridge thick with pines and scaly with outcrops of sharp gray rock. The ground around our feet was littered with pine cones and padded with a mat of dry brown needles. On the porch of #6 a striped chipmunk sat calmly nibbling something held in its miniscule paws.

"Golly, it's groovy up here!" said Trudy.

Sharon sighed, closed her eyes, dropped her forehead against Uncle Waylan's shoulder. "Makes me sleeeeepy!"

Uncle Waylan laughed. "We ain't got time to dawdle, kids. I got a feeling it's an extra-fine day to make some good hard American cash."

He got the girls' bags from the trunk and carried them inside the cabin. I took our two next door to #7. Inside, the chill from the night still hung like a transparent fog in the plank-floored room. Twin beds with iron frames, between them a night stand built from bark-skinned saplings, and an oval hooked rug for your feet. The beds were covered with red and black Navajo blankets. The place looked clean and smelled of Pine-Sol.

I dug out my windbreaker from my bag. At the car, Uncle Waylan was sitting behind the wheel, his boot heel propped upright in the hinge of the open door. I got in the passenger side.

"This is a great place, Uncle Waylan! Our cabin's really neat."

"Glad you like it, Jimbo." He lit a cigarette. "Bathroom okay?"

"I forgot to check."

He nodded toward #6, laughed. "They're giving this one a going-over, believe me."

I drifted serenely off, enjoying the stillness, the freshness in the air, the sunlight, then he said, "Ah, listen, Jimbo, long as I got the chance here to mention something private. . . . " I peered at him. His look said this was between us boys. "Well, it might turn out that our sleeping arrangements could be a little different."

"What do you mean?"

Sharon emerged from #6 wearing her red cardigan sweater and sunglasses, her wooden shellacked purse with the painted roosters hooked on her elbow. She stopped, turned back, yelled, "Hurry up!" through the doorway.

Uncle Waylan said quickly, "You think it'd be okay if you and Trudy stayed over yonder after lights out? I got business to discuss with Sharon."

Letting her down easy? How could I object? But he looked *sheepish*. "Sure. If it's okay with Trudy. There's two beds."

"Thing is, see," he hurried on, for now Trudy had stepped onto the porch and Sharon was locking the door behind them, "maybe it's best you didn't mention anything to Trudy and let Sharon take care of that, okay?"

Because Trudy will hate this idea? "Okay. Sure."

Sharon came down the steps first, but my gaze swooped up behind her to Trudy. I was in shock—I hardly knew what to make of this unexpected prospect, but I could picture nothing more than the two of us sitting cross-legged on a bed in flannel pajamas and wool socks playing canasta and eating popcorn, though rosily, rosily around the edges of this involuntarily conjured mental image was an aura of arousing intimacy. That Trudy and I might "spend the night together" was very titillating in general but not specifically conjugal. True, I'd already imagined fondling her breasts, but at that moment no reality had threatened my fantasy; now circumstances might actually force or extort this. That frightened me.

Trudy was descending the steps quite gracefully; the hem of her sundress flicked across her pink knees and her shins flashed white, her strong calves flexing. She was laughing, her sunglassses were poked into her hair, and she seemed much too old for me (relief: she'd reject me as too young). But she was likewise teasingly available now, "my" girl assigned by circumstances and Uncle Waylan. Mine to possess? Was this possible? I wondered how she would feel when Sharon eventually broached this subject. But then, when the two girls passed my window, Trudy visored her sunglasses over her eyes and immediately looked my way, and though the dark lenses kept me from seeing her eyes, the act of hiding them hinted that our sleeping over there had come up. But what was said?

It was much too heady to consider, and while we drove to the race track, I played out a series of innocent vignettes to relieve myself of the responsibility for anything serious: Trudy and I could play Hangman. Across the road was a bowling alley built with logs like a Iriquois longhouse, where we could bowl until we fell dead from exertion. We could read her book aloud to one another until someone fell asleep. I wished I'd brought my Monopoly set. We could play password. Animal, vegetable or mineral. Stuff like that. No law said we had to do more. In fact, she might sock me in the jaw if I tried.

The track at Ruidoso Downs ran mostly quarterhorses in what

119

the Chamber of Commerce touted as "The World's Richest Horse Race." It was my first of any kind, and my worries about what lay ahead after sundown dissipated in the camaraderie and excitement of the next three hours: we yelped and screamed and grabbed each other and cussed and stood tiptoe to peer over other heads while our horses (picked by Uncle Waylan, who also put down our bets) thundered by in a hail of clods as one great unified brown body along the quarter-mile track in hardly twenty seconds. We couldn't see which horse had won and had to wait to hear it announced. But we didn't care. We drank Coors from cans and, at one point, a midget mountain shower sprinkled us groundlings, and we all scurried under the bleachers and huddled, laughing, with splattered programs held above our heads. Trudy started shivering and rubbing her goosebumped arms, so I slipped off my windbreaker and caped it across her shoulders.

"Thanks!" She smiled.

By afternoon's end, Uncle Waylan and Sharon had won $40 apiece, but Trudy and I were down $20 between us. Having taken a dislike to the name Baffle's Nigger, Trudy had told Uncle Waylan to put her money on Hopeful Struggle, and I'd followed suit so she wouldn't feel alone.

"Dinner's on me and Sharon," Uncle Waylan said when he saw us moping about our losses.

Back at the cabins, I washed my face and swabbed at my armpits and wondered how clean my underwear truly was, then I sprinkled too much of Uncle Waylan's Old Spice on my cheeks, slipped on a long-sleeved shirt, and combed my hair four times.

"Whew!" Uncle Waylan grinned when I came out of the bathroom. "You smell like a French whorehouse!"

"I didn't know it'd pour out so easy."

"I hope we don't drive by any beehives."

"You think I ought to wash it off?"

"Naw, hell, I was ribbing you, Jimbo."

He was lying on a bed, smoking, one arm bent like a wing and pillowed behind his head. He inspected me from head to toe and grinned. "Ready for action, huh?"

"I am hungry, all right."

"We'll make sure you get a nice big T-bone. Young fellow like you will need a lot of protein to keep up your strength."

"A steak would be good."

He kept smiling as if I were a walking joke.

"Here . . . ." His cigarette hand swung out, and he tapped a knuckle against the night stand. "I left you something in here. For later."

"Thanks." I pretended not to know what it might be.

"I guess your daddy has talked to you about these things."

I couldn't imagine my father even uttering the word "rubber," let alone telling me how to use one.

"Well, yeah."

He must have known I was lying. "I've been meaning to take you to Juarez. I'm sorry now we haven't got around to it."

"Juarez, Mexico?"

"Yeah. Place like that, well, a boy can learn how things are done, so when the time comes you'd know what to do. When it comes to a thing like this, somebody needs to be in charge."

He was frowning from worry. "Do you know the most important thing about making love to a woman?"

I swallowed and looked out the window. Dusk made the panes dark enough to mirror my face.

"Wear a rubber?"

He chuckled, ruefully. "That's an important consideration, all right, but I was thinking more about something else. It's this— never go faster than she wants to go." He groaned and rubbed his face with his hands. This was torture for him, I could see. "And I ain't talking about, uh, moving in and out, son. I'm talking about how many minutes or hours or days or even years it might take her to get the idea of starting it up on her own. You see?"

"I guess."

"Oh, mercy! I'm not used to giving lessons on this."

"I really appreciate it, Uncle Waylan."

He sat up and snubbed out his cigarette. "You're a hell of nice boy, Jimbo. I'll be happy if I have a kid half the lad you are. I know you'd treat a girl with kindness and respect. Especially one like Trudy. She's not exactly what you'd call experienced, as I understand it."

I felt guilty already, if for nothing more than cursing my reputation for niceness and yearning for a chance to besmirch it thoroughly. Except for acting like a jackass during my first toot, I'd never done anything in my life worthy of a criminal's admiration, and I was sick of hearing about my sterling character. But his warning made me worry: had my drooly wishes about Trudy's tits leaked out into the atmosphere? Had Trudy complained to Sharon and Sharon talked to Uncle Waylan about my behavior?

He read my stricken look and laughed. "Son, don't worry about anything. Nature has a way of taking care of these things." He looked enviously at the night stand drawer. "Whatever happens, I suspect you'll have a hell of a lot more fun than I will. However hard it is to get started, it's even harder to find your way out. You sure can't learn that in a cathouse, either. *Nobody's* giving lessons in it."

I braved a shot in the dark. "Are you going to break up with Sharon tonight?"

He blew out a long, slow breath; you could hear the air diminish like a deflating tire. "Am I going to break up with Sharon tonight? Damn, Jimbo, you sure get down to the lick log. Lemme say I plan to start on it, anyway. I know it's time to put away the toys."

When we went out to greet the girls, they were waiting beside the car, as if helpless, though it wasn't locked. They now both wore huge party skirts, pullover sweaters and scarves knotted at their necks and had changed from flat shoes to pumps. Around her neck Trudy wore an engraved gold locket on a chain so fine it looked at first like a colored thread. The way the locket lay so delicately between her full, sweatered breasts took my breath away.

"Aren't we lucky fellows?" crowed Uncle Waylan as he cocked open the carriage doors with a flourish. "Ladies, your beauty humbles us!"

"And your bullshit's ten feet deep," said Trudy.

Settling into the passenger seat, Sharon had to weight her skirt with her arms to keep her flouncy crinoline slip from hiking her hem up to the dashboard. I tried to stop thinking of the bad news she might hear later. Every time I looked at her it was as if I knew she had terminal cancer and she didn't.

Trudy got in beside me with a great rustle, and under her skirt I saw acres of corrugated white material.

"God!" sighed Trudy. "I can't believe you wanted to bring these, Sharon! I feel like I'm wearing an open parachute!"

"You look really nice," I said.

Trudy's sideways sneer exposed a pointed eyetooth. Why was it when I tried to be smooth I only seemed a blundering fool?

122

"Well, you do," I persisted, sounding wounded.

"Don't try to be suave, Jimbo." She playfully thumped my head with a knuckle.

We ate big rare T-bones and baked potatoes at a hunting lodge with red checked tablecloths and candles in net-covered glasses. The waitresses wore dirndls and the bus boys had on yodeller get-ups and pointy Swiss hats. The napkins were pink, and on each table stood a tall glass vase containing a spray of daisies. Uncle Waylan ordered champagne. Despite my fervent vow never to let strong drink pass my lips again, I couldn't resist "tasting" champagne, and I had to drink two glasses because he offered a toast to each of our dates in honor of their being female and therefore categorically wondrous and beautiful. The rosy candlelight softened the skin on their cheeks and chins, formed a delicate illuminating cowl around their faces, lit up their eyes, glinted in the moisture on their lips. Every time I looked at them I fell in love with both by still another inch. So despite Trudy's admonition not to be suave, I offered up another toast in honor of her birthday. Sharon then offered one in honor of us men, and Trudy proposed a round to Jack Kerouac.

That suited everybody fine. Everything suited everybody fine. Before I knew it, Trudy and I were looped and silly. This time she didn't reproach me with sobriety: she got tipsy too. We stood her potato upright and dubbed it "Ike" in honor of the president, then decorated it like a snowman using toothpicks and bits of carrot and lettuce and onion from our salad; we played matchbook football and tried to top each other with disgusting dessert names, and her "dingleberry pie" beat out my "pus pudding." Through all this, Uncle Waylan and Sharon sat beaming like proud parents whose lively progeny were their primary source of entertainment. He scooted his chair close to hers, laid his arm along the back, her head dropped to his shoulder, and her gaze grew dreamy and vacant, as if she didn't have a care in the world, poor doomed thing. Of their four upper limbs, only his left arm and hand were visible.

We left stuffed but happy, tight, walking into the night air that hit us like a splash of ice water to our heated faces, and sang Fats Domino's "Mockingbird Hill" and "Happy Birthday" to Trudy all the way back to #6.

In the cabin, Uncle Waylan and Sharon turned on the radio and danced close and slow while Trudy and I sat on the floor and

123

played gin rummy, but that degenerated into slapjack, and then I asked Trudy if she'd played fifty-two pick up. To my astonished pleasure, she said no.

"Here's fifty-two cards—pick 'em up!" I flung the deck across the bare floor, and we both went breathless and near to urping with laughter. Then I relented and helped her retrieve them, both crawling on all fours in and around the legs of the adults. This proved to be our undoing.

"Trudy, why don't y'all go to the office and get us some Cokes?" said Sharon.

"More champagne!" I said.

"Definitely not," said Uncle Waylan.

Trudy put on my windbreaker without asking. I liked that. It made my heart beat a little faster. We stepped onto the porch and breathed the chilly air, waiting to get our bearings in the darkness. On the road a football-field's length away, cars moved in a muted swish, their red and white lights a festive blur.

The zipper on my windbreaker purred metallically as Trudy's hand went up.

"Are you too cold?" she asked.

"Gosh no. It feels great out here."

We clomped down off the porch and walked the gravel road that shone bone white in the light of the moon falling in shafts through the pines. The mood shifted; suddenly I felt sober and shy. Every time I snuck a quick look at Trudy, she'd smile back. I would smile, then turn back to the path before my feet. Three steps later, I'd look, she'd smile, I'd smile then turn away. We repeated the same little ritual. It was weird. It was unprecedented. It was very exciting.

We were side by side though not close, and when I sidled left to avoid a pothole, the backs of our hands brushed once, electrifying me, and I blurted, "S'cuse!" and she said, "S'okay." I waited three more swings of our pendulum arms, and when the arcs of our hands were in sync, I let her hand bump mine, only this time I caught her fingers and sought a grip; my heart was thudding against the top of my skull, and I expected her to yank away, but instead she entwined her fingers in mine and squeezed so that we were sort of shaking hands as we strolled side by side. Soon, though, the contact of her warm soft hand so overwhelmed me (and her, too, I think) that we both let go (it was either that or go zooming into the heavens), and I was afraid I would keel over, reeling, in a faint.

I cleared my throat. "So, uh, how's it feel to be out of your teens?"

She laughed nervously. "Portentous. Heavy with portent." I heard an odd little trill in her voice.

"What do you mean, exactly?"

"Like something big's going to happen, maybe good, maybe not good."

"Soon, you mean?"

She shot me a glance. "Oh, not necessarily."

Reproved, I spaded my hands in my front pockets. I cursed Uncle Waylan and the burden he'd placed on me of shedding my innocence. Every word said now by either of us took on a hue seen only in the light of this.

"You mean like your future, then?"

"Yes."

"What do you want to happen to you?"

We were nearing the office, where a soft-drink vending machine stood on an open side porch.

"I don't know, exactly. I want to be a writer. But I guess that wouldn't surprise you."

"No. But it does seem unusual for a girl."

She laughed in pity at my ignorance. "You've got a lot to learn about 'girls,' Jimbo."

This seemed to be my theme for the day, and I'd almost reached my threshold for taking lessons in the subject. The return of the Trudy who mocked my youth irritated me. I sulked while Trudy fed dimes into the box and handed me the Cokes as they clattered down the metal chute one by one.

On the way back, she said, "Hey!" I looked her way. She gave me her familiar combative grin and jabbed my shoulder with a knuckle. "Shut up!"

"I know I've got a lot to learn. But just because you've been to college for two years doesn't mean you know everything. Maybe you've got things to learn, too."

"Oh, God, don't be so sensitive. Okay? Geez. I'm sorry. I'm always shooting off my mouth. I really like you." She grabbed me around the neck and smacked me wetly on the cheek. The ring of moisture burned cold in the night air. I had a fleeting sensory memory of a doughnut of soft warm flesh pressed to my skin. My heart lifted, and I let go my anger. How easily she could control my moods surprised me. "You're my favorite person here in Ruidoso, New Mexico."

"Thanks!" I laughed. "It's a small field of contestants."

When we hiked back up to the porch of #6, we found a "Do Not Disturb" sign hanging from the doorknob.

"Assholes!" Trudy muttered. She furiously beat her fists on the door. "Come on!" she hissed to me. I knocked mildly against the pine slab while Trudy continued to wham at it, then she kicked the door twice with the pointed toe of her pump.

"Hey, in there!" she yelled. "Sharon! Here's your goddamn Cokes!"

When no one answered, Trudy hollered, "Sharon! Did you hear me?"

I looked toward the office. Trudy apparently had no qualms about creating a disturbance.

"Aw, heck. Let them be," I said mildly. Trudy gave me a withering look, raised her fist to pound the door again, but then we heard the metal chink of a lock, the door cracked open, and Sharon's face appeared. I tried to read on it whether she'd learned her fate. The room beyond her head was dim, though there was a flickering light from a candle. Her arm came through the crack. I handed over two Cokes.

"Crap, Trudy! What's the matter with you? Why don't you guys go play strip poker or something?"

She leaned back as if to shut the door but Trudy pushed against it. For a person who was about to get dumped Sharon was very eager to clear the time and space for it.

"At least give me my bag!"

"It's already over there."

Trudy, dumbfounded, dropped her hand, and Sharon closed the door. There was no doubt now as to Trudy's attitude about our spending the night in #7. Her anger was frightening. I wanted to tell her this hadn't been my idea but even to express awareness of a plan was incriminating.

"We could go to the bowling alley," I said. "Get a Coke or something."

Trudy looked at the two bottles in my hand and snickered. "We have some."

126

"It was a manner of speaking. We could watch people bowl. I bet they've got pinball machines. Maybe shuffleboard and a juke box."

She glowered. To dispel any suspicion that I'd connived, I said, "Maybe when we come back, they'll be through, uh, talking."

"Oh, sweet Jesus, James! They're not talking! They're balling!"

"Bawling?"

"Doing it, dummy!"

I grinned. "Oh. Well, maybe they'll be through with that, too."

"They're going to be at it all night. It's why we came here, don't you know?"

I could understand that Uncle Waylan might want to take all night to prepare Sharon for the bad news. Or to have one last fling before turning his back on temptation. But Trudy's anger discouraged me from saying this.

"I thought it was for your birthday."

"That was the excuse."

She stewed in silence, arms laced over her breasts, gaze launched into a far distance. My toe found a crack in the porch decking that made an intriguing creak when I pressed it over and over with my shoe. I considered opening a Coke with my pocket-knife but realized I was getting chilly.

"I'll be right back." I made for the stairs.

"Where are you going?"

"Get a sweater," I called over my shoulder.

"Oh, hey, I'm sorry. I'll go with you!" After a moment she was striding beside me in the darkness.

FIFTEEN

S oon as we set foot inside, I started babbling. "Hey, listen, Trudy, there's a deck of cards in my bag, or maybe we could read your book, you wanna do that? I've got a pad and a pencil, too, we could play tic-tac-toe. Or if you want to sleep, I could go to the bowling alley. I don't want you to feel uncomfort . . . ."

"Will you relax?" Trudy laughed. "I'm not going to rape you. Open me a Coke, please."

While I pried off the caps with my knife, she went into the bathroom. She came out a moment later carrying the huge, billowy slip and stood it upright at the end of a bed. It looked like a squat Christmas tree in white.

"Can't stand those things!"

I handed a bottle to her. She said thanks and took a long slug of the cola. I realized that she didn't blame me for these arrangements. She shoved a pillow up against one iron headboard, then sat back against it with her legs stretched out on the red blanket. I opened the other bottle. I hesitated, then I gestured to the foot of the bed she'd chosen.

"You mind if I sit here?"

"Course not."

I sat cross-legged, facing her. She was silent, and I felt duty-bound to entertain her.

"What's in your locket?"

She set her Coke bottle on the night stand. Her chin dropped to her breastbone; she looked down, pinched the locket gently between her thumb and index finger and peered at it cross-eyed.

"It was my grandmother's. My mother sent it for my birthday. She's been keeping it for me." She pried it open.

"Wanna see?"

She leaned over her knees and I rose up on mine and crawled forward to see the locket. Our hair caught, and I could smell her cologne and winey breath. Nervous, I took a quick look—a face with old-timey sideburns and mustache.

"It's my grandfather as a young man."

I dropped back to my Indian-sit; Trudy drew her knees up and sat with her chin on the peak they made, pulled her skirt down around her shins, forming a tent-hollow under there for me to imagine.

"I've always thought heart lockets were very romantic."

"They're neat," I said.

Her smile let me know I amused her.

"Why'd you ask me about it?"

"I dunno. Making conversation."

"You weren't thinking a boy had given it to me? Did you think there was a hank of his hair in it?"

"Uh, no." I shrugged helplessly.

"What? You don't think I could have a guy?"

This smile said she was enjoying my discomfort.

"Do you?"

"What do you think?"

"Uh, well, I think you could have any guy you set out to get, Trudy."

She smirked. "You've been around your uncle too long, Jimbo!"

"I meant it."

"That's what he'd say."

"It's true."

"Why should I be able to get any guy I want?"

"You're, well, pretty and nice . . . ."

"Sugar and spice? Oh for God's sake, can't you be any more personal than that?"

I inhaled, summoned my courage. "You have really . . . really beautiful breasts. And hair and eyes, too." I considered stopping there but tossed in, "And skin. I like freckles. A lot."

She was quiet a moment. That may have been the first time I'd ever surprised her. "That's a little better. How about my personality, do I have a cute personality?"

Since candor pleased her, I said, "No, not at all. That's the very last word I'd use to describe your personality."

"What, then?"

"Loud."

"I'm loud?"

"Your personality is."

She chuckled. "Does that bother you?"

"Bother me? No, not exactly. It's just I'm not quite used to it."

"What're you used to, types like Sharon?"

I wanted to say I wasn't used to any kind of girl, but I thought of Louise Bowen. And realized I'd outgrown her.

"What 'type' do you think Sharon is, anyway?" I asked.

"Geisha. A girl who curtsies and does whatever her man wants, little squeaking mouse."

She sounded angry. This characterization didn't fit my picture of Sharon. I thought of Sharon as sexy, mysterious, a little prickly and unpredictable—maybe "unknowable" to me. She'd always been "nice," but her courtesy conveyed clear boundaries, and she never bowed or scraped when it came to me. I thought she could get pretty much what she wanted when she wanted it. Otherwise, Uncle Waylan would have said adios long before now.

"You really think that's how Sharon is?"

"Most of the time. When she's not a slut."

"God, Trudy! She's your own cousin! I can't believe you're saying that about her! I thought y'all were friends."

"We were. I used to respect her and really look up to her. She was always like a big sister to me, and all my life I wanted to be just like her."

"Really?"

Trudy nodded. All her playfulness had vanished. "I used to think that life was sort of against her. I used to feel sorry for her because I thought her luck was bad, what with Aunt Norma dying of cancer and Uncle Richard being such a worthless bastard. I used to feel sorry for her because she was a victim of circumstance. I don't see it that way any more. Now I think she acts like any other stupid slut."

"What made you change your mind?"

Her look burned me. "What do you think?"

I blushed, guilty by association. "You don't think she and Uncle Waylan should be together now?"

"No. He's *married*. Do you?"

"I guess not. No, you're right. And my Aunt Vicky, she's really super, you know. I think you'd like her. I feel sorry for her, too."

"Me too, being married to a guy like him."

I sipped at my Coke and turned over in my mind the news I'd gotten from Uncle Waylan. Should I tell Trudy now? At the least it proved he was loyal to his wife. I felt reluctant to spring it on Trudy, though, maybe because in my mind's eye I could see her leap up and run to #6 to rip Sharon out of Uncle Waylan's arms and console her. I was selfish: I wanted Trudy's undivided attention.

"Aw, he's not so bad," I said finally.

"He's an asshole."

"How come you're so against him? Last time we talked about it you were saying that if he was getting a divorce, then it was okay with you for him and Sharon to be together. Besides, he's helped you guys out, he's really generous, and it's not like he tries to hide anything from anybody. He treats Sharon like a lady, which I think she is!"

Trudy scoffed. "God, I hardly know where to start." She lay over on the bed, stretching out, arms over her head, then she drew up her knees and curled with one palm between her thighs and the other pillowing her cheek.

"What do you think's going to happen with them?"

I couldn't tell if she was soliciting my opinion or leading me somewhere.

"I'm not sure. I guess sooner or later he and Aunt Vicky will get back together."

"You think that's the best thing?"

"Do you?"

"Maybe, under most circumstances. I would always wish for somebody better for Sharon than a guy like him."

I tried to ignore this insult. I wondered if she were trying to goad me into an argument. "I guess I think that would be best because he and Aunt Vicky are married, and I think he cares a lot for her, still. He loves her. I think that if they hadn't had a fight that night or if he'd hadn't let himself get so worked up about it, he wouldn't have gone to Dumas to look up Sharon. And he and Aunt Vicky would still be together. But I think he cares about Sharon, too. I mean he does worry about her welfare." Could she read between my lines? I'd drawn a useful distinction for her to consider.

132

"Bullshit!"

"Why don't you feel that's true?"

"Because she's just easy to him. She's young and vulnerable and has to do what he wants. He's her boss, too, you know. I've been trying to get her to leave."

"That might be the best thing," I said sadly. If Uncle Waylan heaped the bad news on poor Sharon's head tonight, then by tomorrow Trudy would have them on a bus for Dumas.

"I think Uncle Waylan and Aunt Vicky could patch it up if they have to."

"How nice for them!"

Fortunately, her sarcasm required no answer. I thought of changing the subject (and thus the mood), but before I could, Trudy said, "What do you think he'd do if Sharon turned up p.g.?"

"Wow! I don't know! I hadn't thought of that."

"Think of it, then."

"I suppose he and Aunt Vicky could divorce and he and Sharon could get married."

"What if he didn't want to do that?"

"I guess she could get an abortion or go to one of those homes for unwed mothers."

"Just like that?" Trudy snapped her fingers in the air. "Like going to the bakery and deciding between doughnuts or cinnamon rolls?"

"Well, no, of course not!"

"What if she stayed right in Hedorville and walked around with a great big belly and kept on working some place then had the kid and raised it right under his nose, even called it Waylan, Junior?"

That this dalliance of my uncle's might turn into *Tess of the D'Urbervilles* or *The Scarlet Letter* hadn't dawned on me. "Wouldn't she be too embarrassed?"

"She can be a tough cookie. It'd be like her to want to spread the misery."

In a couple of seconds, I got it. "Wow!"

She held my gaze for a long minute. "You've got to promise not to say anything to him!"

"Yeah! Sure. I won't!"

"I'm not kidding, Jimbo. Sharon would kill me if she knew we were having this conversation. She hasn't said anything to him yet."

"Ok. You can trust me. When did it happen?"

"That weekend he came to see her in Dumas. It's why she agreed to come work for him."

"Wow. Double wow!"

"Thing is, I'm really worried about her. I'm mad at her, too, but I'm also worried."

Trudy's eyes welled with tears, and she struggled up onto her elbow and wiped them with the hem of her loose full skirt. I handed her my handkerchief (freshly laundered by Aunt Vicky), and she blew her nose.

"I thought maybe you would help me."

"Sure! Yeah!" My heart bounced wildly in its basket. "What do you want me to do?"

"Help me help her figure out what's best for her."

"I'd be glad to."

She smiled weakly. "That means be a spy. She needs to make a very tough decision, and she needs to know things to make the right one."

"Things like what?" If I sounded suspicious, Trudy didn't appear to notice.

"Like who does he really want to be with?"

Out of weakness, I hedged and squirmed. I didn't want to spoil our intimacy. If Uncle Waylan was telling Sharon tonight that he preferred to be married to Aunt Vicky, then Trudy would find out soon enough, I thought. I felt like a weasel, but I might never have a chance to be in a place like this with Trudy again.

"Okay. I'll do what I can."

I put out my hand to shake. She shoved herself upright into a cross-legged posture. Our knees touched. She took my hand as if to shake it, then pressed it between both of hers.

"How do you feel about this other stuff?" She was smiling and couldn't quite meet my gaze.

"What other stuff?"

"Why do you always make me explain things that I know you already understand? You might as well understand me outright, okay?"

She grinned and flushed. A billow of red curls fell over her brow and she tossed it back with a jerk of her head. Her cheek showed lines where she'd lain on the blanket. She was still holding my hand. I tried to will it numb.

"Okay. You mean me and you in this room tonight, right?"

"What? Me and you here? What about it?"

I flushed. "Okay. You win."

"I win what?"

"I do know what you're talking about."

"What're you talking about?"

"About me and you in this room."

"What about it?" she said.

"Well, I guess we're suppose to . . . to do something."

"What would that be?"

"I don't know. Whatever we want, I guess," I said wretchedly.

"What do 'we' want?"

"I don't know."

"What do you want?" she asked.

I looked her right in the eye. "I want to kiss you."

She grinned. "Copasetic."

In my previous life as a lover at, say, a Methodist Youth Fellowship hay ride, my kissing Louise took one of two forms: I'd be overcome with a tender regard and I'd lunge at her cheek and go "smack!" the way you do with an adorable infant, or I'd bring my face into position with my eyes almost closed, cock my head so that a vertical axis drawn through it would intersect one drawn through hers at a ninety-degree angle, then I'd press my positioned and puckered lips to her firmly sphinctered mouth and we'd push toward one another once, then release.

I knew what had been missing the instant I kissed Trudy. I shut my eyes and did my docking maneuver with Trudy's face but she was moving too (new development!) and so her mouth caught mine before I'd had a chance to arrange my lips, and her mouth writhed and nibbled around the ring of my lips and her tongue tip dabbed at mine and I felt a probe of her warm breath go down my throat. I shuddered with pleasure and began trembling all over; I instantly went so hard that it ached like something sticking into, and not out of, my pubic bone. I felt woozy and curiously inspired to say I love you, Trudy. Was I still drunk? My hand went to her waist but before I could will it to rise and cup her breast, she pulled away.

"Anything else you want to do?" Her cheeks were flushed, and gleaming threads of moisture pearled momentarily between her lips.

"Yes. I guess I want to do it."

"It?"

"Lose my virginity, for God's sake. Quit doing this! What do you want to do?"

"I don't think I want to lose my virginity. I think I want to have lost it, though."

"You don't want to do it?" I was crestfallen. I fell back onto my haunches with my arm hiding the tree limb stuffed into my underwear.

"I want to have done it, to have it done with."

Complexities, perplexities. I hardly knew what to say or do. I was so hard I was afraid it was a permanent condition (wasn't there a disease?) where I'd have to carry this painfully rigid log around for the rest of my life.

"Would you rather play cards or go to sleep or something?" I said, sulking. I was thinking I'd sneak away when the lights were out and flail this thing against a big pine tree to get it to go down.

"No. Let's sit like this for a while, ok?"

"Okay."

We sat, knee to knee, with her holding my hand. She turned it this way and that, inspecting the back of it, the knuckles, the nails. She was trembling minutely. She was a little nervous. That was different. And gratifying.

"Nice hands. I had a boyfriend when I was a freshman. His nails were always dirty."

"How come you and he didn't, uh . . . ."

"He asked but I told him no."

"Did you mean it?"

"Of course."

"You weren't only saying it so he'd think you were respectable?"

"Respectable?" she hooted. "God, no, for me that'd be a reason to say yes! No, I said no because, because his nails were dirty."

"Because his nails were dirty? What happened to your admiration for the workers of the world?"

"I was only teasing you. I'll admit that maybe when I've said no before it only meant *not at this time or not at this place*. Sometimes when I've said no it meant *not in a million years and not even if you were the last guy on the planet*. But most of the time I've said no because I'm scared and feel too vulnerable. I wasn't ready."

"How will you know when you're ready?"

"I guess whenever it happens it will happen because I'm ready. I had this roommate, Sherry. She did it for the first time when she was fourteen. I asked her why, and do you know what she said? 'Because he asked!' Some girls will do it because guys ask and they feel sorry for them or feel generous or hate to think of a guy feeling bad or don't think enough of themselves to say no. Like Sharon."

"No kidding?" Despite how I might've willed otherwise, I couldn't resist the devilish thought of throwing myself upon Sharon's mercy. Maybe after I got beat up on her behalf I should have asked her to console me with sex.

"Well, within limits." She looked up and caught my eye, grinned. "Not me, though."

"I wouldn't think so."

"You shouldn't make it sound like a defect in my character."

I shrugged. This incessant badinage was straining me; I presumed I was getting a "no," and, exasperated, I could take only an academic interest as to which of her several categories it might belong.

If we weren't going to do it, we might as well find something else to occupy ourselves, and I could hope for a distraction powerful enough to unlock the jammed apparatus on my dingus so I could fold it up and put it away.

I decided that, all in all, it was probably best that we weren't going to make the effort, since it was easy to imagine that Trudy would want to talk about it for the next three decades. My champagne buzz had sunk like an airless kite to earth, leaving me with the shadow of a headache and my senses dulled.

I yawned.

"Am I so boring?"

"Mountain air. That champagne made me sleepy."

"Let's go to bed."

I scrutinized those chocolate eyes for a definitive interpretation of that ambiguous phrase. I thought of all the things she might've said: *Let's turn in.* Or *I've got to get some shut-eye.* Or *I'm dead tired* or *I'm asleep on my feet.* I decided to walk the tightwire of that ambiguity to see where it led.

"You can have the bathroom first."

Trudy lugged her overnight bag into the bathroom, and I shrugged out of my sweater and shirt and jeans and into a t-shirt. Bending my cock by its creaky hinge, I got into my sweat pants, seeing on my underwear a half-dollar of dick syrup that I hoped wouldn't seep through. I kept my socks on (it seemed strange to be cold at night) and dug out my shaving kit and sat on the bed waiting.

She came out wearing socks and her thighs were bare up to the hem of a long red sweatshirt with WTSTC on the front. I imagined her panties under it. I was like a giant dick with arms and legs.

"Brrr!" Hugging herself, she dashed for the nearest bed as if she were cold, but I thought her hurry was probably inspired as much by modesty. Everything she did now seemed of infinite interest, as if I could study her smallest gesture over and over and it would yield, over and over, a gratifying bounty of Trudyness.

I brushed my teeth slowly. Now that I had a moment to reflect, the news of Sharon's pregnancy started sinking in. It made me very uneasy to hold a secret from Uncle Waylan, especially one so volatile and so essential to his welfare. How would he take the news? He wasn't an "asshole," as Trudy had said. It didn't seem fair to condemn him before he had a chance to prove his mettle.

I believed he would do the honorable thing when called upon. I supposed that would be to divorce Aunt Vicky and marry Sharon.

That made me ache for Aunt Vicky. Now it was obvious that no one would walk away from this unscathed. I hadn't seen this before.

I thought of the other couple over at #6 and wondered if, at this very moment, Sharon was confessing. Then I thought of Trudy out there waiting. My Trudy. I longed to kiss her again. Maybe I would ask if I could sleep with her, chastely, and put my mouth on hers once more. One kiss. Just one. Then I could hold her. Maybe she'd let me feel her breasts. Do stuff only above the waist.

The condom in the night stand—if Uncle Waylan believed in using them, how had Sharon gotten pregnant? Could there be a mistake? Could someone else be the father? And was Sharon pinning it on him?

And should I be spying on Uncle Waylan for Trudy and Sharon, anyway? I mean, after all, he and I were friends, family, coworkers, and, maybe above all else: fellow males, members of the same tribe. I owed him much. He was teaching me how to be a man. And this is how I repay him?

I kept coaching myself to stay loyal to my true friends. When I came out of the bathroom, Trudy was half-sitting, half-lying in bed with the covers pulled up under her breasts and her hands smoothing out the blanket across her thighs. She gave me a neutral look.

I glanced at the other bed. She had set her overnight bag on it, effectively disabling it as a place to lie in. I read this as a sign. My heart was pounding and my hands were suddenly damp.

"You want the light out?"

"Sure."

I stepped to the switch beside the door and flicked off the overhead light. The dark room lightened as my pupils dilated, and the moonlight laid a pale blue patina across the tandem beds. I thought I heard her murmur. I moved to the ends of the beds and stood between them on the curving rim of the hooked rug. I thought of that stupid short story we'd read in the eighth grade about the lady or the tiger; it seemed a false dilemma now. The choice was truly between lady and the tiger behind one door and nothing behind the other. I detested my cowardice.

"Aren't you cold?"

That she cared about my comfort touched me. I realized her concern had been a recurring melody in the day; Trudy did indeed like me, and, liking me, welcomed me into her bed.

"Yes," I said. "I am cold."

There was a rustle, and in the dimness a white sail appeared flat on the dark surface of the bed as she flung back the covers. Without asking I slid in beside her, and we burrowed deeply under the blankets where the warm womb exhaled the fragrance of her body. Instantly, we awkwardly clutched at one another's heated forms and kissed, then we locked into an embrace so fierce that we were unable to do anything for a long while except cling helplessly and rock ourselves like autistic children.

SIXTEEN

Now I had a song in my heart. I took the words to "I Love You Truly" and sang them "I love you Truuudddy," played the tune over and over like the jingle of an ice-cream truck in my inner ear. No sooner would I start shovelling sand, say, or carrying pipe than my mind would rocket off the launching pad and go whirlagigging out to that luscious fleshy redhead I adored.

How did I love her? I count these ways: her joking bubbly repartee, the backs of her knees (soft, fragrant, wonderful to kiss), her disdain for Elvis, her vocabulary, her musky fragrance on my fingers, her shimmering eyes, her tiny hands, the color of her hair, her seriousness about the world and her interests in things usually labeled masculine such as chess and astronomy.

There'd I be cataloguing these wonders and next thing I knew Slim or Red or Pete would be whanging on my hardhat with a tool: "Hey, Jimbo, wake up!!" Drooling, slack-jawed, I'd be lolly-gagging and loitering with shovel in hand, eyes as vacant as a cow's. Aliens had sucked out my brains and left my body a shell. The guys were quick to know the cause, too. *"Damn if old Jimbo don't act pussy-whipped!"* No, no, no! I thought. My condition is much more shameful: I'm loopy-soupy with love. My muscles dissolve when I think about Trudy and my eyes tear up. Pardon me, but I need to sit down right here so I can watch the movie in my mind of us in the cabin last Saturday night, down to our socks, breasts to chest, leaky loins to luscious nest, neither knowing exactly how it's done but having the time of our lives figuring it out as we groped along, using our tongues the way blind men use white canes.

"Do you agree, Jimbo?"

"Huh? Uh . . . "

I'd done it again! Aunt Vicky and her friend Robert from Baltimore were looking at me expectantly, Aunt Vicky beaming as if I were her star pupil when, in reality, my brain had been pickled in *eau de Trudy* and I hardly knew my name, let alone what events were unfolding in world affairs.

"Jimbo hasn't been himself lately," cracked Uncle Waylan.

We were in Aunt Vicky's living room. It was the Friday night following our trip to Ruidoso, and Uncle Waylan and I had been invited to dinner to meet Aunt Vicky's friend and his bride, who were driving through on a honeymoon trip to the West Coast. Aunt Vicky's friend wore spectacles and a bola tie he'd bought in Fort Worth, but the western effect was spoiled by his wearing wing tips and crossing his legs at the knee. He smoked a pipe with a bowl carved to look like the head of a setter. The fellow's bride was a lumpy looking thing with a bad overbite and a big string of pearls that must have been brand new because she toyed with them every second like rosary beads. Every other sentence noted her new groom's character or habits. "Oh, that's the sort of thing Robert just hates!" or "Robert likes his whiskey neat!" she'd say to demonstrate her intimacy and possession, I guessed, or to point out virtues Aunt Vicky had overlooked way back when. I supposed it wasn't fair of me to dislike them on such short notice, but Uncle Waylan had told me on the way over that Robert was the one Aunt Vicky "left at the altar," and Uncle Waylan was sure the point of the visit from Baltimore's perspective was to prove to Aunt Vicky he did much better by being dumped, and Aunt Vicky's point in asking Uncle Waylan over was to prove she'd been right to come out west. It was a duel: new partners at ten feet across a parlor floor.

Personally, I'd have never chosen Lumpy over Aunt Vicky in a thousand years (not that Mr. Baltimore had a choice). But I had much new insight about love and could easily forgive his choice and his bride her sappy behavior.

"We were discussing Arthur Miller," said Aunt Vicky.

"Oh," I said. "Copasetic." I'd read this chapter. In fact, now that I'd been blessed by Trudy's love, I could understand

Marilyn's picking owl-eyed baldy. For Trudy to love me, she had to overlook a lot of ignorance and inexperience.

To show my worldliness, I said, "I guess love is blind."

Aunt Vicky 's friend from Baltimore tittered. "That may well be true, Jimbo," said Aunt Vicky. "But we were talking about his appearance before the committee. Do you agree that he shouldn't name names?"

Uncle Waylan saved me by saying, "Maybe you should catch the lad up to speed."

Robert leaned forward and fixed me with the condescendingly "helpful" look you get from people who aren't teachers but who think that this is a great loss to the world. He said, "Hewack. The H.U.A.C. That's what we call an acronym." He waited until I nodded at him like a dunce. "For the infamous House Un-American Activities Committee. They've subpoenaed Mr. Miller in an effort to force him to give the names of persons attending a meeting in 1939—"

"Nineteen thirty-nine! Isn't that pree-posterous!!" shouted Aunt Vicky, almost lunging out of her chair. Since she was holding a glass of wine as she did a jumping jack for punctuation, the wine sloshed onto the back of her hand. She frowned at the dribble then licked it off. We were supposed to have had bits of chicken liver on a toothpick with bacon wrapped about them as appetizers, but she'd burned them beyond recognition, as the newspapers say. I think she was drunk. She said we were waiting for the roast to finish cooking. I was antsy to get back to the shop and talk to Trudy on the phone or borrow a truck and see her.

"A meeting in that year at which there were supposedly several known communists," Robert went on, speaking mostly at me and pretending not to be alarmed by Aunt Vicky's outburst. "But Mr. Miller is refusing to give them what they want. They're charging him with contempt of Congress and are having his passport withheld."

Amazing! Hardly two weeks ago I'd never heard of Arthur Miller and now here he was all over the map, marrying movie stars and getting himself in hot water with the U.S. government. Gee, the world was full of wonders! However, none was compelling enough to distract me from my primary mission in life, which was licking my way around the glorious globe of Trudy's lovely form, and as soon as I murmured my gratitude to Robert for the gratuitous lesson in current events, I intended to melt into the woodwork to continue charting my voyage.

But Aunt Vicky hadn't forgotten that she'd asked a question. She repeated it. "What would you do if you were Arthur Miller, James?"

I got the impression I was supposed to represent the brains in my family. Aunt Vicky's cheeks were red, as if she'd had her face in the oven. Her eyes were aswim in a glinty fluid, she was tapping one toe and swinging one leg over the other, all the while drumming her sharp nails on the belly of the wine glass—"tinka tinka tinka." She was wearing a teacherly shirtwaist dress with a full skirt that came to her mid-calf, a new perm that made tight coils of hair on her gleaming forehead, and big white plastic earclips that looked like flattened mothballs. I'd never seen her in so much make-up, and since she didn't have her glasses on, she kept gravitating forward as if slowly toppling and squinting like someone driving in a blinding rain. She seemed like a stranger. Even through the fog induced in my brain by love fever, I could see that she was unhinged.

"About this Hew-ack?" I stalled for time. They nodded. I wondered what Uncle Waylan would answer, but he was nursing his private irritation. He'd had three bourbon and branches, and he sat stretched in his easy chair with his legs straight as if he had rigor mortis while standing and somebody laid him back like a board in his chair. This put his boots plop in the path of anyone who got up to walk, though he'd move them aside or back when necessary (too slowly and not enough). If Aunt Vicky'd hoped his behavior would prove to the Baltimores she'd married a gentleman, I'm sure he'd disappointed her. He was more than a tad surly and had scootched his character an inch or two down the scale the other direction, the way I'd seen him be with my mother. *Whatever you think of me I'm going to prove I'm worse.* It was beyond me why anyone would go out of his way to make a bad impression, but this was a known perversity in his character.

When he caught me looking at him, he drawled, "I don't know about Jimbo, but I didn't get my ass shot off in the Big One so a pinko fairy could lie to the FBI."

Aunt Vicky thrust her face at him the way you'd stiff-arm a tackler on your way to the goal line. "My, Waylan! Please assure us you're not going to show your scar next!" Then she had to beam a smile at the Baltimores brittle as sheet candy and add, "You know he doesn't mean a word of it."

While Uncle Waylan studied the bottom of his empty tumbler as if deciding whether to contradict her, Robert crossed his legs and delicately pointed the stem of his pipe at him. "Not to split hairs, my man, but I do believe that Miller's marriage proves that his sexual preferences are orthodox."

His goofy bride warbled, "I think he's almost as dreamy as Robert!"

Aunt Vicky said, "How sweet" but got right back to me. "Well, Jimbo?"

I'd hoped my opinion mattered so little that everybody would've forgotten I'd been asked. I knew Uncle Waylan's answer wasn't the "right" one. But the issue was: can you rightfully disobey your government? I knew the instant I said "Thou shalt obey thy government," Aunt Vicky would remind me of the Germans who'd known that Jews were being put to death in camps but who hadn't said "no" to their government. And about Ghandi's movement in India and the case for "civil disobedience" in the fight for independence from Britain, a revolution that corresponded with our own. And last year in Montgomery, Alabama, people had started disobeying orders issued by their "government" to sit at the backs of buses and use only designated water fountains.

These cases were fresh on all our minds. I dipped into myself in an effort to sort out how I stood. I felt deep in my bones the westerner's don't-fence-me-in resistance to being governed by anyone for any reason—the highly vaunted "rugged individualism" of the cowboy, farmer, trapper that extends even to such commonly accepted concessions to the rights of the body politic as zoning. But I'd also come of age while men were overseas dying for their country and felt the powerful tug of patriotic adherence to duty. Included in my Boy Scout credo was the vow "to do my duty to God and my Country." I wasn't seasoned enough to recognize that a distinction can be made between one's country and one's government.

It did seem we were in a time of national crisis. People had built fallout shelters in our neighborhood, and at school we held air-raid drills, taking shelter under our desks by assuming a posture (foetal-like, only on your knees) that offered maximum protection from falling debris. Tomorrow, in fact, there was to be a national civil defense drill across the nation as a rehearsal in case of a nuclear attack by the Russians. Many U.S. cities would be "bombed," and the police and civil defense authorities in those cities would halt traffic and herd people into air-raid shelters.

In times of danger, didn't you have to take drastic measures to guarantee the security and safety and surivival of the nation? So if the U.S. government were to inquire into my associations on the grounds that I might be holding information vital to national security, shouldn't I be eager to help?

But Aunt Vicky's question wasn't merely academic. The context was this living room among this company. I didn't want to sound like Uncle Waylan, but I was caught in a maelstrom of conflicting loyalties. Even though I knew he was partly responsible for perpetuating the Baltimores' obvious opinion that he was a redneck, I wanted to be his ally—but without being painted by the same brush. I wanted to be Aunt Vicky's best pupil but also to be known as a man more like Uncle Waylan than like Robert de la Baltimore.

The silence was growing awkward. Lumpy looked as if she might break it by sending up more Hosannas to honor Robert, so I said, trying to please everyone, "Well, here's my opinion. If Mr. Miller knows that the people at the party in 1939 were actually communists, then maybe he should tell the government who they were. If he knows they weren't, then he should tell them their names don't matter."

Uncle Waylan chuckled as if I were a fool. Aunt Vicky said, "I better check on the roast" and rose and left the room without looking at me. I'd disappointed her.

So much for steering down the middle of the road.

146

SEVEN-TEEN

With Aunt Vicky in the kitchen poking the roast, I took my chance to flee. "Gotta wash my hands," I murmured. Down the hall and, sneaking a look behind me, I ducked into Aunt Vicky's office. I dialed The Round-Up, got Wally, asked him to plug me into Trudy's room.

Waiting, I eased onto the desk. A stack of placards leaned against the wall. "Our forefathers fought for freedom of speech!" declared the top one in red fingerpaint. Aunt Vicky and Helen McIntyre made them for their "anti-censorship" protest tomorrow at the library. They'd stepped up their campaign because the library board had bowed to pressure from the citizen's group and had stripped *Peyton Place* off the shelves. I'd agreed to help them.

"Hello," answered Cotton. Had Wally rung the wrong room?

"Hey, Cotton, it's Jimbo," I offered neutrally. It was hard talking to Cotton these days: I had to sound civil but not quite friendly. I didn't want him to think I was afraid of him, but I also didn't want to hint at a rematch. My previous fights had all produced a camaraderie between me and my adversary, as if the fight had been a perilous mutual adventure we'd survived, but Cotton remained stubbornly aloof.

"Yeah, Jimbo? This here's Cotton."

"I was looking for Trudy."

"Ain't here."

To avoid inquiring where she might be, I asked, "Sharon there?"

"She ain't feeling so hot."

Cotton was stubbornly laconic; this natural mode of expression was heightened by his unwillingness to offer a victor's gracious hand to the vanquished. I waited, in vain, for more information. Sharon had missed three days of work this week, and to avoid visiting her at night, Uncle Waylan had a lame excuse that I had been expected to deliver as his ambassador. Lying about his absence stuck in my craw. "He's gotta catch up on the paper work," I said on Wednesday night, an excuse that not only explained his absence but also reminded her that he was doing her chores.

Was Sharon pregnant-sick? I asked Trudy earlier in the week. "Yeah. And heart-sick, too," she said. In Ruidoso, while Trudy and I were falling in love, Uncle Waylan was telling Sharon that he wasn't "good enough" for her, that she'd "be better off" without his "cruddy old self." This was after they'd humped like bunnies half the night, of course. Surely Sharon had heard an overture to leaving in this? Had she told him she was pregnant? Not yet.

"But is Sharon there?" I went on doggedly to Cotton.

"Yep."

I mutely cursed him. "Lemme talk to her, ok?"

He covered the phone and I could hear murmuring. Then he said, "If Waylan's with you, she wants to talk to him."

Aunt Vicky appeared in the doorway, and I almost jumped out of my skin.

"Dinner's on!" she sang. Then she grinned, obviously presuming I was talking to a girl. I said, "Be there in a sec" to her and blushed.

What was I supposed to tell Cotton? I couldn't imagine waltzing to the dinner table and telling Uncle Waylan that "someone" wanted to talk to him. Would Sharon play her last trump now?

"Tell her he'll call in a bit," I said to Cotton. "And tell Trudy I called looking for her," I added gruffly.

It was a long walk down the hall. Where was Trudy? I was sweating around the collar of my white shirt. I hated being in a tizzy, wrought up every moment of the day. Thinking about Trudy had a curiously contradictory effect. One moment it'd be like a soporific drug oozing through my veins and soothing me into a trance-like state or that waking coma lizards fall into when

148

you stroke their bellies. But the next moment I'd be tearing my hair out imagining losing her. Uncle Waylan might send them back to Dumas. Or he and Aunt Vicky might break up for certain and my parents order me home. That my happiness lay in other people's hands wasn't new: but it was suddenly *crucial*, and for the first time I could see that what the adults did for themselves could determine what happened to me. This put my conflict between what I wanted and what was good for everyone into very sharp relief: Trudy and I could be together only so long as Uncle Waylan stayed confused and uncertain, only so long as his ambivalence was endurable to him and to Sharon and Aunt Vicky. My best interest lay in maintaining the shaky equilibrium, propping each angle of the triangle.

But doing this was *wrong*. Neither Sharon nor Aunt Vicky was being treated with the honor and respect due them; five minutes' discussion with my father would shame me for considering any action that didn't arise from this premise: it was my duty as a man to protect women from harm.

Even if I managed to ignore my conscience and to keep the conditions stable, Trudy might fall out of love with me, anyway. My God, how secure could my measly grip be on someone this beautiful, smart, and sophisticated?

Loving someone had an underside of nightmarish projected sorrow and loss I hadn't anticipated. The love of my parents and sisters had always been an agreeable constant I'd taken for granted, but Trudy's love was far more urgent, far more essential to my welfare, I believed, and so without it I might die.

For about a day following our blissful night in Ruidoso I strutted about immensely proud to have learned what making love was all about. When we got back on Sunday I stayed at The Round-Up smooching with Trudy and wanting desperately to find a dark and private corner, but Sharon finally ran me off at midnight. Monday at work, though, I was cross and hungover from being drunk on love. I worried that the instant I was out of Trudy's sight, my effect on her would weaken. I imagined that her love depended solely on my presence. I lived in terror that the smallest thing might make her tumble out of love—she could blink and I'd be yesterday's mood swept aside by a night's sleep or a drink of cold water. I could become as small to her as Louise was now to me.

Monday night Trudy worked a party at the country club for extra wages; by Tuesday evening, it had been forty-four hours since I'd laid eyes on her. I was so afraid that her feelings might change that I wanted to freeze every aspect of her identity, and when, after work, I finagled a winch truck and rushed right over to see my darling, the way she looked slightly different (was it her ponytail or new lipstick?) made her a stranger. But, miracle of miracles, she still loved me! We picked up burgers at the Dairy King and drove the rumbling old heap of metal out to the boonies where we did it twice on the seat with the door flung open. I sang "I love you Truuuuddy," and she laughed with pleasure. Our love drew out a softer, quieter Trudy, not a coquette exactly, but now when I pulled her close and kissed her ear and whispered "I love you darling," she sank into a swoony state that made her seem as helpless as it made me feel powerful. (But she remembered the condoms.)

We stayed out until almost dawn on Wednesday, and we suffered the penalty of working a day without sleep. That night I hit the hay early and she stayed up to nurse Sharon. Last night I hoped to see her, but Uncle Waylan had sent our crew clear to Monahans to hook up a new well and we hadn't gotten back until long past dark. When I called, Wally told me that Trudy and Sharon had gone to see *The Searchers* again. I'd thought I might catch her this morning at Runt and Dot's, but we got a late start and couldn't stop for breakfast.

Now where was she? Was she on the patio with Wally? Some place reading or writing most likely. I hoped! It was possible a new guy had checked into The Round-Up, a college man, and he was sweet-talking her or exchanging notes about the origins of the cosmos or *he's already read Kerouac and can talk to her about him!* Trudy, what about *our* book, the book of love? Now that we'd dipped only into the first chapter, how could you set it aside? Aren't you dying to know what happens next? *I hate this! God DAMN you, Cotton, for not telling me where she is! Goddamn ME for having too much pride to ask!*

At the dinner table, the four adults were civil and would have bored one another silly had there not been such a terrific undertow right below the surface of their chatter. One wrong word, and they'd all go blub. Aunt Vicky had toiled long and hard to make the sort of meal my mother churned out daily: pot roast, mashed potatoes and gravy, cooked carrots and green bean casserole and Waldorf salad and cranberry sauce and those rolls you open by whacking the cylinder against the sink until it pops. Lovesick youths are usually depicted as being wan with loss of appetite, but it wasn't true of me: I went at it in a big way, keeping myself busy partly to avoid being interrogated as to my opinions and partly to stuff back my anxiety about the state of things. I wanted to weigh myself down so I couldn't be blown hither by any small wind.

While I sat in the pickup waiting, Uncle Waylan and Aunt Vicky stood on the stoop under the yellow bug light. Aunt Vicky had her arms crossed over her breasts, and she kept looking off to the side while Uncle Waylan talked. Uncle Waylan had his hands chocked against his hips like a referee about to blow his whistle for an offsides penalty. I couldn't hear what they were saying, but finally Uncle Waylan kissed Aunt Vicky on her forehead, the way John Wayne kissed his sister-in-law—the holy wife and mother— right before she's slain by Comanches.

Several blocks went by while I wrestled with my conscience. I was surprised at how quickly and easily I could be a conniving snake, but then I finally told Uncle Waylan that Sharon said she wanted to talk to him.

He sighed. "Dang."

"Cotton said she wasn't feeling so hot."

"I feel like an absolute turd, Jimbo. I should've been strong enough last weekend to cut it off clean. Trying to let her down easy is just prolonging the agony, looks like." He slammed his fist against his thigh. "Goddmanit! Why'd I have to go thinking with my pecker!"

For one reason or another, we hadn't discussed what happened between them at Ruidoso, and I took this opening. "Aren't you going to get back together with Aunt Vicky?"

"Oh, Lordy, Lord, Lord, Jimbo." I waited for more. I watched the reflections of our pickup flick like a cut-up film in the store windows along the street, and we seemed to be moving in several directions at once.

"Thing is, we still got kinks to work out. No need for us to get in a big hurry. I don't expect she's thrilled about how I acted tonight. And I wasn't too happy to have my face rubbed in the kind of life she likes to think she'd rather be leading."

"That Robert guy—boy, is he a butthole!"

Uncle Waylan brayed with laughter. "You said it, not me!"

"What do you think Aunt Vicky ever saw in him?"

"Fellow like that has a lot to offer a woman, Jimbo," he said seriously. "He's kind and gentle, I'd guess, and probably willing to talk and listen to her problems. I take it he's a very steady fellow, hasn't changed jobs or his address in ten years. Most women like things to be dependable.

"Also, you have to remember that they had a whole way of life in common. And that's important. I'm sure she came out here looking for something new, but now that the new's wore off, maybe the old life looks even better. Right about now I'd guess she's feeling plumb nostalgic about the way things used to be back in Baltimore."

He gave the pack of Phillip Morrises on the dash a practiced shake to bring two butts within reach of my fingers, and I lit one with the dash plug.

After we'd smoked a meditative moment, I said, "Uncle Waylan, if you and Sharon quit seeing each other and she goes back to Dumas, could Trudy do Sharon's work?" I pictured Trudy and me living together at the shop. She could get her rent free, maybe, and we could share expenses for food. Our little love nest. Every day when I came back from the field, she'd be there in the office or in our own place lying on the bed waiting for me.

He concentrated on making a stoplight as it was falling from yellow to red, then he said, "Sounds like you're pretty sweet on sweet Trudy."

"Yeah. I am." I longed to say *I love her with all my heart and soul!* Not saying it made me feel cowardly. "She's really *wonderful!* Uncle Waylan! She's so . . . so, oh, I don't know! Just really *terrific!*"

He smiled. "The lad's smitten to the hilt! I don't mean to pry, Jimbo, but I'm wondering if you, uh, used that, uh . . . ."

"Yeah."

"Good golly!" He laughed uproariously, clapped my shoulder. "Welcome to the club, son! You've crossed the Rubicon! You need any more?"

"Uh, no, thanks. I can get them."

"Fine! Well! This is dandy good news! I'm right proud of you! And what a nice sweet kid she is! Pretty as a peach!"

"Yeah, she's really, you know, *terrific.*" I sounded less enthusiastic on second run, but I was embarrassed by his pride in my deflowering.

"I remember my first time. You don't ever forget that. Me and Noreen. She and her folks lived on a farm down the road from us about a quarter mile or so. I'd known her since we were just squirts going to the same one-room country school. Oh, well, then that saps gets to rising and first thing you know some fine young girl you've been looking at all your life starts to take on a whole new aspect. We were both fifteen. Just plain crazy about each other. Lord, Lord. . . ."

We were going slower and slower down the main drag. Other cars were passing, full of kids out cruising on a Friday night, and I envied them. I wanted to be cruising with Trudy under my arm, snug against my flank, her hand draped lightly over my fly. A couple of cars squealed around us as if impatient with Uncle Waylan's driving, but he seemed oblivious. He hadn't answered my question about Trudy, and he seemed too lost in thought for me to interject.

A sigh rose up out of his ruminations. He smiled and shook his head at me.

"One Sunday she told her folks she wasn't feeling good, so they went off to church without her, and I went over there and we sat in the swing on her porch. She sat in my lap and unbuttoned her blouse, and one thing led to another. After that, godamighty! I was like a puppydog trotting around after her. I thought I was going to bust from loving her so much! We hung tough through the torture of living apart for a year or so, and then we ran off and got married right when the war broke out." He chuckled. "Sixteen years old! My God!"

"You got married when you were only my age?"

"Oh, yeah. With country kids it wasn't all that unusual, especially for the girls." He eyed me balefully. "It's not something I recommend."

If that's so, I wondered, why do you sound so full of regret that it's all behind?

"Believe it or not, I used to write poetry to her. She put an old coffee can upside down behind their barn and that's where I'd leave little slips of paper with my verses on them. When I'd come back to leave a new one, there'd be a piece of paper there that Noreen had dipped in perfume and had planted a big red kiss on.

"Oh, gosh, it all seems a little silly now. Those poems weren't anything more fancy than the 'roses are red' kind of thing, but they sure as the dickens had my heart in them, I'll say that!

"No, a lot of things are going to happen to you before it's all over, Jimbo, but you won't forget your first love!"

EIGHT-
EEN

Aunt Vicky had recruited seven marchers, but Betty Cooper called at the last minute to say she had to wash her venetian blinds, because company was coming. Then Rena Spearman phoned to report that the water pump on her husband's truck went out on his way to Odessa, and she had to take him another. Sandra Goodrum claimed that the sealing ring on her pressure cooker had torn when she was fixing beans last night and shooting steam scalded her hand.

"Washing her venetian blinds! I mean really!" Aunt Vicky snarled to Helen as the three of us and Thurman, the intern librarian, plucked the placards from the trunk of the Mercury.

"I'd say Walter didn't want her out here 'walking the streets,' as Jack put it."

Helen had her head in the trunk when she said this, and when she straightened, she slid her sunglasses over her eyes. Aunt Vicky put her fingertips to Helen's arm as if checking for a pulse in the wrong place.

"Did Jack give you a hard time?"

Helen smiled weakly. "Well, his mother called him at seven this morning raising hell. It teed me off that she wouldn't talk to me about it! She thought she could order him to order me to behave. He told me he wasn't going to stand in my way, but I could sure tell he'll play the martyr all weekend. What he hated worst was having to fix his own breakfast."

"Times of crisis require sacrifice," jibed Aunt Vicky. She scrutinized my face as if looking for cooties, then she switched to Thurman. She whooshed a plume of smoke out the side of her mouth. "How about you? Did you have to run a gantlet to get here this morning?"

Thurman was in Levis, sneakers, and a yellow short-sleeved sport shirt. He looked more like a college kid now that he was outside of the library.

He grinned. "Well, do you remember that I got this summer job because my Aunt Melody's on the board? Guess who voted on the wrong side this week!"

"Oh, dear! Did she say anything to you?"

"She told dad my cousin Peggy had a sudden yen to be a librarian."

"Jesus Christ, these small towns. . . ." Aunt Vicky muttered. While she looked us over, we three stood in a semicircle, as if at parade rest. She glowered at nobody in particular and took ferocious drags off her cigarette. I got the impression that she thought that we were reluctant to serve or had second thoughts. The Baltimores had left for the West Coast early this morning; Aunt Vicky told me on the way over that if they'd known ahead of time, they'd be right here with her, but their schedule wouldn't permit a half day's delay. (Frankly, Lumpy hadn't struck me as a fire-breather.) Aunt Vicky's eyes were bloodshot as if she'd stayed out late drinking or hadn't slept well, and she was chain-smoking.

"James, I want to make sure you're here voluntarily."

"I don't have a hangnail bothering me, Aunt Vicky." Yesterday, Red and Slim had given me a hard time, but I presumed they were joking when Slim said he thought the whole lot of us "ought to be horsewhipped, tarred and feathered, and run out of town." I didn't know what they objected to. So far as I knew, neither had ever read *Peyton Place* or had even heard of it before this week. Red said we were "just stirring up trouble," and Slim said with a sneer, "Some people always gotta be different." Uncle Waylan said, "Don't call me if you wind up in the pokey."

I decided not to report these reactions to Aunt Vicky. Late last night when I finally got to talk to Trudy on the phone, she'd wanted to join us this morning but we both believed that it might be awkward.

Aunt Vicky smiled brightly but falsely to whip us into better cheer. "Look, you guys. Is the sun shining?"

It was. The day had emerged as a gloriously fresh rendition of a summer morning. A waft of cool breeze, the fragrance of honeysuckle riding on it. Mockingbirds on the phone lines, butterflies flitting over the lantana snug against the library flanks. Loose dogs trotting with tails awag along the street, collars a'clinkin'. Hardly any other human was out and about; the library hadn't opened yet, and though a few children were playing in the park, we had the sidewalk to ourselves. Over the tops of the Dutch elms along the street, the town's big-bellied silver water tower stood rigid and solid, like a big metal globe on legs, with "Srs '53" daubed in black across its waist like a wrestler's belt buckle. Looking about you'd think this was a *Saturday Evening Post* Saturday morning in America.

"We're engaging in a perfectly legal activity, guys. Not only is it permitted, it's our obligation as citizens to speak out! Right?!"

"Right!" responded Thurman.

"Do we want library books to be censored by any Tom, Dick, or Harry who takes a notion to be offended by something he hasn't even read?"

"Nooo!" we answered in unison.

"Now, I'm not a fan of *Peyton Place*," she went on. "But that's not the point. Right?"

"Right!"

"Good! Fine. Now let's hoist these signs and walk around the building here. If somebody wants to talk about what we're doing, then that's an excellent opportunity to recruit. We've got more signs in the car. But be polite even if they get nasty. The Civil Defense drill's starting at eleven, and they're using the library as a shelter and command post, so we'll get some traffic later on, anyway."

My sign said "Today *Peyton Place*—tomorrow your Bible!" I doubted that such a thing would come to pass, but I could see the point and had chosen to walk this idea around the park over another dreamed up by Thurman: *Sin? Or Cen-sorship?*

Carrying a sign with an idea on it evoked novel sensations. I felt extremely visible, for one thing. I'd never been a showoff and didn't like giving oral reports, and carrying this sign made me fairly itch with the discomfort of being in the public eye. People passing in cars pointed me out to one another, sometimes slowing and swerving to the curb and following along while they read my sign, idling right at my heels like a motorboat burbling by a pier.

Curious, I guessed. Could be they were photographing me or fixing me in the cross hairs, too. (My first taste of political paranoia—not many years later it became familiar when I carried posters against the war in Viet Nam and saw men in dark suits shooting me with telephoto lenses.)

I tried to be nonchalant; I ignored some and waved howdy to others. My embarrassment then took an odd twist. The more discomfort I felt, the more I grew angry at them, and the angrier I became, the more *righteous* I felt. I hefted the sign higher, glaring and daring them to watch me.

A pickup slid to a screeching halt past my post then rolled backward until the driver's door was three feet from my left elbow. We were strung out along the walk and I was last in line.

"Hey! What's this all about?" The driver hollered at me, squinting at my sign. He had a three-day stubble and a roll-your-own tucked behind his ear. "You giving away Bibles?"

"No, we're protes . . . ."

He peeled away before I could finish.

Kids in a powder-blue Pontiac convertible cruised by, jeered and hooted. One girl ducked down in the seat, and I guessed she knew Aunt Vicky from school.

Ever since I'd announced that I was committed to doing this, I'd been gathering impressions that surprised me. *People didn't like what we were doing,* and their dislike seemed unrelated to the issue. What could those kids object to? Did they want censorship? Probably not. Did they hate *Peyton Place?* Like Red and Slim, they probably hadn't read it.

We were only stirring up trouble. We were only doing it to be different. For the likes of Red and Slim and those jeering kids, the social order was a placid lake and fish were not supposed to leap out of the water and take to the air. They hated us for making ourselves visible; they hated us merely for being unconventional. I was getting a small taste of what it meant to be a pariah, and the injustice of that was like a string dangling from a tapestry of a previously intact world, a string I was tugging on.

The library opened; soon several cars parked along the curb, and we drew various responses from patrons going into the building. Some stopped to chat with Helen or Aunt Vicky or Thurman about entirely unrelated matters, as if politely ignoring our bad manners. (Thurman later said, "It was like I had a big booger hanging out my nose but they weren't going to mention it.") Others such as Larry Pustley, today's civil defense warden,

158

showed their disapproval by sashaying by in a huff and refusing to speak to us. Now and then somebody would flash a thumbs up or an okay sign, but most were oblivious, indifferent, or hostile.

Around ten-thirty a delegation of Baptists arrived to pray for our souls. They outnumbered us two to one and were led by a very tall fellow with an Adam's apple the size of a lemon and long wrists with hairy white knobs that showed at the ends of his cuffs. This was, Helen told me, the Reverend Jess Wright, and his flock consisted of Mrs. Harold Page, Mrs. Charles Wain, Mrs. Archibald Moore, Mrs. Thomas Lovell, Mrs. Eddie Bickley, and a Miss Rita Showalter, a thin brunette about my age who kept secretly rolling her eyes at me. Except for the captive teenager, this same crew stalked the hospital for hell-bound souls to snatch from the jaws of Satan.

The Reverend Wright's flock struck up *"Are You Washed in the Blood of the Lamb?"* Alone we'd not drawn a crowd, but two opposing groups sent out a scent of danger or excitement on the breeze, and within minutes we had a big herd of on-lookers. The civil defense drill would soon begin; two sheriff's cars and an ambulance pulled into the staff parking lot beside the library. A platoon of Boy Scouts piled out of a station wagon wearing yellow CD armbands.

The Reverend Wright's auxiliary sang all the verses to the hymn as a warm-up, and then circled seamlessly back to the top when he signalled for them to set the needle back in the groove. He left the flock at the mercy of the shrillest soprano, who could not be musically contradicted, and he took up strolling alongside Aunt Vicky and Helen, dogging their steps. He was dressed in dark suit pants, a white dress shirt and a blue tie, black wingtips, and he carried a Bible open in one palm.

"I want you to know that I am not angry with you," he said.

"That's good," said Aunt Vicky.

"No, but I am afraid for you."

"Don't be."

"We're praying for your souls."

"Aw heck!" spat Aunt Vicky. "I wanted to do that! Now you've gone and spoiled it!"

Helen laughed, but the Reverend Wright was undaunted by the sarcasm of a godless schoolmarm, being armed with the Holy

Writ. He smiled indulgently, the way he might if forced to hear a risque joke in a barbershop.

"I wish you'd see it in your heart that we're concerned for what's best for our community."

"I don't know why you're here, Reverend Wright. After all, you've won, haven't you? As a result of your personal efforts, I can no longer read a book in this *municipal* library built and supported by *public funds* and *my taxes* without having to check with you first to see if it meets your approval!"

She'd hiked her voice considerably, and her head snapped from him to the gathering crowd. "What do you want me to do? *Like* it and praise you for it?"

"No, of course not. I want no praise for me! But we can praise —"

"Don't tell me—"

"—the Lord," they finished in unison, and he added "Jesus Christ."

He beamed, pleased she knew the lines. He walked backward in front of her, looking out to the curbside and gesturing to the bystanders—kids on bikes, women with toddlers on their hips, and some Shriners with what looked like upside-down red slop buckets on their heads who'd arrived to help with the CD drill.

"I'm worried that you especially, Mrs. Kneu, can't see the need to protect our community from moral degradation. If someone was pouring sewage into our water supply, wouldn't you speak up? If someone tried to poison the food in the school cafeteria or set fire to your pupils' desks, wouldn't you call the police or the fire department?"

He came to a halt in the walkway, forcing Aunt Vicky to stop or run into him. He stiff-armed her with the Bible held in his outstretched arm, as if to hold her at bay and immunize her, and turned to the crowd. "I'm very concerned when somebody we've entrusted the minds and morals of our youth to goes around aiding and abetting pornographers!"

"Pornographers!" screamed Aunt Vicky. "You know, if you had a brain you really would be dangerous!" Some onlookers laughed. She was shaking with fury. For a moment I thought she'd whack him with her sign.

She glared, batted his Bible aside and stepped forward to challenge him. He hopped off the walk to let her go. Helen passed by, and he looked her up and down as if memorizing every feature, and when Thurman reached his station, he shook his head sadly and went "tsk! tsk!"

Me he didn't know, of course, and I'd presumed that he'd have no interest in correcting that. But soon as I came alongside he locked into step with me.

"Son, I'd like to talk with you," he murmured at my shoulder. "It's James, am I right?"

I gave him a suspicious sidelong glance and nodded curtly. How'd he know my name?

"Well, James, we've not met, but I'm the Reverend Jess Wright, and I'd like to welcome you." His arm came across my path and the back of his hand was splayed at my waist like a school crossing guard's, but I knew he wanted to shake, and I was not the kind of person who could refuse. I got a grip and thought I'd make it painful for him, but he'd attended too many Rotary luncheons to be caught off guard by a bone crusher; he held his own surpassingly well, though the earnest expression he wore to accompany it was supposed to make me associate strength with righteousness.

He glanced at my poster. "I'm glad for your message, I truly am. I worry myself about those who are planning to take away God's word, whether they live in Rome or Moscow!"

He was missing the point, or twisting it, but I didn't feel free to correct him.

"We'll be having our regular Sunday services tomorrow. And of course the young folk meet in the evenings at the Pearl Street annex. Won't you join us?"

"My folks are Methodist."

"Well," chuckled the Reverend Wright, "if you've been sprinkled, you've at least gotten damp, we always say. But"—here he leaned close like he might propose something indecent—"what we hope is that you'll accept the Lord Jesus Christ as your personal savior. Have you done that, yet, James?"

"Uh . . . ." I recalled a special Sunday communion service when my class was welcomed into the congregation. "Well, I guess so."

"You guess so?!" He reeled back in alarm. "Son, believe me, you'd know it!"

"What's he want!" demanded Aunt Vicky.

"He . . . ."

"I've invited the lad to church, Mrs. Kneu, and I'll give you the same invitation. Would you—"

"Tell him to kiss your hiney, James."

"Gosh, Aunt Vicky, I . . . ." I bit back the rest—*don't want to be rude!*

"Now, now, Miz Kneu . . . . " Reverend Wright had a pretty evil grin for a preacher: he was glad he'd gotten under her skin.

"I'd appreciate it if you'd not molest my nephew," Aunt Vicky said more calmly. "Your invitation has been received."

Then we heard a shout and a flapping noise. Thurman was wrestling with some fat guy with his shirttail out who had a hold of his poster, too, and they were spinning around in a clumsy dance like a top wobbling off its axis. The guy kept hollering, "My chirren use this liberry! My chirren!" and Thurman yelled, "Let go! It's mine! Let go!"

Somebody hollered, "Kick his ass!"

The whole bunch swarmed over the curb to follow the fight as Thurman and the fellow careened over the lawn, and when Thurman booted the guy's shin and made a grunting yank to reclaim his property, the guy let loose and staggered backwards. Then he came charging at Thurman, trying to claw his way through the poster that Thurman held like a shield as he backpedalled like crazy. The guy had a Porky Pig face with a crop of bristly blonde hair down between his eyes, and he was chuffing and cussing, face cherry-red and shining with sweat and slinging drool like a feral hog as he came. He swung wild at Thurman, windmilling, wasting haymakers on the empty air as Thurman danced back.

Soon a deputy sheriff and a fellow with a yellow armband—it was Larry Pustley—dashed up to separate them.

"Thurman, calm down! Ed, you too, you hear me?" The deputy sheriff, Bud Darling, was a slight fellow who wore a hat so big it made you think of Yosemite Sam. On his bicep was a large red tattooed heart with "Darlene" on it, plainly visible because he rolled the cuffs of his short-sleeved shirts almost to the shoulder seam.

He looked at us gathered to watch and made motions with his fingers pointed down, as if shooing chickens. "Y'all go on." He turned to Thurman. "Gimme that sign, son. You're just raising a ruckus with it!"

Thurman balked. Aunt Vicky stepped in front of him. She said, "We've got a right to picket, Bud, and you know that."

Deputy Darling hesitated, chewing on the side of his cheek, studying his options.

"It's time for the siren to sound, anyway," said Larry Pustley. He ostentatiously pulled out a large pocket watch, clipped the strap of it under the lip of his clipboard, and scrutinized it critically. "I count less than sixty seconds."

According to Aunt Vicky, in real life Pustley was the Yellowjackets football coach and the high school's sole history teacher. He and Aunt Vicky had been nursing a mutual disrespect since she arrived at HHS and refused to pass a star tailback so he could qualify for a homecoming game. He smoked Camels and humiliated boys who wore glasses and believed that his Korean service made him an expert in oriental culture. Wally had told me Coach Pustley was fond of telling his charges about the "sideways nookie" he'd enjoyed on the other side of the globe. He was large—he'd been a tackle at Texas Tech—but his wife outweighed him by fifty pounds. She ran the S&H Green Stamp redemption center. Last year, they'd celebrated their tenth anniversary at the La Fonda Hotel in Santa Fe and rumor had it that their conjugal relations were so boisterous that they'd been billed $200 for broken furniture. She had fists the size of cow hooves.

The crowd milled, not sure the action was over, when Coach Pustley held up his finger as if to begin a footrace, and, eyes on his stopwatch, counted down, "Three, two, one . . . ."

NINE-
TEEN

We watched him. Nothing happened for seconds; he looked worried, then his face bloomed like an ugly thistle as the "awwoonnnn" of a siren rose over the rooftops. Mounted under the water tower, it had been paid for by the government to be used in a "national emergency" and (more likely) when anyone spotted a tornado. Loud, penetrating, it wormed down under your flesh and into your bones and roared like a twister in your brain, and, from the war movies I'd seen, I flinched to hear it, saw in my mind's eye Londoners frantically scattering hither and yon as the buzz bombs howled and sputtered in from across the Channel.

I knew we'd see no Messerschmidts or Red Chinese stars on MIG-17s. No, what we pictured was an unearthly silence as a lone phantom bomber inched across the rim of space like an aphid on an upside down fish bowl, invisible to us. Like Hiroshima and Nagasaki: silence then a horrific, fiery whoosh!! that turns all substance to agonizing ash.

"All right, people, let's go to our shelter!" Coach Pustley hollered through the megaphone of his hands.

Other CD workers and a few Scouts came out to direct people into the building, and as our crowd broke apart, the kids on bikes raced for the front door, laughing, eager to get inside where they might get Kool-Aid while waiting for the all-clear.

Coach Pustley strode up to Aunt Vicky, Helen, Thurman and me with a bouncy step that made me suspect he was enjoying this too much.

165

"I'm gonna have to ask you to come on inside now. Leave these signs out here."

"We're not through picketing, Larry." Aunt Vicky hoisted her sign and almost stepped off the curb, but he reached out and tugged at her sleeve.

"Then I ain't *askin.* I'm *tellin'* you! Take shelter in the library."

The grounds were emptying, slowly at first, then quicker, the way bath water gradually trickles down a drain then gets in a hurry; meanwhile, the siren went on whirling overhead like a ominous dirigible of dark tornadic sound. Helen and Thurman and I fidgeted uncertainly.

"You don't have the authority, Larry. You just want to put a stop to what we're doing."

"Naw, Vicky," Coach Pustley said earnestly. "You can go back to doing whatever it is when the alert is over."

"I wouldn't take shelter even if I weren't picketing! You don't actually believe that this building would offer actual protection from an actual nuclear attack, do you?"

"That's not the point. This is a preparedness drill. In case of an attack."

"Okay, so it's not a real shelter or a real attack. So then there's no real need for me to take non-shelter. If it's okay with you, I'll just *pretend* to take non-shelter. But tell you the truth, I believe that as long as people have the *illusion* of safety they're not going to work to stay out of a real war! The only *real* shelter is peace, Larry!"

"Fine! Tell it to your friends the Russians!"

He slapped his thigh with the clipboard as if spurring a horse and whirled on Helen and Thurman and me. He could make us do something.

"Time to take shelter, folks," he said grimly.

Thurman lowered his sign to the ground. Helen said, "Coach Pustley—"

"It's the law," he cut her off. "Your husband would appreciate that, I know."

Helen couldn't look at Aunt Vicky, but she held her sign high as she headed for the library doors.

Coach Pustley smiled thinly and bore down on me: surely I was not going to resist after the others had surrendered?

Aunt Vicky said, "James, you better go inside."

"What are you going to do?"

166

"I don't know yet."

"Vicky, you'd best follow the proper procedure," Coach Pustley warned. "You should set an example."

"Exactly!!" she declared.

"Or I can cite you for failure to obey."

"Failure to obey!!?"

I cringed. He grinned. She was easy to bait today.

"There's more to it." He held his clipboard higher and read. "To expedite the vital work in the period following an enemy attack, the president authorizes the try-out in Operation Alert of an executive order which gives the Administrator of the Federal Civil Defense Administration extraordinary executive powers. It also directs *all executive departments*"—Coach Pustley gave us a meaningful glare—"that's all executive departments the power to carry out these responsibilities to the maximum extent. The Civil Defense Authority will assume and exercise all necessary governmental functions to maintain law and order and to protect public health and safety."

He grinned and knocked a knuckle against the pages. "All right here. Until that siren sounds the all clear, yours truly is in charge!"

"I'm not going inside. Arrest me if you want."

"I will, believe me!"

"Aunt Vicky," I said, suddenly recalling Uncle Waylan's warning not to call him if this should happen.

"You go in, James."

I carried my sign like a shovel, horizontally by the handle, and started for the library. I didn't object to obeying the authority of a civil defense warden during an air-raid drill. But I could see that Aunt Vicky was right. The library would be useless if an H-bomb were dropped on Hedorville. Why this sorry little dried-up place would be a target was another question, though everybody here flattered themselves that it would be on the hit list because the Russians "sure would want the oil fields!" How the Russians could utilize these oil fields after such an explosion nobody ever said.

So why didn't they dig a big cavern? Half the houses in my Dallas neighborhood had underground shelters in prefab concrete or metal, stocked to the roof with fresh water, canned goods, kitty litter, an arsenal of guns (to be used on neighbors who hadn't dug a shelter and who tried to crash into yours when the "big one" blew), candles, batteries, condoms, comic books—the whole rigamarole. Stay down there for months while the heavens are aflame and the oceans boil.

But even if Hedorville didn't have a real shelter, I could see how the authorities might need to practice herding people. They needed to try out the Conelrad alert network and to rehearse the exceedingly awkward transition from the elected political structure to that scary system where the Yellowjackets football coach, a moron, gets to be king for a day.

And I took Aunt Vicky's point that all this playing at being safe kept people from working at real security. I stopped after a couple dozen steps and looked back at them. Aunt Vicky had reached the sidewalk and was calmly parading with the sign, though no one was there to see it. Coach Pustley was storming toward the back of the library in a jog that made his change jangle; he was on the way to fetch Deputy Darling and the handcuffs, I guessed.

I didn't know what to believe. Did I have sufficient cause to disobey legitimate authority? And I wondered all at once about Aunt Vicky's mood and motives: if Robert and old Lumpy hadn't shown up last night and obviously gotten her in an uproar about her life out here, would she be so feisty today, so cantankerous, so quick to show her claws? Maybe she's only hung over, or didn't sleep enough, and tomorrow she'd look back and wonder what all the fuss was over. For all I knew, she was having her period. Didn't women do a Jekyll-and-Hyde once a month and say and do things they later regretted?

On the other hand, did it matter if the personal motive got mixed up in the action? I mean, who could do anything without being partly moved by powerful undercurrents that the person probably wasn't aware of? Like Coach Pustley—what made him want to be the warden? Only a desire to serve his country?

I didn't feel right going inside, but I also didn't feel right plunging into the chilly disfavor of men with the titles of "warden" or "deputy." The consequences of that were still unknown and might be unpleasant. I wished Uncle Waylan were here to make me do one or the other, but he'd taken a crew down to Wink today to help clear off a pad after a well blew out, killed a roughneck, and burned a jackknife rig.

What would my father do?

I looked back to where Aunt Vicky was parading slowly along the walk. The siren had wound down, and an eerie quiet, stark in contrast and accentuated by traffic's having ceased on the street, shrouded the scene. It was heavy with portent, as Trudy might say, pregnant with malign possibility. You could imagine the bomb falling soundlessly through cold blue space in this silence. Aunt Vicky was the sole human figure in my vision, and, from this distance, she appeared small, her head half the size of her poster.

Back at the library, Coach Pustley had obviously reported Aunt Vicky's refusal, and everyone jammed up to the windows to see what would happen.

It wasn't hard to figure out what my father would do and why. Or what Trudy might say if she were here. So I sighed, took a deep breath, and walked back out to the curb. When Aunt Vicky turned at the end of her loop, she saw me and beamed.

"Thought I told you to go inside."

I shrugged. I wasn't happy to be here, but I didn't want to play the martyr. I raised my sign upright as if in defiance (it wasn't), and we stood at the curb watching as the library door opened and Coach Pustley and Deputy Darling came through it, then strode purposefully toward us. They had matching pruney scowls, though even from this distance you could see a tic of unseemly triumph tugging at the corner of Coach Pustley's mouth.

"Are you sure this is the right thing?" I tried to joke.

"It is for me, James. I can't answer for you."

"What do you think they're going to do?"

"Try to reason with me, with us, I mean. But they'll have to put up a good show and save face."

I scanned the crowd at the library window and saw Thurman but not Helen. I wondered if he felt more safe than sorry to have chickened out. I wondered if I felt more proud than afraid. I'd been a law-abiding kid all my life; once I turned in a wallet that had a $100 bill in it. It wasn't easy to become an outlaw.

When the two men were about halfway to us, the siren went up again to sound the all-clear, and Aunt Vicky laughed. The door to the library burst open like the lid to a popcorn pan, and people surged out to go on with their business, though a sizeable group veered our way to get good seats for the second act.

"End of the reign of Czar Pustley!" Aunt Vicky declared.

Coach Pustley didn't want to relinquish his throne. Soon as they got about as close as Ping-Pong opponents, he yanked at Deputy Darling's elbow to steer him right at Aunt Vicky.

"Failure to obey!" he crowed. "Get her for failure to obey!"

"The drill's over, Larry." Aunt Vicky gave him a saucy smirk.

Deputy Darling said, "Vicky, you put me between a rock and a hard place, here. I—"

"Arrest her!"

"— wish you'd of done what you're supposed to do."

"Bud, *I* could've arrested her, but I came to get you. Now, dang it, do your job!"

Deputy Darling cocked his head at Aunt Vicky and looked mournful with regret, rolling his eyes back toward Coach Pustley, and said, "I'm going to charge you with failure to obey a lawful order."

Deputy Darling had handcuffs hanging from his belt, but he made no move to unlatch them.

"Whatever you feel is right, Bud."

"The boy, too!" Coach glared at me. "I told him to go inside and he ignored my orders."

Deputy Darling said, "How old are you, son?"

"Sixteen." I swallowed hard.

"Don't be ridiculous," said Aunt Vicky. "You want to arrest me, fine, but don't make yourself a laughingstock by hauling a child to jail for carrying a picket sign!"

"Maybe you should think twice about contributing to the delinquency of a minor! Bud, cite her for *that,* too, damnit!"

Aunt Vicky's mask of defiance slipped and for the first time she looked afraid. "Failure to obey" Larry Pustley might be a laughable offense, but even I, a novice law-breaker, knew that a charge of contributing to the delinquency of a minor could be devastating for a teacher. Aunt Vicky had miscounted the trumps.

"Don't go telling me what to arrest people for, Larry," snorted Deputy Darling. "We'll let Judge Bickley sort it out."

He didn't cuff us. We all walked to the deputy's radio cruiser at the back of the building, and he put me and Aunt Vicky in the back seat, but when Coach Pustley wanted to ride up front, Deputy Darling told him that if he was coming to the station, he'd have to get there on his own.

"Insurance!" he yelled out the driver's window at Coach Pustley's back, supposedly to explain his refusal.

The city hall, the police and fire departments, the municipal court and the jail were all housed in the same new two-story building made of blonde brick (a source of civic pride) and its angular newness and solidity made a daunting impression.

Deputy Darling's wife, Darlene, was the jail's bookkeeper and receiving clerk; when we came into the foyer to the cells, she was sitting at the reception desk listening to "There Stands the Glass" pouring out of a radio on the counter and was crocheting an anti-macassar with an aqua yarn. She looked up and smiled as if we were company she'd been expecting for lunch.

"Well, hi, Vicky!" She stood and set aside her needle and yarn.

"Hi, Darlene," said Aunt Vicky.

Deputy Darling took off his hat; he was bald, with thin greasy strands plastered on a pate the color of mushrooms and a distinct tan line that made the top half of his head look like a lid.

"Darlene, I've arrested Miz Kneu here, so you need to get her to fill out the damned forms."

"Oh, I am so sorry!" she offered to Aunt Vicky. "What in the world for?"

"Failure to obey a lawful order," Deputy Darling said sourly.

Darlene looked bewildered; she had very thick glasses that magnified her blue eyes, and they were abob in a sea of salty fluid. "Is that a misdemeanor or a felony?"

"Misdemeanor."

"I never realized it was a crime," Aunt Vicky said. "At the Nuremburg trials, they convicted people for *following* orders."

"Of course it's a crime! It's a fancy way of saying you're a royal pain in the bee-hind!"

"Then you should've arrested Larry, too!"

"Yes, yes," he murmured, though the way he waved dismissively at her you'd have thought he was disagreeing.

Darlene opened the gate for Aunt Vicky to step behind the high counter and they both sat down at a desk as if Aunt Vicky were applying for a bank loan. Deputy Darling stepped into a side office with glass walls, where he slammed his hat down on the desk and pulled a cigar out of a humidor.

After a moment, I cleared my throat loudly and called out, "Sir? Deputy Darling? Am I under arrest, too?"

He gaped in surprise as if he'd forgotten me, then he came out of his office with his mouth all twisted into a grimace that cranked his nose a quarter-turn to eight on the clock. He stopped and looked me over.

"Son, do you have a dollar on you?"

"Yessir."

"Then why don't you go down the street and get us all some soda pop."

"Uh. Okay. What kind?"

"Anything will do."

I turned to leave and heard him say, "And if you don't come back I won't cry about it."

When I emerged from the building I felt relieved and disappointed at the same time. No telling what interesting aspects of outlawry I'd miss because I was the little fish and they'd caught the mastermind. Now I wouldn't be able to have Trudy nurse the bruises I got from my being beaten with a rubber hose, and I'd have no lurid anecdotes about my fellow inmates to impress her with.

As I stepped off the curb, I saw a car pull into the lot behind the municipal building. Coach Pustley was driving, and Reverend Jess Wright was in the front seat. Out of the back stepped a portly grey-haired fellow in a western-styled suit and boots and bola tie, and they went into the jail.

When I got to Stinky's Good-Time Bar I started worrying. Something in the sprightly and nimble steps of that trio fixed in my brain. I called the shop from Stinky's. To my surprise, Sharon answered by saying, "Kneu Well Service." I hadn't expected her to be working today. I asked her to please raise Uncle Waylan on the two-way radio because Aunt Vicky needed him. Considering their tangled-up lives, I didn't like giving Sharon this responsibility, but I had no choice. I told her about ignoring Coach Pustley, and "he got Deputy Darling to arrest her for failure to obey a lawful order. Me too. Maybe. I'm not sure yet." Actually, I was reasonably sure I wouldn't be arrested, but it was pleasureable to flaunt the possibility.

Deputy Darling had more or less urged me to become a fugitive, but I was too curious and concerned about the outcome to vanish into anonymity and leave Aunt Vicky alone, so I carted two Dr. Pepper's and two Orange Crushes back to the jail.

Mrs. Darling wagged her head no when I offered her a bottle.

"Where is everybody?"

"They're all in talking to Judge Bickley." She crocheted while I sat in the criminal's chair and sipped a Dr. Pepper. The other three bottles stood sweating on the desk. It occurred to me that maybe I shouldn't have had Stinky pop their caps.

"They're cooking up something." She kept her eyes trained on the minute needlework between her fingers, so intent you'd think she was spying on a tiny world there.

"What do you mean?"

"Judge made Bud put her back in the cells. He's pretty hot about this whole library thing to begin with. His wife's in Reverend Wright's choir."

"Shit!" I blurted. "Oh, pardon me!"

She shrugged. "So have you called her husband?"

"Yes ma'am." I got a rush of fear all the way down my spine that wedged into my sphincter like an ice-cold enema. What was she trying to tell me? If she was worried . . . "But I couldn't reach him directly, and his secretary has to call him on the radio-phone."

"He's going to need to post her bail."

"Oh. Could I, you know, see her?" I wanted to let Aunt Vicky know that I'd called Uncle Waylan and that I was still here.

Darlene hesitated; I thought she was deciding whether to allow this, but then I understood she was working herself up to violate her husband's standing order. (Failure to obey!)

"I guess. But not for long."

"Can I take her this?" I held up an Orange Crush bottle.

"Yes, but I'll have to pour it into a paper cup."

173

TWENTY

Darlene Darling led me through a locked steel door and down a hall laid with green-and-white checkered linoleum. One side had high windows, the other empty cells—no catcalls, cons banging cups, no tattooed forearms waggling like tentacles through the bars. Eventually we turned a corner, and I followed Darlene's gaze to a cell where Aunt Vicky was sitting on a bunk with her elbows in her lap and her face in her hands. Her shoulders were shuddering, and I heard something like a kitten mewling.

Before she could look up, Darlene yanked me back around the corner and said, much louder than necessary, "Now you just wait right here, James. I'll go get that cup."

I waited, surrounded by empty cells. I listened closely, heard shuffling, then the unmistakeable sound of a woman blowing her nose softly and gently.

"Aunt Vicky?"

"Yes. Is that you, James?" Her voice sounded high and trembly but almost merry.

"I brought you something." I peered around the corner holding up the bottle of Orange Crush. She was standing now, dabbing at her cheeks with a handkerchief. She smiled. Behind her glasses, her eyes were a net of red lines and her makeup was smeared. She daintily pressed her fingerpads against her eyes as if to squeegee tears from under her lids.

"Thanks! I *am* very thirsty."

"Deputy Darling's wife had to get a paper cup. They won't let you drink from the bottle."

"Afraid I'll cut my wrists, I guess."

175

She sighed and sat on the bunk. The cell had an outside wall and a very narrow window of glass blocks high up near the ceiling, and when she turned the back of her head to me, she appeared to be looking at it. It took me a minute to realize she was composing herself.

"Nice place you got here," I said.

She laughed, then started bawling. She fairly sobbed for a while with her face in her hands, then banged on her thighs with her fists to make herself stop. "Oh, I'm sorry!" she burbled, laughing through her tears. "I know this makes you uncomfortable. Waylan sort of *writhes* when I cry. I'm only relieving the tension. You understand?" Her lips, quivering, curved unevenly in a ragged smile. Her face was soaking wet. "It's been a hell of a day, the whole last twenty-four hours."

Darlene arrived with a little Dixie cup you unfold to use. "Sorry, this is the best I can do."

When she left, Aunt Vicky held the cup through the bars and I poured it full three times in a row. She drank it so lustily that it dribbled an orange trail down her chin and neck and mixed with her tears in the hollow, and she had to dab at her throat with the handkerchief.

"My God, I'm a mess!"

"I called Uncle Waylan."

"What'd he say?"

"I didn't talk to him directly. I had a call put out to him in the field. Mrs. Darling said he'd have to post your bail before you could get out."

"Well, thanks, James. I knew sooner or later I'd have to call him or Jack. You spared me having to decide."

We lapsed into silence, she staring pensively at the wall and me wishing I'd brought cards so we could while away the time. It was like visiting someone in the hospital. You didn't know what to say and there wasn't much to do.

Aunt Vicky turned and gave me such a sad and earnest look that it rattled me. "James," she sighed. "They didn't arrest you, right?" I shook my head. "That's good. They're trying to charge me with contributing to the delinquency of a minor, and unless they charge you with something I don't see how I can be contributing to anybody's 'delinquency.' You're not a delinquent."

She rubbed at a spot of orange on her blouse. "Have you ever said anything to anyone about my suggesting that you read *Lolita?*"

176

I burned. Sure, I'd mentioned it to Trudy, to Sharon, to Wally, to Uncle Waylan. I remembered her warning to me in the library and was suddenly afraid that I'd betrayed her.

"No. Well, I mean, you know, to friends and such. Why?"

"Oh, I'm just speculating, I guess." She shoved her glasses up onto her forehead, then she pressed her temples between her thumb and middle finger and massaged them for a moment. Then she blew out a big breath to fortify herself. "James, you wouldn't ever make up stories about me, would you?"

"Ma'am?"

Absently she put the empty cup on her thigh and ironed it flat with the heel of her hand, then she ran the creases between her thumb and index finger.

"I mean that sometimes, boys, and men too, well, they get to talking and get carried away in wanting to top each other, and maybe before they can catch themselves they might say something they'd really didn't really mean. Or isn't true at all. And they might even be sorry about it."

"Oh, God, Aunt Vicky! I'd never say crap like that about you, honest!"

"I knew you wouldn't. He's just bluffing. The Reverend Wright, I mean." She looked away. "He told Judge Bickley that I should be charged with committing an indecency with a child."

A child? One of her students? The charge itself almost propelled me backward like a big wind. Then I realized he meant me. And *Lolita,* in which (irony of ironies) I had yet to reach the twentieth page. Then my overheated fantasies about her seemed to have leaked into the public arena for the casual inspection of all. If they had a device that turned my thoughts onto a movie screen, they'd find me guilty as all get out.

"Boy, that really stinks!"

"Yes, it does. But it has sort of jerked my chain. I have been irresponsible. I've been so caught up in this business about Waylan and me that I really haven't been a very good aunt, I'm afraid."

"That's not true! You—"

"No, no. I appreciate your loyalty, James. But being an aunt is a parental role, too. And this situation has made me realize that we're going to have to discuss things with your folks."

I thought I was going to faint. I almost dropped the empty bottle in my hand. I'd forgotten I had parents! Well, not that I had them, certainly, but that I needed their permission to come and go.

"What're you going to tell them?"

I know I sounded petulant, and I must have looked alarmed. A stinging pressure rushed up behind my eyes and my chin quivered minutely. Aunt Vicky had suddenly become the enemy; she'd been a pal but now she wanted to play the responsible adult! And it was too late, anyway. I'd already gone beyond her ken and made a life of my own!

But the worst part—she could cause me to have to leave Trudy. I was ready to turn on Aunt Vicky in an instant, I realized.

"Well, I can't avoid telling them that I've been arrested on this particular charge and that you were with me at the time. Maybe they'll understand that this was about politics, not morality. I'm sure you know them better than I do. Wasn't your dad a member of the Young Communists League when he was a student?"

"What?" If she'd said he was a transvestite I wouldn't have been more shocked.

"Oh dear," chuckled Aunt Vicky. "You know, a *lot* of people who came of age during the Depression flirted with being communists. It was the thing to do. I thought Waylan had told me Frank joked about it once. But I'm probably not remembering right."

"He's not one now, I can tell you that!"

I was being hit by surprises right and left and felt the fight-or-flight rush of those under seige.

Aunt Vicky laid her head back against the cinderblock wall and closed her eyes. Her hands curled about the edge of the bunk and her knuckles were knobs of white bone. I stewed about this new development; compared to my having to leave Trudy, my father's dallying with being a Red way back when was a BB next to the planet Jupiter. Their response to this arrest would be horrrified dismay, and they'd want me on the next bus home.

"Could we write them a letter, Aunt Vicky?" Maybe I could find a fancy-stepping way to put it so they'd see things my way, or, barring that, I could hope that the post office would lose the letter.

She gave me a sad clown's smile. "Don't think so. They'd know it was an evasion."

"Thing is," I said, pushing as close to the bars as I could get. "I'd really really really hate to have to leave, Aunt Vicky. I really would!"

178

"You like it here that much?" Her brow squiggled into a puzzled frown. "With all this uproar?"

Lord, what this woman didn't know! "Well, I'd hate to leave you and Uncle Waylan, sure, you know. But I've made some really good friends."

Her face canted off to the side as if I'd cuffed her cheek. "Good friends?" she asked, as if wondering why she hadn't heard of them until now.

"One friend in particular." My cheeks popped out as a gigantic sheepish grin stretched my mouth from one earlobe to the other.

"Ah hah!"

My face felt hot. I leaned over to retie my shoe lace.

"Are you in love?" It was not a taunting question such as Cotton would ask but, rather, a request for information. She knew enough about me, I guess, not to make a gooey celebration of it.

"She's really terrific. She's about all I think of day and night."

"Is this the girl who works at the diner?"

I nodded.

"Tell me about her."

It came by fits and starts at first, but then it flowed with a gush. I praised Trudy's hair and eyes and skin and freckles and her "figure" and how cute her mouth was, leaving out how much I loved to have her stick a nipple in my ear or drag them across my stomach. Then I told her how we liked to argue about things such as abstract art (she liked it, I didn't) and whether Ike was a good president (I said yes, she no), but we liked the same candy bars—plain Hershey's—and we liked to pour a bag of Tom's salted peanuts into the mouth of a Coke bottle, and she was good in math and science, loved to read books (I knew that would appeal to Aunt Vicky), and she wanted to be a doctor or a writer, and that even though she would be a junior at West Texas State College next term, she treated me like an equal, and that she'd taught me to like jazz—did Aunt Vicky ever hear The Bird play?—and jug wine, "and we're reading the coolest book, by this guy, Jack Kerouac. It's called *On the Road*. We read parts of it to each other. Trudy wants to be a writer, did I say that? She's actually writing a novel right now."

"Oh, how nice!"

Her declaration had an air of finality, a cap on our conversation.

I waited for her to ask more. Now that I'd gotten started, I wanted to talk to her about Trudy. I wanted her to milk me of all the burgeoning new impressions and sensations that I could hardly contain. Once during the night in Ruidoso, Trudy fell asleep with her head on my shoulder and drooled on my shirt and I had such a tender feeling for her swell up in my chest I thought I was going to burst into sobs. I loved to kiss her hands; she had short fingers and very pink flesh. I loved the way she toyed with the doghairs on my nape—it sent chills down my spine. I loved how she'd sometimes throw a French word into a conversation in a jokey way or use a cartoon voice. *(Sacre bleu, mon frere!)* And we had plans, very important plans.

"Anyway," I said to break the silence, "that's why I *really* don't want to leave."

She was quiet, considering, I hoped, that she might renege on her vow to tell my parents, but then she said, "You know, James, sometimes separation is a very useful tool. It can allow you see things in a new way."

This made me shudder. I already worried that Trudy would come to her senses from eight hours of sleep; God only knew how potent an influence a change of venue might be.

Then we heard Uncle Waylan hollering all the way from the front desk. "Goddamnit, Bud, what the hell do you mean locking up my wife? I can't believe you'd let yourself be pushed around by a pencil-dick Baptist preacher and football coach who dudn't know a goal line from a chow line, and, as for Judge Bickley, he has to by God stand election next year and he damn well knows it!"

There was further grumbling and cursing and counter-carrying-on —Deputy Darling replying too quietly to be heard— but then only minutes later we were all out on the sidewalk under the large blue dome of the open western sky breathing fresh air as free men and women.

TWENTY-
ONE

You'd think the speedy bail-out would've put Uncle Waylan in Aunt Vicky's favor. But as we rode in the pickup to the library to retrieve the Mercury, she was mute as a stone. Every other block or so, Uncle Waylan would cuss Deputy Darling, Coach Pustley, Judge Bickley and Reverend Wright for having his wife jailed for no better reason than standing up to half-wits and little Hitlers.

Clearly, he wanted her to say, "Thank you, Waylan!" Each time she failed, he'd go at it again. I felt sorry for him. He was waving his indignation about with wild abandon to get it noticed, but she was looking the other way. Her silence seemed bitchy to me. By the third time he lit into the filthy four, I thought she'd respond if only to shut him up.

When she didn't, I said, "Thanks again, Uncle Waylan, for bailing us out."

"Aw, hell, it's okay, Jimbo!" he gushed. "I'm glad y'all called me quick as you did. I'm sorry it took so long to—"

"We didn't call," put in Aunt Vicky. "James did."

"Well," murmured Uncle Waylan. "whoever, you know. . . ."

"No, not whoever. *James.*"

If I'd been Uncle Waylan, I'd have screeched that pickup to a stop and invited her to walk. (Or I liked to think I would, anyway.) But he only frowned—bewildered, I could see.

"Dadgumit, was I supposed to leave you in there, Vicky?"

She crossed her arms and leaned into me as he shifted from second to third.

181

"They wouldn't have held me long. I still hadn't made my official call to a lawyer."

"I'm sure as hell glad you hadn't. It's bad enough that Jack McIntyre thinks you're leading Helen astray what with—"

"Not Jack, no, for God's sake, I wouldn't have called him in a thousand years, Waylan. All these local good ole boys are smoking the same cigar!"

"Aw, you mean some Yankee, then! Oh, *there's* a good idea!"

I couldn't believe Aunt Vicky was pretending that she wouldn't have called him or Helen's husband, especially when she'd admitted otherwise to me. Was she too ashamed to thank Uncle Waylan? Did it give him too sharp an edge in their negotiations? Or did she resent that what rankled him most was how these good ole boys had shamed him by doing this to his *wife?*

When we pulled up beside the parked Mercury, Aunt Vicky said, "James, thanks for supporting me."

I thought that her gratitude was misdirected or was meant to prick Uncle Waylan, so I only nodded.

"And about that call to your parents. Come over tomorrow night and we'll do it. It might not turn out as bad as you imagine."

Easy for her to say! I did have a twenty-four hour reprieve, though, and I was grateful. I said "Thanks" as I stepped down to let her out my side. She walked around the front of the truck and to the driver's door. I saw her hand come up and Kilroy-drape across the sill. I couldn't see her face.

"Poor Waylan," I heard her sigh. "I'm such a bitch!" His head turned and he was facing her. I studied his twisted shoulder under the oil-splashed work shirt, his uplifted thigh in the dirty jeans, his scuffed boots, his manly tallness and solidity, and I wondered how it could all be at the mercy of her whims. He stretched over and outward, and when he'd crawled almost halfway through the window, I knew that they were kissing.

As he and I were driving on to the shop, I said, "She was pretty darned upset in the jail. It's a good thing you got us out, Uncle Waylan. They had her in a cell, and she was crying a lot. She told me she was going to call you or Mr. McIntyre."

"Yeah. It was silly of her to act like she was going to ring up the New York ACLU to take care of this piss-ant deal." He chuckled, then he started laughing. "Damn if she ain't a pistol, son! I wish I'd been there when she told Coach Pustley to take those orders and stick 'em where the sun don't shine! Did he have a fit?"

"I thought he was going to bust a gut if Deputy Darling didn't put the cuffs on us."

"You gotta admire a woman with that gumption." Grinning, he shook his head over and over, chuckling as he imagined (I suppose) Aunt Vicky rebuffing Coach Pustley and the coach stomping on his cap like a cartoon character in impotent fury.

"Even if you do have to bail them out of jail?"

"I wouldn't have no other kind."

Bad news! Sharon definitely was not that kind. It made me nervous to hear Uncle Waylan be so certain about his preferences now. Since the Ruidoso trip, he'd inched farther away from Sharon (and Trudy) and closer to Aunt Vicky. The visit by the Baltimores had been a hole in the road, for sure; though it hadn't slowed him down, it had obviously made Aunt Vicky slam on the brakes.

I remembered Sharon answering the shop phone hours ago. All this dithering by the adults, swinging and swaying, sidestepping, backstepping, leaping over the abyss with their eyes closed, and meanwhile, a particular set of cells went on steadily dividing, multiplying, ceaselessly, according to their own inexorable pace and their own preconceived plan, oblivious or indifferent. Pages from my sophomore biology text. No matter what these adults did, those cells would hew to the straight and narrow in a most determined way, accumulating weight and force like a drill puncturing their plans.

"Did you see Sharon when you came back in?"

"For just a minute."

"How's she feeling?"

He looked puzzled. "Oh, okay I guess. She didn't say anything about being sick."

"Why'd she come to work today?"

"She said she wanted to do make-up from missing this week."

Maybe she'd planned to tell him she was pregnant when he came in from the field, and the crisis with Aunt Vicky intervened.

"Are you going to see her tonight?"

"Well, I was hoping your Aunt Vicky might agree to go dancing, celebrate getting sprung from the hoosegow."

I tried to joke. "She didn't seem real friendly, Uncle Waylan.

Maybe she needs a night to herself." And then he could go out with Sharon?

"That's true. But I see that as a good sign, Jimbo. It tells me she's warmin' up to me inside, and she's just resisting it, see? I always take anger in a woman as a sign of hope. Maybe she even thinks we might make a couple again some day, and so in the meantime, she's gotta punish me. I can take it, son. Most likely I deserve it, too. And I gotta try to make up for how I acted last night. I was a gen-yeew-ine horse's patootie, and I know it. It just riled me, you know, seeing her with that Robert, and every second I knew she wished I was more like him and less like me, and it plain stuck in my craw. And I'm sorry about it. I want to make it up to her. First date we ever had I took her dancing out at Al's, and the biggest fight we've had was because I wouldn't."

"She told me."

"About the fight?"

"No, about your first date. She said she drank too much."

He laughed, hugely, with relish. "That's what hooked me! I always was a sucker for a good-time gal. Noreen was sure that way! I didn't figure on finding it in a respectable schoolteacher. It was what you might call a devastating combination, and it sure made my head spin!"

When we got back to the shop, Sharon wasn't there; all the trucks were parked inside, their crews gone for the day. Uncle Waylan immediately went to phone Aunt Vicky, and I walked back to the bunkhouse. Shut up all day long, it was dusty and stuffy; I had to yank up three windows and start the squirrel-cage cooler to make it bearable.

I lay on my bed. I was sinking into a very sour humor. I'd been hoping that Trudy had told Sharon to leave a note for me ("Trudy says she loves you!") or at least give a sign of wanting to see me, of having missed me since our call last night. I hadn't seen her since dawn on Wednesday when we said good night, so long ago it could've been last year.

I was weary of Uncle Waylan's pinball-bouncing from bumper to bumper, as he held my own fate in his hands. To save myself a lot of future sorrow, maybe I should go ahead and die right now. Save myself that dreaded phone call home, too.

"Trudy, I love you, darling," I murmured aloud to the empty air. I felt weepy.

Uncle Waylan came back, grinning big. "I got a probated sentence!"

he thundered. He yanked up the tails of his work shirt and the pearl buttons went *snick! snick! snick!*

"Stand back! Dancin' Dan Magrew's on the loose tooo-night!" He plopped onto his rack (his term, from the Navy), tugged off his boots, stripped off his dirty jeans and shirt, started bellowing off-tune *I'm an old cow hand, from the Riooo Grande,* at brain-blasting volume, pranced into the bathroom in his jockey shorts, started whooping in the shower. *I'm a honky-tonk man/And I can't seem to stop . . . . Loves to give the girls a whirl to the music of an old juke box. But when his money's all gone* (right here's the nub!), *he's on the telephone, cryin' Hey hey Momma, can your Daddy come home?*

His boisterous good humor drove me into a funk. It baffled how a man in his situation could carry on like he didn't have a care in the world. Of course, he didn't know as much about his situation as I did.

I made myself get up, took a Coors out of the refrigerator and sat at the table drinking from the can and smoking a Phillip Morris, acting like an easy-going hombre with nothing but relaxing on my mind. When he came out of the bathroom barefoot but in clean jeans, I said, "Okay if I take one of the trucks out tonight, Uncle Waylan?"

"Gonna see your honey tonight?" Before I could reply, he was singing an answer to the tune of "Camptown Race Track." *Well, Jimbo's seein' his honey to-night, honey to-night, honey to-night. . . .*

"Hope so," I muttered.

He flicked on my radio. It wasn't dark enough or late enough to get "The Louisiana Hayride" from Shreveport, so he jiggled the dial a minute to tune in the one Hedorville station. Little Jimmy Dickens. Next to those stupid chipmunks that sang, he was about my unfavorite, and I had adopted Trudy's utter disdain for any music that wasn't East- or West-Coast cool.

"You need some do-re-mi, son?"

Uncle Waylan flipped his wallet up from his rack, dug into it, and handed me a ten-dollar bill.

"Thanks."

"You're welcome to it, Jimbo, but only if you spend it in a truly frivolous fashion such as on wine and women, and you better not have a dime left when you come crawlin' home!" He clapped me hard on the back. "Quit mopin', lad—it's Saturday night!"

185

This sent him into a redneck rendition of Little Richard's song on the same theme. *I'm gonna rock it up! I'm gonna rip it up! And ball tonight!* I slipped the bill into my shirt pocket. I chugged on my beer to empty the can and left to call Trudy. On the way I took out the bill and put it in my wallet. I wondered if I was spending Uncle Waylan's money or my own. As usual on the subject of money, he was full of grasshopper advice. But he was talking to the proverbial ant. So if this was my ten dollars he was advancing to me, I'd spend five and save the other half. If he was giving me his ten dollars to blow, then maybe I'd save only two. Since I had free room and board, Uncle Waylan had been paying me only part of my wages each week; he was setting aside the rest for when I went home. My weekly "allowance" hadn't been quite enough to support a girlfriend, and, though Trudy often kicked into the pot, I was always low on cash. By his accounting, my savings account now had $150, less than I'd hoped to have this far, but if I kept on at this rate for all the summer (now a very big if!), I'd go home with enough to buy a car or to put away for next summer when Trudy and I were together.

"Hi, darling!" I gushed when Trudy answered their phone.

"Hi, my sweet boy."

"Say it again!"

She laughed. "What? 'My sweet boy?'"

"Yeah!"

"Okay, but not until you get over here!"

I was so excited I was dancing in place like a five-year-old who needs to pee. "Man, oh man, I've got a million things to tell you, sugar!"

"Hurry! Cotton and Wally and Sharon went to see *The Searchers* again."

That meant—well, it's obvious. Is there any exasperated impatience more itchy and twitchy and hair-tearing than that felt by a lover enroute to meet a lover he knows is eagerly waiting in a private place? I meant to ask Uncle Waylan about the money but was too frantic to get away; I yelled "Later!" into the bunkhouse door and leaped into Terrible Red, the old Ford winch truck whose front seat Trudy and I had christened Wednesday night, and, of course, I flooded it by trying to hurry it to start.

The town only had two lights, I ran up on them right when they clicked to red, and the cold truck coughed and died twice between them. Then I nearly rear-ended a grandma in a '49

Packard because the truck's windshield was featuring a movie of Trudy's creamy plump shoulder and the side of her jaw and her delicate earlobe under my face as I lay between her warm soft legs.

I swung the truck under The Round-Up's adobe archway and slid into a parking slot in front of #7, shut off the engine, remembered that Wally asked me not to park the truck there because it blocked the drive, thought *Oh fuck it! He's gone to the movies.* Then I leaped from the cab and was about to reach the motel door when I realized that when they came back he'd see the truck and come bang on the door wanting me to move it. So I went back. Trudy was peeking out the window, fingering the blinds aside, looking perplexed as I got back into the cab, so I hollered, "Just a sec," cranked up the Ford, reparked behind the motel, dashed across the courtyard to where my darling waited.

I presumed (or hoped) Trudy would be naked under the covers or wearing only a robe (not that I'd seen her in one!), but when I burst through the door she was standing beside it in shorts and a big t-shirt and we whooshed into one another's arms like barbeque fire-starter. But our meeting had a strangely alien air. We tried to look each other in the eye but our gazes ricocheted away like bullets off a granite slab, and so we embraced as if the recoil tossed us into one another. I pulled her close, felt her warm breasts on my chest, my chin over her shoulder, holding her around the back and waist; she felt heavier, more solid, even taller since last I'd seen her, more strangely *other*. We were hugging and kissing each other's necks and moaning, then she said "Ouch!" and joggled backward—I'd stepped on her bare toe—and we broke apart.

She held my hands out between us; we were separated like players in London Bridge, and we still couldn't meet each other's gaze. She was wearing her hair in a ponytail; her nipples poked through the thin T-shirt. My cheeks flamed, and I went hard.

We were both jittery, swallowing over and over, twitchy, hands busy busy busy, flitting like buzzing bees, shuffling our feet, dancing in place, about to bust out of our skins. Since I hadn't expected it, I didn't really know how to banish this frenetic crackling case of nerves that stood like that stupid electric Id thing in *The Forbidden Planet* like a force field sparkling between our arms that we were both afraid would fry us to touch it.

I decided to barge right through. I stared right into her brown eyes as if daring the alien thing to make itself known, challenging it, I guess. Then I stepped right up, pulled her close again, and slid my right palm over the smooth curve under the hem of her shorts.

"I love you my darling sweet Trudy," I murmured into her face. Then we tongue-kissed pressed loin to loin with our hands moving incessantly until at last everything seemed familiar. We did a clumsy entwined dance to her bed and fell onto it, where we rolled about like one form, two logs bound tightly by our arms and legs, while our mouths were grafting lips to lips, then her hand wriggled down under my jeans to stroke me, and I, wailing out her name, shot off.

We started again more slowly. This time stripped naked and lying breast to chest under the sheet. It was still twilight outside, and even though the blinds were closed and the curtains drawn, I could see where I was kissing as I worked my way down her sweaty mottled neck and over her rubbery nipples, down her fragrant ivory belly and into her coppery pubic hair. I scooted down between her legs while she lay back, eyes closed, quiet, expectant, very interested to see what I'd do. I blew gently on her curly hair and she giggled. I scrutinized her pink and cloven mound, having never been this close in person, thinking with wonder *This is what It looks like!* adoring the two curved humps and the dips at the juncture of her thighs, seeing the tiny pink tongue protruding from the lips—the thing seemed strangely exotic, like a fragrantly musky flower or a sea creature—immensely attractive, fascinating. Then, catching my breath for courage, I savored her flesh, favored, for the first time, her private places with my tongue. I was afraid she might disapprove, but she whispered, *Jimbo Jimbo Jimbo!* And when I took that for encouragement and lapped at the firming ridge, she breathed *Oh god yes!* I surrendered wholly to my lust; I squirmed and wallowed, horribly ashamed and deliriously happy, feeling the world recede farther into the dim distance, as if we'd crawled into a capsule that had been sent zinging far out into mute black space.

Soon she slipped a condom on me then guided me inside her. But even while we were rocking wildly on the bed and yelling one another's names into the empty room, I still had an inexplicably weird afterimage of how we'd been the minute I came through the door; I was haunted even in the depths of our intimacy by the notion that when we were apart we each grew an odd, transpar-

188

ent outer skeleton, like an invisible manifestation of our *otherness* from everyone else in the world, and to get back together required that we crack open these shells, burn them away with this ferocious hot flame of desire, and it wasn't all that easy to do.

TWENTY-
TWO

B y request I was walking naked but for sneakers down a
two-rut road. The waxing moon tossed a white neon glow
on nearby mesquites whose limbs lifted with the breeze,
rattling their clusters of beans. Whiffs of sulfur dioxide. Far in the
distance flares of refineries. Crickets going *chick chick*, the low of
a cow in the dark. Now and then a whir of bullbat wings overhead.

It was a mysterious summons, but because I was in love I took
pride in not questioning whatever peculiar motive inspired it. The
truck was at my back. Trudy was in the cab watching me. We'd
driven out to the boonies when Sharon and Wally and Cotton
had returned from seeing *The Searchers*. First thing we'd done
was to do it again. That third time had milked us of our urgent
need to couple (also left our parts a little sore where they weren't
numb). But no sooner did I feel the urge to speak in our after-
glow about the weirdness of the day at the library and the jail,
she'd asked, "Would you walk naked down the road for me?" I
said sure, but how far? She said she'd honk to let me know.

This was a novel experience so I didn't know what attitude to
strike. I didn't ordinarily think about being observed when I was
out in the world merely getting my body from one place to
another; sometimes, sure, if I thought someone was watching in
the hall, I did a jively shuffle to look cool. And when I walked up
for Communion or down the aisle for an award at assembly I was
aware that my walk should express a gravity befitting the occasion.

But how did I walk naked down a country lane in bright

moonlight so a girl can observe me? My ass felt big as a bushel basket and very *noticeable,* as if I had a string of blinking Christmas lights looped around it. Was she paying me back? Was this an object lesson, or was it the source of a weird pleasure for her? Should I waggle it? Should I, uh, *clam up*? Flex my cheeks and make my ass travel steady as a caboose on a slow-moving train? Should I stroll? Or stride? What in the world should I do with my arms and hands?

I tried to walk in a natural fashion, but what was "natural" for an exhibitionistic naked moonlight stroll? It seemed disturbingly feminine, the way I had to think about what somebody was thinking of my body as I went about simply walking, knowing she was watching and knowing she knew I knew.

I thought it best to walk in a manly way but couldn't shake off the suspicion it looked foolish.

She honked at around the fifty-yard line. I crisply executed a military U-turn. My limp weenie flopped about. I doubted Trudy could discern much detail from this distance, but as I strode toward the looming hood of Terrible Red, I could feel her gaze and my peter shrank to a cigarette butt.

"Thanks a bunch, sweetie," she said through the window when I was beside the truck slipping on my shorts. She scooted over a tad when I slid in beside her. Though we'd worn ourselves out, I still couldn't keep my hands off of her. My palm sought her warm thigh and a current ran through my skin, charging my battery. It was unthinkable that I should have to leave her. We could be like Kerouac characters and run off to Mexico.

"Why'd you want me to do that?"

"Just a whim."

"Will you write in your journal about it?"

"Oh yes."

"What'll you say?"

"Ummm. That you looked like Endymion."

"Who's he?"

"This Greek kid."

"What's his story?"

She hesitated. "Kiss me."

I did. It was a playful kiss, with cartoonish smacking. I'd not known there were so many kinds.

"I missed you today," she said.

"Really? Why?"

"Maybe because Sharon was so upset that Waylan gave her the brush-off when she was down at the shop. I thought about him and about you and how you're not like him and how I'm glad of that. And how lucky I am to have you."

"How lucky you are?! Oh, man, Trudy, you're not half as lucky as I am to have you!"

She grinned. "Wanna arm-wrestle for it?"

We joke-tussled a minute, but it ended in an affectionate squeeze.

"He had a lot on his mind," I said. "He had to bail me and Aunt Vicky out of jail."

I told her about the picketing, the preacher and his choir, the CD drill—she'd heard the siren but she was washing dishes at the cafe and they ignored it—the arrest, calling Uncle Waylan, and so forth. I tried to sound nonchalant, as if I were used to being hauled to the pokey for failing to obey a lawful order. Then the business about calling my parents popped back into mind, and I must have visibly slumped.

"What's the matter?"

I told her that my parents didn't know my aunt and uncle were separated and that Aunt Vicky had gone along with not telling them. "But now she thinks we have to let them know she was arrested and that I was with her on the picket line. She wants me to come over there tomorrow night and call them."

"What do you think they'll say?"

"God! What do you think? What would your folks say?"

"I really don't know, Jimbo. I'm not a kid any more."

She didn't play that card often. But it always crushed me. One thing I'd come to hate about being in love was how close to the surface my feelings were these days. Like a five-year-old, I could swing in a second from happy laughter to hot and angry tears.

"So maybe you could be my guardian," I said snottily. "God, Trudy, don't you even care that maybe they'll make me go home?"

"Sure! But maybe I oughta go somewhere else, too!"

"You mean you'd come to Dallas if I had to?"

"Well, I wasn't thinking of that, exactly."

She turned her head and her face was hidden. She put her hand on the lower crescent of the steering wheel, absently rocked it.

"What then?"

"God, Jimbo, I don't have any *plans.* I'm going from day to

193

day. I was thinking more about Sharon." Now she turned to look at me, very earnest, frowning. "She's got to get out of here. Waylan's obviously trying to dump her."

"Aw, maybe he only wants a cool-off period."

"Oh sure! Don't be naïve."

I guessed she didn't believe I might lie to her about this and endure the guilt. She went on as if to make me see the truth. "She can't face up to how he's through with her. I've seen her like this before. Right now she's kind of giddy with denial. It's the last stop before she bottoms out and turns into a vegetable. Meantime she's got a very serious problem that needs to be solved *immediately!*"

Trudy seemed as worried about Sharon as she did about us. I suddenly understood how much Trudy's connection to Sharon had to do with our future. I'd thought everything hinged on my parents allowing me to stay, and if they did, then Trudy could stay too even if Uncle Waylan and Sharon split up. Now the future was a darker mystery because it would be formed by decisions and events that I hadn't yet conceived. I'd imagined I was in the driver's seat of my life and that all I had to do was to obey the traffic laws and keep the backseat drivers pacified. Now I saw that the windshield was painted over and I was roaring down the road at sixty miles an hour watching the road whiz by through a hole in the floorboard!

"Shouldn't she tell Uncle Waylan that she's pregnant? Maybe that would help him make up his mind who he should be with. If he and Sharon wound up together, everybody's problems would be solved." Except for Aunt Vicky's, of course.

"She's too proud. She says she doesn't want him to be with her only because he has to be."

Considering her condition, her pride seemed overly particular in setting the terms for negotiations. But, then, maybe her pride was sensitive because of that condition. We'd had this conversation in Ruidoso, and I'd promised to spy for Trudy. Sharon was one week more pregnant, and Uncle Waylan had shown signs of ditching her.

"What if she went to one of those homes? I think there's one in Fort Worth." Though I'd mentioned this last weekend, I decided to be more forceful now. "There was a girl in our school my freshman year, Joyce Bartlett. She was looking a little plump, then she left school supposedly to live with her aunt in Fort Worth, but everybody was sure she'd been knocked up by Louis Keys. Anyway, she came back to school last year really slim and trim like nothing happened." I didn't add that nobody would talk to her and that Louis had joined the Navy.

Trudy shrugged. "She says she doesn't want Waylan's kid walking around the world where he might give her a nasty surprise some day. I also think maybe she would want to punish Waylan by not having his child."

"Having a kid is a pretty big thing with him, all right. But it doesn't seem fair for Sharon to punish him before she gave him the chance to do the right thing."

"What would that be?"

"Accept responsibility as the father and marry her." Of course, after my talk with Uncle Waylan earlier today, I wasn't sure he would assume this responsibility. He wouldn't *like* it, that was certain.

"Is everything always so simple to you?"

"Just because it's simple doesn't mean it would be easy."

"What if they don't love each other?"

I thought she was grilling me to make my ideas look foolish, but then I realized she'd asked this of herself. And I felt guilty withholding what he'd told me about letting Sharon down easy and wanting to be with Aunt Vicky.

I said, "She loves *him*. I know he cares for her."

"I can't really speak for his feelings except that I'm sure they're shallow," said Trudy. "But I think I understand Sharon's. I think she picked Waylan because she knew that he'd leave her the way her father always did."

"That sounds really stupid, Trudy. Who are you, Dr. Freud?"

"Too fancy for you, cowboy?" She was smirking.

I snagged a cigarette from the pack and lit it to add a few years to my age. "Why would she do that? It's self-destructive."

"The question answers itself, Jimbo. For me 'the right thing' might be for her to get him out of her life and come to see why she picked him in the first place, then somewhere down the line meet somebody she knows truly cares for her. If she and Waylan get together now, then it makes that harder to happen later."

I wanted to tell Trudy that she was a genius but I had too much pride (like Sharon?). Once again, something she said set my mind working in a new way.

"Okay, then, if you guys are so smart about knowing the right thing, what's to be done about her problem?"

She sighed. She took the pack of cigarettes off the dash and lit one with a book of matches tucked inside the cellophane. I thought her silence meant she hadn't worked that out, yet.

"Wally heard of this Mexican doctor in Seminole. Guy Wally knows over there, one of his old Marine buddies, told Wally about him."

The flurry of pronouns momentarily confused me—it was uncharacteristic of Trudy to jumble her syntax—and I wasn't quick enough to read into it that she was scared.

"God, isn't that illegal?" I thundered.

"Yes."

"And isn't it also dangerous?"

"Yes. Both of those, Jimbo. If I remember right, last weekend you said it was all easy as—" She snapped her fingers.

"Yeah, well, that was then."

"What you left out is that because it's illegal and dangerous, it's also expensive."

"How much?"

"Wally says three hundred, about."

I whistled. You could buy a good used car for that! "Where will y'all get that kind of money?"

Trudy blew out a long thin stream of smoke, tapped her ash out the window sill, lay her head back against the seat and gazed at the headliner.

"I don't know. I've got a little. She's got a little. Maybe we can come up with two hundred or so between us."

"Oh, man, now for sure you guys have got to tell Uncle Waylan. I mean, this is his kid, his problem! He ought to be the one paying!"

" '*Ought's* another way of saying zero, Jimbo. It's for her to ask him and tell him she needs it. She won't do it. She doesn't want to be in his debt."

"His debt!" I screeched.

"Her words, not mine."

I swung open the door and hopped to the ground to pace in the grass beside the truck. I was furious with Uncle Waylan. And with Sharon, too. I smoked two Pall Malls in a row, savagely, spitting tobacco bits and screaming "Fuck!" as I stomped up and down the lane in my shorts. As I was lighting cigarette *numero trés*, my hands were shaking and my breathing was ragged and shallow. I'd run out of my anger, and I was seeing something out of the corner of my eye, figuratively speaking, that I didn't like the looks of: Trudy wanted me to donate to the cause. My outrage at Uncle Waylan was partly fueled by my deep and bitter reluctance to do that. This was not my mess! If I gave up my savings, what about our plans to travel next summer together? And what would I tell my father: *No, Dad, I didn't save any money. I spent it all on an abortion for Uncle Waylan's girlfriend! She didn't mind being in my debt but she didn't want to be in his!*

I went back to the truck.

"Couldn't she borrow the rest from Wally?"

"I don't know."

"Or Cotton. Aren't they big pals?"

"You think Cotton has a savings account?"

"Well, why not! People have them, you know! All you have to do is walk right into a bank and tell somebody you want one! It's not like you have to pass an exam or get a license!" I was on the verge of adding *Even I've got one!* when I realized that this was precisely the point.

"True. But you have to put money in them," she said, snide as a schoolmarm.

"Well, then, goddamnit! Why is this my responsibility?"

"Nobody said it is."

I turned away, crossed my arms, glared at the flickering odiferous flares on the night horizon. But I was ashamed of my outburst now. I'd focused selfishly only on how this might affect me and Trudy. I kept willfully forgetting how much Trudy felt attached to Sharon—they were more like sisters than cousins— and how Trudy took on Sharon's burdens. Then I knew that to be in love with Trudy meant that I had to accept those burdens as my own. Whether I wanted to or not. This was not good news. And creeping into my awareness was the nasty surprise of this ugly streak of smallness in my character. Someone who supposedly loved Trudy should have leaped to make the generous offer to help, even been *eager*, for God's sake! If my spirit was too pinched to take on the responsibility of love, then I didn't deserve it. I had intelligence and imagination enough to see how I should have responded, how I should have felt, but also how I lacked the generosity of spirit to have done it spontaneously. All that was left me now was to try buying respectability.

197

"You didn't say it, Trudy, but I'm guessing that you guys would like for me to help, too."

"If you're willing. We'd be grateful, very grateful, Jimbo."

She turned in the seat and looped her arms around my head and shoved my face into her breasts. I inhaled—my reward for being a nice guy.

"How could I say no?" I murmured. I lifted the hem of the T-shirt and tickled my cheeks with her stiffening nipples, nuzzled and nibbled at them. This went on for a while. But before I completely lost myself in my lust, I did have time enough to feel my old unreformed self slip back over me: I began to resent that Sharon had not had to ask me for help. She hadn't even had to ask to borrow the money. Her emissary who was now tenderly caressing my dick had extracted a pledge of support with absolutely no cost to Sharon's precious pride.

Going back to the The Round-Up about two, Trudy sat with her cheek on my shoulder, one hand in my lap and the other absently stroking my bicep as she hummed to herself. She seemed wholly content; I tried to be as happy, pretended to be so, but under my pretense was a pedal tone, barely audible, that issued from my worry about our future. Without money how could I hope to go away next summer with Trudy? And had she considered that? If she had, what was her solution? If she hadn't, why not? Had the crisis atmosphere swept aside all consideration of our future? Was planning for a future only a bourgeois luxury? Sal and Dean would surely say so. Was I ready to *live* according to values I found appealing in the abstract?

I couldn't bring myself to ask Trudy about our future. I didn't want to hear her answer that she'd blithely pried loose my savings with no thought about it; I also didn't want to hedge on my gift or show it wasn't offered freely; I wanted Trudy to feel that I'd given it as an expression of my love for her.

When we got back to #6, Sharon was sitting cross-legged on her bed in a long pink nightshirt filing her nails. Her hair was dark with dampness. Her face, scoured of makeup, looked blanched, her lips colorless. Her eyes seemed smaller and her nose sharpened at the tip, like the features of a fox or a ferret.

As the generous benefactor I was fairly swaggering, and Trudy wasted no time in telling Sharon that I would help them.

"Oh, Jimbo!" She bounded up from the bed and leaped

barefooted to me and did a hit-and-run embrace, leaving the ghost sensation of her breasts against my chest but hugging too quickly and lightly for me to measure any swelling in her belly. She stepped to the radio and turned it down. Patsy Cline was falling to pieces.

"I've only got a hundred," I said, without calculating, then immediately wondered why I'd set that amount.

"Oh, that's so much help! I mean, just knowing it would be there. I'm hoping I won't need it. I mean, if worse comes to worst. But I'm hoping." She held up crossed fingers.

Trudy came out of the bathroom toward me rolling her eyes behind Sharon's back, then passed to the door, saying, "Back in a sec." I sat at the desk. Sharon resumed her Lotus on the mattress. An open magazine lay between her knees.

I lit a cigarette and smoked in silence for a moment. Sharon stayed intent on her nails.

"Don't you think you should tell Uncle Waylan?"

"Yes," she said immediately, to my surprise. "And I will, you know, soon as the time is right. I want to tell him when it will make him glad."

I had no idea whatsoever how her mind was working on this problem. I said, "Well, I meant that maybe he'd be willing to help with the cost."

She stopped tinkering with her nails and the file became a little dagger upright in her fist. She peered up at me, puzzled. "Oh, he'd never pay for this, because he'll want the baby. That's my first choice, too. I'm hoping I won't need anybody's money for that. I really appreciate the offer, and, you know, like I said, if worse comes to worst. But I'm hoping it won't."

If I was ever going to tell the truth about what I knew, this would be the moment. *Sharon, Uncle Waylan has told me flat out that he's going back to Aunt Vicky if she'll have him.*

"But if he doesn't know about your, uh, this, you know, deal, then how can he be glad or anything else?" I insisted.

"Jimbo . . . ." She sighed with exasperated impatience, then folded her hands in her lap, leaned her head far back and inhaled deeply, as if taking in clean fresh mountain air. Then her gaze swung down on me as if she were sighting in a rifle. "When he says he loves me, that's when I'll let him know we're going to have a baby."

"What about doing it the other way around?"

"It wouldn't be fair. I don't want him to feel trapped. That's why he's with Vicky."

"What do you mean?"

"He thinks she can't do without him."

"Really?" This was news, for sure. If Aunt Vicky had convinced Uncle Waylan that she couldn't live without him, then she'd sure fooled *him*. She seemed a hundred times more capable than most women of getting by on her own. Maybe this was the excuse he'd given Sharon.

"You probably know him well as I do, Jimbo. But one thing that really wrecked their marriage was how she acted about having a kid. Didn't he ever talk to you about that?"

"No," I said, though I hated to admit it.

She got up from the bed and pranced over to the cooler they kept by the bathroom. She leaned over to open the lid, the nightshirt rising to disclose slim calves and the white backs of her knees, a sight I absorbed with a mild appreciation but without any rise in my libido. She took out a Tab, held it up to offer another to me, and I shook my head. She popped the cap using an opener hanging from a nail by the bathroom door, downed a swallow and flopped onto the bed with her back against the headboard.

"He's always wanted kids. That's why him and his first wife broke up, I think. She didn't want them; she was too busy partying."

"Yeah, I do know that."

"So when Vicky and him got married, he said she was all for it, but she never got pregnant. She went to a clinic over in Lubbock to be checked out, and the doctors put her on a schedule, where you take your temperature and count the days between your menstrual cycles, and then there's certain positions you do it in to better your chances."

She slugged on the Tab, again showing her soft white throat threaded with a lace of tiny blue veins. Seeing her drink made me thirsty. I dug a Coor's from the cooler, punched it open and took a sip, dimly aware that the bitter stinging carbonation had grown familiar to my palate.

Sharon had a habit of never completing a thought aloud and you sometimes had to prompt her. "So?"

"So then she kind of made Waylan perform on demand, according to the schedule. Like a circus monkey. They could only do it certain days of the month, and she had to check her temperature, and it had to be in a certain position and all. He said he felt like he was back in Navy or was punching a time clock. She took every bit of the joy out of it for him." Sharon grinned. She slumped, tucked her chin against her breastbone, looked down to her abdomen and smoothed her long nightshirt over a swelling so slight it might have been caused by gas. She caressed herself tenderly.

"We didn't have no trouble," she said wryly, pretending regret but sounding proud. "Looks to me like we're a pretty good fit. I'm fertile as granny's hen. And I admit we had fun while we were at it."

She gently palmed her belly and drifted away, her eyes half-closed, smiling like the goddamn Mona Lisa. Off to some mind movie, and the plot was this: the father of the unknown unborn child at last comes to his senses in the final reel, rushes to the girl who has heroically kept silent about her condition (playing the wronged and martyred would-be bad girl), then the reformed rascal pours out his love and his regret, proposes marriage (this is her reward for forbearance and self-denial). She waits a beat to torture him, then accepts—and tells him that she's got a bun in the oven! Wedding bells and shots of the ecstatically happy almost-family behind the rolling credits.

Who was I to holler "Fire!"

TWENTY-THREE

B y Sunday evening, I'd drafted a strategy for handling this dreaded phone call. My parents always said being an adult meant taking responsibility for your actions, so I'd decided not to sit passively by while grown-ups determined my fate.

That was the gist of what I said as we lingered at the end of Aunt Vicky's supper of chicken a la king on rice. Pecan pie and vanilla ice cream were still to come.

"So because this involves me, I want to be the one to discuss it with them, Aunt Vicky. I know them better. And it's my life they're going to be deciding."

Uncle Waylan looked as proud as a poppa whose Little Leaguer just whacked one over the fence.

"Good idea, Jimbo."

Aunt Vicky was going to and from the table to the sink, taking our plates and scraping them. I'd scooted back my chair and Uncle Waylan was enjoying a postprandial cigarette. (To my aching envy: I still hadn't the nerve to smoke in front of Aunt Vicky.) He was also lapping at a shot glass of Kahlua. So far they'd been jovial together—Uncle Waylan had brought a rose he'd clipped from a bush at the library on our way; he'd pulled out her chair and promised to repair a screen, and he'd taken out the trash without her asking. She kept touching him—bracing herself with a hand on his shoulder as she leaned over behind him to pick up a dropped fork, stroking his forearm to punch up a point, patting his cheek to feel his shave, and digging a finger into his waistband when he complained of feeling skinny from a lack of home cooking.

I was hoping the spillover from these good spirits would inspire her to endorse my plan.

"I'm afraid your mother would take it amiss if I didn't speak personally to her about this," fretted Aunt Vicky, apparently back to square one. "I'm bound to the conditions of my role in *loco parentis*." When she saw my questioning look, she added, "Being a substitute parent. It wouldn't be to my credit if I ducked out of telling her what I did to be arrested and how you came to be there with me. I feel bad enough not having told them Waylan and I are living apart."

"I doubt that'd surprise her any," put in Uncle Waylan. "If I read her right, she thought you were about ten steps above me anyway, so she's more than likely expecting you to have tossed in the towel. You'd get an A for it."

Uncle Waylan's caustic attitude toward my mother often pained me, but then it was an oblique shot in my favor.

"Besides," I rushed in, "nobody will care if you got arrested or anything—you're an adult. And it wasn't your fault, anyway. It's not like you robbed a bank or stole a car. It was a stupid civil defense drill, and they wanted to stop us from exercising our legal right to say you thought it was wrong to take the library books off the shelves!"

Aunt Vicky might presume my passion rose from my convictions; seeing me this worked up might sway her to my side. I wasn't faking my outrage, but it was inspired by a fear of leaving Trudy.

When she didn't respond, I leaned farther into the wind and stuck my chin out. "And it was probably a good thing you didn't tell them about you and Uncle Waylan, because, I mean, you're together right now, and when I've seen you together lately, you've been like any other normal aunt and uncle I ever had, or even better, and I'm over here all the time and you know as much about what I do as any parent does, Aunt Vicky. I mean, I tell you everything."

She looked pleased. I was getting good at this. Eddie Haskell had nothing on me. "What would really bother me would be having you speak for me like I was a child. Since this was something I did by choice, then it's my responsibility to explain it as best I can. If you have to do it, then that lets them know I wasn't mature enough to have made up my own mind in the first place, right?"

Uncle Waylan laughed. "Vicky, lawyering sure seems to run in this family."

Aunt Vicky cocked one fist on her apron-clad hip and gave me a wryly canted smile.

"What would be your explanation to them of why I wasn't living up to my responsibilities as an adult in not speaking for myself?"

Count on a teacher to be one step ahead of you.

"You don't need the practice."

They laughed.

After I wolfed half a pie topped with a pint of ice cream to fortify myself, I went into Aunt Vicky's "office" and shut the door. I was woozy from being stuffed—it was like being drunk—so I crashed into her desk chair and stared at the phone for several minutes, plotting my ploys and postures. I'd never acted in a school play but I watched rehearsals while people "got into character." I could try that, too, but no doubt those actors had been cautioned against eating half a pie before going onstage.

What was the character I had to play? With my father, I'd be The Dutiful Son: "But I was only doing what I thought you'd want me to!" I could do that sincerely, partly because it was true: I believed my dad wouldn't have left Aunt Vicky to walk alone no matter how perversely or willfully she'd gotten herself into that pickle. As for her arrest, I might toss in that business about his being a communist in college. But that was playing catch with lighted cherry bombs.

I'd put myself at risk to protect her—surely he'd respect that. Well, maybe he would. He was a lawyer, after all, and there'd been precious few occasions when I'd tried to run an explanation around him that he hadn't tripped it, yanked it up by its lapels, and demanded that it stand a white-glove inspection before proceeding on. It was easy to anticipate his objections: if she jumps off a cliff, will you have to hold her hand on the way down? If she decides to rob a bank, will you drive the getaway car so she won't feel vulnerable and alone?

And if my mother answered? Would the same argument serve? Could I claim that I imagined my own mother standing out there and how she'd yearn to have her son beside her?

Could I say I presumed the order was for children, to keep them safe from the, uh, army trucks and stuff on the streets? Or that Coach Pustley hadn't shown us a badge? Or I hadn't heard the order? Probably with my mother, my best chance lay in pleading guilty and begging for mercy. She hated lame excuses or a heated defense of what she took to be indefensible conduct. So my most credible stance to her was this: I'd been true to my nature as a worthless, childish boy by "acting up," and I was sorry and ought to be punished.

That was the song of a ten-year-old and would guarantee I'd be sent home immediately.

I belched and smelled the foul cloud around my head. I was so stuffed I could hardly think straight. I laid my hand on the receiver. Maybe I could trust my instincts for extemporizing according to the mood of my respective parent. I might have to grovel—so be it. I could make outrageous promises, including being a better brother to Alise and Diedre and cleaning out the garage without being told, mowing the grass, not whining about drying the dishes.

I dialed the long-distance operator and told her the number I wanted in Dallas. It was an hour later there—8:30. On a Sunday night. They were probably watching Ed Sullivan. I could see our living room, with the big bay windows looking out onto Amherst, the two wing chairs with the smoking stand between, the burnished leather hassocks—Alise probably sitting cross-legged on one—and my mother and father sitting on the sofa that faced the Magnavox mahogany console. Diedre would be lying on the floor on her tummy, legs in the air, hands under her chin. My place—one of the wing chairs—would be empty.

Pang! Did they miss me at all? Of course I didn't want to have to go home, but all at once I wished I could go, for one night, to make sure they all existed, that things hadn't taken on some malign aspect in my absence. I'd bet that my mother had made sandwiches out of the leftover pot roast they'd had after church today, and maybe they were eating in the living room on TV trays. She'd have taken two pieces of white bread and put slices of beef between, added a big scoop of mashed potatoes on the side, then drizzled rich brown tasty gravy over all. My dad would be smoking his pipe; he liked a fruity Borkum Riff that produced blue aromatic wreaths like fragrant dirigibles hovering all over the house when he fired it up.

The phone kept ringing, apparently in a house empty of inhabitants I'd so vividly imagined. Where in the world were they? Sometimes there were programs at church on Sunday evening. There was a service, of course, but they never attended. I hoped nothing had happened to them.

Soon I turned cross. Here I'd worked myself into a sweat making a presentation only to have it postponed. I'd have to endure the torment of calling again, later on this night or another, and although I was relieved, I'd never liked to put a hard thing off: pain dreaded was pain doubled in my book.

I also worried that Aunt Vicky might call when I wasn't here to head her off or to ameliorate the damage. I couldn't trust her to argue my case because she didn't know how desperately urgent it was. On the way back to the kitchen, I realized what I had to do. (And saw what I would've done had they answered.)

"Well, there's good news and bad news!" I crowed. I was beaming heartily. They smiled back. "Bad news is they're both pretty steamed up about it all." I grinned like a jackass, pulled a chair out from the table, spun it around and mounted it like a saddle, laid my arms cool-like along the back of it, anchor-manned my grin from one to the other. "I told them what happened, and, you were right, Aunt Vicky, about Dad—I told him that I'd wanted to be with you when you were arrested because you were family and a woman and Uncle Waylan wasn't there to stick up for you, and it was for a good cause and all, and you know I believe he was a little bit proud of me, but he couldn't really let on, and he said—you'll like this—he said, 'Hellfire, Jimbo, if she went to rob a bank, would you offer to drive the getaway car just so she wouldn't feel lonely?'" I slapped my thigh and guffawed.

"That sounds like Frank, all right," said Uncle Waylan with a smile.

"And your mother?" said Aunt Vicky, with far less enthusiasm. I had a sick feeling in my gut.

"She, uh, couldn't come to the phone, she was giving Diedre a bath. She said, I mean he said he'd talk to her. He'll take care of it."

"I thought you said they were both steamed up about it."

"Well, he was, at first. I was just speaking out of knowing how she'd feel. Could I have a Coke?" Without waiting for an answer, I got up and rummaged about in the refrigerator. I found the Cokes quickly but kept my head in the box for a bit, shuffling them around.

"What's the good news?" Aunt Vicky's voice was saturated in teacherly irony.

"He put me on probation. He said if he heard another word about my doing something this stupid, he'd make me come home and scrape and paint the trim on the house. He didn't want to have to hear another word."

"I'd sooner eat a tub of chicken squat than scrape trim on a house," murmured Uncle Waylan.

"Tell me again exactly what you told him, James. I want to make sure I know what he knows. Your story went by in a rush."

I took the bottle of Coke from the icebox and walked it around the kitchen like a colicky newborn while pretending to search for an opener.

"Okay. Here's what I said." I pulled out the utensil drawer and fished in the metallic sea of odd spoons and paring knives and ice tongs and such, raising a racket. "I said that we went to the library today to, you know, let people know how we felt about those people making the librarians take some books off the shelf." I paused to yank the drawer another six inches toward me and bent to peer into the dark cluttered rear of it, my hand swirling to rattle the gizmos and whatnots, nut crackers and ice picks and shrimp forks. "And of course when the Civil Defense drill came— Oh!" I straightened and gave her a wide-eyed happy look. "Yeah, they had one, too, in Dallas. And he was at the hardware store and got really p.o.'d because the police wouldn't let people leave the store while it was going and he had to get back home so he could take my mom to get, to her, uh, eyes checked. Anyway, I said that they'd tried to make you go inside just because they wanted you to quit embarrassing them, and then I told him that I stayed with you because, uh, I was afraid somebody might get rough and Uncle Waylan . . . " I nodded toward him and realized belatedly that I was making this argument at his expense, "wasn't there because he had to work."

I picked up the bottle opener and eased the cap off the Coke, hearing the hiss as if it were coming from somebody displeased with a vaudeville act. I took a long slow swig. The bottle held six ounces and my gut and esophagus had only an ounce of space. When the carbonation bubbled down there, I felt a burp erupting and was afraid I'd spray the room with a barrel of puke.

"I see," said Aunt Vicky.

I fine-tuned my ear and chanced a glance at her face. She was skeptical? convinced? I'd have to say uncertain, reserving judgment maybe. My heart was thundering against my ribs.

"You got to admit the lad deserves a merit badge for honesty," Uncle Waylan told her.

"So your motive was apolitical?"

"Ma'am?"

"Your motive was personal—you were afraid for my safety?"

"Well . . . yeah." Was I was stepping into a noose?

"You wouldn't have stayed out there protesting if I'd gone inside?"

"No. I guess not. Did I do something wrong?"

"Oh, no, James. Not really." She smiled sweetly in a way that made me feel twelve. "But being the beneficiary of your chivalry, I suppose I need to write and thank them for bringing you up so well."

"Aw, Aunt Vicky—he said he didn't want to hear another word."

In response, she said, "Waylan, there's still more pie—why don't you take it with you? You and Jimbo can have it with your lunch tomorrow."

Back at the shop, while Uncle Waylan reworked Sharon's bookkeeping in the office, I lay on my bunk as jittery as I'd be were a tractor battery jumper-cabled to my toes. I worried about Aunt Vicky's little love note to my folks, how I might head it off, alter it, squelch it. Best I could hope she'd procrastinate or even forget it, or write it and let it sit around before mailing it and maybe I could filch it off her desk or offer to post it, ha ha ha.

Liar!

For God's sake, what was happening to me!? I'd crossed yet another Rubicon; I was now the shameful possessor of a darkly criminal mind. I'd lied to them about the call, just as boldly and baldly as a con man! Stood there in their kitchen and pumped them completely full of hooey! My dad in the hardware store— my God! The crap that spewed out my mouth!

I was sinking deep in sin.

Here's how much a liar I had become: when I was holding that phone and waiting for it to be picked up in Dallas, I suspected that when my parents answered, I would flood their ears with a river of bull hockey, too. Quick as a wink. I'd never in a hundred years have told them what I claimed to Aunt Vicky I'd said.

I was a desperate man. Now I knew what that phrase meant.

It meant I was willing to descend into the deepest pit of hell to get what I wanted!

And my parents, my mother, this was her fault! She must have known that this would happen if I spent the summer here; this was exactly what she'd feared! I'd become her worst nightmare; I'd sunk so deeply into the abyss that I could never face her again. My dad was a dupe, a fool to have talked her into letting me have my way.

I smoked now. I was hooked. A nicotine fiend.

I'd been drunk at least twice and still I stepped right up to the bar for another. This despite my mother's stories over the years about her and Uncle Waylan's father and her own mother's grief about it! This would break her heart!

Worse yet—I'd gone from pulling my pud to wallowing in nasty things with an actual girl; I'd committed horrendous acts of perversion upon her womanly temple, and I'd relished my descent into animal lust.

Was I becoming a Starkweather? Would I burn buildings, get hooked on dope? Torture animals, cheat widows out of their savings? Rape and murder?

Was that stupid Reverend Wright really right? Should I have gone to his church tonight? Why oh why weren't my parents home when I called? Did that fateful absence seal my destiny as a man on the downward corkscrew to hell? Sure, I was glad when I didn't have to lie, but now, realizing clearly how far I'd walked off the path of righteousness, I was terribly afraid I'd missed my chance to let them know by a hitch in my voice or by telepathic signal that I was in trouble, big big trouble. Please make me come home!

Tears crawled past my temples and tickled my ears like gnats. I draped my arm across my eyes and zipped my mouth shut so my whimpering wouldn't be heard. Dimly I knew that it was officially within my power to rise from my bed of wickedness and go to the phone and beg forgiveness. But I felt limp inside and down deep so thoroughly enamored of my sins that I could only wallow in sorrow and self-pity. It seemed my only salvation lay in Aunt Vicky's writing that note to my mother.

TWENTY-
FOUR

In later years I learned to go easy on myself for lapses into vice (what's the good of mellowing if you can't step under the autumnal umbrella of forgiveness?), and if the '60s taught me anything, it was the moral superiority of disobedience. At sixteen, though, my conscience had a wicked bite that made me wince as if from a flu shot. I lay awake half the night that Sunday regretting how I'd disappointed my parents and myself by succumbing to temptations.

But I also had a ferocious hunger for all the world could offer, so, despite my orgy of self-recrimination, by Tuesday night I was drinking beer and playing poker with Cotton, Red, and a fellow I'd just met called "House." He was called that because, I supposed, he was big as one, though his salient feature to me was his collection of "Mexican fuck books," in which Popeye and Olive Oil, Maggie and Jiggs, and Blondie and Dagwood were depicted in an educational array of sexual practices using outsized genitalia.

These I pored over with burning embarrassment and enormous relish. Aside from the lure of the lurid, the temptation was to imitate the men to gain acceptance of the tribe, a temptation far more powerful than my vow, now forty-eight hours stale, to obey the Scout laws.

We were staying over at a squalid inn deep in the vacant wilds around Pecos, Texas. The inn was a gas station/grocery of wood frame and galvanized tin situated at a remote crossroad; above the station and accessed by a rickety outside staircase were four tiny, curtainless, rugless, bare-walled rooms each furnished only with an army-surplus metal bed on which lay an acned mattress naked of linens. The rooms shared a common bath (stool and sink only) at the end of a hall, a hall suffused, when we entered, with a dusty yellow light teeming with motes. The building reminded me of those on Gunsmoke, though it stood alone in a many-mile square of mesquite, flat-topped mesas with scrubby skirts, and red-banked arroyos over which buzzards wheeled like strolling cops on the beat. We'd arrived late in the afternoon after working near Odessa; we were one of two crews on loan to a trucking company, and we were to join Uncle Waylan and the other crew tomorrow near McCamey to move a jackknife rig.

Our supper had been potato chips, beef jerky, and salted peanuts washed down with Coors from cans. Now we were sitting on the floor in the room Cotton claimed because the window looked out onto the highway. I'd peered out that window to assess this prized feature and saw only a bumpy, charcoal-colored ribbon stretched out endlessly to the south, heat still quavering in ghostly distortion above it, the road moving straight to the vanishing point at the horizon on its way to nowhere.

I was learning to play poker, a painful rite of passage for all young fellows. No boy wants to admit he doesn't know how, yet playing without knowing how is disastrous. Your ignorance will be flushed out soon and your losses mount quickly. As usual, Cotton was a year ahead of me on this, too, and each time I had to stammer and ask for a run-down on the heirarchy of hands, he'd snicker. During a game of five-card draw, when the showdown came, he swept up the pot with a wink at the others and said, "Sorry, Jimbo, but your two pair won't beat my ace-high half-flush." I conceded humbly as the others burst into jackass hee-haws. This was the poker equivalent of the snipe hunt. Sometimes it seemed my initiation into manhood would never end.

I don't know what my mother's bridge club chatted about when they played. I'd overheard them talking but presumed my eavesdropping altered the character of it. The men wondered if the Yellowjackets would beat Odessa next year, or had Coach Pustley lost his only good running back when Larry Dowell went off to study engineering at Socorro? Pros and cons, my stats against your stats, my info's a whole lot bigger than your'n. It struck me as odd then that Cotton struggled to hold his own with Red and House in this debate, odd because he was a working man who'd not finished the ninth grade and who had no family or historical ties to the city or to the team.

Then they turned to Ford vs. Chevy, a perennial favorite debate, and once again Red and House struggled to beat each other over the head with a mastery of trivia. Hunting and fishing stories followed—first buck, biggest rack, biggest fish. Since my father owned no guns or fishing tackle, I was at a loss to contribute and wished that Uncle Waylan would pursue these hobbies rather than his current one of adultery.

Then Red and House told drinking stories. Here they clearly considered Cotton and me as inexperienced equals. Red once drank two mayonnaise jars of moonshine. We boys didn't know what moonshine was, did we! Nosir, you boys don't know what the old white lightnin'll do to you! But House of course had once *chugged* a quart of Jack Daniels black and went into a dad-blamed coma for two days and woke up to find he'd busted all the furniture. Red drank terrible bad beer in the Phillipines; House had worse—"like horse piss!"— in New Orleans. Red and this buddy got drunk on sake one night in Okee-fuckin'-ah-wah and wrecked a jeep; House put away one of them big, you know, grassy bottles of Eye-tal-yan wine in San Francisco and wound up fucking an Indjun gal in the back of a pickup. Red ever fuck an Indjun?

Naw. Fucked a gook or two, though.

Jever fuck a nigger?

Naw. Hell no!

Damn—I did. Took a week to wash off the stink!

You must of been drunk!

Haw haw haw.

That inspired a memory from House about Spanish fly. Did we boys know what Spanish fly was?

"Heard of it," declared Cotton for both of us. He put just the proper twist on the inflection: you didn't want to claim a knowledge so deep it made the coming story irrelevant or redundant.

"I got some from this Messkin down in Juarez," said House. "Just a little powder down in the bottom of a little bottle. He said use a pinch in your gal's drink, you know, when she's not looking." He leered at us. "He said only thing you gotta watch out for is don't let her out of your sight."

He waited a beat for effect.

"Why's that?" asked Cotton.

Red beat House to the punch. "She'll be humpin' anything that moves."

"That's right," House shot in quickly to let Red know he was still in the saddle. "And you want to be right in her line of fire."

"I tried some on this old gal in Memphis," Red said. "Fellow who sold it said it was extra-potent."

House leaned back on his elbow and belched; the eruption was in proportion to his size, and it was aimed at Red—it might have been a bark or a pistol shot—so Red withered in the noxious fumes and trimmed back his plans to snatch the story away from House.

House said, "Well, dose I give was plenty strong. Wouldn't want nothing stronger, nosir! Whew! Lord!"

"What happened to your gal?" Red obligingly asked.

"I picked her up from her ma's house. I was driving this old Harvester pickup, you know, with the shift on the floor?"

He went on, but my heart sank. He was telling a bald-faced lie; he was stealing a piece of folklore probably familiar to all. The guy slips the Spanish fly into the girl's drink, then they go for a drive in his floor-shifting vehicle; on the way he stops at a drugstore for cigarettes (condoms, liquor), and when he comes out, the girl is dead; she'd impaled herself upon the gear shift rod. In House's variation, when he came out of the drugstore, the girl was riding the knob and hollering for him to jump in and give it to her good.

Undaunted, Red cranked up the press for his edition, but I got up as soon as he started laying out the exposition and murmured, "Gotta piss."

I went down the hall and took a loud leak with the door open to make my excuse solid; then I went out onto the staircase landing and down in the darkness to the lot behind the building. A pale violet light still eeked up from the far horizon and several stars glittered as diamond pinpoints against a navy sky. The moon was a tipped-over crescent face down over the silhouette of a mesa miles away. I still heard their murmur, so I put my back to the building and stepped cautiously out into the mesquite, threading through critter holes and dim scarecrows of prickly pear.

I lit a cigarette. I could hear my breath; it was very still, the air cool but lax, ruffled only by a whir of wings overhead and something sailing past too fast for me to sight it.

I was trying to shut out the picture of that hard cold metal ripping such tender flesh, flesh that I knew now to be delicate as
rose petals. I wondered if I had what it took to become a man. I
wasn't sure I was up to it. You had to contemplate cruelty with
serene equanimity, or, better yet, relish it. The tales about Spanish
fly turned my stomach, and I wondered if something were missing in me. These were supposed to be sexy stories—stories about
sex, anyway—but the girls in them had been cheated of the power
of volition and were, well, *tortured* by the tellers of the tales, tortured to death, and there were no bystanders saying *tsk tsk what
a tragedy*. I'd heard that Spanish fly yarn a dozen times. Usually
it happened to a friend of the teller's brother or such, and in no
instance did the teller express any repugnance or indignation
about what the protagonist had done. Nor was it a cautionary
tale. Instead, the listener was to be amazed and fascinated by
what the girl *had done to herself*, so passionately lusting that she'd
torn out her own organs with a metal shaft. It was one for
Ripley's.

The picture made me shudder. I worried that I didn't have
enough male hormones trickling through my system. Barbershop
machismo only made me cringe with inadequacy. I didn't know
enough about any sport to assert authority in a discussion. I was
trying to learn; I stayed alert and studied the talk, but, truthful-
ly, style seemed as important as the content, and I lacked the will
to win. You had to climb into the ring and jab another guy with
what you knew, and he socked you back with what he knew. You
went at it for a few rounds to a draw or somebody won or lost.

I did know about sex, now, but I shied away from talking to
them about Trudy. When Red or Slim or Pete or even Cotton
ribbed me, I'd clam up and grin sheepishly. "Jimbo, heard you're
going steady. That mean gettin' it steady?" Har de har har. At
least once a day I was accused of being pussy-whipped. Curiously
enough, you could be both proud and ashamed of that.

Sometimes I felt as if a great battle were being waged for my
soul, my allegiance. The women of the world, or the females in
my life—Mother, Aunt Vicky, my sisters, Louise, Trudy,
Sharon—stood on one side of a line and called out to me, sweetly, with gentleness and humor, the siren song of their desirability.
Come join the fun! We smell good! We look good! You'll like the
way we laugh, and you'll enjoy talking to us! The men stood on

the other side hailing me as heartily. Stay away from them! Come join the tribe! You'll like the way we roll about in sweat and blood and dirt, use our muscles and get to be in charge of everything!

I knew I would wind up with the men, but it seemed that with every inch that I went in that direction, the gap between me and the women yawned wider. In becoming a man, I didn't want to have to forsake the company of women or stamp out my dormant interest in their lives. But it seemed increasingly necessary. Of the four of us playing poker, I was apparently the only one disturbed by the Spanish fly stories. To become a man, I'd have to grow a shell.

I stood in the darkness for several minutes; eventually I planned to go upstairs and get right back on that horse, you could say, but before I did, the door at the landing swung open and light spilled onto the pasture.

I heard somebody clomp down the stairs then the softer, sibilant shu shu shu of footsteps in the dirt as he crossed the lot and traced the orange point of my cigarette to where I stood.

It was Cotton. In fairness, I should say now that this was his last night on earth. Tomorrow at mid-morning a hundred tons of metal would crush and kill him instantly. And this was our last conversation. That's the reason I recall it so many years later, though nothing about it seemed prescient then (or now)—no hints, no harbingers, no dark allusion or signs from Heaven. It was typical of our conversations: a thrust, a feint, a split second of dropped guard when I had to choose to hit or not, a handshake at the end of the match that might or might not turn into a test of strength.

First I heard water drilling the ground, his big sigh, then, "Ahhh! Nothing like bleedin your lizard in the woods!"

"Downright civilized!" I joked.

"Got a smoke?"

I shook the pack at him; his Zippo clinked, then his face glowed in an orange halo against the dimness for a second.

"Ain't that House full of shit?"

I laughed. "You need hip-waders to be in the same room with the sucker."

"So how come you left?"

He expected me to justify it. As if he knew I was too tender to take it.

"It was either leave or call him a goddamn liar and I'm not near big enough for that. Was that you I heard clapping all the way down here?"

"Sheeeit! Red's the butt kisser."

We were quiet a moment, both gazing into the heavens. If we were on better terms, I might have mentioned how big the sky was at night here; you felt like you were on the top of a glass globe looking out into an infinity swimming with tiny lights. It made you dizzy, aware that without gravity anchoring your boot soles you'd soar off the planet into space.

I wondered why he'd left Red and House to come out here.

He asked, "So when are you going back to Dallas?"

The question startled me, but I took care not to show that. How'd he know about my problem? Did Uncle Waylan report that Sunday night call to Sharon and she told Cotton? Or did Trudy tell Sharon and he'd overheard? It wasn't his business, and I couldn't glean the spirit of the question: did he mean to embarrass me by alluding to my need for parental approval? Or was he expressing sympathy in an oblique way? Or if he wanted information, how would he use it?

"Well, I don't have to go yet. Probably at the end of the summer, right before school starts." I blew out a long drag. "Why?"

A beat hung between us and he kept looking up. I got the feeling he was deciding whether to say something revealing. I was suspicious. Did he have the hots for Trudy?

Finally, Cotton shrugged. "Just wondering."

"I'll be around for a while yet." (Sharon later told me he'd talked of saving rent by moving into the bunkhouse but felt uncomfortable so long as I was staying there.)

"What about your girlfriend?"

"What about her?"

"Y'all gonna be pen pals or what?"

"We'll work something out."

"She's pretty sweet on you, you know."

I went at his words from every conceivable angle looking for a fuse. Poking fun? Warning me not to trifle with her? Congratulating me?

Carefully, I said, "The feeling's mutual."

"Maybe she'll come visit up there or something."

"Maybe."

He chuckled. "Y'all could go to the 'Cotton' Bowl!"

For a second I feared he was slyly alluding to having done something with Trudy behind my back, read into his words the most appallingly sinister and unlikely deeds.

"What's it like, anyway?" he went on, then I realized that the pun was only benignly innocent and corny, and that it revealed, no doubt unwittingly, his longing to be included.

I gave him a thumbnail sketch of the stadium and the fairgrounds, then—realizing suddenly that the lessons from upstairs didn't have to go for naught, that I did indeed have material to exploit—I enthusiastically lit into a manly tale half-real and half-baloney about going to the Cotton Bowl for a New Year's Day game between SMU and Oregon with my dad and Uncle Waylan. My tale mishmashed at least three different games, this one complete with a mile-long colorful parade, hip flasks, and big-titted cheerleaders, with a rousing play-by-play of the fourth-quarter series that won it for SMU, in which there was a crucial long, long, looooong pass—this was reenacted as Cotton and I stood in the dark, my arm arcing overhead between us, me trotting out from him and yelling, waving to mime the ball's howitzer trajectory—a fifty-six-yard pass from Number 37, the great Heisman Trophy winner and All-American Doak Walker to, uh, Lloyd Carlson, I said (having lost the name of an actual receiver), who caught it and dived into the end zone a millisecond before the final whistle blew!

The point was not who won or how it was done; the point was that I'd been an eyewitness in the company of two men—my father and uncle (and never mind that I was only eight!)—at an important game held at an important place, and that I'd passionately relished it. *And don't you wish it'd been you?*

Cotton was quiet. Properly defeated and envious, I hoped. Feeling safely one up and thinking of his pun, I asked, "Is Cotton your real name? I mean, what's your *real* name, anyway?"

"That's for me to know and you to find out," he said without an instant's hesitation.

TWENTY-
FIVE

W hy's he keep saying it was his fault?" Sharon asked me
for the umpteenth time.
"I don't know. What's he say when you ask him
that?"

"He just shakes his head."

Sharon and I and Trudy and Wally and a few others from the
motel and the shop were at Stinky's bar on Friday evening. No
funeral was held in Hedorville for Cotton. His body had been
shipped out this morning, so we were holding a wake or memo-
rial service. We were playing Cotton's favorite records on the juke
box—mostly Carl Perkins, Patsy Cline and Johnny Cash, but he'd
also loved Tennessee Ernie Ford's "Sixteen Tons." Every time
we'd play it, though, the lyrics would scrape my nerves like chalk
against a blackboard: *St. Peter don't cha call me 'cause I cain't
gooooo/I owe my soul to the comp'ny stoahh. . . .*

Uncle Waylan was mourning with Aunt Vicky in private. He
told me she wouldn't feel comfortable here tonight, though she
and Cotton had been very friendly when she worked in the office.
I supposed Uncle Waylan was feeling too low to sort out the eti-
quette, but to me Aunt Vicky had as much right to be present as
Sharon, and wasn't The Other Woman supposed to hide so The
Wife could preside on ceremonial occasions?

On the other hand, Uncle Waylan had agreed to go to Sitting
Bull Falls tomorrow with Aunt Vicky and Helen's family, and I'd
bowed to considerable pressure to tag along as a sitter for Helen's
kids.

"What's he say to you?"

"Same stuff, Sharon."

"You were *there*, Jimbo."

Her probing made me itchy. She was angry, exhausted, worked up, about an inch away from bursting into hysterics. I wish she'd shut the fuck up about it; I didn't want to think about it. I didn't want to see it any more.

"He's got no call to blame himself," I said. "You heard what everybody's said. He tried to do what he could do. Nobody could fault him for not trying. Will you get another pitcher?"

"Why's he *think* it's his fault, then?"

"I don't know! God, Sharon, why ask me? Shut up about it, will you?"

She got up to refill our pitcher but also to let me know she was irritated, and I was glad to see Trudy coming out of the door marked "Heifers." She was wearing the sundress she'd had on in Ruidoso, and I hoped that when she sat down by me again I could sneak my hand under the table and put it on the first available place on her body.

I wanted to ease away and be alone with her, but I had to bide my time and do it with good grace. Though I couldn't tell anyone, I was strangely and inexplicably angry about all the mourning over the death of who the paper called "Hedorville man Alfred (Cotton) Manley." Roustabout for Kneu Well Service, age seventeen, who was "fatally injured Wednesday morning in a work-related accident near McCamey when the derrick of a drilling rig being lowered to the bed of a truck fell and crushed him." (If he'd been a student they'd have called him a "youth," and I guess Cotton would at least be proud to have earned the name of *man*.)

The story was only a few column inches on the second page of Wednesday's paper, but Uncle Waylan sent a copy of it with Cotton's body back to North Carolina. Looking through his belongings, Sharon found letters from an elderly great-aunt and learned that Cotton had run away at fourteen from a foster home but had kept writing to this relative. Uncle Waylan had the funeral home put the coffin on the train this morning and had set Sharon to work sorting out the knotty insurance details. Since the accident happened on a job site officially contracted by the trucking firm and Cotton was "on loan" to them, Uncle Waylan's insurors argued that Cotton was that firm's responsibility, and they, of course, argued he was Uncle Waylan's. Meanwhile, he'd paid for the funeral home and the shipping and had wired money to the relative for Cotton's burial.

Sharon came back with the pitcher and, to my surprise, sat next to me in the booth so that when Trudy arrived seconds later, she had to sit opposite. That was okay, too, because I could rub my knee against the inside of her leg if I slumped forward enough.

Sharon's eyes watered all at once, and she chewed on her thumbnail.

"Why didn't we ever do this when Cotton was alive?"

"Do what?"

"All get together here and talk and listen to music."

Sharon said "all," but two important principals were absent. Trudy shot me a look of long suffering; she'd been consoling Sharon since Wednesday and had told me that it annoyed her how Sharon commandeered all the grief space for herself, as if she were the only one who felt it.

"I guess it takes something awful like this to make you know what's important," Trudy answered.

"I really understood that kid. Something about him made me want to mother him. You know?" Sharon's voice cracked. "You looked at him and you realized that nobody in his whole life ever ironed him a shirt or reached up to tuck the label back under his collar or made him a pie or gave him a Valentine."

My foot was tap-tap-tapping on the floor, calf muscles flexing-relaxing, over and over. If she didn't shut up, I was going to blast off like a rocket.

I said, "Aw, you don't know that! That aunt might have done a lot for him when he was a baby." I meant to be reassuring, but I sounded impatient, as if I were scoffing at her sympathy. Sharon pulled a napkin from the metal dispenser, blew her nose, and levelled a withering look at me.

"Jimbo, he's dead. He won't beat you at anything again, don't worry!"

She shot up and scurried off to the women's john, fists clenched at her sides.

"Jeez," I muttered. I looked at Trudy, my head leaning over the table, drawn by her large brown eyes. She looked delicious in that sundress. "I don't mean to sound harsh, but she's really off the deep end with this stuff. I mean, I'm sorry too that Cotton died, but . . . ."

She smiled, sympathetically I thought. "It's complicated. She's sorry she didn't feel about him the way he felt about her. She's going through her mother's death all over again, too, I think. And she's feeling, you know, *tender.*"

I took this to mean *pregnant.* I plunged my arms under the table, slid my palms under her dress and caressed the warm smooth skin inside her thighs.

"Can't we go now? I want to kiss you a bunch."

"Restrain yourself. You're jumpy as a cat in a room full of rocking chairs."

One tilted brow and a tiny smile put quotation marks around this cornball simile—maybe it was an allusion to Tennessee Ernie Ford. I looked to see if anyone was watching us; the fellows from work were in the other booths all faced inward, and Wally was dancing with a widow who subbed for him at the front desk. I leaned closer to Trudy's face, put my gaze at work tracing the delicate lines around her lovely bow-shaped mouth.

"I'm in a state of . . . what's it called? *Tumescence?*" I scooted forward so I could touch her mound, but she squirmed aside.

"Behave yourself!" She slid to the end of the bench and got up, brushed her skirt smooth, rolled her eyes at me. "I'm going to check on Sharon."

"I can't help it if I love you so much."

"Take a cold shower while I'm gone."

I watched her cross the tiny sawdust-salted dance floor and vanish beyond the corner of the bar. I loved how she looked from the back, the way her red-gold hair cascaded down her neck in frizzy coils and lay between her shoulders, those rounded but strong-looking shoulders that conveyed a milkmaid's vitality. The hem of her skirt fell to the backs of her knees and showed her strong curved calves. Though she didn't like to hear me say it, she looked like she belonged on an Iowa farm. That look moved me deeply. It dazzled me that I had possessed her, that she loved and desired me.

I considered pouring my glass full again and joining Red and Slim and Mex and Pete, or Wally and June, but I was afraid they'd talk about Cotton. Sitting alone I could play a man so deep inside his sorrow that he doesn't want company; he wants to nurse his wounds with silence and strong drink. The John Wayne model.

I guessed if people really knew what was going on in me I'd feel ashamed. For whatever reason (something missing in me?) I hadn't cried over Cotton yet. Everybody else had, even Uncle Waylan. I kept *trying* to. I kept *expecting* to. I'd never lost anyone close to me, so I hadn't been prepared for *an absence of an identifiable emotion*. Other people's grief seemed flamboyant, theatrical, their behavior driven by a very large swell of feeling. What I felt was that I wanted people to *shut the fuck up* about it! I didn't want to *talk* about it. I didn't want to *think* about it. I didn't want to see it again, that human variation on the theme of *road kill*. I wanted to forget it, drown myself in sweet living Trudy. You see it down the road, a lumpy thing, then there's fur and dark red meat and a leg sticking out where it shouldn't and you get too much of a glimpse of exposed bone—so *white!* who'd have dreamed bone was so white when it's ripped fresh from its sleeve of muscle, with some weird slick sheen of dampness glistening on it—knobby joints knit with bloody gristle, a furry ear, skull crushed like an egg.

"Sharon wants us to take her home." Trudy stood beside me shaking my shoulder.

"Be glad to," I said. "Would you mind driving?"

It was a strange to be sitting in the pickup between them, hip-deep in girls, you might say, weirdly thrilling in a secret way you wouldn't want to advertise around a campfire on a hunting trip. I had my hand draped over Trudy's thigh, my palm soaking up the heat from it under the thin soft cotton, felt her bicep brush my chest as she shifted the lever fixed to the steering column. No floor-shift here. No black knob. I blinked away my thoughts. Sharon seemed small, slumped into the corner of the seat, but she smelled of Wind Song. I remembered she was supposed to meet Uncle Waylan later.

"What's this about the cable drum?" she said.

"I don't know. What'd he say?" I wished she'd get off this subject.

"He said the brake slipped and that's why the derrick fell."

"Crap wears out, Sharon, for God's sake. It was an accident, you know? As in something nobody intends to happen!"

"I'm just trying to figure out what's going on with Waylan." Sharon leaned beyond me to pass Trudy a look. Having known each other since they were toddlers, they could speak volumes with the smallest glance. I thought this signal might be *I thought you said your boyfriend was supposed to help us!*

Trudy said, "Why does it matter, Sharon?"

After a tense silence that agitated me, I said, "Sharon, Uncle Waylan risked his life trying to get to Cotton before the goddamn thing fell on him, goddamnit! He risked his goddamned life!"

"I didn't say he didn't! I'm asking why he blames himself. Whose winch truck were y'all using, ours or theirs?"

"Terrible Red." I knew she already knew that. This was courtroom procedure, and she was taking a deposition.

"Did y'all know the brake on the winch needed fixing?"

"I don't know. I didn't. Ask him."

Sharon dug into her purse for a Pall Mall and lit it with the dash lighter. "I'm not trying to *investigate* nothing, Jimbo. You talk to insurance people all day long about a fatal accident that happened on a job and see what kind of mood you're in."

"All right. I'm sorry. He's upset, you know? Because Cotton was like a son to him, and, well, you'd feel responsible when something like that happened to anybody who worked for you, too."

"Would that include an office manager you'd knocked up?"

What could I say? "Sure."

"I'll remember that."

Just as Trudy was wheeling the pickup under the adobe arch of The Round-Up, Sharon said, "I told him, y'all."

"Wow!" was all I could reply.

Trudy pulled the truck up to the door of #7 but left the engine idling.

"When?" she asked; it sounded like an accusation. "You never said anything."

"Last night."

Sharon opened the door and climbed down, shut it behind her, then strained up on her toes to squint through the open window at us. I kept re-running pictures of Uncle Waylan from last night and through this day. He hadn't uttered a whisper about this to me. He certainly hadn't looked like a man who'd gotten such news, though I wasn't sure how a man in such circumstances should appear. Was he discussing this new development with Aunt Vicky right now? Then, involuntarily, the thought came that I might not have to give Sharon my hundred dollars after all. I'd talked Uncle Waylan into withdrawing it for me so that I could supposedly send it home to be added to my savings in Dallas. Five $20 bills were still hidden in my footlocker. If Uncle Waylan were to step up and do his duty . . . .

"What'd he say?" I asked.

"He said he had to think about it. It was kind of shocking news."

"No doubt," said Trudy.

"He said we'd talk about it more tonight."

"Do you want me to stay with you?" asked Trudy.

"No. Y'all go on." She waved vaguely, though we all three could have easily supplied the "location" her gesture referred to. "He wouldn't say much with you around, anyway."

"We'll get back soon. Okay?"

"Don't worry." She chuckled nervously. "Maybe he'll have good news."

Trudy's silence was a thundering denial.

TWENTY-
SIX

The McIntyres had a seven-year-old boy and a ten-year-old girl who instinctively recognized that I was a species of child but also a spare adult who could be abused at will; Helen McIntyre had them ride with me in Uncle Waylan's car while the four adults went in the McIntyre's new Pontiac. Normally, being at the wheel of the Mercury for a couple hours' road trip would've pleased me, but it was too easy to imagine these kids' brains splashed across the windshield.

It'd been a while since I'd been in charge of children. It only took a little pinching, choking, or tickling to keep my sisters in line, but I doubted Helen McIntyre would allow me to discipline her brats this way. I was directed to follow the Pontiac, and if in trouble I was to flash my lights. Before we even started, they argued over who was to sit in the front.

"You both stay back there!" I drew an imaginary line down the middle of the rear seat. "Jackie, this is all yours from this line to that door, and Gladys, this is all yours from this line to that door. After a while, maybe I'll let whoever is the quietest sit up here." I was sure I'd never let either sit in the suicide seat.

We went along in relative peace for a while, cruising at sixty. Jack McIntyre drove steadily and patiently, like my father, and I was relieved to follow at his stately pace; I kept both hands at ten and two as I'd been taught and clenched my jaw when I had to steer around the hamburgered bloody humps of rabbits and armadillos.

To get my mind off this, I imagined my family back home. On such a beautiful Saturday, they might barbeque in our back yard. Mother would be making potato salad or lime congeal, other neighborhood mothers with her, all wearing aprons and drinking coffee and stirring pots while they chatted. Dad would light a fire of hickory and oak in our brick pit so it would die back to perfect coals for grilling steaks. There'd be a watermelon and Neopolitan ice cream. My dad would lie in his hammock, smoke his pipe, and tell knock-knock jokes to the kids, maybe drink one beer all night. The kids would wear swimsuits and play with the garden hose or run through the sprinkler. The fireflies would show up at twilight and the children would chase them holding a jar in one hand and a perforated lid in the other. After the party my mother would be long in the kitchen cleaning dishes and storing leftovers, and my dad would put out the fire, dump the ashes onto the flowerbeds, store the extra lawn chairs, hose off the patio, bundle up the trash: neither would go to bed until the work had been finished. They never waited until tomorrow to do anything; they never left anything undone. They took perfect care of their two young daughters and of their son, whom they trusted, even though he lied to them and had sunk into behavior that would deeply distress them.

I looked in the rearview mirror at my face, then behind my head I saw these utter strangers whose lives were literally in my hands. It seemed inconceivable that I'd passed so swiftly from being a child who is someone's responsibility to being an adult responsible for someone's child. Now I was a young man in love with a young woman with whom I had adult sex. I flashforwarded to a decade later: I was married and had these two children and was driving them somewhere. The passenger seat was occupied by a ghostly generic wife, nameless and faceless, a blank to be filled in. Who would it be? What would she be like? Trudy?

I glanced at the empty seat as if expecting to see my "wife," but Cotton materialized for an instant before vanishing back into the other world. It was odd to feel him looking on from out there, but it seemed typical that I couldn't read his attitude toward what he saw. If he could speak a single word, like Citizen Kane, what would it be? "Possibility," maybe. Or "Hurts." Maybe "Wait!"

I wanted to be home safe. I had a Rip Van Winkle fear that my parents had grown aged and my sisters already had breasts and periods and beaus, and I'd missed it. Thinking of my sisters growing into women made me realize that my mother had been a girl—did she have a boyfriend before my father? What if, say, she'd been another fellow's Noreen? Or another fellow had loved her and left her? And was this woman I called "Mother" and my father called "May" the first he ever loved, or only the best? Or the last? Or only the latest?

My own birth no longer seemed the inevitable action taken by the best possible cosmic conjunction: it could have been an accident. Frank might have wound up with Woman X instead of Y, and May might have married Man A instead of B. Sharon's coming child—whether Uncle Waylan and she were married or not—that child will grow up with no necessary awareness of all that happened this summer while he or she slept in the womb. Sharon might marry someone else and never tell the kid about its real father. And I will carry this kid's very early history in my memory. Someone might be doing the same at this moment about me.

The decisions these adults faced now seemed impossibly hard. I'd deluded myself that I could figure out what was "best" as if "best" could be located someplace outside them, but since then I'd come to see that all their definitions of "best" were mutually exclusive.

I didn't know what had gone on last night between Sharon and Uncle Waylan because when Trudy and I got back, Sharon wasn't there. I woke up this morning realizing that Uncle Waylan never came home, but he soon arrived with Aunt Vicky, and I didn't know whether he'd spent the night with her or had picked her up this morning after spending the night with Sharon.

After watching the legally marrieds bill and coo today I decided that he'd stayed with Aunt Vicky. Bad news for Sharon. I thought of Sharon and Trudy packing their suitcases.

I shut out the scenario by keeping my mind on my driving. Since Cotton was watching, I'd make him feel he hadn't died in vain. *Both hands on the wheel, see?* I told him. *Eyes up!*

After we left the Artesia highway out of Carlsbad, the road to the falls was gravel, and the summer had been dry and a coat of white dust lay upon it and the surrounding shrubbery. Choking in the wake of the Pontiac, I dropped back and jounced slowly over potholes through a valley between arid brown ridges. We wound down through arroyos and flash-flood gulleys and along stands of cottonwood and mesquite and salt cedars. After we'd come to the campgrounds, we hiked along a trail that curled around a mesa. We heard the falls before we saw them; the stream led away from them, running over boulders and spreading over the rough terrain like water spilled across a table. The falls were no wide Niagara: a sheet of shiny liquid plunged off a lip of the mesa to a pool far below. Damp, moss-slippery steps had been cut into the bluff so that we could climb, slowly, gingerly, hand to hand up the cliff behind the falling water. The cool damp air was a blessing after the heat and dust, and soon we reached a cave. We stood at the mouth looking through the shimmery cascade into the heated light beyond.

"Is this an Indian's fireplace?" Jackie tiptoed on a ring of blackened stones. We all laughed. I toed dirt over a used condom.

"Indians did use to come here, son," said Uncle Waylan. "But I suspect people like us made the last fire."

The boy's father stepped between them and added, "The falls are named for Chief Sitting Bull."

"That's a silly name!" declared Gladys.

I stood entranced by the tumbling water and then noticed that Uncle Waylan and Aunt Vicky had disappeared into the dimness of the cave.

"How far's this cave go?" I asked Jack.

"Fifty yards maybe."

He and his wife exchanged a glance. Helen wore a tiny smirk.

"Let's go back there!"

"We don't have a flashlight," his father told Jackie.

"But they went there."

"They're grown-ups."

Another glance. The smirk again.

"Uncle Waylan's got his lighter. That's enough when your eyes are used to the darkness."

"Daddy, can we use your lighter?"

"Jack, let's take them down to eat." Helen smiled at me like a hostess. "You ready to eat, Jimbo?"

"I guess."

Jack McIntyre started down the slippery stairs with his daughter and son following. Helen hesitated on the brink, cupped her hand to her mouth and called out, "Vicky?"

After a moment, a muted voice said, "Here, we're back here."

"Do y'all want to come eat now?"

Uncle Waylan answered, "We'll be along in a bit."

Helen said to me, "Maybe you better wait a minute and then

remind them." She spoke as if they were careless children who might lose track of time and I was their older sibling.

I stayed by the fire pit not knowing whether to wait or to go exploring. I realized that Uncle Waylan and Aunt Vicky had gone off to be alone. However, my new role as purveyor of secret information drew me irresistibly back to the perimeter of the darkness to listen. Water was dripping, trickling. A cheep, like a bird, then the scritch-scratching like a lizard through leaves. The falls maintained a sibilant rush, obliterating sounds. I stepped deeper into the darkness, feeling the damp, rough walls of the cave. I could see nothing. I thought I heard a murmur, low voices, urgent. Something like a kiss ending, the snap of elastic against flesh, a sigh, a rustle of clothing. A groan? A moan? I could have been hearing things. Something white, deep within the cave. For a moment. Or was it on my eye? I stared and projected onto the darkness a couple embracing passionately like somebody on a movie poster: she against the wall, head over his shoulder, eyes shut in transport, he with his thigh between hers, his hands on her ribs. Any minute she will murmur *Oh take me!*

"Aunt Vicky?" I blurted out. "Uncle Waylan?"

Because I got no answer, I thought maybe they hadn't heard, but before I yelled again, Uncle Waylan called, "What do you want?"

"We're all going down to eat."

"Okay!"

I leaned into the darkness, cocked one ear: they were laughing softly. I decided I'd already made too much of a nuisance of myself, so I said, "See you below."

I picked my way over the rock-strewn floor back to the fire pit. Uncle Waylan yelled, "Wait up! We're coming."

Far in the darkness a tiny light flickered, then their shapes emerged, Uncle Waylan holding his Zippo aloft like Liberty holds her torch as he pulled Aunt Vicky along. He grinned.

"It's dark back there. Can't see your hand in front of your face!"

"Find anything?" I tried to sound ingenuous.

"I don't know." He turned to Aunt Vicky. She was smiling with one side of her mouth. She kept looking out of the cave and into the light. "Did we find anything?"

Her blouse was rumpled and damp in the back. Maybe she looked flushed; it was hard to tell in here. She squinted at one palm, then wiped it on the seat of her jeans. Though it wasn't characteristic of her, she'd not worn her glasses today, maybe out of vanity. She said, "It didn't go very far."

"Dead end," Uncle Waylan said happily. "Them Indians didn't have to worry about anybody coming in their back door."

Aunt Vicky kept her eyes down in what seemed a display of modesty, and, adding that to Uncle Waylan's merry humor, I got the impression that they'd actually *done it* back there. She could get pregnant, too! *Then* what?

"This place'd be right cozy on a winter night, with a nice big fire and a couple of buffalo robes."

"Too damp."

"Well, you get thirsty you don't have to walk but a dozen steps to running water."

"You always were high on domestic comforts. It makes a person wonder how you can tolerate living in that shop."

"I ain't there all that much."

We all gazed about like contractors planning to remodel the cave. The roof was blackened with smoke. "I wonder if cave men ever made pictures on these walls," I said.

"Found a couple back yonder." Uncle Waylan was grinning.

Aunt Vicky sat on a boulder and slipped off her shoe, shook it. "Vulgar graffiti."

"It'd be neat to find cave paintings nobody'd seen."

"Why would you like that?"

"I don't know." I'd commented without forethought, and her unexpected question sent me back to a schoolroom.

"You could sell tickets," said Uncle Waylan.

"I guess it'd be like being a Spaniard and coming here for the first time, you know, being an explorer, a conquistador. Don't you think it'd be neat?"

She looked at the wall opposite where she sat. People had scratched words and signs onto the charred and dusty slate. *BJ + NS. Tulsa. Srs. 51. Kilroy was here, '48. Betty sucks.* A heart around the names Bobby Joe and Ginger. I suddenly imagined these scribblings under the scrutiny of an extraterrestrial visitor or an archeologist in 2242.

Aunt Vicky said, "Being the first wouldn't matter much to me. Understanding what the paintings meant would. I'd like to see some and know what the person who was drawing them was thinking and feeling."

"One thing is they'd all be dead."

Aunt Vicky chuckled dryly. "Gosh, Waylan, that's a cheerful thought."

Pleased to have delighted her, he smiled. "Well, I didn't mean to sound morbid. Kind of on my mind, I guess."

"Me, too. Poor Cotton."

"Let's go eat," I said.

TWENTY-SEVEN

Aunt Vicky sheepishly helped Helen lay out the food on the concrete picnic table, and while we ate she posted herself on the end of a bench so she could hop up for what was needed.

Then the women put away the food, and we men removed to the open-air drawing room: we lit cigarettes (I decided to quit hiding from Aunt Vicky) and finished our beers around the open hood of the new Pontiac. We looked deep within the cavity, admiring the clean metal, the unblemished paint on the valve covers, the black hoses and belts. New motor smell of clean oil, baked paint. Jack cranked up the engine so that we could belly up and watch the belts whir and the generator and water pump go around, listen to the purr of the V-8 and feel the vibrations in our loins as we pressed against the fenders.

"What you had her up to?" Uncle Waylan asked Jack McIntyre.

Jack McIntyre shot a glance toward the women and leaned toward us conspiratorially. "A hundred and ten. You know that stretch between Odessa and Wink? I mighta pushed her butt to one-twenty but I was outrunning my sonofabitching lights."

"Huh!" Uncle Waylan chuckled. "I never cared much for GM cars myself, but if you say a Puny-ak will go a hunnerd ten, I'll have to take your word for it."

Uncle Waylan's contempt for GM cars escalated in direct proportion to their cost and social standing. He was an enlisted man to the core. He could tolerate a Corporal Chevy, but he had a deep distrust of the officer class—your Lieutenant Pontiac, Colonel Oldsmobile, General Cadillac. I'd heard him wax blue-streak eloquent about the McIntyres: they were social-climbers, country-clubbers, little-finger-crookers. Among Jack McIntyre's many sins were practicing law and playing golf in Bermuda shorts. That he drove a "Puny-ak" seemed perfect to Uncle Waylan.

Uncle Waylan deeply resented that the McIntyres had resisted Aunt Vicky's becoming involved with him, and he resented that they still had an influence over her. He must have known that his affair with Sharon made him look bad, and he must have been struggling to keep from being hangdog guilty in their presence.

An added complication was Jack's criticizing Aunt Vicky's behavior and arrest to Helen. Though Uncle Waylan himself disapproved of it, he didn't like Jack McIntyre's talking about her "unhealthy influence" on Helen. (The charges hadn't yet been dropped because Aunt Vicky wouldn't promise not to protest again, despite Uncle Waylan's trotting between her and the district attorney begging each to relent.)

Today, though, Uncle Waylan had been exceedingly civil to the McIntyres, and, barring the one incident where he molested their friend in the cave, he'd been a perfect gentleman.

For his part, Jack McIntyre seemed to want to meet Uncle Waylan halfway. Out of Helen's earshot, his accent had ripened, and he seasoned his speech with curse words. But he cursed like a preacher who wants to be known as a regular fellow; to my ear it rang false because I'd been working alongside virtuosos in the art.

Despite their mutual efforts to be civil, Uncle Waylan had flung down the gauntlet about how fast Jack McIntyre's new Pontiac would run, no matter how conciliatory he sounded.

"Could've been faster than a hunnerd ten." Jack McIntyre took a swallow of his Coors. "That was just the last I looked." He glanced at the dust-blanketed black Mercury. He looked as if he might ask how fast Uncle Waylan had driven it, but he was too good a lawyer to give away such an opening.

Uncle Waylan volunteered it. "I pegged out that Merc a half dozen times at least."

The speedometer registered to 120, where a little metal teat then stopped the needle. I wondered if this claim was a fib.

Jack McIntyre clucked his tongue, wagged his head. "That's sure tough on the old machinery."

Uncle Waylan laughed. "Never had a Ford fall apart on me yet."

They next jousted with their comparative service records: in this corner we've got Uncle Waylan's carrier duty in the sub-infested waters of the Pacific, in the other Jack McIntyre's stint with the Army Air Corps in buzz-bombed England as an air-traffic control officer. The art of this verbal Indian-wrestling required that each work into the conversation the extent to which each had been exposed to danger. But the trick was not to appear to brag; they were merely sharing war stories. As it had been with Red and House last Tuesday night, I was the audience and judge. I was content with the role, though I didn't want to hear a Spanish fly story.

Uncle Waylan introduced his trump card with the phrase, "The scaredest I ever was . . . " which I admired as a sly way to open a story meant to establish your bravery. As for the tale, I could have told it to Jack McIntyre word for word. The fleet was attacked by kamakazis off the New Hebrides, and one slammed into the gun turret next to Uncle Waylan's station, killing many pals and setting fire to much of the ship. He sustained a burn on his ribs—here he pulled up his shirt to show the scar—when he and a buddy pulled another friend out of a flaming compartment.

I wondered how Jack McIntyre could top this.

"You get a Purple Heart for that?"

"Yeah." Uncle Waylan winked at me. "Wish I still had it. Ex-wife stole it off me and probably hocked it."

"Guy I know works down at McBee's Hardware told me he got one when a damn mayonnaise jar fell on his big toe when he was working in the sonofabitching galley." Jack McIntyre laughed. "Doesn't that beat all?"

"Yeah, I reckon perty near everybody who got close enough to action wound up with one. They're a dime a dozen if you're where the shells are exploding."

"You get a Navy Cross, too?"

"A Navy Cross?"

"Yeah, for you and your buddy pulling the guy out."

"Aw, naw. Hell, we didn't think anything of it."

"Your C.O. didn't write you up?"

"Aw, hell! We weren't heroes. We were just doing what we had to do."

"You ask me, what y'all did deserves the Navy Cross. Didn't he find out about it?"

"Naw. We never said anything."

"Huh. Nobody knew about it! That's something, it really is."

Uncle Waylan was frowning. "Fellow we saved knows about it, all right."

"Waylan, I think you and your friend ought to get credit for that. It's not too late. I'm not a lawyer for nothing. Give me the friend's name, why don't you, and we'll start a campaign. Congressman Larkin's a good friend of mine—hell, we can get you that Navy Cross in no time. Let me write your friend and ask him to write a letter for us, that's all it'd take."

"Aw, naw," Uncle Waylan said quietly. "Hell, I'm no hero."

Jack McIntyre nodded, but I couldn't tell if he agreed or conceded to Uncle Waylan's reluctance to pursue the issue. I had the peculiar idea that he was toying with Uncle Waylan, calling his bluff. I wanted to speak up and tell Jack McIntyre how only Wednesday morning my uncle had deliberately chosen to run right under many tons of plummeting metal trying to reach Cotton before Cotton was pounded into the truck bed like a soft nail and Uncle Waylan was almost smashed into road kill himself, but no sooner had I remembered it than burning bile shot up my throat and I had to turn away and clench my teeth to keep from upchucking.

Jack McIntyre said he'd been in a control tower at an air base in East Anglia that was strafed by Messerschmidts. The attack killed everybody in the tower but him. He raised his pant leg all the way up his thigh and showed us a hairless white zipper scar that reached from his ankle to above his knee.

"The look on your face, son!" he said, laughing at me. "Flying glass. Broke my leg in three places."

Uncle Waylan whistled softly. "I reckon you got a Purple Heart, too, then."

"Yeah. But closest I ever came to saving somebody was when I talked a Mustang pilot into a landing because his eyes'd been shot out. But that sort of thing happened every day."

"How many horses you say this thing has?" I asked Jack McIntyre.

He answered some number and to my relief they moved on. As I'd witnessed often this summer, this dueling could cover as many different events as the Olympics: fistfights, whorehouses, who paid the least for a tire, who paid the most for a fishing rod, brushes with celebrities, bets won—the categories were almost infinite. Uncle Waylan and his adversary had just turned to deer hunting when Aunt Vicky and her pal strolled up, luckily before I had to hear any more about hot chunks of metal ripping into flesh. The wives were ready to hike above the falls.

"What're you fellows doing?" Aunt Vicky beamed at us proudly. It pleased her to see Uncle Waylan and Jack McIntyre together.

"Just chewing the fat," said Uncle Waylan.

"Comparing their scars."

"Oh, my!" said Helen. "Waylan, do you have a big one?" She and Aunt Vicky looked at each other and giggled.

Uncle Waylan did something I'd never witnessed: he blushed. He put a sour twist to his lips and looked toward the falls.

"It's as big a one as I'll ever have."

Aunt Vicky leaned into him and curled her hands about his arm as if clinging to a pole. I was amazed at this transformation in her demanor. She grinned. "I'm sure it's all you'll ever need, darlin'."

"That's what I've been told."

Helen said sweetly, "I hope we haven't stirred up a hornet's nest."

"Naw, hell, Jack and I were just admiring this Genral Mothers product, right, Jack?"

"Waylan was telling me all about the war."

"Oh that!" said Aunt Vicky.

We followed a trail that moved through an arroyo near the falls and up to the stream above. The country there was surprisingly lush along the water, a rich green gash carved out of the arid surroundings, and the stream ran clear over a limestone bottom and collected into green pools like beads on a chain of water. Cottonwoods and peeled madrones stood along the banks, Pampas grass and Spanish dagger, yucca in bloom, with small groves of Spanish and live oak. The kids and I saw small mule deer that sneezed when they spotted us and bounded over the boulders, showing white tails. The kids dogged my heels as if I were their personal guide. I'd not been told to take them under my wing, but soon we were separated from the two pairs of adults. My wards treated me like a rented docent, no doubt the result of being carted to and from various lessons.

"How many gallons of water are here?" asked Jackie. Gladys was whacking at the heads of Pampas grass with a stick as we goat-footed up the rocky trail.

"I don't know."

"You think there are more than there are miles to the moon? Or less?"

"I don't know."

I wanted them to shut up. I had things to consider. I missed Trudy. If she were here, then I wouldn't have minded baby-sitting. It would be like playing house and they were ours. I resented that Uncle Waylan and Aunt Vicky had each other and so did Aunt Vicky's friends. If I'd known that while I was being a nanny today the other grownups were going to make out in caves and such, I'd have stayed back and gone to see Trudy. I had a bad feeling about what might have gone on last night while I was sleeping. I'd never seen Uncle Waylan and Aunt Vicky so lovey-dovey. How would pregnant Sharon fit into this picture?

"Is that a blackbird?"

"Yes. They call it a soldier bird."

"Why?"

"Why do you think?"

"Because of the red things on his shoulders!"

"God, Jackie!" whined Gladys. "You're soooo smart!"

"Up your nose with a four-foot hose!"

"Look!" yelled Gladys. "There's an eagle."

"It's not an eagle. It's a buzzard."

"They eat stuff killed on the road."

"That's right. Hey, you wanna play a joke on it?"

Is the Pope Catholic? Yes! Yes!

"Okay, here's what you do." I looked around, saw a flat limestone embankment. "You guys lie here and pretend you're dead. Pretty soon, that buzzard's going to notice you, and he's going to get really hungry." Their faces looked stricken, so I said, "Don't worry! He's just going to be curious. So he's going to land right beside you so he can decide if you're something to eat. And about the time his mouth starts watering, I'm gonna jump out from behind those bushes and knock him in the head with a rock. Whata ya say?"

This trick met with enormous enthusiasm. I laid each down on the rock bed and arranged their limbs so they'd look "dead" and yet be comfortable.

"Okay, now you can't talk, you understand? And don't move! That's the most important part. If you move, the buzzard'll think you're alive, and a buzzard has absolutely no interest in anything that's living. Get it?"

240

I left them lying beside the stream and hiked with the ghost of Cotton trailing right behind me a few dozen yards up the hill out of their sight but where I could keep my eye on them. I only wanted to get off alone to think about Trudy, dream about what she and I might do tonight. If we got back in time and they hadn't gone!

Buzzards. Hunkered on a road around a bloody lump. "Get out of here, goddamnit!" I cursed with my jaw clenched.

I sat on the hillside in the shade of a madrone tree poking at the ground with a stick. Below, Jackie and Gladys were lying dutifully dead. I scanned the surrounding shanks of visible stream for the others. In the distance, Jack and Helen moved slowly among the boulders and scree where a bluff had collapsed into the canyon floor. Farther west, in the distance a nude figure hopped nimbly into sight then vanished as it jumped from a ledge. Probably Uncle Waylan. He and Aunt Vicky must be skinny-dipping in a pool. Must be fun to have fun. If Trudy were here, we could find a natural tub hidden in the shrubbery, and we'd press against each other in the water and French. My main goal in life these days was to kiss every square centimeter of her body. I still had a way to go. If they'd left town while we were here today and I never saw her again, I didn't know what I'd do. I'd go to Dumas looking for her. I'd go house to house, hitchhike from city to city, take a tramp steamer. I'd be John Wayne and Jeffrey Hunter wrapped in one heartsick fellow riding year after year from place to place showing a tattered snapshot and saying, "Have you seen this girl?" (Which reminded me that I didn't have a photo of her!)

I groaned. I felt heart-sick with anticipated sorrow and woozy with lust. I had an aching hard-on and I strangled it to make it behave. I considered literally spilling my seed upon the ground for relief but Cotton was watching. Then the weird thought came to do it for him, in his stead. He was becoming somebody who stood for unrealized possibilities, and I was starting to feel a survivor's obligation that—unknown to me then—would persist over many years.

They were restless below. Jackie swatted something away from his face. They would tire of this soon and start looking for me. I hated these children, and I hated their childish parents.

I sat God-like watching them gradually come to the awareness that no buzzard would alight beside them as if perusing a menu; they fidgeted, they leaned up on their elbows, they sat up, they scanned the sky, Gladys got to her knees, Jackie stood, then it wasn't long before they were both yelling, "Jimmmmboo!" They'd discovered the trick. I decided I wouldn't answer until they called for "Mister Proctor!" It took minutes for Gladys to think of this.

I growled like a mad dog from the shadows of the tree, yipping now and then like a coyote, barking like a hyena, and eventually led them in this manner to where I sat like a truculent Buddha on the hillside.

TWENTY-EIGHT

The McIntyres beat us back to the picnic table, but Uncle Waylan and Aunt Vicky strolled in later, holding hands. Aunt Vicky's hair was damp.

"Where'd y'all go?" Aunt Vicky asked Helen with a phony innocence: "y'all" was not a usual component of her vocabulary. "We looked all over."

"I could ask the same of you, but I can see you took a swim."

"Got pretty hot climbing those hills," said Uncle Waylan.

"I can well imagine."

Chastized, Aunt Vicky brought out the lunch leftovers, then the four adults played bridge. Uncle Waylan kept winking at Aunt Vicky in a stagey way that drew complaints from their opponents. I sat at the end of the table reading *On the Road* but couldn't concentrate because it reminded me of Trudy and our vow to see the world with one big sleeping bag and a couple of knapsacks. Once I leaned over to fish Jackie's balsa glider from under the table and caught Aunt Vicky hurriedly withdrawing her bare toes from the inside of Uncle Waylan's thigh.

Around twilight we loaded up. To my relief, the McIntyres rode in their Pontiac, and I had the Mercury's back seat to myself. This afforded an unavoidable contrast to the Ruidoso trip, when I'd had Trudy beside me and Sharon was the front-seat passenger. I felt Trudy's absence now. Aunt Vicky didn't sit the way Sharon had—almost in Uncle Waylan's lap—but she did lean her torso into the center space and stretch her arm across the seat so that her fingers played with the curly dog hairs at his nape. She hummed. By the time we hit the blacktop, only a faint violet glimmer hovered over the horizon, and Uncle Waylan hit the headlights.

I was tired and cross and bored and worried, contradictory though those emotions might seem, so I yawned and lay curled on the back seat with my hands as a pillow thinking I'd sleep, or, in pretending to, I'd be left alone to think about Trudy.

It wasn't long before Uncle Waylan asked, "Jimbo asleep?"

"Seems to be."

An impulse arose to say I was awake but I fought it back. It wasn't curiosity about what they'd say that motivated me: it was anger, an anger whose origin I didn't understand then. (Now I know it was because they controlled my life by unpredictable, capricious whims.) It would serve them right if they babbled embarrassing stuff. It wasn't my job to save them from making fools of themselves.

"Babe, I'm sure glad you asked me to come with you today."

"I'm glad I asked, too, Waylan."

"It was like old times to me."

"Me too."

A rustle, then a smacking kiss. "That's for being such a prince. Helen was awful today!"

"Heck, they're not so bad. I can't fault them for wanting the best for you."

An interim, humming. I opened my eyes. Her head now lay against his shoulder.

"Now, hon, I can't drive when you do that!"

"I've missed you, Sugar Bear."

Sugar Bear? I was trapped, now: I'd already heard too much and was past the point of no return playing possum.

"Maybe we can make up for lost time."

"Umm." She giggled. "Such a big, big scar."

"Darn it all, Vick, you're gonna make me run off the road."

Should I pop up to watch the road? (Somebody should!) A squeak of the seat. Aunt Vicky sat upright, and I relaxed. "I talked to Mom the other night."

"Does she know . . . ?"

"No. But she misses me. I miss her. I've been thinking it might be good to go home for a visit. You and Jimbo could come back to the house. It would be a lot more comfortable for you."

"How long a visit?"

"I don't know. It depends, I guess."

"What on?"

"Well, I thought it might be good for us to be away from one another where we could think things out."

"I'm pretty tired of thinking, myself."

"What's that mean, Waylan?"

Uncle Waylan sighed. Big. "I guess it means I see I've been a fool. I let this thing with Sharon hang on way too long." When she said nothing, he added, "I told her last night to go back to Dumas."

"And that you loved only me?"

"Yes, darlin', that's just what I said."

It was all I could do to keep from bolting upright like a corpse popping out of a coffin. Last night he told Sharon to go back to Dumas? Then they'd had all day long to leave! Could Trudy walk out of my life without seeing me?

"How'd she take it?"

"Not too good. She claimed she was in a family way."

"Oh my God!"

"Now, don't get excited. I wouldn't take a bet on it. It seemed like something she threw out, kind of, well, desperate."

"Christ, that's pitiful, Waylan! You make me so goddamn mad!"

"Well, hon, you'll have to get in line behind me."

I wanted to scream, "But it's the truth!" I was so tense and alert I thought surely my rigid form was sending off waves of crackling consciousness from the back seat.

"Okay. I want to be constructive about this. Let's talk about why you left in the first place."

"I don't know, I really don't. It's like I told that counselor. I wish I did."

"I do, too. Maybe you could figure it out if I wasn't here to confuse you."

"Aw, naw, that wouldn't help, believe me!"

"Have you thought about it at all? I mean, all I know I was in the kitchen up to my elbows in dishwater and I wanted to go dancing, and the next thing I knew you'd stomped out of the house. Why did that set you off? And if you had a gripe why couldn't we talk about it?"

"Aw, hell, I don't know, really. I wish I did. I'm sorry, really I am. Must have been something at work, you know?"

"No, I don't think so. And Reverend Abbot didn't, either."

"Then why don't you tell me what was wrong with me?"

A rustle. A click as the dash lighter popped out. Then the thick smell of cigarette smoke. "I can see you're not ready to listen."

"Okay, okay. I'm sorry I got a little riled up."

"It's okay to get riled up, Waylan. But we can't move back in together like nothing happened only because we're missing each other."

Uncle Waylan chuckled. "Seems like a good reason to me."

"Well, the reason's good, all right. But whatever was wrong won't go away by itself."

"You know, that's the problem with being married to you."

I got the feeling he regretted blurting this because he didn't follow it up.

"What's the problem?"

"You make everything so damned complicated, Vicky. I mean, we had a real good time today. At least I did."

"I did, too! In fact, I told you so."

"Well, why not leave it at that? How come we have to spoil it by dredging up the past?"

"I'm very sorry that you feel I'm making up problems."

"Aw, it's not that. Damn! Are you gonna punish me for the rest of my life?"

"Waylan, I'm not trying to punish you, for crying out loud!"

"Shh!"

"He's asleep. I'm only going to say this once. Waylan, I'm not ready to be your wife again, even if you told Sharon you never wanted to see her again. We've got to figure out where we went wrong before. I wouldn't want to wake up six months from now and find out there's another woman again."

"I understand, I do, I mean it."

"So I believe that if our marriage means anything to you, you'll think about what happened while I'm gone."

"I could think about it a lot better if you were here."

"I don't think so."

"How long, you think?"

"I said I don't know. But you and Jimbo—"

"Oh, I don't think we'd do that."

"No? Why not?"

"Just because."

"You'd be more comfortable. You'd be very welcome. After all, it's your house too, Waylan."

"Well, the bunkhouse is good enough for us. Couple of fellows batching it, it's got all we need."

There was a long silence. I thought maybe they'd simply worn out the subject for the moment, but it turned out that Aunt Vicky was stewing in all the implications aroused by this dispute over where we'd stay. I heard another rustle as she scooted back to the passenger side and leaned her head against the window. I didn't know she was crying until she spoke again.

"You go ahead, Waylan, you diddle around all you like. I don't care, if it means so much to you. I hate giving up on things, but you're a goddamn brick wall and I'm tired of butting my head against it!"

"Aw, hon, I didn't mean nothing. If it makes you feel better, we'll stay in the house."

"I know she's still there one way or another! If not her, someone else. I'm not blind, for God's sake!"

Uncle Waylan sighed helplessly, and Aunt Vicky wept in silence for a while. She blew her nose quietly.

"Vicky?"

"Go to hell, Waylan!"

"Now that's real mature."

He lit a cigarette and turned on the radio to crackling static and cornball cowpoke music, and I knew each was angrily nursing wounds in private. After a minute, he turned the radio off.

"Vicky, I want to try to explain it. If I can. I mean, it might not make sense. I can't guarantee it will. I don't understand it myself, you know? Half the damn time I don't have any idea why I do one thing or another. Yeah, I've had thoughts about it, but you can't hook them up in a neat little train that's going some place in particular. They're like a bunch of loose marbles rolling around in an empty space that's tilting one way then another."

I thought he might be grinning when he said this. When she didn't exploit his straight-man opening, he went on. "But I know this is important to you. So I want to try."

"I would appreciate that, believe me."

He went "ssssshhhhhh" blowing out a long breath. Cleared his throat. "I'm not sure you're gonna like it."

"Take a chance."

"Noreen figures pretty big here."

"That doesn't surprise me."

After a moment, Waylan said, "I didn't feel up to going out. I wanted to stay home. I'd had a hard week. I was looking forward to being alone with you, you know?"

"I wanted to be with you, too."

"But dammit, Vicky, I didn't feel up to putting on a damn tie and sitting around that goddamn country club."

"Waylan! I never said a word about the country club! We could've gone anywhere you wanted! The Corral or the State Line. I wouldn't have cared! I could've gone dancing on our own patio and been happy! How come you couldn't have told me that you wanted to be with me?"

"I didn't want to be begging you."

"Begging me?"

"Yeah, you know. To stay home."

"Well, if you'd have wanted us to stay home so you could spend time with me, why didn't you come into the kitchen and help me do the dishes and talk to me and tell me how much you love me?" I could hear a minute tremolo in her voice. She stopped to blow her nose again. "You could have come and talked sweet instead of sitting in there with the paper and grunting when I tried to discuss going out! Why didn't you?"

"It's really hard to explain. I wish to hell I could be like you and have all the right words for every which occasion and every little goddamn thought. I really do. I know I'm short, way short, when it comes to that sort of thing." He sighed, hugely. "If I had it to do all over, I'd crawl into that kitchen on my knees and beg you to marry me again, babe. I love you, Vicky, I really do."

"Okay. What about Noreen?"

After a long silence Uncle Waylan said, "I'd had a dream about her. The night before. Sometimes it's like she won't leave me alone, like she's sitting out there in Bakersfield or wherever the hell it is and she's got this little Waylan voodoo doll and she gets up in the middle of the night and decides to stick pins in it and twist its little pecker."

I snuck a glance over the top of the seat. He was turned to her as if checking for permission to tell this, and she was gazing back with encouragement.

"Well, I have memories about Robert, too, of course."

"One difference being you never told me about him until he showed up here, Vicky!"

"Did you imagine I was a virgin?"

"No, but—"

"Let's not get sidetracked. This dream about Noreen . . . ?"

"I'd say that there's not much to it, but I know you'll pick the bones clean," he said dryly, with begrudged humor. "She and I were back home, kids again, in somebody's house. It was summer, pretty hot, and we were in a kitchen, and she danced up to me and stuck her tongue out and grabbed a sandwich out of my hand and took off laughing, so I chased her outside. But when I started down the road after her, a black dog came running out of a corn field and growled and snapped at me, and I had to stop and let her go on."

"And?" Aunt Vicky prompted after a moment.

"That's all there was."

"What does that have to do with me and you?"

"This is the part you won't want to hear."

"Quit presuming that, Waylan. Even if it hurts, it's important that I know what's going on in you."

"Okay. I woke up early. I mean that the dream was one you have pretty near time to wake up, so I woke up sooner than our alarm and I just lay there with the dream hanging in my skull. It was just as real as a Technicolor movie. It was still dark. I couldn't shake it off, and while I lay there waiting for the alarm to go off, I went back over my marriage to her, the whole sorry mess of it, starting with the time we did anything more than kiss and her family'd gone to church on a Wednesday night. We sat on her porch swing and next thing you know we were in her bed. I was so happy I up and proposed to her then and there. Fifteen goddamn years old, Vicky. Fifteen! Couple of stupid kids! Then I jumped to the last chapters. We didn't have a middle—the goddamn war cheated us out of it. You know, coming home after working my butt off that day, walking through the house calling out her name, and her not answering but it wasn't all that unusual for her to be out supposedly with her pals, the ones she'd met when I was overseas, and half the time she wouldn't be home until midnight, but, anyway, I was hoping she'd be there for once, and I was going from room to room until I finally got to the kitchen and there she was standing in the back door with her hat and purse and for just a split second I was happy, thinking she was just getting home, too, same as me, but then she was saying, 'I got to leave, Waylan,' and me thinking she meant to go out for the evening, and then she was closing that door in my face and getting in that car that was in the alley. To this day I don't have any idea who was behind the wheel of that goddamn vehicle!"

Uncle Waylan groaned. "Man, oh man, I'll tell you! Whew! That morning after the dream it all came back to me. Like being hit with the flu. I was lying there in the dark waiting for the alarm to go off, and my eyes were watering. I came within a quarter-inch of waking you up and spilling my guts and making love to you."

"Oh, God, Waylan! I wish you had!"

"I know. But you'd have known I was all shook up and you'd have wanted to interview me, sure as hell. Besides, it wasn't on our fertility schedule."

There was a beat of silence, then she said tightly, "I can see why you thought this might be painful for me."

"Oh, darlin', you've gotta know this: while I was lying there feeling sorry for myself, I was also thanking the good Lord that I was waking up beside you and not Noreen. I was counting my blessings, and you were, and are, the very biggest and best one of them. If Noreen hadn't dumped me, I'd have never met you. You're smarter, classier, sexier, and funnier than Noreen, and one hell of a lot more interesting, besides. I thought I was one lucky SOB to have you, and I still do."

"Sexier? You think I'm sexier than Noreen?"

"Yeah. She was strictly missionary."

"But not afflicted with a fertility schedule."

"We never got around to it. She didn't want kids."

"Maybe that was my mistake."

"Aw, it wasn't a mistake, hon. It just—"

"Let's keep that can of worms closed right now, okay? So you were thinking good things about me . . . ?"

"Well, I got to thinking about you and me and how we'd gotten together, and so all during breakfast I got to looking at you and—you know how that robe you've got shows your legs when you're sitting down?—I got to thinking good thoughts about you, hon, and I started thinking that I'd do a little hocus-pocus on that ghost of Noreen when I got home later that night, that you and I'd have a nice quiet night being together and making love and we'd just slam the door in her face when that bitch came knocking. I thought about you all day long, I did, I honestly did, Vicky. Every time I'd have a bad Noreen memory."

"I take it they weren't all bad. Bittersweet, maybe." He must have given her a warning look, because she said, "Sorry. Go on."

"I kept thinking tonight. Hell with Noreen! Just you and me there in our house, maybe I'd catch you right when you're coming out of the shower, kind of slippery and wet, or I'd climb in there with you and to hell with that goddamn schedule. It was all I could do to keep my mind on my work, Vicky. I was looking forward to coming home that night."

"You were horny." She sounded vaguely deflated.

"Oh, it went way beyond that. Like I said, Noreen had that voodoo doll, but I had a good angel on my side and I was bound and determined that bitch wasn't going to get the best of me. I was pretty pleased with how I climbed up out of my blues like hiking rung by rung straight up a twenty-foot ladder with a dead man on my back, and by the time I got home that Friday night, I was feeling pretty worn out but happy. But also kind of, I don't know, mad way down deep, mad that she'd put me through it again. And sad that you'd had to inherit it all. I remember pulling up in the driveway and sitting there a minute counting my blessings and thinking what a nice house, what a nice wife, what a good life I had. And I was thinking how grateful I was to have this, to be able to spend the day out wrestling 'gators and come home to a clean and quiet place with rugs and pictures on the wall and the smell of fried chicken. You had that nice dinner ready, and I remember how good it was and even, oh this is going to sound so queer, I was admiring your arms. I know I never said a word to you about them, but they're beautiful, they truly are. And anyway, after we ate I went and sat down with my paper thinking I'd skim it and later on we'd, you know, get to the other. I sitting in my chair sort of burrowing into our life—am I making any sense at all?"

"Yes! Oh, yes!"

"I remember once I kind of closed my eyes and laid my head back and listened to you washing the dishes. You were humming something, and I could hear the little clinks and such. I felt so happy I could've busted into tears, Vicky. This was the way things were supposed to be. When we were dating, it seemed like things were always inside-out—we were always out roaming the world. Your home was a goddamn hotel room and mine was that damned bunkhouse. Neither one of us had any kind of place we wanted to be in. Now, this was our home, and you were part of it, a very big part of it. I could appreciate how you'd put it together piece by piece, damn nigh every stick of furniture and the samplers on the walls. It was like I was a permanent guest, and you were the hostess. We had a nice big new bed. We'd romped in it a few hundred times already, and I was thinking about how later on we'd do it again."

He fell silent. Aunt Vicky said, "I know what happened next."

"You told me you wanted to go out."

"No, Waylan, I asked you what you thought of our going out!"

"Same difference."

"Well, hardly."

"All I know is I was having a nice daydream about us being in our home and all of a sudden I look up and there you are standing by my chair wanting to go out. I guess it hurt me. I wanted to stay home with you. I wanted you to want to stay home."

"You said you were too worn out. Why didn't you tell me your real reason?"

"Aw, I don't know, Vicky. Like I said, I didn't want to be begging you to stay home with your own husband! I've got some pride!"

"Pride!?"

"Damn it all, haven't you heard a word I've said? When you started wheedling and whining and carrying on—"

"Waylan! I was only joshing! I was trying to—"

"talking about not being ready for the old folk's home and all, then I—"

"My God! I was kidding!"

"then I heard Noreen all over again, like you were saying being married to me wasn't enough for you any more! And it about broke my goddamn heart!"

TWENTY-NINE

We mulled that over. My thoughts whirled like paper scraps in a dust devil. Uncle Waylan had stormed out of the house because of a dream from the morning before!? And he was only now putting it all together? And his running off to Dumas and knocking Sharon up, drawing her here, and thereby bringing Trudy, too, and so bringing us together—all this came not from a plan but from his gut reaction to a bad dream?? And the ripples from it might include Cotton's being on that truck bed that morning, who was to say?!

Oh, worse yet: he'd made these events happen acting under the influence of a bitter memory *without even knowing it?* Because his first wife had abandoned him, maybe because of the war, because they'd grown apart when they had to be apart . . . .

Oh, man! This was horrible! Grown people living and dying and making things happen and having things happen to them with no idea of why!

Cotton hadn't asked to be born, and he hadn't asked to die. Nothing essential about his life had been left for him to decide!

And how about me? Meeting Trudy was a happy accident in my life. Having a rig fall on his head was an unhappy accident in Cotton's. It could as easily be vice versa, and precious little I could do about it! I'd thought my helplessness was a necessary condition of childhood; now I saw that these adults whom I'd always presumed to be in control of themselves and of the world (and of me!) were weak and stupid and impulsive, and their lives were like chaff upon the wind!

I'd been so eager to learn the secrets of adulthood and so

proud to achieve my small measure of knowledge. Now I wanted to stay a child, but trying to take shelter from the violence and chaos by putting my life in the hands of these adults was like hiring a pyromaniac to guard my home.

I curled into a ball and felt a weird internal prompting that urged my thumb up to my lips. Up front they weren't talking. I had to divert my mind from the black horror I'd blundered onto, so I tried to think of Trudy. Even if she went to Dumas, I could visit; it wasn't prison. Next year we'd be tramping about Europe talking to people wearing berets and ordering meals from waiters with handlebar moustaches. We'd make love in that sleeping bag. We'd sit in sidewalk cafes with the Eiffel Tower showing over the trees in the distance. We'd ride a red Vespa in Italy, she pressing her breasts into my back and her arms around my waist, wind in our hair . . . .

Dreaming of this calmed me, but my therapy was interrupted by honking and yelling. The commotion gave me an excuse to "wake up," so I thrust my head over the back of the seat and said, "What's happening?"

The McIntyre's Pontiac was cruising by in the passing lane. The brats hanging out of the back window were sticking out their tongues.

"Somebody ought to give those kids a whipping with a willow switch," said Uncle Waylan.

As the Pontiac veered back into our lane ahead and its taillights began to recede, I felt the Mercury accelerate. Uncle Waylan flicked his lights to bright, then we started around the Pontiac.

No sooner were we around it and into our driving lane than the flicker of the Pontiac's lights behind signalled that Jack McIntyre was going to pass us.

Uncle Waylan glanced into the rearview mirror. He half-turned toward me, grinning. Aunt Vicky was sitting upright, staring dead ahead.

"What you think, Jimbo? Think he can take us?"

A wave of nausea swept over me so strong I thought I'd faint. "I dunno, Uncle Waylan," I mumbled.

Luckily, the road was straight, flat, and empty but for car lights dim as distant stars far ahead. The Pontiac surged up on our left. We were cruising at seventy-five. The kids had their heads out the window, Gladys' hair whipping around her face. In the front seat, Helen McIntyre was looking through the windshield.

Uncle Waylan goosed the Mercury up to the Pontiac's speed.

And, of course, Jack hit his again, and soon we were sailing along door-to-door at eighty-five. Those distant car lights ahead had anaphased into distinctly separate cells. Helen turned and ordered her children out of the window, and the glass rolled up. They mashed their faces against it, making pig-noses, gleeful and oblivious to the danger. What innocence!

I had to turn away. Aunt Vicky was stiff like a stone thing. I was afraid for her, there in the suicide seat. At least in the back I could drop into the floorboard. I tried with all my might to send telepathic messages to Uncle Waylan: *Stop!* And to Aunt Vicky: *Make him stop!*

I looked ahead. Somebody had to give soon. Jack McIntyre punched his footfeed to the floor to hit the passing button, and his Pontiac bucked and leaped ahead, then Uncle Waylan did the same. I slumped down so I couldn't see the road. I was maybe twenty yards away when Cotton was standing on the truck bed while the derrick of the jackknife rig was being lowered crown-first onto the truck, and Cotton was supposed to guide it down and unlatch it; the din was horrendous from the truck motors and they had the rig motor running, too, using the main cable to help lower the derrick, and with the two-way radios and the yelling Cotton couldn't hear everybody screaming *Jump!* Uncle Waylan sailed past me fast, scrambling right for the bed, and in that instant I saw what I should have done, but Cotton had his back to us, and Uncle Waylan had just reached the step-up on the cab when the crown on the derrick hit Cotton like a giant hammer, hit him so hard it went right through, bounced up from on the bed, and knocked Uncle Waylan ten feet into the air. I had to make myself run with all the others to get there, but I was glad everybody else was first and I couldn't see much through their legs or over their shoulders except blood and something too white and didn't really want to.

I blinked back the memory. I lifted my head: now we were racing at ninety-five. The sage and mesquite were a white blur, fence posts flickering by like cigarettes in a newsreel production line, and as I glanced ahead into the darkness we were frantically gobbling, I hoped nothing big stood or lay in the highway like a deer or a cow. Smaller bloody heaps of road kill popped into our lights and sailed by us before I could identify what living creature they once had been. I was afraid I was going to be sick. When I shut my eyes I saw a butcher's hammer pound a slab of beef.

We went fender to fender for what seemed several minutes—no doubt only seconds, since I was holding my breath—with the traffic ahead looming closer, until, at last, Uncle Waylan's eyes caught mine in the rearview mirror.

"I'm sick, Uncle Waylan!"

I groaned and clutched my gut; he braked to the shoulder, and I tumbled into a weedy bar ditch, slapped my palms to my knees and splattered my ankles. After a second he was beside me.

"Damn that was stupid of me, Jimbo! Sorry. That guy gets my goat."

"Okay," I choked out. When my gut was empty, my knees were shaking and my calves were Jell-O, so I plopped back on my ass. I bent my head between my knees. I gasped for breath for a minute, then, when I seemed to get it back, inexplicably, I started sobbing.

Next thing I knew Aunt Vicky's warm soft hand was stroking my neck and patting me on the shoulders.

"Jimbo," she said gently, "it's okay."

She knelt and tried to hug me. I let her, but I felt resistant, half annoyed by her effort to console me. I kept on weeping but felt oddly detached, as if this were something my body was engaged in, but, in the meantime, I'd left it there and walked off to smoke a cigarette, the way you might let a bucket fill from a slow hose in your absence.

"I'm okay now." I meant *go away!* I clenched my jaw to hide the trembling. "Guess something I ate went down wrong."

But she wouldn't go away. She sent Uncle Waylan back to the car and hunkered in silence beside me. A small sliver of a moon stood over the horizon, but it was too dark to see anything in the field. Cars passed behind us, their lights making a visual roar that matched the noise and the wind they stirred. A big truck thundered past and the backdraft rocked us both and for a second I hallucinated that it had veered off the road and was plunging down the embankment at us.

"You don't believe me?" I was still blubbering and couldn't seem to shut off the valve that would stop it. I tried breathing deeply but my intake was ragged and spastic.

"I didn't say that. Do you want to talk about it?"

"About my stomachache?"

"About anything."

I turned and saw that her brows were squiggled in maternal concern. I thought that I might as well milk it. I knew she wanted me to break down and tell her I was upset because I'd seen Cotton killed; by telling her, I could gain her sympathy and bask in her attention. I felt cynical and phony knowing that it would be so easy to manipulate her and feeling the irresistible temptation to do it. (Did I actually only hope my disturbance was a pose? By pretending to exploit Aunt Vicky's tender regard, was I able to let her know that I'd been shaken to the bottom of my being but didn't have to face that yet?)

"It was so horrible, you know, the way Cotton died."

"Yes, I know," she murmured. "It must have been terrible to see."

I waited for something to bubble up from under the cover I was keeping on myself. "I wish I hadn't fought with him that night at the motel."

"You and Cotton had a fight?"

"Yeah. I thought he was, well, trying to . . . to turn Trudy against me."

"Did you shake hands when it was over?"

"I guess."

"Then no harm was done, Jimbo."

I couldn't admit there was a sin of omission as well as one of commission: me, standing frozen while the derrick fell and Uncle Waylan ran past to save Cotton.

"But there might have been, Aunt Vicky. One of us could have killed the other accidentally."

"You were both lucky."

"That's just it!" I wailed. "I don't want things to happen because of that!"

Cotton's luck was that the closest person to him had been me.

THIRTY

They dropped me at the shop, and I dashed into the office to call The Round-Up. The front desk phone was answered by June. "Room seven," I told her, not bothering to identify myself or to ask about her grandchildren and her toy poodle, Oodles. I let the phone ring twenty times, dancing in place, about to explode. "Come on! Goddamnit! Answer!"

June broke in. "I guess they're not back yet, Jimbo."

"Not back? Where'd they go?"

"Wally took them somewhere."

"Where? Were they carrying suitcases? Did they check out?"

"I didn't see them leave. Hold on."

Clunk! went her receiver. I paced to the end of the cord like a coyote on a chain. I hoped she was checking the books to see if the girls still occupied their room.

"Somebody wanted their key," she said.

"Did they check out?"

"No, they wanted their key."

"No, Sharon and Trudy!"

Rattling, rustling. A squeaking hinge. "I can't tell. Wally don't keep the best of books on his permanents."

Permanents! I liked that word!

"Didn't he say when he'd be back?"

"He said he wasn't sure."

Good! If he'd gone to the bus station, he'd be right back. And if he'd taken them to Dumas he'd have said he'd be back tomorrow, most likely.

"I'm coming right over, June! If they get back before I get there, please, please, please! tell them not to leave again!"

"All righty." Her bovine calm exasperated me.

I ran into the bunkhouse, tripped over that damn little hairless mutt and sent it yipping under Uncle Waylan's bed. "Sorry!" I yelled at it while I dug into my footlocker for the five twenty-dollar bills. I was sorry I'd been too stingy to give the money soon as I'd gotten it, as if that might have kept them here, allowed them to stay, or at the very least required them to say goodbye. And I realized I should have already given it because they might need it for any number of reasons now and having it would have put me in their mind as a friend, someone they owed and would want to stay in touch with. Sal Paradise would've handed it over in a second.

I jumped into the cab of the smallest truck available; heavy wooden boxes of valves and fittings were chain-and-boomered to the bed, and as I went tearing off the lot and onto the highway all that metal bounced and sang a horrid clanking chant. It was full dark now, about "dark-thirty," as Uncle Waylan would say. It took only ten minutes to reach The Round-Up, and I roared into the gravel lot with my head swiveling wildly to survey the scene. Wally's car wasn't parked outside the office. Trudy's room was dark. I slammed the brakes and slid to a halt at the back and cut the lights and jumped out into a fog of white dust.

As I trotted to the office, my heart was hammering and I felt breathless. I hoped I'd beaten them back, though there was the slim chance that they'd come and gone and June hadn't given them my message. As I scurried across the lot, I inhaled deeply to slow my pulse, and, at the office door, I blew out a gust to get a grip.

"Did they get back yet?"

Seated behind the counter, June was knitting something which might serve as a sweater for a ham. I batted a tendril of Swamp Thing out of my face. When her gaze swung up to take me in, she looked dazed, like someone who's been reading all day.

"I, uh, didn't hear nothing."

This was only partly reassuring. On cross-examination the witness would confess to wool-gathering.

"I'll go wait in Trudy's room, okay? If you see them or they call, will you please, please let them know I'm here?"

"Okey-dokey."

Their room was unlocked as usual, and it seemed stuffy and

warmer than the night air outside, so I left the door open and hoisted the bathroom window. I switched on the lamp atop the night stand, recalling how the corner of it gouged into my kidney when Cotton and I wrestled that night (and I kept trying to recreate in recollection that sharp ache). Aloud I said, "That hurt!" surprising myself and wondering if I weren't going batty because I seemed to be talking to an invisible presence.

Sharon's bed was neatly made, and Trudy had slung the spread up over the pillows, her usual way. This probably happened when they'd gotten up, hours after Uncle Waylan had told Sharon he was going back to Aunt Vicky, so I hoped this was a sign they hadn't planned to check out.

Trudy's journals weren't on the desk, but while waiting I could snoop. I balked. I went outside and stood in the lot smoking to resist the temptation, hoping they'd return while I was out there.

I told myself that if I could find them in an obvious place—under the bed or the mattress or in the nightstand—then I might take only a peek. But when they weren't in those places, I went to their chest. Trudy had the bottom three of the six drawers; when I slid open her topmost drawer, her scent billowed out and weakened me. I plunged my hands into the soft disheveled heaps of her panties and bras, socks and T-shirts, not fishing for the journals so much as yearning to grab up fistfuls of my elusive darling.

My hand brushed over the cover of a Big Chief tablet. I held it for a moment without looking into it. Reading it would profoundly violate her trust. And if she caught me I could hardly argue that I hadn't read anything—she'd say I hadn't had time. I'd already be guilty of having searched for it, and I couldn't claim that I'd found it by accident, that my true purpose had been to root around in her underwear!

I looked out to the lot. The rising moon was bleaching the bone-colored caliche silver-gray. Lamps glowed yellow in other rooms. I closed the door.

I sat on the bed with the tablet on my knees. I had nothing specific to look for except for what she really felt about me. Why couldn't I trust what she'd said? Why couldn't I believe her?

I got up, jerked open her drawer, and slid the tablet under her clothing. As much as I wanted to pat myself on the back for doing the right thing, I couldn't shake the memory of Sharon sitting

261

here on her bed—before Cotton was killed, before she'd told Uncle Waylan about being pregnant (could it have been last week? It seemed a year!)—filing her nails and thanking me for pledging the loan but still dreaming that Uncle Waylan would see the light. And I was in contempt of her then because I knew better.

She was happier at that moment than she was last night when she learned the truth. The truth was the crunch under the hull as the ship runs onto a reef, that thump and squeal beneath the tires when you hit a squirrel. When you're a kid you dash off after the truth willy-nilly, but now I was wary. The truth was supposed to set you free, but if I had to learn something painful about me and Trudy, I'd rather the truth have to send out a search party. If Trudy's journal showed she loved me, then it would only confirm what she'd said. If the journal had bad news, I wanted to wait until the last possible second to hear it.

I went out onto the stoop again. I smoked; I paced; I chucked pebbles listlessly into the lot, considered going to the office, even talking to a dopey adult female such as June might be preferable to aimless fretting.

At 10:45 Wally's old Chevy coupe with the windshield awning pulled under the arch and he parked in his slot. He cut the lights and the red tail lamps went out. The dome light came on when the passenger door swung open, and Trudy got out, pulled the seat back forward so that Sharon could shimmy out from the rear, bent over, face first, like something emerging from an egg. My heart thundered. I wanted to scream hooray.

"Hey!" I yelped. They looked over; I waved. Trudy held up her hand in what I took to be a hello but then it seemed to signal "wait a second." She and Sharon talked briefly, almost nose to nose, before they turned to pad toward me. Wally stood behind the screen door watching them.

They walked side by side, the same height. Trudy usually gave the impression of having more flesh than Sharon, though now when they passed into the light, Sharon's neck and face looked bloated.

"God I'm glad you guys are back!" I crowed as they came up to the stoop. "Where've you been? I was worried. I heard about what happened last night, and I was afraid that you guys had checked out!"

Sharon glided past as if I were invisible—she looked like someone about to lose her lunch any second—and Trudy might have followed her inside if I hadn't snagged her elbow.

"Hey!"

"Oh Jimbo!" she groaned and collapsed into my arms. I held her tight to my chest and we rocked. I couldn't tell if she was crying or not.

"Oh I love you, sweetie!" I murmured into her hair. I was shamelessly vulnerable and didn't care. "Where have you been? I was so afraid you guys would go back to Dumas and I wouldn't see you again."

"I wouldn't do that."

From inside the room I could hear Sharon bawling. It unnerved me. I thought Trudy would want to console her, so I released her; she stepped to the threshold, ducked her head inside, said something, but then eased the door shut.

"What's the matter with Sharon?"

"Give me a cigarette."

I lit two Pall Malls, then she leaned against the door frame and slowly sank until she was sitting on the concrete with her back to the wall. I folded down to Indian-sit beside her. Her face was in the shadows but when a car sailed by a pale white searchlight swept over her features. Her eyes were swollen and the skin on her cheeks mottled.

"Where did—"

"We went over to Seminole," she cut in. "You remember when I told you about Wally knowing this guy who knew a doctor?"

"The abortion? Y'all went to get an abortion? Already? I brought the money if you needed it. How—"

"Wally pawned his guitar."

"Did you . . . get one?"

"It turned out his friend only knew of somebody who knew of somebody. We were supposed to go first to a drug store and call a number from the phone booth inside. When we did that, somebody on the other end told Sharon to go to this particular street corner. When we got there, she was supposed to wait for a while, and then somebody would drive up and ask if she was the party with the package, and she was supposed to say she was looking for Mr. Lumpkin. It was all very cloak and dagger." She toyed with the lighted end of her cigarette, shaping it to a point against the concrete. "We found the corner out on the edge of town in this rundown neighborhood. Sharon said we'd have to give this Lumpkin guy a deposit."

"How much?"

"Half of it. A hundred fifty."

"I brought my money if you want to pay Wally back." It seemed urgent that I establish I'd done this. "Or if you need it for anything, anything at all."

"You're sweet." But my reward was perfunctory and she seemed to be brooding.

"Then what?"

"We waited a while. Can you imagine what all this was doing to Sharon's nerves? Anyway, this car drove up, and the guy in it pulled right up to Wally's window and asked if we were looking for Mr. Lumpkin. Wally said yes. Then the guy said, 'Where's the girlie with the package?' Wally pointed to the back seat. The guy got out of his car and stuck his head through Wally's window. 'You the one?' he asked Sharon. She said yeah. And he said, 'Got yourself a heavy package that needs delivered, do you?' She said yeah again. And he said, 'You got shipping money?' She got the bills out of her purse and said, 'A hundred and fifty, right?' He said, 'You were supposed to be alone. A crowd makes the post-man nervous. He wants two hundred fifty right now, the rest when the package gets sent.'"

"Who was this guy?"

"He had on tan khakis and brown Wellington boots and a yellow nylon see-through shirt, had a flat-top and smoked Luckies. Horseshoe ring on his left middle finger." Trudy touched that knuckle with the fingers of her other hand. "He was about six feet and maybe one-ninety. Somewhere in his forties, I'd guess. The way he kept saying 'package' with a little sneer made me nervous, so I took a good close look."

"You think he was a doctor or something?"

Trudy scoffed. "I think he was a con man who despises women."

"Why? What happened?"

"He told Sharon to get into his car. It was a '54 Olds hard-top, white over blue, in case anybody needs to know. This really made me nervous and Sharon had this sort of quiet doggedness she gets when things go wrong. It's like she's resigned and ducks her head and keeps on trudging forward right into that quick-sand. I kept telling her we could figure something else out, but she kept saying, 'No, I've got to do something now!' and so she got out of our car and got into his. I yelled at this guy, I said, 'Where are you taking her?' He said they were going to 'the post office'—he had that smirk—and that we were supposed to wait there and he'd bring her back after she 'dropped off her package.'

"Well, you know how she is about asking for help. I kept saying, 'Sharon, don't you want us to come with you?' and the guy kept saying, 'You people weren't even supposed to be with her— you stay here!' but I kept seeing the look on her face as she was sitting in the guy's car. She was really scared and almost paralyzed, and I was about to raise hell and I was trying to get Wally to help me make this guy realize that Sharon was somebody that people cared about and we weren't going to let this complete stranger who obviously thought she was just another knocked-up tramp drive off with her like nobody gave a shit about her and he could treat her any damned way he pleased. I mean think about it—she was asking a stranger to do something illegal so she had no protection from the law. And if the guy was to rape her, she couldn't go to the police. She had no idea where she was or who she was with and she was going to let this guy take her to some other stranger who was going to poke around in her. I mean, they could do anything they wanted to her and she couldn't complain. I was trying to get her to think about this, and I kept saying, 'But Sharon, you need somebody with you!' The guy started to get mad at us, and he was saying, 'Well, you're the one with the problem, not me, I don't have to do this!' and leaning over Sharon and opening her door and trying to shove her out. She said, 'No! Go—let's go!' And so he took off.

"I made Wally follow him at a pretty good distance. It was a goose chase, really. We drove out of town a few miles, and then he started going down little country roads through the cotton fields. He must have turned a hundred times. It was so dark out there we had to use our lights. He knew we were following him. We kept driving, and when we came to this one corner, there was Sharon standing by the road. He kicked her out of the car.

"We had a pretty big fight. She thinks he was taking her to a doctor out in the country and that he decided not to when he saw us following them. I told her he was going to dump her, maybe after he'd, well, done whatever he wanted to. She's really pissed off at me."

"Trudy, maybe you saved her life! Even if he'd taken her to

this doctor, no telling what might have happened. You hear stories all the time!"

Her hand came up and her soft warm palm clapped gently over my cheek. She bent forward and her lips brushed mine. I was gratified to have consoled her.

She sighed. "Now I'm responsible. I promised to help her."

I pictured Trudy calling homes for unwed mothers, Trudy sitting at Sharon's side in the hospital dabbing Sharon's sweating brow, Trudy chauffeuring Sharon to the doctor's office, going for pickles and ice cream at midnight, etc.

"I guess I'd like for you to help, too."

"Sure! How? If you need more money than I brought, I can probably get some more."

"No, it's not money. I want you to stand by, I guess. In case."

"In case what?"

"I dunno. In case we need you."

"Sure." Easy enough. Be Prepared—my Boy Scout motto. A chauffeur?

"Okay. Fine. Thanks, Jimbo. You're a sweetheart."

She raised herself to her feet and I followed suit. "I've got to go talk to June and call Dot. Why don't you go convince Sharon she's better off without Waylan and anything or anybody associated with him."

"Sure," I agreed, though it was on the tip of my tongue that I too fit this category.

Sharon was curled in a fetal knot on her bed, her rounded rump to the door. She was wearing jeans and ballet slippers. The tails of her rumpled pink cotton blouse had worked out of her waistband to reveal the pale smooth skin of her back, the knobs on her spine making a long sad smile. One flattened hand was jammed between her thighs and the other lay under her cheek. I stayed on her blind side and eased onto the bed. She was no longer sobbing but her cheeks were wet. She staring fixedly into the space framed by the opened bathroom door, as if at the commode.

"Hey, Shar," I whispered. "Do you need anything? A Coke?" Shook her head.

"How about a beer?" No. "Do you want to talk?" Apparently not. "I don't want to bother you, but I'm worried about you. Trudy told me what happened. Can't I get you something? I brought that money you needed. You can pay Wally back with it or whatever."

After a moment, she asked, "Did you see Waylan today? Didn't you go some place with them?"

"We went to Sitting Bull Falls with the McIntyres and their kids."

She sniffled and squirmed into an upright slump against the headboard as if dragging herself into another mental mode. Then she blew her nose.

"Did y'all have a good time?"

"Oh, it was okay."

She stared at the ceiling for a moment. "So do you think he really did tell her about us?"

"Yeah."

She pulled her ankles toward her crotch so that her soles pressed against the insides of her thighs. She wiped her cheeks dry with the tips of her fingers, then used them to brush at her hair, snapping her head in tiny jerks to clear her ears of errant strands.

"Did he say anything to her about me, I mean about what I'm like or how he felt?"

I busied myself by going to the cooler and rummaging in the tepid thaw for a bottle of anything and found an Orange Crush. I hardly knew what to say. I wanted to be reassuring but not raise false hopes. An impossible task.

"I don't know for sure what he said to her." I went back to the bed and offered the bottle to her. She declined, then changed her mind and took it, sipped with her pale lips covering the little glass hole; I took the bottle back with the unbidden thought that she might be diseased. "I just know from listening to them that she knows."

"I wondered if he made me really small to her, like I was trash he picked up at a bar when he was too drunk to know what he was doing. Or I was somebody he was trying to help and I threw myself at him. Or we only did it once and it was my idea."

"I don't know what he told her."

"That hurts the most, to think about what he might be saying about me."

My guess was Uncle Waylan probably thought the less said the better. I knew the less I said the better.

"Especially considering what he told me about her," Sharon went on, "and she's the one he wound up picking! God knows what he's saying about me! He told me things about her that she'd die if she knew I knew them."

Were "these things" on the order of Aunt Vicky's nude vacu-uming? I hesitated to ask. But it seemed to animate Sharon to go on in this vein.

"Huh!" I said. "Like what?"

"She puts Hershey's chocolate syrup on him when she sucks him off."

I did not want to know this! "Maybe he's lying," I blurted out and instantly saw my mistake.

"Why would he lie? You think she's too high and mighty?"

"Aw no, it's not that! It's just he's a terrible liar—you ought to know that!"

"That's for sure. He's a lying bastard and a dirty son of a bitch! But I'm going to get him back." She stared into space, frowning. "I'm going to get him back, believe me."

I furtively wiped the lip of the bottle clean with a swatch of the bedspread then sipped from it.

"Do you think he told her I was pregnant?"

"I don't know."

"I doubt it. It sure wouldn't be much to his credit."

"He'd be afraid it would make her too mad, considering how they tried so hard to have their own baby."

Sharon snickered. "Yeah, well, tough titty! Have I got news for them!" She frowned and chewed on her thumbnail for a moment. "Where's Trudy?"

"Went to the office."

She fell silent and stared into space again with the intensity of a cat watching something invisible to humans. Then she said, "You know when I was with him I really didn't care what he did to me—rape me and slit my throat, it wouldn't matter."

"Gaw, Sharon! He's a liar, not a killer—come on!"

Sharon looked shocked. "Not Waylan, Jimbo."

"Oh."

"Did Trudy tell you what we're going to do?"

"No." Instantly, terror shimmered up my backbone: they had a plan? Leaving? Getting him back?

"She told me she was going to ask you to help."

"Oh, yeah, she did—yeah, I'll help!" I fairly babbled. "Sure, whatever y'all need!" I was uneasy to have signed a blank check, though.

"I guess right now I'm supposed to take a real hot bath." She rose from the bed, wearily, in stages, like someone getting up in the morning, and, dumbly, I held out my hand to help her as if she were an invalid. I cupped her elbow as we trudged to the bathroom, where she murmured "thanks" and gave me a strained smile before gently palming the door shut in my face.

THIRTY-ONE

Trudy came in hugging a brown paper bag. "Where's Sharon?"

I pointed to the bathroom. Water cascaded behind the door and you could smell steam.

Trudy set the bag on the desk, plunged her arms into it and brought out two motel towels, a pint of whiskey, something silver like a short welding rod, a spool of thread, a bottle of a clear liquid, and a jar of Vaseline.

"How is she?" Trudy twisted the cap on the whiskey bottle. I'd never seen Trudy drink hard liquor. She poured a tumbler about half full.

"Jimbo?"

"She's okay, I guess. She was crying but she stopped and wanted to talk about Uncle Waylan." I snagged her gaze then nodded at the items. A diabolical booby trap for him and Aunt Vicky? "She said she was going to get him back. She seemed pretty bent on that."

"Good!"

Carefully, as if it were a urine sample, Trudy carried the glass of whiskey to the bathroom, knocked once then opened the door and took the tumbler inside. I'd never known Sharon to drink straight whiskey either. Coming back out, Trudy called over her shoulder, "Keep the water hot as you can stand it, Sharon."

"What're you going to do?"

Sharon lifted a book off the desk, then she sat on the bed with her thigh pressed to mine and laid the book on our knees, as if it were a family photo album she planned to guide me through. She opened it to a page she'd marked with a slip of paper. "See this?"

I canted my head and glanced sideways: cross-section of a human female—sheaths of muscle, looped tubing and folds of tissue in exotic, horrifying hues of the red and purple family.

"Jimbo, look! It won't hurt you."

"Okay."

"Do you know anything about the human reproductive cycle or gestation?"

"Not much." Goofy, I sang, *First comes love, then comes marrrrriiage, then nine months and a baaabby carriage!* I cackled. "That's about it. Oh, yeah, and I know about the curse." I giggled. I felt jumpy, wished I had a tennis ball I could be tossing at the walls and snatching on the bounce.

"This is the uterus." She pointed to a lemon-shaped organ, then tapped a nail against what would be the stem tip. "There's the isthmus that leads to the opening, and that's also the cervix, and that leads to the vaginal canal."

I blushed. "Yes, Herr doktor Buschwackt! Der vaginal canal! Ja-wohl!" I did a "Heil Hitler" salute. Isthmus! Canal! What? A geography lesson?

"These are the Fallopian tubes, and they produce the eggs that the sperm fertilizes. When the egg is fertilized, it fixes itself to the wall of the uterus." Trudy was frowning at me, but I couldn't help myself: I was twitchy as a ten-year-old.

"Der uterus! Ya yah yah!"

"Right now the egg in Sharon's uterus is about the size of the end of your little finger."

I waggled my little pink digit, imagined a face drawn on the nail. "Hello!" I yelped. "Little Timmy Fingertip!"

"Sometimes they get dislodged. That's what happens in a miscarriage. That's what we'll try to do. We'll encourage her to miscarry. Then the body kind of flushes itself like it does when you get your period."

"I don't have periods!"

"You're lucky." Trudy slammed the book shut and clenched her jaw. I thought for a moment she was going to cry or belt me, and I suddenly felt very ashamed. I knew she wished then that I was five years older. I wanted to act mature but I felt out of control. "You're very lucky, Jimbo. A girl in the dorm last year got pregnant but none of us knew it, and she went to Lubbock to get an abortion and came back to school and the next thing we knew she was in the hospital. She almost waited too late to get help and the infection about killed her. I told myself that if that happened to me or somebody I loved I wasn't going into this blind and ignorant. You can be if you like; it's a luxury you can afford."

"Aw, I'm sorry. This makes me nervous, Trudy."

"I bet it makes me even more nervous."

I cleared my throat, adopted a serious demeanor. And the instant I shook off my antic humor, I started trembling. I was terrified of what I might be asked to do.

"Okay, what? I mean how would you do this?" I glanced at the window. The blinds were closed but the door wasn't locked.

"We're going to . . . introduce something into the uterus that will make it react."

"Introduce?" Had she used the right word? "What do you mean?"

Trudy set the book aside and went to the desk. When she sat back down she handed me a slender silver rod with a tiny hook on the end.

"It's a crochet needle. I got it from June."

Hair rose on the nape of my neck. "You're going to put this up there?"

"The smooth end. I'll tie some thread to the other."

"God, Trudy—won't it hurt?"

Trudy swung her face at me. Her brown eyes were swimming in tears and her lip was quivering. "I don't know, Jimbo. I hope not much, anyway. I mean, it's bound to, some. Even though I'll try to be really gentle and go a little at a time. Dot was a nurse in World War Two and she told me how to do it."

"Couldn't she come help?"

"She didn't volunteer, and I didn't want to ask or tell her any more and implicate her."

"Can't Sharon go to one of those homes?"

"She says it's too easy for her to picture Waylan going around later on looking for this kid and finding it or the kid coming to look for her and finding her."

"What about a doctor here, Trudy? This girl back in Dallas was supposed to be pregnant and I heard her folks took her to the family doctor and because she was supposed to have complications, they took care of it in the hospital."

"Yeah, well, I guess lots of nice rich girls with family doctors who've taken care of them for years probably don't have to drive around cotton fields in the dark of night looking for a greedy butcher to help. They can get a D&C in a safe and sterile environment, with an anesthetic. Find some reason to call it anything but what it is. Nice folks, you know, like the wife or daughter or sister of your district attorney or Baptist preacher, somebody like that."

"A dee-and-see?"

"Never mind."

We sat in silence. She bent over the book with her elbow on her thigh and her chin in her palm and leafed through the illustrations. I sensed that she wished she hadn't included me in her plans, that I was only another problem. She was disappointed in me, and I burned with humiliation to realize that. But there was more to my objection that merely my fear of the unknown and the forbidden.

"Trudy, I know this is going to sound really strange, but suppose Sal Paradise is right? You remember that first passage in *On the Road* you read to me in the car that day, about living and dying and passing from one state to the next, and coming back again and again to life from the other side? I've had this really weird feeling all day long that Cotton is right here." I waved around the room as if to point out his present position, but of course saw nothing. "And what if this baby, this egg in Sharon's womb, is his chance to come back?"

"Sal was hallucinating. He hadn't eaten in four days," said Trudy. But then she took my hand and held it in her lap. "I know this is hard. It's hard for me, too. And if it's true that Cotton can come back, he'll get plenty of chances later and time means nothing where he is."

"And what about Uncle Waylan? This kid is his, he—"

"It's not a kid, yet. And Sharon gave him a chance to stake a claim in this. He chose not to."

"He didn't believe her."

"He doesn't want to. It simplifies things for him to deny it."

"But everything is happening too fast. Maybe Sharon should sleep on this."

"What do you think she's been doing for a month and a half?"

Well, she couldn't have spent all that time considering an abortion. As late as last week she was dreaming that she and Waylan would start a family with little Timmy Fingertip. But I felt trapped into silence: any objection seemed a betrayal.

"Trudy, I love you."

I couldn't get her to lift her eyes from the book. "Trudy, I do

274

want to help. Tell me what you want, and I'll do it, I promise." I automatically signed the Boy Scout honor pledge with my first two fingers pressed together and my hand held up. "What happens then, what do we do then, after you, we, put the, uh, thing inside?"

"Mostly wait and hope for the best. Pray if you're not too hip."

"What will happen?"

"Dot said she should start cramping then she'll bleed."

"Bleed?" Against my will, I sounded alarmed.

"It's her system's way of purging itself."

She went to the bathroom again, knocked lightly and slipped through the door without waiting for a reply. After a moment their voices rose in a murmur; though no words were distinguishable, the tone was umistakably grave.

The book was heavy in my lap. I opened the front cover: the volume was not to be taken from the special collections section of her college library. Lord! A book thief to boot!

I tossed the book onto the desk. I wanted events to freeze so I could consider everything, but then again the last thing I wanted was to think about this. To pitch yourself off the high dive, you get up on it and you pace about, drumming up your courage, you yell at yourself Do it! Do it! Do it!, stir up your energy until it's swirling around like a leaf storm inside your body. We were on the verge of a life-threatening and very illegal act; or, rather, I had agreed to be an accomplice. Definitely not the mastermind. Usually when I had to make decisions about morality or ethics, I'd ask myself what would my parents do or say? What would be their opinion?

They would be outraged. But I believed also that it lay so completely outside their experience that their quick, judgmental response would be flimsy. I had to believe that if they had lived through this past month and knew as much about this situation as I, they wouldn't condemn us. If they were the compassionate and rational people that I believed them to be, they would understand why I agreed to help.

May the Intrinsic Mind forgive us, I murmured to myself. And may Cotton get another shot real soon.

Trudy stuck her head out of the bathroom door. "Jimbo, bring me a sheet."

I stripped off the bedspread, yanked the top sheet loose, gathered it up and passed the bundle to Trudy.

275

"I'm going to cover the windows," I said.

"Okay. Good."

She shut the door. I scooted the desk chair to the window, climbed up and hung the bedspread over the rod, bunched it up around the opening so that no light leaked out. Then I eased the door open like a thief checking the getaway route and surveyed the lot, the other rooms. Did Wally know what we were up to? Trudy must have talked to Dot from his phone, and she must have given June a reason to borrow a crochet needle.

Somebody's radio was on. Elvis. "Heartbreak Hotel." Heartbreak Motel, I thought. The moon was still rising, and the light made day for night on the lot.

I shut the door and jammed the chair up under the knob. What next? Boil water? Rip a sheet into strips?

Trudy's head appeared again. "Hand me the needle and the alcohol and the thread."

"Are you going to do this in there?"

"No, I'm sterilizing things."

"What about the lights?"

"I don't know yet."

"Are you going to use the bed?"

"Yes. I guess."

She ducked back inside the bathroom but left the door ajar. Splashing, then the glug-glug of water draining. I tried to picture an operating amphitheater; I turned on the overhead lights and the desk lamp, then I cleared the furniture back from the unmade bed. I tuned Trudy's radio to the 50,000-watt clear channel station in New Orleans—Moonglow With Martin was on—and I came into the middle of Thelonius Monk's "Round Midnight." I couldn't decide if that cool and melancholy mood was right for performing an abortion, but the sound might drown out our noises (such as?), and it seemed a better accompaniment than the banjo and mandolin hoe-down by Lester Flatt and Earl Scruggs I dialed past.

Sharon came out swaddled in the sheet, strands of damp hair plastered to her forehead, her cheeks rosy from the heated water; her arms were tucked under the material to tug it close about her neck, making her look like a mummy. She tried to smile encouragingly at me but her eyes darted off and I could see that she was suddenly shy and embarrassed. I thought of baptism or a pagan sacrifice.

Trudy, following her, said, "Go lie on the bed."

She looked uncertainly from one bed to the other, and I said, smiling, patting the mattress like a bell hop, "Here. This one. We got it ready for you."

She sat gingerly on the edge. Trudy was carrying the crochet needle and the bottle of alcohol. She opened the jar of Vaseline and balanced the silver rod across the top.

"Maybe I should have more whiskey," said Sharon.

We were hyper-aware of each individual motion. Sharon and I waited side by side on the bed while Trudy wove around the furniture to return to the bathroom for the tumbler; then she came back to the desk, not looking at us and her mouth forming a soundless whistle; then she unscrewed the cap on the whiskey bottle, tilted the neck against the tumbler, making a clinking sound, while Sharon cleared her throat and clenched her fists. This was like an odd communion service or that moment in the movies when the scientist gets the volunteer to test the new formula.

But while Sharon was drinking from the tumbler, gagging and coughing, I had an image of an old western where a cowbody has an arrow in his side and his cohorts are giving him whiskey before they cut it out.

"Turn out the overhead," said Trudy.

I did. Sharon scooted up on the bed, and Trudy lifted the shade off the desk lamp. When she did that, the light flared up wild all over the room and flashed us, flung unfamiliar shadows about everywhere that spooked us suddenly mute. It was as if an invisible photographer had just stolen a snapshot of us. We froze, Sharon half-reclining against the headboard, Trudy standing by the desk, me standing at the foot of the bed not knowing what next. We were a tableau for a long moment.

Sharon finally said, "Trudy I want this. Whatever happens, I'll thank you for trying. I'm ready."

Trudy blew out a lungful of pent-up breath. "Okay. Let's make a kind of tent with your sheet, okay sweetie?"

She arranged Sharon's body so that she lay across the towel-draped mattress with her hips on the edge and her legs spread and her feet stirruped on the two desk chairs. I turned my back to give them privacy, and they draped the sheet over Sharon's knees and the chairs. Trudy dragged the shadeless lamp down off the desk and set it on the floor beneath the tent. Now the room was dim but for a glow through the sheet that reminded me of Christmas luminarias. Trudy went to her knees and disappeared.

"What should I do?"

"Come hold my hand, Jimbo," said Sharon.

I knelt on the floor on the other side of the bed from Trudy, bent near Sharon's head and clasped her hand between my own. My face was close to hers. Her grip was strong, and she kept clenching my hand as if milking it, steadily, with a rhythm that might have matched her heartbeat. Trudy poked out from under the tent to reach up to the desk for the crochet hook. She dipped the smooth end into the Vaseline, then she ducked back under the sheet. The gearshift rod, I remembered, and Cotton's head squashed like. . . . My stomach swirled but I gritted my teeth and concentrated on Sharon's hand gripped in my own: she counted on me.

"I need your left hand, Sharon," Trudy said. Sharon's hand moved under the sheet to below her belly. "Hold right here."

I heard them both breathing. Light under the sheet made formless silhouettes. Then Sharon took a sharp breath. Trudy said, "I'm about where I need to start pushing a little, okay?"

"Okay!" Sharon gasped. Sharon's hand and face registered every motion Trudy made, and I read her winces and groans and her vise-gripping fingers like a terrible book. It was as if deep inside Sharon a clotted scab were being pried away from its anchoring tissue particle by particle.

"Sorry!" Trudy kept saying. "It won't be long! Be as still as you can."

"Does it hurt?" I asked.

Her head jittered up and down. She hissed, "Yesss!" Then gasped. "Go on, Trudy! Do it!"

Sharon stiffened and her hand clamped mine so hard that her nails cut into my palms. "Ooo!" she hissed. She bared her teeth. "Oooo aiii! Oww!" she cried, like, I realized, a woman in labor, her head thrashing while Trudy pleaded, "Be still, sweetie!"

"It'll be over soon," I murmured to her, like an expert.

"Almost there!"

Sharon's body went stiff as a wooden box; her eyes were squinted shut and her breath was stopped. Then she yelped, her hips convulsed up off the mattress, and Trudy said, "Okay, I think that's far enough."

Sharon sank back down. Her arms struggled free from the

straight-jacket of the wrapped sheet, and when her hands were clear she clapped them over her face. Her shoulders shook, then her torso, and she started weeping.

"Oh, he's going to hate this! God damn him!"

"Atta girl!" mumured Trudy.

"That dirty son-of-a-bitch!" Sharon yelled. "I hope to hell he just hates this!"

Then she burst into gasping sobs that made me want to run from the room; she pressed her hands against her face and tossed herself from side to side, her bawling winding around our heads like a police siren; I'd never heard anyone wail with such profound misery in my life; it came from the bottom of her feet and surged up through her gut and she was turned inside out, as if an awful festering thing she'd been keeping tight in a box for a long time had now gushed out like floodwater. I was dumbstruck. While she sobbed wildly, Trudy scrambled up beside her on the bed and grabbed her shoulders to still her thrashing, all the while cooing and shushing her, "Shh! shhh! Take it easy, baby, try not to move, sweetie! Oh, he will hate it, you know he'll hate it all right, believe me!"

This didn't console Sharon in the least.

THIRTY-
TWO

While Trudy rocked Sharon, I pulled the chair from under the doorknob and stepped outside. The moon had cocked itself up another notch in the sky but nothing else had changed: God was not rattling the heavens with wrathful thunder, and the stars were not reeling dizzily along their appointed courses. The police were not mobilizing, and Reverend Wright and his sheep were nowhere in sight.

For a moment, it seemed we'd gotten away scot-free, then I wondered if I weren't deluding myself: who knew what consequences—what punishments!—awaited around a corner?

My hands were shaking; my right palm was scored by three deep tender nail marks; one was seeping blood; I pressed on the cuts and winced, but the sight of my injury consoled me: it might immunize me from damnation.

I kept whispering, "Oh wow, oh wow!" as I feverishlly sucked on my Pall Mall. I didn't know what to feel. I was mostly relieved. But I knew something important had occurred though no sirens wailed across the sky. If we had done our job, a person would not become in the world, and the "survivors" wouldn't be the same. Sharon would not bear a child in a home for unwed mothers, Uncle Waylan would not be a father (of this child, at least), I would retain my own experience forever, or until senility had erased it from memory. But I couldn't say if it was "right" or "wrong" then. I thought that maybe I'd have to wait for years until the fallout had all fallen out, then I could tote up the pluses and minuses. (Four decades later I still have no answer.)

Yellow light splashed over my back and when I turned Trudy was peeking through the blinds. She'd removed the bedspread from the window. She crooked her finger at me.

Sharon was reclining on her side, propped up by one elbow, still swathed in the sheet. She had the air of someone receiving visitors. She smiled wanly but with welcome. Both lamps were on now, giving the room an ordinary, domestic air. Coming inside was like entering a hospital room, and my hands felt empty, as if I should have brought flowers or a magazine.

"How're you feeling?"

"Okay. I guess I was a pretty lousy patient."

Trudy said, "You were a trooper."

"Thanks y'all. Both of you."

"Aw it's okay," I said.

Sharon looked as if she might start crying again, and Trudy said, "Remember, we're only part way through, guys."

I groaned. "What now?"

"We wait."

"How long?"

Trudy shrugged. "I'm no expert."

Sharon asked, "You think I should jump up and down?"

"No," said Trudy. "Not with a crochet needle in your uterus."

It was 11:30 by now. Ella was singing that she gets too hun-ngrry for din-ner at eight. We decided to play Monopoly. Sharon was the shoe, I was banker and had the racing car, Trudy took the flat iron. The "Go To Jail" card had an especially sharp resonance for us. By 1:00 A.M. Trudy was a utilities magnate who also owned the west side of the board, I had the low purples with a house each and two oranges and Sharon had Park Place and a scattering of single properties that Trudy and I were eager to pry from her. When we'd hear a car come crunching into the court-yard and its lights would flick across our walls, we'd say "Wait!" or "Listen!" And we'd freeze for a second, then continue—after all, what were we guilty of, playing Monopoly? Was it illegal for Sharon to be wearing a crochet hook?

Sharon landed on Boardwalk and buying it almost wiped her out, so she sold Vermont Avenue to me for four times its going rate; as I was buying a hotel for it and one sister site, Sharon sat up straight, held her body very still.

"What?" asked Trudy.

"Maybe I just need to pee." Sharon gingerly eased off the bed and trundled with geisha steps. "Don't cheat," she tossed over her shoulder. "Trudy, watch him."

When Sharon shut the door, I squiggled my brows at Trudy—is it happening now?—but she shrugged. We sat mute on the bed, each gazing fixedly at a point six inches before our noses; Trudy's legs were crossed and both bare dusty feet were hands of a body clock ticking off the jitters under her skin.

"Trudy?" Sharon called.

"Yeah? I'm right here, cuz."

"Trudy, I'm bleeding—isn't that supposed to be good?"

I shivered; icy mice skittered up my spine.

"How much? Is it a lot?"

"You better come see."

Trudy bolted up and scrambled through the door. I checked my watch: 1:36 A.M. And twelve seconds. I branded the numbers on my brain; it seemed a crucial part of an elaborate procedure, the way a doctor performing an experimental brain operation for the first time would note the time upon commencing.

I got up and paced, peeked out the blinds. By now most of the regulars had returned from carousing and lights were on in the three rooms Wally reserved for his usual Saturday one-nighters, most of them bachelors who came in from ranches. The lot was full of vehicles; country music from three warring radios tuned to Odessa, Shreveport, and Tulsa boiled and coiled above the lot like smoke from a tire fire. Saturday nights at The Round-Up were pretty rowdy and usually by now Wally would have had to break up a fight. It worried me that I couldn't tell whether it was a fortuitous coincidence that we'd done this tonight or an unlucky roll of our dice.

Flushing water crashed and Sharon emerged, smiling sheepishly. "False alarm, I guess."

"Are you okay?" She nodded, but I peered over her shoulder at Trudy, trusting her to answer candidly. Trudy waggled her hand in the air, but I had no way of judging what "more or less" meant.

By 3:00 A.M. Trudy owned all the reds and yellows as well as the west side of the board, but I still clung to my purples and pinks, and Sharon was still alive by the luck of our unlucky lands on her hotel-filled resort on the Boardwalk down by the sea of Go.

Sharon kept distracting us by palming her abdomen as if testing for air pressure, frowning, hissing "ssss!" through her teeth. Twice between three and three-thirty she left off playing to go into the bathroom. Trudy I would freeze to hear the sink faucet squeak, the clank of the commode lid against the tank, then a muted rustling and the flush water's coughing glug.

Around four Sharon went to the bathroom and stayed for a long while; Trudy was on the verge of barging in when Sharon finally came out looking very pale.

"You okay?" asked Trudy.

"Mmm." Sharon had no sooner sat back down when she clenched her teeth. "Owww!" she howled. "Damn!" She clutched her abdomen. Trudy and I sat frozen, waiting.

"Are you cramping?" asked Trudy.

"I don't know," moaned Sharon as she tested herself for pain. "Something. It's aching."

"Like cramps do?" Trudy asked hopefully.

"I dunno. Sort of. But different. I think I'm swelling—is that good?"

"I hope so."

"You hope so?" I trusted Trudy so much as a female and a college student that it rattled me to be reminded she was winging this.

Sharon sat motionless for a long moment as if listening to a message from deep in her gut, her fingertips pressed to her stomach. She frowned, closed her eyes. Sweat broke out along her hairline, and her throat pulsed as she swallowed. She winced, took a quick breath between her teeth.

"Ow! Shit!" she yelled, then both hands clapped over her belly and she bowled over on her side across the board, sending the cards and houses and little red hotels skittering onto the bedspread. She convulsed and curled into a ball, rocked herself against the headboard. Her eyes were screwed shut and her cheek muscles were taut under her eye sockets. Her lips twisted and wrenched to show her gritted teeth.

"Are you sure you're supposed to leave that needle in there?" I asked Trudy. She ignored me. "Is that what you're supposed to do? Is that what Dot said?"

"Oh shit, Tru!" gasped Sharon. "It really hurts, oh, it hurts! Oww!"

"That's good, sweetie," gushed Trudy and leaned over her.

"Get some aspirin!" I yelped. I leaped from the bed. Sharon's yowling filled all the spaces of the room now. "Where's the aspirin? Let's give her some aspirin!"

"Oh shit it hurts, Tru!"

"I know, baby, I know," murmured Trudy. She stretched out behind Sharon and hurriedly spooned her, wrapped her arms about her while Sharon grunted and panted with the spasms of pain.

"Does it feel like regular cramps?"

Sharon's head waggled violently. "Worse!"

"Where's the aspirin? Don't y'all have aspirin? Give her some aspirin!"

"Quit yammering about the goddamned aspirin, James! Look in the bathroom, goddamnit!"

Trudy sounded half-hysterical, and that shook me to my shoes. If she flips out, who's in charge? Where's the nearest responsible adult?

I lunged for the bathroom, desperate to find something to ease Sharon's torture. Once a bunch of us Cub Scouts were playing football in the street after a den meeting, and Jerry Bradford's mutt got hit by a car and had its hind leg crushed, and it howled and dragged itself around in circles with the splintered back leg showing bone and scrawling a spiral of blood on the pavement while we stood gaping at it, dancing up and down, not knowing what to do, and I wanted to plug my ears that mutt was baying so piteously as if pleading, *Don't just stand there—do something!* I ran to get our den mother, Mrs. Rainey, and she sent Mr. Rainey out to look, and he ran into his garage and came out with a shovel and cracked the poor mutt's skull open with one big lick.

I shoved open the bathroom door, but then I reeled back at what I saw: the white porcelain rim of the commode was slathered and splashed scarlet with blood. The bowl was a chalice of pink water. In the trashcan lay soggy wads of blood-drenched tissue.

"God!" I hollered. "There's blood all over in here!"

My heart started hammering. Sharon would bleed to death if we didn't do something! I yanked open the medicine cabinet, located a bottle of Bayer's, shook out four aspirin. I poured a tumbler of water, keeping my gaze off the toilet, and hurried back with four aspirin in my palm.

Sharon was moaning and chanting, "It hurts! It hurts! It

hurts!" She rocked to and fro. Her fists were pressed to her stomach. Trudy had sat up and continued to purr consoling endearments and to stroke her back, but now she too looked bewildered and frightened.

"Sharon, take this." She opened her eyes and saw my extended palm with the four loose tablets before her nose, grasped them, tossed them down, gulped the water—as if I'd offered a magic potion, and, as much as I hoped aspirin would help, at bottom I knew it wouldn't do enough.

Sharon started groaning again, hissing, grunting, pushing her fists against her stomach.

"Trudy, there's blood all over the place in there!"

"Hush!" said Trudy, nodding vehemently toward Sharon. Don't scare her! As if Sharon didn't know her blood was spilled all over the fixtures in there!

"Shouldn't we take the needle out?" I asked Trudy. "Maybe that's what's causing all the blood? Did Dot say to leave the needle in? How far did you push it, anyway? Should you leave it in like that? Maybe you should take it out, what do you think, Trudy? You think maybe the needle punctured something, and—"

"Shut up, James!" roared Trudy. She held up her hand like a traffic cop then rubbed her forehead. "Yes! No! I don't know! Sharon, is it still hurting the same?"

"Uh-huh!"

"Trudy, the blood—"

"Okay, James! We heard you! Yes, all right, let's take the goddamned needle out!"

Trudy coaxed Sharon up and they stumbled together to the bathroom with Sharon moaning and doubled over with pain. I stood at the partly opened door, but Trudy had her back in the crack.

"Just stand right there," she told Sharon. "Hold on to me." Sharon was apparently straddling the commode, and I saw one arm come up and loop around Trudy's neck.

"It'll only take a second. You could probably do it easier than me."

The door was bumped almost closed and I couldn't see, but I heard Sharon say, "Okay. Oww! It's out."

"Throw it away!"

"It still hurts. Bad."

"Do you want to go back to the bed?"

"Just let me sit here. Oh shit, my hand's all bloody!"

Trudy turned to glare at me through the doorway.

"Out now! You happy?"

I felt unjustly accused of chickening out and thus guaranteeing the operation's failure by not allowing it to run its course. Trudy opened the door to come out, but stopped when Sharon started yelling.

"Oh shit, Trudy! It hurts like hell!" Sharon started bawling and leaned over and grabbed herself under the knees and rocked on the commode seat. Then she stopped suddenly and cried out to Trudy, "Oh oh oh help! Now I can feel it squirting out of me!"

"Hang on, sweetie!" Trudy almost knocked me down dashing to the phone.

"Nobody's on the switchboard," I said when she yanked it up and held it, puzzled, to her ear.

"I've got to talk to Dot!" Trudy ran out of the room, leaving the door wide open. Sharon's crying was so loud I was afraid everyone would hear, so I jumped up and shut the door. I felt abandoned and helpless and very afraid, then it flashed on me how much Sharon was feeling those things this instant, so I ran back to the bathroom.

I knelt beside the commode. Sharon was shivering, bent over, rocking herself, her blood-streaked hands gathering the sheet up under her chin, her fingerpads making stains on the white sheet that looked like crimson dog-paw prints. Her lips were blue. Shock, I thought. She's going into shock! Oh, shit! The Boy Scout handbook said lay them down with their feet above their head and keep them warm.

"Take it easy, Shar." I helplessly pat her shoulder. I was shaking all over but luckily she was oblivious to my condition. I tried to sound calm. "Trudy's gone to get help. I'm right here. Let's go lie on the bed."

"Hurts too much!"

When she sat up and moved a fold of the swaddling aside to rub at her belly, the sheet showed a beaded chain of blood roses arcing across it.

"But you need to!"

"Did she call Waylan?"

I almost said who? "Yeah, yeah, she called him." What possible good could he be to us right now? "Now come lie down, okay?"

I nagged and tugged her up from the commode and half carried her into the other room. Glistening threads of crimson trailed down the tops of her feet. I had just laid her back and was elevating her bloody feet when Trudy came bursting through the door looking frantic.

"Dot says we better take her in!"

THIRTY-THREE

Trudy and I leaped from the truck onto the floodlit emergency driveway and helped Sharon slide down from the seat; she left smears of red on the torn tan bench; the front of the sheet looked like a butcher's apron, and on the back where she'd sat was a huge rough blossom big as a bushel basket and so wet it blotched my arm when I passed my hand across her waist to help her.

Her eyes were rolling back, she was sinking limper by the second, so we had to hoist her between us while we banged on the door. It was a small hospital, and by this time—about 4:30—the resident on call had lain down for a nap and the admitting nurse had dropped her head into her arms at the desk.

The minute we were let in I felt a gigantic surge of relief to be safe in institutional hands, and the admitting nurse, Nancy Albright on her nametag, swiftly got Sharon onto a bed and rousted out another nurse and the groggy rumpled resident, a fat guy with a twelve-year-old's face like Pudge in the Superbubble comics.

Trudy stayed with them, and the nurse called me to the desk for paperwork. Though no one was in the waiting room, a Levi jacket was slung over one chair and I heard a masuline moan from deep within the building. I was still jangly from the breakneck drive, my heart was thudding, and I was supercharged from hyperventilating. I tried to act calm and casual as I fell into a chair beside the counter and, dizzy, knew that if I hadn't decided to sit right then or had started a millisecond later I wouldn't have landed on the cushion.

Name and address? For a second I thought she meant mine. I wondered if I should lie and instantly saw that our panic to get here had swept aside any thought to plot our stories. Before going on with this interview I wanted to ask the nurse to let me confer with my lawyer, that redheaded girl.

I gave her Sharon's name and The Round-Up Motel, #7, as the address.

"What's the matter with her?"

"She's bleeding!"

"When did it start?"

The nurse had a long thin nose and a hairdo that looked like a black swimming cap with feathery fringes, and she'd eaten off her lipstick while dozing, I guessed. She had piercing little black eyes that glittered with liveliness once she'd come sufficiently awake to take an interest in her surroundings.

"I say when did—"

"Uh, about two I guess. I don't know exactly." I wondered if I should say they'd called me only moments ago to bring them here. "We were sitting around playing Monopoly at their place and all of a sudden, she, Sharon—" I dipped my head toward the long dim corridor—"started crying from the pain and the next thing we knew there was all that blood." Blood that I could see gleaming in red ragged dimes on the floor near the counter and making a Gretel-like trail from here to the door.

"Huh." The nurse was writing with an automatic pencil and her lead broke so she stopped to rotate the cylinder and inspected the result with a cross-eyed scrutiny. "Was she pregnant?"

"Pregnant? Was she pregnant? Gee, I don't know!" I declared. "I really don't know them all that well."

She peered directly at me. She was standing at the counter to write, and her higher plane reminded me of a judge sitting behind his bench.

"Sometimes they say they were riding a horse or a bicycle or accidentally fell down some stairs."

They? The nurse had grouped Sharon with other hemor-ragettes, and I was intensely curious to know what qualified one to belong other than this shockingly copious bleeding: were "they" and their accomplices serving time now?

"No, no falls that I know of," I said finally. "I guess you ought to ask her."

"Oh, I'm sure the doctor will."

She continued to make entries. If the doctor was interviewing Sharon, then Nurse Albright's interrogation was gratuitous—satisfying her curiosity? Or were they doing a cop-shop Mutt & Jeff deal here to snag us in contradiction? I noticed now that she had one big pearly earclip with a fringe of metalwork like the brown lace on a fried egg. I saw the other lying loose on the floor in front of the counter, but I wasn't going to point it out. I ostentatiously leafed through an old *Life* magazine with Rita Hayworth on the cover; it was atop a stack in the red vinyl seat of the next chair. The furniture might have been salvaged from an old barbershop.

"Religion?"

"Excuse me?"

"What religion is she?"

Sharon had that little gold cross around her neck; her father had given it to her when she was ten, Trudy said, in a rare appearance between binges or wanderings, but I'd never heard her profess a denomination.

"Protestant, I guess."

Now this strange question scared me. Was Sharon near death? I was about to ask why she wanted to know when she asked, "Who is the responsible party?"

Responsible? "Beg your pardon?"

"Does she have Blue Cross?"

"I don't know. I don't think so."

"Who is the responsible party, then?"

I considered this. I hadn't thought long about it before a rage came boiling up from my gut. I slapped the magazine down and jumped to my feet.

"Put down first name Waylan, last name Kneu! That's K, N, E, U!"

She chuckled. "Waylan?"

She was acquainted with him. I wasn't going to ask why, where, or when.

"What's the address?"

"Do you have a phone I could use?"

She pointed to the black phone on the counter. I picked up the receiver and spun out the numbers on the dial and heard it ring maybe seven times before Uncle Waylan picked it up.

"Hawnh?"

"Uncle Waylan, this is Jimbo. I'm at the emergency room of the county hospital. You better get down here right away— Sharon's about to bleed to death and you need to come take care of it right this goddamned minute!"

I slammed down the phone. The windowpanes shivered from my blast. From the sidelong twisted grin the nurse was slyly offering I got the idea she relished Uncle Waylan's getting a comeuppance.

"What do you think the doctor's doing?" I was sweating and jumpy, and all my outrage had holed itself up in the caves of my blood and bones, counting the rounds of ammo left, breaking out the dynamite kegs and tossing up barricades.

"Trying to stop the bleeding, of course. Waylan's your uncle?"

"Is it hard to stop?"

"Depends."

"What on?"

She shrugged. I wanted to strangle her. "On what's causing it. But you can't tell me that, can you."

It wasn't a question. "You think she'll be okay?" I asked, though it gave her another chance to toy with me.

"That depends, too."

What a smart-ass! "Yeah, I'm his nephew, I'm afraid to say."

"Oh, now, he's not all bad."

I wasn't in a mood to hear the evidence she might have to the contrary and thought her ambivalence bewildering and wholly irrelevant: she must be another of his understanding women. I couldn't hear anyone crying or talking or walking in and out of the rooms down the hall, and I didn't know whether that was good or bad. I leaned into the counter and pushed my face as close to hers as I could without rudely violating her territory or scaring her with my nervous energy.

"Nurse Albright, would you please go back there and find out if Sharon's going to be okay? Okay? Please?"

"Why is he the responsible party?"

"Sharon's his office manager!"

"Oh! Was it a job-related accident?"

"Yeah! You could say that."

She clipped her pencil into the breast pocket of her smock and strode down the hall; her white shoes had thick crepe soles the color of art-gum erasers and gave off a muted squeak. I went to the windows to watch and to wait, and it seemed hardly seconds later that the dusty black Mercury was wheeling into the drive, the headlights splashing over my face. Aunt Vicky was with him. Behind me, a door squealed open, murmuring voices echoed in the hall, and I turned to see Trudy and the doctor and Nurse Albright trundling like a shaggy three-headed beast toward the desk.

Trudy walked right into my arms and buried her face in my neck. Her shoulders were shaking and I could hear her mewling. I held her and patted her back helplessly. Pudge and Nurse Albright held a whispered conference over the forms.

"She gonna be all right?" I asked. "I called Uncle Waylan."

Trudy's head bumped my chin twice when she nodded. "He said he's supposed to report it, like gunshot wounds and stuff, because it's illegal," she murmured against my chest. "She's okay, yeah, I mean she's not bleeding any more and he finished the job—he said he 'scoured her out'—so she won't get infected. What good can *he* do?" she said, and through the glass door I saw Uncle Waylan and Aunt Vicky cross the driveway. He had on jeans and a denim welder's shirt with the tails out and his hair stuck up stiff like a cockscomb; Aunt Vicky had a scarf tied over her head and was wearing a sleeveless white blouse and a red skirt and was hugging her arms as they walked in. I drew up tense all over. It was one thing to impulsively shout at him over the phone and still another to face him down.

"Jimbo, what the hell's going on?" roared Uncle Waylan.

My calves were quivering and my hands broke out in a sweat. I swallowed and licked my lips. "I called because, Uncle Waylan . . ."—my arm shot out straight but started trembling as I pointed down the hall, outraged, but also scared of him and scared I might start bawling—"because Sharon's back there about bleeding to death, and you need to take care of this!"

"What happened to her?" he asked me and Trudy, then turned to the doctor at the counter, who was observing with mild interest. "Doc, what's going on?"

"You family?"

"No, but he's the responsible party," said Nurse Albright. She lifted the form and tapped it with her pencil. "Says so right here, Waylan."

"Will somebody tell me what's—"

"She had a miscarriage," said Trudy. "And we'll thank you to pay the bill."

"Oh, Waylan!" gasped Aunt Vicky. She fell back into a chair.

"Me!? Why me?" Nobody spoke, but we all gave him a mute answer by our looks. "Oh, hell's bells! Why didn't she tell me, for God's sake!"

"Uncle Waylan," I said, "She did tell—"

"I mean tell me in a way that made me believe her, goddamnit!"

No one said anything. Then the doctor said to Nurse Albright, "Keep her down for a couple more hours. I'm beat." He gave the nurse a clipboard, waved to us all and turned down the hallway. I wondered if he'd actually report the attempted abortion. I wondered how many years you could get for it.

"How is she, Nancy? Is she going to be all right?" Now Uncle Waylan's brow was all squiggly with anxiety. "She's okay, isn't she?"

"A lot you care," said Trudy.

"She'll live," the nurse said.

It didn't sit well with Uncle Waylan to be the object of so much scorn. He kept slowly revolving in the center of the room like a lighthouse beacon, basting us with an expression of bewilderment and injury that said *Why is everybody always picking on me?* Then he glared at us.

"Hey, I take care of what's mine to take care of! How much is that damn bill?" He went for his wallet like Quick Draw McGraw, but Aunt Vicky stood and held his arm.

"Do it later, Waylan. You should go see the girl now."

"She doesn't want to see him," said Trudy.

"Let's say it's part of his payment," said Aunt Vicky.

"She's had punishment enough!" argued Trudy. She'd pulled away from my arms and planted herself in the mouth of the hall as if to stand guard. "She doesn't need to see him. Just let him take care of what he owes us."

"Trudy, dadgumit!" moaned Uncle Waylan. "I never meant for her to have to go through something like this, not in a million years! If I'd a known . . . ."

"What would you have done?" Aunt Vicky put in when he failed to finish his thought aloud.

"Well, damnit, I don't know, but it wouldn't be like this!" I thought maybe he meant it wouldn't be with a half dozen people glaring and making him feel guilty. "Now, Trudy, I need to let her know I'm here."

I glanced at Aunt Vicky. She'd sat back down and was looking out the glass door and past the lot where a faint glimmer of dawn was pushing over the lower rim of sky like a city burning far in the distance. Her jaw was clenched and unspilled tears formed a second surface on her eyes.

Uncle Waylan and Trudy stood in a face-off. For a second I thought he might shove her out of the way, and so I gulped back my fear and moved to her side ready to protect her. Then I saw from the hangdog anguish on his face that he really hoped to get her permission, because it would amount to approval or at least amnesty.

"It's okay," I told her. "We'll go, too."

She shrugged, then turned and led us down the hall about a hundred feet or so past a few rooms where patients lay sleeping. She opened a door to her left, and we walked into a room with pastel green cinder-block walls like those in the city jail. Sharon lay under a clean white sheet on a narrow metal bed. She was awake, and she was pale, very pale, but her eyes were red and puffy. You wouldn't think she could've had any more tears in her.

"You bastard!" Her lower lip quivered.

"Now, darlin', don't start in on me! If I'd a known you were in trouble, I'd a helped you I swear to God!"

He glided to the bed and tried to take her hand, but she snapped into a ball like a hedgehog with her back to him.

"Darlin', I didn't know!"

"Yes you did! I told you!"

"Well, yeah, I know, but—"

"But you thought I was lying? God, Waylan! You think I'd actually want any man I had to get by lying about such a thing! You think that little of me! You bastard!" She broke into furious sobs and pounded her fist against the mattress.

"I wish you would of told me—"

"I did!"

"Told me again, you know, louder! I'm so goldanged hard-headed, things don't always sink in right away, and—"

"Oh, you didn't want to know!"

"Now that's not right, darlin', of course I did, I—"

"We could've had a baby together, Waylan! Don't you see that?"

"Yeah, I see it, I know, I—"

"I hope you're happy!" She thrashed and flailed at the sheet covering her and finally spun herself over, raised up, shoved her furious face at him as if it were a branding iron. "I hope you're happy because I took care of it! You won't have to worry about that any more!"

"Oh, darlin', I wish I could—"

"I do not want anything from you, Waylan! I want to get out of your life, and I want you out of mine! You're a sorry son-ofabitch, and I pity your wife! You owe us for what we spent! That's all I want! And you tell that doctor not to go telling people why I'm here, do you understand? I better not have to explain this to anybody or your name is gonna get a lot of mention!"

She started crying again, then she lay back shuddering. When Uncle Waylan reached to lay his hand on her arm, Trudy elbowed him aside and wedged herself between them; she stroked Sharon's brow and began to murmur.

"Waylan, you've upset her," said Nurse Albright, entering the room. "I could hear her all the way up front. I'm going to give her a sedative."

"If you got a pill for the galloping dumbass, give me one of them," he muttered.

"Your case is terminal," she said calmly.

296

THIRTY-FOUR

Monday morning, fewer than twenty-four hours after Sharon checked out of the hospital, she and Trudy left for Dumas. Trudy and I held a feverish vigil at Sharon's bedside at #7 Sunday night, and while Sharon dozed in one bed we made desperate, furtive love under the sheet in the other; we didn't want to leave her, but we ached for the privacy to say good-bye and clung to one another all night.

By mutual agreement, I worked Monday and didn't take them to the bus station. After staying up all night, neither of us could have endured that parting. Despite not sleeping, though, I jammed a frenetic energy into work. We were sent to shovel a sludge of oil-drenched sand out of the bottom of a holding tank we entered through a bolt-lined hatchway, and when I punctured the muck with the point of my shovel and shoved it in to get a bite, the stuff clung like taffy and made a nasty wet smack when I heaved up a glob. The top of the tank was open, and the sun bore into the cylinder and bounced off its aluminum sides. The fumes made us dizzy and sick. Our boots sopped up goo the color of cockroaches.

I fought the sludge like an angry man, sweat gushing from my pores, stinging my eyes; I wanted to work myself into passing out, then maybe I'd wake up on the other side of my grief, where consciousness without the pain of loss was possible.

As soon as I came in from work and cleaned up, I called Dumas to see if Trudy had arrived. The woman who answered said Trudy couldn't come to the phone right then, but could she take a message?

My parents' son rose up in me to say, "Is this her mother? Hi! I'm Jimbo Proctor, ma'am. I'm a friend of hers she met in Hedorville. I'm sorry to intrude on your dinner or your family quiet time. I was calling to make sure she got home safely."

I was afraid that everyone and everything in Hedorville now had an unsavory reputation to Trudy's mother, but she said, "Why yes, I'm her mother. It was nice of you to call. I'll be sure to tell her."

My manners had apparently gotten me past her first line of defense. I wanted to ask, "Where is Trudy? Can I hold? Can she call me back?" but I was too bashful, and Trudy's mother left no opening. Did she know what I was to Trudy?

"Well, thanks, ma'am," I said. "Uh, good night."

"You're welcome. Goodbye."

It was six o'clock. An hour later in Texas. Uncle Waylan had already gone to Aunt Vicky's house, and I was facing my first night out of touch with Trudy since we officially fell in love in Ruidoso; we'd rarely gone a night without at least talking on the phone.

I paced inside the shop, even encouraged that weird, grizzled mutt to tag along (without success) as I trudged about in the junkyard, huffing breaths, making weird noises, snapping my fingers, for what seemed hours, though when I returned to the office to wait for her call, it was only six-fifteen. I thought there was a chance she'd called while I was burning off steam, but, then, I'd have heard the ring.

I watched the phone for forty-five minutes. Surely Trudy would call back. But maybe their phone stood in the center hall where everybody could eavesdrop, and her folks might be strict about long-distance calls.

I set my hand on the receiver. I wanted to call again. Maybe she'd be free to talk now. But then maybe her mom would think I was being a nuisance. Could I pretend to be somebody else? No. If her mother recognized my voice, she'd be suspicious from then on.

I walked from wall to wall inside the office for a bit. With Sharon gone, there'd been no secretary or dispatcher, so Uncle Waylan had sat here all day. On the desk papers were scattered like wind-tossed leaves, and the wastebasket was empty except for coffee grounds dumped out in a newspaper, so I knew he hadn't accomplished much.

I fretted for another hour or so. Around eight I decided to tell her mother that Trudy could call me collect. I cursed myself for not thinking of that sooner.

This time a man answered. I said, "Hello, sir? This is Jimbo Proctor calling from Hedorville, New Mexico, and I'm a friend of Trudy's. I called earlier and talked to her mother because I wanted to make sure she—Trudy, I mean—got home safe, safely, today, and I guess she did, but I wanted her to know she can call me here collect at Kneu Well Service any time. Collect." When my mouth uttered "Kneu Well Service" I realized I'd unintentionally but luckily stumbled onto a way to sound mature.

The man said, "She's out right now, but I'll sure let her know you called, Mr. Proctor. Does she have that number?"

I gave it to him, wondering if he now thought that Trudy and I had business to transact.

Then I fidgeted for another hour waiting for her to get home from being "out" and get the message and call collect. When my watch read 9:03, I translated it to Central time and wondered darkly where was this "out"? My stomach rubbed itself together and howled for mercy. I'd not eaten since lunch. I could take a truck and get something from the Dairy King, but I was afraid to leave the phone.

In the bunkhouse I looked into our refrigerator. Iddybit crept out from under Uncle Waylan's bed and tiptoed to the box to stand patiently by while I inspected the interior.

"What do you want?"

Silently, the mutt looked at me with its one good bulging brown marble.

"Godamighty, you're the ugliest damn dog on the planet, you know that?"

She waited.

"You poor sap. You're like all the rest of them, aren't you? Just waiting around hoping he'll notice you."

A six-pack of Hamms, a carton of Sharon's cottage cheese, a head of browning lettuce, a package of baloney whose pieces were dark and leathery on their rims. I trimmed off the dried perimeters of two slices, then cut them into wedges to fit on crackers. I cut another into thirds and tossed the pieces into Iddybit's bowl and she leaped to wolf them. I opened a beer and took it and the cracker sandwiches back to the office. While I babysat the phone and dampened the squawking in my stomach, I read at a newspaper but couldn't get past the first paragraph of any story. Ike would run again and wanted Congress to pass his foreign aid bill and had no criticism of Nixon as his running mate. Former President Harry Truman was prescribing "woodshed treatment" for "wayward youths." I noted this with interest because I had become one and seriously doubted that a few whacks on my fanny would discourage my errant behavior.

At 10:30, I clutched the phone again. 11:30 in Dumas. Trudy was still "out," or she'd come home and either hadn't gotten my message or didn't feel free to call. Or for some reason—what reason would that be?—she didn't want to talk to me.

It was imperative that I learn whether she'd been given the message. If I called again, what could I say? That a wild rumor was circulating here that Trudy'd been hurt in an accident and that I was calling again for the third time, I know, yes sir, yes ma'am, sorry about it! just to make sure this was only a rumor and that she'd arrived, uh, safely and was, uh, safe asleep in her own bed, sure hope I didn't wake anyone up!

At midnight I gave up and trudged into the bunkhouse and lay down. If she was home now, she probably didn't feel free to call. If she wasn't home, where would she be?

Maybe their phone was out of order.

Or maybe ours was out of order now!

I leaped out of bed and dashed into the office, lifted the receiver and heard a dial tone.

Back in the bunkhouse, I lay alone in the dark and worked myself up into a whimper that stung my eyes wet. Hundreds of pictures of Trudy swirled in the darkness, but eventually the day's hard hot work and the wear and tear on my emotions wore me down and I surrendered to a fitful, sweating sleep riddled by fragmentary dreams. In one Cotton and I were out in the fields with a crew and I took a 36" pipe wrench from the truck bed to use. It was so new the red paint on the long handle was still so fresh you could smell it, and Cotton complained, "Jimbo always gets the new stuff! It's not fair!" over and over to everybody else.

Uncle Waylan woke me only minutes after I'd dropped off, it seemed.

"Hey, Jimbo! You slept like a Russian."

He meant I never took my clothes off. I got up, groggy, heart-sick, and, while I toyed with breakfast at Runt and Dot's, Dot said, "Dang, Waylan, we miss that Trudy!"

Same job site, only now, day two of Trudy's having gone, I moped and groaned and felt completely listless. The shovel I would manage to embed in this gooey muck became glued upright so hard and fast that all I could do was lean on the handle the way you do a crutch and hope my weight would break something free.

"We gotta make that boy quit loping his mule," Pete cracked to Red and Slim. "He's turning puny right before our eyes."

"Aw, hell, Pete, what he needs is to get married," said Red.

"First time I ever heard you recommend that particular remedy," said Slim.

"It's the lesser of two evils. Just look at that pore youngster!"

They kept joking about my moonstruck exhaustion, my groggy fog of apathy, but I never rose to the bait. I worked only enough to keep from having to claim sickness and lie down. When lunch came, I crawled under the truck to nurse my wounds while the rest went to a nearby mesquite thicket. I no longer cared what they thought of me; I no longer wanted to impress anybody with how hard I could work. I was sick of work, sick of their stupid redneck jokes, sick of this place, sick of feeling heartbroken and exhausted. I decided this would be my last week and that starting tomorrow I would offer to (beg to) answer the phone, do a clerk's work, and clean up the shop during my remaining days.

I considered proposing to my mother either or both these plans: I go to high school in Canyon where Trudy attends college, or Trudy comes to live with us and goes to North Texas State or SMU, only blocks from our house, so she could easily walk to and from class.

When we came in from the field, I suspected Pete had a chat with Uncle Waylan about my performance, because Uncle Waylan drove me over to Aunt Vicky's to get the Mercury and said he wanted me to change the oil in it that evening. He either wanted to help me keep my mind off Trudy or he wanted to punish me for dogging it at work.

Alone in the quiet shop with all the crews gone home to their wives and children, I changed the car's oil as quietly as possible so I could hear the phone.

It didn't ring. I sat behind the wheel of the car and drank a beer. I got lightheaded because I hadn't eaten.

Didn't she even care enough about me to let me know how she was doing and to reassure me? I couldn't make myself to call again.

If she called now, I told myself, I'd let the phone ring for a while before answering it. Let her worry about where I was. Then, as an hour dragged on and the phone didn't ring, I couldn't stand waiting and fretting any longer. I strode into the bunkhouse, plucked the rest of the six-pack of Hamms from the refrigerator, and went back to the Merc. I fired it up and peeled away from the shop, slinging gravel against the tin walls. Now when Trudy called, the phone would ring in the hollow empty space of the office, and by God she could sit stewing on the other end as I'd done all last night and all day today and so far this night. It would serve her right to imagine the worst!

I drove aimlessly around town for awhile drinking the beer. I sat at the city park brooding. Cotton gone, Sharon's would-be kid gone, Trudy and Sharon gone. There was a reason—wasn't there?—why I'd been left. I looked into the sky, remembered the sky that night when Cotton and I had stood jawing outside the inn. If he were alive, I'd go pick him up and buy him a beer, I swear to God I would. I swear, God, I would. If he'd not been killed and he had come to Dallas to visit, I'd take him to a game at the Cotton Bowl and we'd cruise Forest Lane, and I'd introduce him to the girls I know. I swear I would! And now can I go?

Was it possible that my punishment for being among the living and for not thinking fast enough to save Cotton was to lose Trudy? After all, I'd stood by while he died and I'd helped kill Sharon's fetus. How could this not cost me something? Nothing was free! All debts must be paid sooner or later.

As twilight fell, I drove out to the Odessa highway. I tried to conjure up Trudy's face but everything in my memory had grown fuzzy. The person Trudy had been to me started to evaporate, and in her place came another phantom made of my fears. The boyfriend with the dirty fingernails—was it possible he'd had a manicure and had come calling in Dumas?

When she was here I'd felt secure of her love, but she seemed to have taken that with her. Maybe her love ended at the state line. Maybe she had already forgotten me or was trying to. Maybe she was angry about something I didn't know I'd said or done;

her silence was fraught with a thousand ambiguous possibilities, an agonizing emptiness into which I was far too free to pour myself. I was too young for her. I didn't know enough to keep her interested. And I didn't deserve to have her!

What if I loved her more than she loved me?

What if she was only making up stories about our going around the world?

What if she was trying to let me down easy and had gone home to see this old boyfriend?

Oh, how could I make her love me and keep her promises?

And she too had participated in giving Sharon an abortion. Were we Adam and Eve tossed out of our Garden of Eden? I mean even if she loved me too, would "fate" or "chance" or "luck" or God intervene to keep us apart forever? To even the score?

I had all the windows down, and the wind was whipping through the compartment like a gale, flapping my shirt collar against my cheek. Traffic was sporadic, and my lights cut a white swatch through the bug-speckled darkness as the road rushed under the carriage of the car. I jammed the gas pedal to the floor, thinking of being in a jet fighter and pulling back on the stick and lifting the nose and rocketing out of the earth's orbit and into deep dark space where Cotton lurked, hovering, always looking on with envy. Why me and not you? It isn't fair!

It'd be so easy to jerk the wheel left when a tanker comes roaring by. She'd cry and realize what she'd lost. The phone ringing in the empty office. Too late, goddamnit, just too goddamn late!

"Trudy! Trudy!" I bawled. "You've just got to love me!"

I reached up to clear my eyes of tears, and when I looked back to the road, the curve had lurched up unexpectedly and I snapped alert too late to amend any sort of mistake.

THIRTY-FIVE

When at last Trudy came to the phone the next night, I said, "Sorry I didn't call last night." I ached with the righteousness of being the martyr, since she had apparently not tried to call me once since being back in Dumas. It was big of me to apologize. "I would've called, but I was in a wreck." I chuckled.

On cue, she asked, "My God, Jimbo, are you okay?"

"Sure. Few scratches. Kinda banged up my ribs." I hoped she thought I was underplaying the true extent of my injuries.

"Did you go to the hospital?"

"Nah. They wanted me to, but it seemed like a waste of time and money."

"They?"

"The people who pulled me out of the car." I was tempted to add "right before it exploded" but that it was too easy a lie to catch, and it would be gilding the lily.

"Are you sure you're okay? Are you in bed? You know, sometimes people get injuries that don't show up until later. It'd be a good idea to get x-rays, Jimbo, really."

I glowed in her concern. "No, I'm fine." I pressed my bruised arm against the desk to make myself wince enough to be barely audible. "A little stiff and sore, but otherwise whole."

"Were you alone?"

"Yeah, in Uncle Waylan's Merc. Man, you ought to see it. It's completely totalled."

"How'd it happen?"

"Aw, hell, I was out at the State Line sopping up some brew and some dumb redneck started bragging about how fast his Chevy was. I got to thinking about that trip that Sal and Dean Moriarity make from Denver to Chicago, you remember? in that Cadillac limo that the rich guy has paid them to drive, and Dean keeps getting into races with people and drives so fast that the speedometer breaks? And they pick up hitchhikers, the college boys, who are scared shitless because he's driving like a maniac?"

I was hoping to hear a response that matched all the pathetic ploys I'd packed into that one small burst—I'm like the guys in *On the Road*, so you have to love me! And aren't you worried about my devil-may-care air? I could lose my life on a lark!

But when she didn't respond, I felt compelled to stack the bullshit even higher. I didn't know why I couldn't tell her the truth: that I was drunk but didn't realize it and was wallowing in self-pity and wasn't watching where I was going because I was too worried about whether she still loved me, and because it seemed only fair to throw myself into danger, to risk my neck, to give the something, someone, someforce a chance to make things equal.

"Well, anyway, I couldn't resist calling this redneck's bluff, and so we went out and went dragging, and soon as I started pulling ahead of him like I knew I would, he lost control and tapped my back bumper, and the Merc ran off the road and flipped about three times." I laughed. "Landed rightside up, though." Actually, it hadn't flipped—the car went sailing over a bar ditch and broke a barbed-wire fence and ploughed through a mesquite thicket and into the side of a tin stock tank. Knocked me silly for a while, but some people following had brought me back to Aunt Vicky's and she'd put an ice pack on the big blue lump on my forehead. The car was driveable but bent up here and there.

"Jimbo! You're crazy!"

"You know what Uncle Waylan said?"

"No."

I conjured up his whiskey baritone. "Only thing I want to know is did you outrun him or not, Jimbo?"

"You were lucky. And so were the people you didn't kill."

Replaying my story in my inner ear, it struck me that in Trudy's absence I'd become horribly juvenile, a far cry from the kind of person Trudy might admire. Why'd I want to scare her? I'd wanted to picture her sitting by the phone last night, biting her nails, pacing, picking up a magazine, trying to read, sighing, tossing it aside.

"What did you do last night? When I didn't call. Did you go out?"

"Read."

"What'd you read?"

"A book."

"Wise ass."

"It's by Camus. About existentialism."

"Oh," I said. "I've been reading, too," I lied. Since Trudy left, I'd been unable to concentrate; the printed word had a power of negative magnetism, instantly repelling my gaze. I was in a dither, my thoughts jittering and skittering crazily inside my skull.

"What're you reading?"

"*On the Road* again because it makes me think of you and our plans, you know? God, I can't wait, Trudy!"

"Jimbo, you're so sweet."

"And you're the smartest and most beautiful girl who ever lived."

"Shut up."

"I'm sorry if I made you worry."

"Don't do something like that again."

"Don't worry."

"Promise me you won't do it and I'll promise not to worry."

"I promise I won't do it." I shifted, bent closer to the desk and hugged the receiver as if to press myself through the sieve of the mouthpiece and burrow into her brain like an earwig. "Trudy, I miss you something awful. I love you, honey."

I waited, hearing the hum and crackle, the hiss and pop—the silence was anything but silent—of sunspots, cosmic rays, errant shortwave ejaculations, someone else's laughter as if at the bottom of a well, all this like a sound screen, while, holding my breath, straining to hear through the noise and beyond it, and at last she said, "I miss you too, Jimbo."

"Is everything okay?"

"You mean here?"

"With us."

"Yes."

"Why didn't you call last night?"

"I can't explain right now."

"Is somebody listening?"

"Uh-huh."

I collapsed with relief. This could explain so much!

"Why won't you write me?"

She laughed. "God, I've only been gone three days. Even if I'd written the day I got back—and I did write something—and mailed it, you still wouldn't have gotten it. Are you writing to me?"

"Yes." In truth, writing was as impossible as reading.

"I've written you something every day."

"Maybe I'll get it tomorrow."

"No, no, I haven't mailed anything yet."

This inexplicably struck cold fear in my heart. "Why not?"

"It's like a novel. Every time I try to end it, it keeps on going."

"So send me chapter one."

After a beat, she said, "Okay."

"I wish I had a picture of you. Do you have one you could send with it?"

"Oh, God, nothing I'd want you to see."

"Please?"

"I hate the way I look in photographs."

"I don't. I mean I know I wouldn't."

She muffled the phone with her hand, and I heard her call out, "Okay, just a minute!" Then, back in my ear: "I have to get off. Mom's home from church and she wants to use the phone."

"Okay. Trudy, I love you!" It was not a declaration; it was a demand for acknowledgment, a demand for her to recognize my state of vulnerability.

"Me too," she murmured quickly, and I could picture her mother advancing on Trudy and driving her love for me underground.

THIRTY-SIX

The next morning, I felt so blue that I invited myself to Aunt Vicky's for dinner. Uncle Waylan had trucked down to Jal overnight with a crew, and I'd been working in the office the past two days. The lump on my head had gone to yellow and receded, but my mirror reminded me of what stupid stuff I'd told Trudy and how stupid I'd been to drive drunk. That knot was a badge of stupidity.

I needed to spill my guts, and this might be my only chance: I planned to work Saturday until noon, draw my pay, then board a bus for Dallas via Dumas, and I had the retiring cop's fear of my luck imploding the last day of active duty.

Uncle Waylan's marital status was ambiguous. He'd spent two nights in a row at their house, but his clothes still hung in the bunkhouse, where, in my nights alone there flailing about in the dark, they seemed like limp skins shed by those who had deserted me. He claimed he and Aunt Vicky were "working things out," but it was hard to gauge the truth of that.

Aunt Vicky fixed my favorites—fried pork chops, mashed potatoes and gravy—and I tried to do the meal justice but didn't have an appetite. While I toyed with my food, she quizzed me on current events. Had I read or heard that Dr. King's bus boycott in Montgomery had forced the company into laying off workers after six months? No? What did I think of it? Did I know that the Senate had been fighting about cuts in military aid to Marshall Tito? I did know about Marshall Tito, and the odd little niche he occupied in our policy of containment, did I not? The Japanese were claiming that we were testing nuclear bombs at Bikini: was I aware of that?

I shook my head sadly.

"I'll let you off the hook this time," she said. "After all, you have been busy."

This clearly referred to my recent activities and to what Aunt Vicky jocularly called my "love life." The gleaming eye and smirk of sarcasm were softened by an underscoring chuckle.

"I do suppose you're aware that Elvis is going to be on "The Steve Allen Show" Sunday night."

"I heard Wally talking about it."

"Would you like to come to the McIntyres with us to watch?"

Though this event was of nation-shaking importance, staying until Sunday would mean another twenty-four hours without seeing Trudy. Also, Trudy's disdain of Elvis as a redneck who "flat-out stole black cats' music" would prevent me from enjoying the spectacle.

"I'm leaving Saturday, Aunt Vicky."

She nodded and sat mute and self-absorbed, brows crinkled, her gaze absently fixed on the small cityscape of condiments—salt and pepper shakers made of black and white glass and shaped like Scotties, bottle of A-1 sauce and Heinz catchup, a sugar bowl—huddled like a lunar outpost at the hub of the table. Then she brightened, shrugged, rose without picking up her scrap-littered plate, and said, "Shall we have brandy and cigars on the veranda?"

When we went out onto the patio, I noticed a girl's blue Schwinn with a wicker basket mounted on the handlebars; it was leaning against the fence. For a moment I thought someone was visiting her. I don't know why, but Trudy flashed to mind, as if Trudy had been hiding here since officially leaving town or had sneaked back to surprise me. Then I realized Aunt Vicky had been riding it. It seemed mysterious, that she'd be riding a bike.

I didn't know where to start talking. I sat dumb as a rock but agitated inside. She seemed to wait patiently. In the pale twilight air nighthawks were diving for insects, and the western sky was scarred with bloody streamers. The summer evening was a backdrop of silence on which the cries of children at play made a dim and comforting music. I could smell the fumes from the flares at the Phillips plant, meat burning on somebody's grill, the burgher's sacrifice, you might say. Beneath the placid surface of the dusk lay an undercurrent of unease, as if you could sense heat lightning but not yet see it.

"What do you hear from your friend?"

My heart syncopated a beat or two. "She says she's been writing a lot since she got back to Dumas. A novel," I declared proudly, though that was stretching what Trudy actually said.

"A novel? Really! She must be a very smart young woman."

"Oh, yeah, Aunt Vicky. She's about the smartest girl I ever ran across." I wanted to add that I wished they could have known one another, but that would call attention to why they hadn't.

"You must miss her."

"Oh, well, yeah." Her direct question startled me into flinging up my guard. My answer was so offhand that it suggested the mild condition of a man who suffers a loss with stoic bravery. Such a blasé dismissal of my pain seemed to lessen Trudy's importance, so I added, "Yeah, I do miss her. A lot. I'm going to stop and see her on my way home."

"Is she your first girlfriend?"

"No, I've had girlfriends before. But, you know. . . ." I flushed.

"You never loved them the way you do her."

"Yeah."

"Is what you like about her most that she's smart?"

"I don't know if that's the best thing. But it's sure a handy tool, her being that way."

Aunt Vicky smiled. "For emergencies? In case yours breaks down?"

"I suppose."

"I envy that mane of wild red hair and all those freckles. She has a very nice full figure, too. She's awfully cute."

"Yes ma'am! She's awfully cute! And ditto about her figure!"

"So your relationship isn't merely Platonic?"

"No."

"You're blushing. I better quit prying." Aunt Vicky grinned. "I really hope it works out for you, Jimbo." She looked as if she might say more but lit a cigarette instead.

I wanted her to query me, because I wanted to tell her my fears, but something in me lagged far back. I wanted to know if being in love always meant getting yourself into a state such as I was in Tuesday night, or was that peculiar to me? I also wondered if there were ways to make somebody love you back nonstop and eternally.

"I hope it works out, too," I joked. I waited a minute, then I said, "We're going around the world next summer."

"Around the world?"

"Yeah, you know, on the road like Kerouac's characters. Just me and Trudy. Hitchhike and sleep in hostels and in parks and such and climb to the very top of the Eiffel Tower. Carry everything on our backs in a pack. We're going to keep journals and write about things as we go. We'll get jobs washing dishes or whatever. I'm gonna take French again this fall to get ready." I felt reckless revealing this. I feared she'd next ask what any sensible adult might: what do your parents say?

"My god, how wonderful, Jimbo! That's about the most romantic thing I've ever heard."

"Really? You think it's a good idea?"

Alarmingly, Aunt Vicky's eyes teared up, but she wiped them with the heels of her hands and blotted her palms on her shorts. She smiled weakly. "It's about the best idea I could possibly think of."

"Great! I'm really glad you think so."

She dug into the pocket of her shorts for a tissue and used it to blow her nose.

"Aunt Vicky, do you believe that absence makes the heart grow fonder, like they say?"

"Are you worried about how distance will effect the way she feels about you?"

"Yes."

"Well, it will change things. It has to. But maybe in ways that will surprise you. Some of the dreaded things that happen turn out to be for the best in the long run and some things we wish for turn out to be more pain than they're worth."

"I'm afraid that she'll forget me when she gets back to college."

"Oh, I doubt that she'll ever forget you, Jimbo. Her feelings may change, yes. It might be that you'll be away from one another for several years and meet other people, but then some day you may meet again and get back together."

I wasn't hearing the answers I'd hoped for.

"I'm worried that maybe I don't deserve her."

"Oh, most people in love feel that way. Or they're supposed to, anyway."

"But maybe we did something wrong, you know, to Sharon . . . ."

She knew I wanted her judgment about it. She took a long while to decide what to say.

"I don't think it was wrong per se. I guess what bothers me is how nobody considered whether Waylan and I would have or could have raised this child."

"You really would have!?" My voice squeaked and I had to clear my throat.

"I really would have considered it."

"I don't think Sharon would have ever agreed to that!"

"No, she was far too angry. And that bothers me, too. Getting an abortion out of anger just to spite the father. It's not a decision that should be made that way any more than people should have a baby to save their marriage or without considering what kind of life it will have."

"She and Trudy would say there wasn't time." And, I thought, you said consider.

"No, I suppose not."

After another silence, she said, "James, what happens between you and Trudy is neither a reward nor a punishment of any kind. It's what the two of you make."

"How do you know when something is right or wrong?"

"It's hard. Sometimes I think it's the hardest thing I have to do. Good things sometimes result from bad intentions and bad things sometimes come from good intentions. Actions have unforeseen consquences, almost always, and they're often more important than the ones you'd intended or expected. And the tough part is that you've got to accept responsibility for what you do without knowing what the outcome will be: you have to make a pledge of responsibility for your actions whether your plans pan out or not."

"I wish to hell Cotton hadn't died, Aunt Vicky!" I blurted out. "And I wish I hadn't helped Trudy and Sharon. Everything seems so bloody!"

"You wouldn't do it again?"

"I don't know!"

"You know both the surgeon and the mercy killer can use the same knife. Maybe Sharon was Alexander cutting the Gordian knot."

When I looked blank, she rose and beckoned for me to follow her. In her office, she slipped a book from a shelf and read aloud a passage about Alexander the Great visiting the kingdom of Phrygia on his travels, where he was shown the chariot of King Gordius. The yoke of it was lashed to the pole by a knot whose ends were hidden, and legend said that only the true king of Asia could find the ends and untie it. Alexander pulled out his sword and whacked right through it.

"Sometimes it's so hard to tell where right and wrong are and where a problem starts and stops that all you can do is to act and hope for the best."

"Even if you do it only because you're frustrated and angry?"

Aunt Vicky sighed. "I don't know, James. Each situation has to be judged according to its circumstances. I guess you and Sharon and Trudy and Waylan will have to sort this one out as best you can."

She sat back on the sofa. Next to me. The coffee table held a cardboard box full of books. Several wall shelves had been cleared and the items put in boxes that sat under them.

"Well!" she declared, fanfaring a segue to a new mood and subject. "Are you looking forward to school starting?"

"Not really. How about you? Do teachers ever get tired of summer?"

"Oh yes! You wouldn't believe how tired I am of this particular one!"

"Well, it won't be long."

"Yes, it won't be long," she echoed. I couldn't tell if she agreed or mocked me in a way I didn't understand.

"What do you know about Yuma, Arizona?"

"Not much. Actually, nothing. Why?"

She picked up an atlas lying open on the coffee table. She flipped to a dogeared page and said, "Look." Her finger moved to the border between Arizona and Calfornia, down in the lower lefthand corner. We were hip to hip on the sofa, and she leaned close to show me. I flashed back to when Trudy and I had sat on the bed looking at the medical text. Aunt Vicky was wearing the wide-legged shorts, and the back of my hand inadvertently brushed her thigh. I felt oddly upset by this.

Yuma stood off the tip of her finger like an angular amoeba.

"It's where two rivers meet, the Colorado and the Gila. There's an Indian reservation, too."

"Huh."

"There's also a small college and a Marine Corps aviation facility.

The part I like best is this, though—look here." She guided my gaze to smaller print. "Gila Mountains, Copper Mountains, the Yuma Desert—don't those sound positively western to you?"

She fixed me with a searching look that bewildered me. It was as if she were speaking in a language I didn't understand about something of great urgency to her.

"There's a high school in Yuma."

I blinked. How was this news?

She shrugged after a moment. "Just a thought." She closed the atlas. "Did Waylan tell you that the school board isn't going to renew my contract."

"Oh, man! You're kidding me! Why? Because of our protest at the library?"

"Yes."

"That's not fair!" I wailed. "You weren't doing anything illegal no matter what they say! It's your right! Can't Uncle Waylan do something?"

She gave me another penetrating look. "Well, he could try, I suppose. I've got a hunch he thinks that this is a way for those silly charges to be dismissed. It's a tradeoff. If I acquiesce then my legal problems will go away."

"Oh man! Aren't you going to fight it?"

"Everything in me wants to, James. But not alone, I don't have the strength. Waylan also thinks it wouldn't hurt for me to stay barefoot and in the kitchen for a while. That's what he'd like. He swears it would make him a better husband."

"What are you going to do?"

"I don't know. It's very hard for me to consider being dependent in this . . . situation." Did I understand? Her arched brow was a curtain rising on a scene in Sharon's hospital room. "When I get balky and fuss about it, he tells me to be patient about the board's decision. He gets irritated. He thinks that because he rejected Sharon I have to be glad he chose me." She blushed and looked away. "He says I need to be more understanding."

I grinned. "I'd say you understand plenty now, Aunt Vicky."

"Yes." She absently reopened the atlas and idly leafed through the maps. "Thing is, James, I really need to teach, and not only to have an income and be independent. It feeds some need way down deep in me."

"I bet you're a really good one, Aunt Vicky."

"Think so?" She was smiling slyly. "How so?"

"Well, you've taught me many things."

"About what?"

My declaration had bubbled out of a fountain of good will and without forethought. But it was easy to extemporize.

"About how hard it is sometimes to do the right thing when nobody wants you to and when you don't know what it is for sure." I was thinking of how alone I felt and how small our group was at the library and of how much torment I had spent over what happened with Cotton and with Sharon. "And that there's a world out there that needs to be attended to." I waved vaguely toward the front door. "Lots of things about girls and women, too."

"Oh, really?" she chuckled, beaming. This was highly amusing, I could see. "Name some."

"I can't pin it down exactly, Aunt Vicky." I couldn't mention vacuuming in the nude, of course, or that business about the chocolate syrup. "But I guess I've learned that girls and women are complicated and full of surprises and that if you're going to understand one, you really have to pay attention. I'd guess you could say each one bears watching. Each one deserves close study."

She looped a long tan arm around my shoulders and leaned into me to smack my cheek with a damp kiss. Then she bounded up and strode toward the kitchen. "You may have learned those things, but I won't take the credit for teaching them," she called over her shoulder. "I believe I've got some dessert. I believe you like peach cobbler with vanilla ice cream."

"I believe I do."

I followed her into the kitchen and sat at the table while she cleared away our supper plates and then pulled the ice cream carton from the freezer and lifted off the foil from the dish of cobbler sitting on the stove. I smelled cinnamon and sugar; the fluted pastry rim on the Pyrex dish was browned and crisp. From under my tongue jets of saliva flooded my mouth. I was suddenly ravenous. I imagined my mother's cobbler and realized that I was about to run out of time to talk to Aunt Vicky.

"I don't understand everything, though, about girls and women."

"That's encouraging!" she boomed heartily and without sarcasm. "For instance?"

316

That's encouraging? She could say the most baffling things! After a moment, I ventured my follow-up. "Well, like that guy Robert."

She had started scooping out big globs of cobbler into two white bowls without respect for the integrity of the beribboned layer of pastry on top (my mother would have used a spatula and carefully lifted out retangles despite the liquid viscosity of the filling), and my implied question made her hesitate. But then she knocked the spoon against the bowl to tump over its gooey, stewy load.

"What about him?"

"Would you mind telling me why you guys didn't get married? Weren't you in love with each other?"

"Yes, I think so." She doled out one tablespoon of ice cream to top off one serving—hers, I hoped. "I guess I ran out of patience, got tired of waiting and waiting and waiting for him— we're talking about five years, here—to stand up to his mother."

"Didn't she like you?"

"Oh, she had nothing against me personally. But she was jealous of anyone who might take her precious boy away. His father died when he was ten, and he was an only child. She didn't want him to move out of her house and she didn't want any other woman to move in with them."

"Are you sorry you didn't wait longer?" I knew this was an extremely personal question and I asked it in a quiet rush that might allow her to pretend I hadn't. But I felt compelled to ask for reasons unknown to me. (No doubt I was worrying about whether Trudy would wait for me.)

She shrugged, then gouged out a satisfactory baseball of ice cream and perched it atop the cobbler heaped in the other dish.

"Yes and no. The irony of the situation annoys me."

"What do you mean?"

"I think that his losing me pushed Robert into action, so his present bonny bride got the benefit of it."

"Did you hope that leaving him was going to make him marry you?"

"I'm not sure. I guess when I was at the end of my rope I was willing for either thing to happen. I came all the way out here, you know. I didn't exactly make myself accessible. Some days I'd imagine that he'd show up to claim me and I'd welcome it and then other days I simply wouldn't give a hoot. Then I met

Waylan, and of course Robert just went pffft!" She flipped her fingers in the air; their tips burst open like flower petals in accelerated film.

This is what happened to the "love" Aunt Vicky felt for this Robert? Pfffft!

That little hiss of air that escapes when you put the nozzle to your tire, that brief, insubstantial whisper escaping instantly into the diluting atmosphere—it becomes as wholly lost and irretrievable as a glass of water poured into the ocean! It was enough to give me a heart attack!

"I'd hate for you to go teach in Yuma, Arizona," I said as she put the bowl before me, then, tantalizingly, made me wait while she put hers down, and, belatedly, opened the silverware drawer to retrieve a spoon for each of us. She held the two spoons in her grip and still didn't sit but instead filled a green glass Woolworth's mug with coffee, looked at me—did I want coffee? and I shook my head—lifted a carton of half and half from the refrigerator and set it on the table. In the interim, my ice cream moon was making a smooth glassine liquid globe of its own surface. I had no spoon, and even if I had, manners would prevent me from digging in until she sat.

"Why is that?"

"I like having you as an aunt."

"I like having you as a nephew. Not to worry, no one's done anything irrevocable yet. I'm sure everything will work out."

I could tell this was a parent's reassurance to a child that above me in the clouds where gods tended to the stability and order of human events all was well. I was vaguely insulted that she thought so little of my new maturity that she'd try papering over the cracks with such transparent stuff. She'd grown unwilling to talk about her love life with me. I doubted that I'd get straight answers were I to persist.

Yet I was no closer to solving the mystery of how or why people fall out of love. The phrase suggested that you were riding on a vehicle called "love" and that you "fell"—kerplunk!—out, down, to the ground, landing somewhere below or beyond where you'd been. When you "fell in" love, it would be like tripping in the dark into a hole or a pit, but when you "fell out," you were falling from a point of transport above. You went down in both cases. Like food—in at the top and out at the bottom. This was hard to fathom and to articulate clearly enough to ask about. There was also the question of volition: you didn't "jump" in or out of love; it was a "fall," like a household accident off a ladder or down the cellar stairs—not, in either case, of your choosing. The first time I saw Trudy behind the counter at Dot's she was like someone from another planet, smoking those Kools and dressed in overalls and using words such as "copasetic," and if anybody'd told me then that she'd be the girl I'd fall headlong in love with I'd have said you're crazy.

Aunt Vicky had grown tired of waiting for Robert. Had she warned him? Given him an ultimatum, a time table? Had there been a particular moment when she reached what transatlantic pilots called the point of no return? Something he said or did? Wiping his nose with the back of his hand or misusing a word one too many times? And she then "fell" out of love? Pffft! Perhaps when she moved out here there were days when she'd imagine him coming to reclaim her, but in truth their love was like a gyroscope that had received its last boosting spin and had begun to churn all wobbly.

I couldn't ask any more. Not only did I feel I'd be crossing a line that protected her privacy and separated us as adult and child, I was afraid of what I'd hear.

Working away at my cream-drenched cobbler, I kept hearing Pssst!—once in the brief spat from the kitchen faucet when she flung on the tap to dash her coffee with water, another time in the odd scrape of shrub across the brickwork under the window at my elbow: the very woodwork was trying to signal me. Or mock me. Pfffft!

My stomach lurched about a half-cup through my two-cup portion of cobbler, and I had to back off from the job a second. I felt that swooning nausea that results when the insatiable sweet tooth meets the unfinishable portion, but I'd go on to eat this dish beyond hunger and then beyond any semblance of appetite, eat it as a kind of strange punishment, eat until the bowl was empty, and I'd still be looking hungrily about for edible substances.

Aunt Vicky was standing at the sink, her loins and her flat abdomen pressed to the countertop, one hand fisted on her hip, the mug curled in the other lifted to chin level but not to her lips. She'd left a cigarette smoldering in the ashtray on the table and had walked away from the syrupy muck heaped high in her bowl.

She was squinting—she who could turn her back on her own

cobbler—and was looking out the window as if someone had arrived to the curb. But when I glanced through the café curtain, the street was empty. A vacant, absent pass of her fingers across her brow to sweep her hair out of her eyes suggested she was long gone already. She looked like a stranger, and that angular profile made her seem a determined, steel-willed person. Superwoman, able to leap strong men in a single bound.

THIRTY-
SEVEN

Earlier on Thursday afternoon, before going to Aunt Vicky's, I drove to Buford Pharmacy to buy a "broken-heart locket." A single gold heart the size of a quarter had been halved in a zig-zag jagged way, and you and your lover each had a gold chain and one side of the heart to wear. When you put the parts side to side, the serration matched and the heart looked whole. Each side had the other's name engraved on it. That had to be done at the jewelry store, and I'd been afraid that the engraving wouldn't be finished before I left Saturday.

But I was able to pick them up after lunch as Uncle Waylan was driving me to the bus station. The clerk, Mrs. Sanford, beamed at me as she got me to check the scripted names. I'd had trouble deciding what Trudy's would name me. "Jimbo" seemed fine scrawled on a cowboy's belt but too colloquial for a gold heart locket. Trudy called me "James" only to sound stern or comical, as in "First to the Waldorf, then back to The Round-Up, James." What made up my mind was hearing her voice in my memory, whispering, *Oh Jimbo, yes, do that!*

When I got into the pickup carrying the two small white boxes, one gift-wrapped, Uncle Waylan asked, as I suspected, "Picked up something for your honey, did ya?" Iddybit was standing in his lap with her paws on his chest, and he was massaging her ears. Her eyelids were drooping.

"Yeah." I blushed.

"Well, you get a chance you might get a little present for your mother. Your sisters, too."

"Okay," I murmured. The last thing I wanted from him was advice on behavior toward females, be they mothers, daughters, sisters, girlfriends or wives. I was angry with him still. All week I had avoided talking to him about anything substantial. However, I was writhing in the peculiar grip of feeling guilty about damaging his prized automobile while simultaneously disapproving of how he treated Sharon and Aunt Vicky. I couldn't recall ever having to feel grateful for being forgiven by someone I didn't respect. (It was still another "first," and I was leaving Hedorville as I'd come: someone who keeps unexpectedly confronting his own experience.) The need to be forgiven made me look for reasons to excuse him, because as a villain he lacked the moral authority to absolve me.

"How long's Aunt Vicky going to be in Baltimore?" Unexpectedly, she'd asked Uncle Waylan to drive her to the airport in Midland yesterday, hardly twelve hours after I'd eaten with her.

"Don't know." He sighed. "She wasn't in a mood to clue me in. Seems like everybody's taking off on me." He smiled wryly.

Poor Uncle Waylan! "Well, you'll always have Iddybit, anyway."

"Yep." The cur had stretched out on her back beside his thigh to better enjoy having her belly scratched. "That's right, ain't it, darlin'? She's outlasted ever damn one of them. She was supposed to have been Noreen's pet, but Noreen never was one to take care of things."

When the bus station came into view, I said, "Uncle Waylan, you can let me out in front. I know you've got stuff to do."

"Hell's bells, Jimbo! I wouldn't do that!"

If he imagined that I was trying to spare him the effort, he was mistaken. He parked a few doors down from the station and hoisted my foot locker from the bed of the truck while I carried my duffel bag. Even after checking the locker and buying my ticket, fifteen minutes remained before the bus would arrive. He was set on keeping me company. To my mind the most useless clause in the social contract is that obligation to see someone off this way. To a person burning to leap into the future, the present was dead time, and those who occupied it mere moving corpses.

We sat in silence, smoking and watching others in the waiting room. He kept antsily crossing and recrossing his legs, tapping his boot heels on the lineoleum, clearing his throat, knocking the ash

322

off his cigarette every second or so, and when I realized that he was working up to a speech, my heart sank. Then I realized that I too was required by social convention to pretend to appreciate what he said, and, moreover, to thank him for this opportunity.

When the agent announced the arrival of the bus from El Paso to Amarillo, I leaped up.

"Well," said Uncle Waylan. He stood, laid one hand on my shoulder, half-turned me, grabbed my hand to shake it, pulled me close to his chest, and then he clapped my back in that awkward hug-shake males do when a handclasp is not enough and a hug would go too far.

"Well," I said back.

"Jimbo, darn it! I wish you didn't feel you have to go home! With the women gone, no telling what trouble we could get into!" He grinned. "And there's a big pile of work still got your name on it."

"I know, I know," I murmured. "That extra money would be nice. And I'm glad I got a chance to come out here and do that, Uncle Waylan. You and Aunt Vicky were really nice to me. Thanks a lot!"

"Aw, hell! Our pleasure!"

We were crabbing off sideways toward the entrance where the bus loomed so close to the building that the silvery side of it shut off the light and cast a gray pall over the interior of the room. The agent in a blue uniform shirt and dark blue cap shouldered through the door bringing in a cardboard box tied with rope and an invisible cloud of diesel fumes. The bus was idling fast. I thought we'd eased safely past the cusp of my departure without mentioning Trudy or Sharon or his marriage, but Uncle Waylan tugged me to a stop and forced me to look at him.

"Jimbo, I want you to know something. I ain't one bit proud of what happened between me and your Aunt Vicky and Sharon. It shames me to think about it, and I won't be sitting on a bar stool bragging of it, either. This is not how a man should behave. I wouldn't want you to think for one minute that what I did was a good example."

I cracked a nervous, painful grin, danced in place. I wanted out of there! "Don't do like you do, do like you say?"

He tried to smile back but he was too morose to let my off-hand joke close the subject. "Something like that." He started to get teary and I longed to bolt through the door and bound up the bus steps. "Thing is, you see, the love of a woman is the only true treasure a man can have."

"I'll remember that, thanks Uncle Waylan, see ya! Take care!" I bellowed over my shoulder as I dashed away, my duffle bag jouncing on my shoulder: good God! Was I never going to get away from him?!

I didn't look out the window when the bus pulled away. Once we reached cruising speed, I took my half of the locket and hung the fine gold chain around my neck, tucked the white box with Trudy's half-heart into my jeans pocket. My plan was for Trudy and me to be undressing each other, and when she unbuttoned my shirt, she'd see my half. Then she'd ask about it and I'd give her the one with my name.

I'm a ding-dong Daddy from Duuu—mas, and you oughta see me strut my stuff!

The Bob Wills tune kept sawing away in my skull like a half-tuned radio as the bus inch-wormed along the Llano Estacado. The route passed through tiny Hereford and Canyon, where Trudy went to college and where, as we passed, I imagined coming soon to finish high school. Then in Amarillo I got off one Greyhound, watched while my foot locker was routed on to Dallas, then, with the duffel potato-sacked on my shoulder, I boarded another bus minutes later for the short trip north to Trudy, Texas.

The bus stop in Dumas was actually a cafe and service station, and when I stepped off into High Plains dry, dusty heat in the late afternoon I saw no one I knew. But before I could make my way into the cafe and find a phone, Trudy pulled up in her family's big black Buick. She shoved the shift into park and leaped out, leaving the driver's door open and the motor running while she hugged and kissed me. She was wearing cut-off shorts and a big green t-shirt that set off her strawberry hair.

"Oh, darling," I whispered in her warm, pink, unadorned ear. I almost swooned with the sense of my adulthood to use this word here, now, arriving, meeting after being separated. "My darling, I've missed you!"

"Me too, Jimbo! Come on!"

324

We trunked my duffel, and I slid into the passenger's side. Moments later, at a Dairy Queen we sat in the car and drank cherry Cokes in too loud a quiet.

"How's Sharon?"

Trudy shrugged dismissively. "Gone."

"Really? Where?"

"She said California."

"California?" I chose Hollywood rather than San Francisco. Sharon might become a starlet but never a beatnik. "How come?"

"She said she wanted to start over." After a minute, Trudy snickered and added, "At square one, I guess. She said there's nothing here."

"Maybe not for her!" I wanted to make Trudy feel better about being deserted. "For me there's plenty! I could spend the rest of my life right here! I think it's a great place!"

"God, you're so sweet!" Without looking at me, she reached over and squeezed my hand.

When we pulled away from the drive-in, Trudy drove fast and jerky; you'd call it reckless if you thought she was showing off, but she was really only inattentive. I scooted over once to kiss her peachy cheek but it felt weird—unmanly—to be the one squeezed up close to the driver.

"God, I've missed you!"

"What'd you miss about me?"

"Oh, man! This a long list, Trudy!"

"We've got time."

"I don't know where to start. Okay, looking at you? Touching you, listening to you, talking to you, touching you—"

"You said that one already."

"Okay, well, only goes to show. Smelling you—"

"James!"

I laughed. Loosened up a little, I felt almost delirious with happiness to be in her presence, as if I'd downed a jug of champagne. "Kissing you. Licking you!"

"My word!" She mock-fanned herself with one hand. "I sound like a storehouse of sensual delights."

"Oh, you are!"

"Light me a cigarette, okay?"

I poked two Pall Malls between my lips and pushed in the lighter of the car. As I waited for it to pop out, I saw that we were on a road heading out of town past barren brown fields studded with pumping jacks dipping down for oil. Did Trudy's folks live in the country?

"What'd you miss about me?" I asked when I slipped the smoking cigarette between her lips.

"Hmmm," she said after a moment. "Your hands."

"My hands?"

"Yep. On all my needy places." She cocked her head, squinting against the upward curl of smoke. She reached up and scissored away the cigarette with two fingers. "And also there's the way you seem to feel that everything you encounter is so worthy of attention and appreciation."

I'd never heard anything of this sort said about me, and I puzzled over it then filed it away.

"I think I'll always remember that," she said.

She arced the wheel and the windshield gave me a vista that overlooked a valley. We'd turned off the blacktop and had come down a caliche two-rut road that hugged the rim of a mesa, and when she stopped, we were on the promontory overlooking several miles of flat earth below. She didn't shut off the engine. I thought maybe we were only pausing, but she set the parking brake with her foot and turned the air-conditioner down one notch from full blast.

"This is where everybody parks."

Descending from the flanks of the mesa were ruddy palisades dropping into a valley where a river of sand snaked through pale green thickets of mesquite and salt cedars. The packed caliche around the car was littered with beer cans, butts and papers. Since it was after six o'clock but before nightfall, we were alone. We faced east, and the sun shot almost horizontally through the Buick's rear window. Outside, the heat radiated off the plains below in fume-like streamers, and overhead buzzards rose on invisible columns of rising heated air.

I was surprised that we'd come here first, but pleased. I was eager to have her notice my locket, then I could present the other half and put it around her neck and let it drape down in that damp and freckled place between her breasts I loved to kiss.

She scooted out from under the wheel and over to the passenger side.

"I've been thinking about you," she said.

We kissed and fondled one another until we were half-undressed. She had a condom in the glove box. We clambered óver the hump and fell into the back seat, me on top of her, between her legs, both of us sweating and lying in a slick wet wallow on the vinyl seat, my locket swinging now and then between us, but neither of us had an ounce of attention to spare for it. The afternoon light was yellow and strong on my back, the beams pumped up with motes and glistening on the red upholstery, but not even the urgency of wanting her so badly kept me from being worried that someone would drive up or that the car, still running, would lose its footing and hurl itself in wanton acceleration over the rim of the mesa.

Later we stepped out, each using a rear door, and stood under the large blue sky in the baking air to tuck ourselves in. The car between us went on idling quietly, faithfully. The bluff we stood on now threw a dark, spear-shaped shadow onto the land below. I tugged off the condom and, without looking, tossed it away onto the ground behind me. Then, just before I got back into the car, I was compelled to turn to see if I could spot it, saw it lying glittery wet and white, sand already clinging to the dampness, admist the older litter.

When we were back in the front seat, Trudy flicked the air conditioning back to high and released the brake. She shifted into reverse and turned toward me to twist her neck and look behind us. The exposed whites of her back-flung eyes showed red veins. I don't know why, but I wished we hadn't made love so quickly and furiously; I wished we'd waited.

"Are we going to your house now?"

"How about a really cold shake?"

"Great."

When she had the car back on the road for town, Trudy said, "What's the dealie around your neck?"

I grinned: talk about stepping into it! I wished she wasn't driving, though, so I could show her. "It's a heart, or half of one."

I pinched it between my fingers, held it out, remembering suddenly how she'd shown me her locket that night in Ruidoso. "Maybe you can't see what's on it."

She took her eyes off the road and squinted at it.

"It says Trudy," I told her.

"Awww!"

"You don't know about these?"

"These what?"

I thought I'd surprise her later at the restaurant or her house when I showed her the one she would wear. "Oh, it's just a fad."

But instead of going to a cafe or to her home, we went back to the Dairy Queen, only now early diners had pulled into the carhop stalls. We ordered chocolate shakes and sat in silence waiting for them. I kept thinking I'd get out her locket, but I wanted the moment to be special, and all the moments that were ticking by right then were poor crippled things unable to hobble to their feet. They couldn't sustain themselves, let alone play props for an important occasion.

It seemed we ought to have more to say, I thought, considering we'd been apart for a week. I'd imagined telling her about every minute I'd spent away from her and listening to her tell me the same. Now each thing I thought to tell seemed too insubstantial to bear the weight of her scrutiny or seemed too distant, even though it might have happened only yesterday.

Our silence seemed to have its own terrible momentum: the longer it lasted, the stronger it got, all the harder to break. We'd just made love, maybe desperately, trying to peel away that film that divided us each from the other, but now it seemed to grow back. She seemed a long way from me. I thought maybe this was only due to the strangeness of seeing one another after being separated, but I didn't know how to get us over or through it. She seemed different, as if she'd changed, not necessarily in respect to her feelings about me, but merely on her own, evolving, assimilating solitary experiences I knew nothing of but which had formed a newness that was the current Trudy.

"So what've you been doing? Your mom said you were out with friends."

Helping the carhop position the tray on the window excused her from answering, and she passed the hop a dollar bill, wrapped a glossy tissue around one coldly sweating glass and handed it to me.

"Reading and writing mostly. Arguing with her."

"About being out with your friends?"

"Not so much that. She's mad that I went off with Sharon to begin with."

Did that mean I'd automatically be in the doghouse? My hint

about "friends" hadn't inspired any exposition about her pals or what they did when they were "out." I wanted to hear her say she was dying for them to meet me.

"Where do you write?" As strange as this question might have sounded to her, I was fishing for an invitation to her house. I wanted to see her room, her desk, her bed. I wanted to meet her mother and father. I wanted to sit down to a dinner and show off my manners, maybe set aside her mother's misgivings about Trudy's having gone off with Sharon. I wanted to take away a vivid mental picture of Trudy's habitat, wanted to know the very aroma of her self that might pervade the fixtures of where she slept and read and dreamed (so I hoped) of me.

"Where?" She laughed. "Different places. There's a little park with a couple of picnic tables, and I've been going out there sometimes in the evenings. Too hot in the daytime. Dumas has no sidewalk cafes, that's for sure. I've sat in the library a couple afternoons but Miz Beekman gets all atwitter that 'a young person' would voluntarily set pencil to paper and wants to go through the stacks digging up supplementary materials for me like the thesaurus and Notable Quotes for inspiration."

"I thought maybe you wrote at your desk at home."

"Oh, I do. But my mother thinks a person who is reading and writing is actually only bored and needs something useful to do. She thinks it's her responsibility to fill my waking hours with practical stuff like learning how to use a pressure cooker."

"I'd like to meet her sometime."

"No, you wouldn't."

"No, really, Trudy! I'm good with mothers! I'm a regular Eddie Haskell!"

She smiled. "Okay. Sometime maybe."

For a long moment we seemed to be in a contest to determine who could take longer to lift a milkshake glass, put it to our lips, mouth a glop of the contents. Finally, I asked, "What are you writing about?"

She'd won by a large margin. And she ran up the score by taking still more time to complete her swallowing unit. "You didn't get my letter, did you?"

The way she glanced at me from the corner of her eyes made my heart stop. "What'd it say? Dear John?"

"No, of course not!" She leaned over and pecked my cheek; her lips were cold from the shake. "I told you it was like a novel."

"Are we the main characters?"

"Yes and no. Characters are characters, Jimbo."

"What happens to them? Do they hit the road and hitchhike around the world together?"

She shrugged. "I'd rather you read it."

"You don't want to spoil the ending?"

"Right. I don't want to spoil the ending."

THIRTY-
EIGHT

fter arriving in Hedorville, the letter must have languished in the stacks of incoming mail at the shop; not until early September did someone cross out the old address and write a "forward to" note on the large manila envelope.

Then the mailman discovered that it wouldn't fit in our box by the door, so he left a yellow slip in its place and took it back to the post office.

By this time, my senior year had started. Day after day I'd watched for the letter because she had referred to it in each of the two conversations I'd managed to have with her by phone. (I'd caught her only twice and had to explain my long-distance extravagance to my parents by admitting I had a "girlfriend.")

I presumed that it explained why she hadn't taken me to meet her parents or friends, and, instead, had coaxed me back onto the bus that very night. I ached to know whether she had another boyfriend or if we had a future. As I was stepping onto the bus, I'd given her the box with her half of the locket. I couldn't bear to watch her unwrap it, so I'd told her to open it later.

Was she wearing her half of the heart? I couldn't bring myself to ask on the phone, and in my increasingly painful letters I resorted to pathetic ploys: "Wearing my half of our heart makes me think of you always" and "I always know where my 'heart' is," but they failed to draw a response. My daily letters grew whiny and obsessively nostalgic, insisting that she remember this and that as if to remind her of clauses in a contract.

I furtively took the yellow slip to the post office myself, and, heart thundering and hands all damp with sweat, paid sixteen cents overdue postage. Then, because I didn't want to have to explain or describe it, I drove to a deserted park to read it.

Desert Stop, an excerpt from a novel by Trudy Wilson, ran twenty typewritten pages. The heroine, Billie, is driving an old "roadster" of unspecified make to California, where she hopes to become a rich Hollywood screenwriter. The car breaks down in tiny Sunrise, Arizona. There's a café/gas station, and Billie waits tables to pay for repairs. The auto shop is run by a vulgar, swaggering redneck, but he has a shy and handsome son about Billie's age. Joey's a sweet cowboy who aspires to ride broncs in a big rodeo up in Calgary, and he practices in a corral next to the cafe.

One evening after work, Billie watches Joey practice, one thing leads to another, and they pair up. He teaches her to ride horses, and they ride for hours in the wilderness. He teaches her the names of trees and desert creatures. They watch sunsets, and she teaches him celestial navigation and bebop jazz. She loves his wildness, his sweetness, how he makes everything he encounters seem worthy of appreciation. They make love, a first for both.

He wants her to stay in Sunrise and be his wife, but she can't forget her ambition to be a writer. Eventually, he feels he has to force her to choose between her love and her ambition, so they part.

However, the story ends when she's miles away from Sunrise heading for Los Angeles, and she realizes that having loved Joey has deepened her ambition. She no longer wants crass commercial success: she wants to capture the beauty of Joey's wilderness and to write about what the omniscient narrator calls "the transforming and redeeming power of love."

I checked the envelope. Had I overlooked something? I was profoundly disappointed. Not a word from the person who was "Trudy" to the person who was me.

I had absolutely no interest in the story's literary merit. I read it several times; the words were like a translucent screen upon which silhouettes played, and I wanted to rip it away to disclose the true shapes of the people behind it.

Did she intend for it to stand as an explanation of herself? I was so furious that this was all she had to "say" about us that I wanted to scream. Of course, I could see how that couple was similar to us, but the differences offered a wide latitude for revision: to me, so long as Billie wanted to write straight from the heart, she could do that just as well in Sunrise, Arizona, as Joey's wife as anywhere else! I sure wouldn't have stopped her! Here, sweetheart. Take this pen and paper and blow, man, blow!

It took many readings and weeks of worry, but the message in the story sank in. Not only was Billie moving on, she'd already changed when Joey saw her in Dumas. I was haunted by memories of my behavior when Sharon needed our help and knew that night marked the beginning of the end of Trudy's romantic regard for me.

I reheard snatches of our talk ("Oh God, you're so sweet!") and suddenly unearthed the underlying reality: Oh God, you're so nice and that's why you're boring! and Oh, God, you're much too young and innocent for me! And, of course, the clincher: Oh, God, you don't deserve the knife I'm about to stick in your back!

The truth sank in, sank me down, sat on me one night like a sumo wrestler, and I didn't leave my room for three days, just kept saying, "I'm sick, don't feel good!" when Mother asked why I was in bed. (Transforming power of love? Yes, like a poison "transforms.") "No, I don't need a doctor!" (Unless, of course, there was something to voodoo, after all!)

My parents couldn't distinguish my sulky sorrow from my general adolescent malaise, but since the phone calls stopped and I sent no more letters, they probably rightly guessed I'd been stunned by the death-ray of unrequited love.

It took years to see that poor hapless Joey had failed to recognize the essential integrity of Billie's self-determination (and self-doubt), attributes that had been present all along. The pressure Billie felt from Joey came not from him but within herself, and what he expressed was not so much his hope of containing her but rather the author's own fear of being trapped.

I've always wondered how she managed this conflict later in her adult life. By the time I got over my anger and pain a decade later and curiosity had driven me to find her, the only Wilson listed in the Dumas directory said Trudy's parents had moved to "somewhere in Utah" years before.

In the late 1960s I saw an AP wirephoto of Trudy standing in a picket line of teachers at San Francisco State. The cutline didn't identify the picketers, so I couldn't know for sure, but it certainly

looked like the Trudy I'd known plus a dozen years and a different wardrobe. Yet there was the possibility that my memories of
her had merely constructed such a future for her in this setting
and situation. Was she writing? Single, married, or divorced? Or
gay? Buried in my desk drawer, inside a cigar box along with old
campaign buttons, gnawed pencils and ink-dried pens, I keep my
half of the locket. It seemed a little foolish, but I did take a mag-
nifying glass to that photo in an effort to detect any jewelry
around "Trudy's" neck, but the closer you look at such a picture,
the more the image dissolves into a mesh of discrete gray dots.

THIRTY-NINE

It took even longer to hear from Aunt Vicky. In October, I got a card from Yuma, where she was teaching. *Dear Jimbo, No doubt you've heard from your Uncle Waylan that we're kaput.* (I hadn't, and if my parents knew, they hadn't told me!) *I couldn't wouldn't stay, and he couldn't wouldn't leave. It's very western here. I feel like Annie Oakley. Hope your school year's going well and that you keep your dreams intact even if your plans don't work out. Love, "Aunt" Vicky.*

I wanted to hide the card from my mother; I cringed to consider how many nimble evasions the information might require from me, and, too, by that time the events of the summer nested in my memory as a tangle of images whose powerful evocations of shame, desire, horror, and loss formed a, well, Gordian knot best kept hidden.

My mother read the card when she brought in the mail, and said, not on handing it to me but later, when it might seem that her information was gathered by tribal mental telegraphy and not by snooping, "Jimbo, did your Aunt Vicky ever say anything to you about her and your Uncle Waylan having marital trouble?"

"No."

We were all lounging in the living room following supper. She was embroidering a pillow case, little gold-winged bluebirds lining the cuff of it, the working area a circle about the size of a salad plate caught taut in a wooden hoop. She bent close, reading glasses perched upon the end of her nose, while I prayed her question wasn't the overture to a symphony of censure.

Or that she would ask me to explain the reference to "dreams and plans." My homecoming had been astonishingly unrewarding and unexpectedly empty; months later I was still nursing a private bewilderment that kept me from believing I had come back to where I'd started. It was as if my real parents and sisters and our home on Amherst had been whisked away in my absence and a mysterious arm of the government had installed an authentic mock-up with skilled imposters who knew the lines but somehow couldn't locate the precise inflection employed by the original players. I moped, sorrowed, holed up alone in my room which I'd stripped of all the puerile fixtures of boyhood—matchbook cover collections, model airplanes, pennants of baseball teams, comic books—and lay with my ear pressed to the speaker of my portable radio every midnight when Moonglow with Martin came on, my skull a hollow sounding chamber for Brubeck's "Blue Rondo a la Turk" and "Take Five." Desmond's wispy alto was a cool, melodic, taunting nag that I was nowhere near where or when I really wanted to be and might not get there soon. I drove the family's Oldsmobile late at night up and down McKinney Avenue slowly, windows open, smoking furtively, listening to the jazz flowing out the doors and windows of the clubs, and often I'd park and simply hang about the fronts watching musicians come and go and listening to their licks. I imagined Trudy right beside me and often included Cotton, too. I started growing a moustache and a goatee, which my mother "abhorred." I discovered *Downbeat* and *The Village Voice,* called my sisters and my teachers "man" regardless of their gender.

I came and went from the house without announcement, snarled and snapped at everyone. I nourished my alienation as if it were a religious faith Trudy and I had created together and which I had a duty to keep strong. There was so much about what I'd done that I couldn't and didn't wish to discuss; so much of me was hidden from the view of my family and teachers and acquaintances that they seemed like strangers, people who had no idea who I really was, and, yet, even while I dragged myself about in this slough of despair and alienation, I didn't wish to be grilled, debriefed, or coaxed out of hiding. I blamed them for not knowing me, for insisting I was the boy who'd left. My wrist shanks showed when I put on the old shirts in my closet and the shoulders were too tight; the coat on my Sunday suit wouldn't button, and all my old pants looked high-water stupid (did Trudy realize that while she knew me I was literally sprouting?); but even still they all seemed to disbelieve I was no longer me despite my new daily habit of shaving and despite the fifteen pounds of muscle I carried back home. I wanted to scream "I am no longer a nice boy!" I was stumbling about in an empty life as I mooned about the past and sky-larked of the future.

This is not to say that they didn't recognize that I was different. To them I had devolved into a perfect example of this relatively new breed "the moody teen." But it was, of course, "only a phase," a phrase they used that made me want to take an axe to them. To my dismay, my behavior was a source of joking pride that humiliated me. They melded my individual sorrow into a national malaise, speaking of me in third person even if I were within earshot as if my skulking were a harmless fad, an emotional hula hoop, the latest style (an internal accessory to match the mania for pink and black); by making me a mere sociological phenomenon, they made themselves members of a huge, mutually commiserating society of put-upon parents. They joked to their friends who were likewise afflicted by this new-fangled invention (Be the first on your block to own the new sulky adolescent!) "Oh, these teenagers!" they'd gush with a mock alarm that didn't hide their masochistic glee. "You know how they've got to have their privacy! Lord forbid that we might ask him where he's going!"

God forbid that my mother would use the postcard message from Aunt Vicky as a springboard into an investigation of the summer's events. *Hope you keep your dreams intact even if your plans don't work out.*

"Well!" declared my mother after biting off a honey-hued thread. I was slumped on the sofa pretending an interest in Ed Sullivan's show, where that stupid foreigner with the box that talked ("Sawright!") was drawing brays of jackass laughter from a herd of howling morons. Outside, a brisk hot wind peppered the window with oak leaves; Halloween would arrive at the end of the week and put an end to summer. On hearing this "Well!" I steeled myself. She could pack a lot into them.

"I said myself I didn't think she was Waylan's type."

Oh I hated her smug self-congratulation! How she was gloating! (Serves him right for being him!) I longed to contradict her.

I seethed with mute indignation at how she reduced what happened to Aunt Vicky and Uncle Waylan to the simple equation of class: "finer" manners, concern for education and culture, "higher" recreational pursuits and more fastidious scruples.

I hated it all the more because even with my thicker dossier on them, in trying to refute her I might be forced to say what I had thought in an unformed, hazy way the instant I'd read Aunt Vicky's card: she and Uncle Waylan had met at a time in their lives when each yearned to have a partner, but the shallow pool of available applicants precluded an ideal match. Didn't that amount to about the same thing as my mother's gloss on it? (And my mother became more right the older we both got.)

I wondered then about Aunt Vicky's giving me that lesson in geography: had she already taken the job in Yuma? Or was she only considering it? Was I supposed to have told Uncle Waylan that she was about to bolt? Was I supposed to talk her out of it? Or had she merely wanted me to know that she'd taken control of her destiny?

These and other questions I planned to ask her at Uncle Waylan's funeral (he died of lung cancer in 1995), but she sent word at the last minute from Seattle that her ancient mother-in-law was too ill to be left by herself. (Aunt Vicky retired from teaching in 1987, and she and her husband opened a bookstore that specialized in mysteries.)

But more than ask for answers to old questions, I wanted to tell her of something that happened that fall (and so I'm telling her now, I hope).

When I returned to school in my new identity as a beatnik manque, I was suddenly aware that my city had been embroiled the past year in a controversy of national proportions, a controversy to which I had been blind to because I hadn't been paying attention. (There is what I call the "red Taurus wagon" phenomenon—buy one and suddenly you see them everywhere.) The Dallas Museum of Art had agreed to sponsor "Sport in Art," an exhibition underwritten by Time, Inc., and *Sports Illustrated*, of work by eighty-five artists in various media celebrating athletics. After touring U.S. cities, the exhibition was to be sent by the U.S. Information Agency to Australia for the Olympics.

Prior to its arrival in Dallas, though, the exhibit was attacked by a local chapter of the American Legion, an organization called

The Dallas Patriotic Council, and another known as The Public Affairs Luncheon Club (a women's group sponsored by the famous reactionary and eccentric oil-man, H.L. Hunt). They demanded that four works be removed from the exhibit because the artists (Ben Shahn, Yasuo Kuniyosh, William Zorach, and Leon Kroll) were known communists or members of communist-front organizations. The attack was twofold. One thrust was at the artists ("The works of the Red hand and the black heart hating America do not deserve to be exhibited to our citizenship," said Colonel Alvin Owsley in a speech to the council. "Let those who would paint a Red picture supplant it with the Red, White, and Blue. White for purity, blue for fidelity as blue as our Texas bluebonnets.")

The second effort was aimed at drumming up resistance to all modern "isms" in art as subversive influences. Handbills and letters to the editor and broadside pamphlets and radio commentators insisted that since the origins of these "isms" were in eastern Europe, they were unhealthy "foreign" influences; they said that the social ferment in Europe following the first world war allowed artists to consider using their art as a means of holding power over the masses, so the artists invented mind-altering, morally debilitating art forms such as Cubism, Dadaism, Symbolism, Futurism, Expressionism, etc. As one letter-writer to the *Dallas Morning News* had it, "The more you try to find the subject in these paintings the fuzzier you get in the head, and this is the way the Communists want you to feel, for when you are feeling fuzzy in the head, you are ready for infiltration."

As absurdly laughable as these words sound now over forty years later, it would be risky to consider them neutered by time. (Think of Bob Dole at the Republican National Convention of 1996 saying that Hillary Clinton's book title *It Takes a Village to Raise a Child* expresses a "collectivist" idea.)

Due to efforts by curator Jerry Bywaters, the museum's board of trustees, and civic stalwarts such as Stanley Marcus, the show had nonetheless arrived during the spring (oh, where was I? It was astonishing to realize all this had gone on right under my nose!) and had opened at the museum in an atmosphere of tense conflict observed and recorded by *Art News, The New York Times,* and *Newsweek.* Because the show came to Dallas intact and went on untouched to other U.S. cities, the affair might have been considered a triumph of reason over fear, but the USIA. canceled plans to send it to Australia in the fall, apparently because of the charges that it was "subversive."

When I came back from Hedorville, this hurricane had passed. But it spawned a large tornado in its wake. In early November the Dallas Public Library mounted an exhibition of textiles by Max Ernst, Alexander Calder, Fernand Leget, and Picasso, among others. The library received what the local papers characterized as "a deluge of protests," and so the library director, James D. Meeks, removed two of Picasso's works from the show. His board supported him, calling the display "a mistake."

I followed the stories in the *Dallas Times Herald,* which I'd begun reading each morning in the school library before my first period. Naturally, the stories reminded me of Aunt Vicky and our protest. I wished she were present to lead another one. It was a shame we didn't have her around to stand up for free expression, I thought.

Subsequent articles revealed that the library board had decided to omit "all controversial art" from future shows, though the prohibition would not apply to books. The event quickly fanned the embers of the previous spring's controversy back into flame, and NBC sent "Today" show reporters and a camera crew to cover the story.

I thought of writing to Aunt Vicky. I guessed she'd read about this in her *New York Times,* or she might have a television set in Yuma, but, as much as I wanted to impress her with my interest in these events, I kept putting the letter off for a reason it took me a week to see: she would expect to hear what I was doing about it.

I floundered in planning, fretted on the sidelines. The textiles exhibit closed, the presidential elections brought Ike another term, and everyone seemed to turn their minds away from politics and toward Christmas. I was half-relieved that by the time I realized that I had a civic obligation to perform, the arena for it had closed. Next time, I thought. (And so I slipped into the comfort of duty deferred, Aunt Vicky.)

Just before school let out for the holidays an awards assembly was held in the gymnasium. It was on a Monday afternoon, and we'd be leaving for the Christmas holidays Wednesday noon. All our tests were over, and we planned to spend this shank of a week partying in class, exchanging gifts. The assembly was officially an opportunity for teachers to give out awards for the semester, but the choir sang "God Rest Ye Merry Gentlemen" and "We Three Kings" to open the hour, and the assistant principal, Miss Browning, not usually known as a cut-up, presided over the occasion wearing a Santa Claus cap.

We were dressed for winter, but it was hot in the gym, and the students in the bleachers were restless. You could hear scrambling about under the risers and giggling as pranksters supposedly searched for and retrieved dropped pens, wallets, or books. A dozen teachers and administrators were seated in metal folding chairs out on the gym floor, each taking a turn at a floor microphone that kept screeching. You could hear a muted thrum of saddle-oxford heels on the risers, and paper wads sailed from the upper rows to the backs of heads below. Smell of sloppy-joe sauce and athletes' foot powder, bubble-gum and chlorine.

I was absently following the proceedings with a jaded, cynical eye and with half my attention expended on the present and the other wondering what Trudy would be doing for the holidays. Mr. Baker, sponsor of the auto club and shop teacher, gave what he called "The Silver Piston Award" to Randy McClain for souping up his '47 Chevy; Mrs. Cox gave Joyce Malone a set of Pyrex measuring cups for winning first place in her "special desserts" bake-off (submissions to which were being sold in the hallway to benefit the Park Cities Baptist Church charity pantry); Mr. Goodman gave Johnny Masterson a "toga" his wife had sewn from a sheet to honor Johnny's making the highest marks in Latin II. Louise Bowen walked out onto the floor in one of those wide skirts with a poodle on it to accept a certificate for her typing skills. (She didn't seem the least hurt that I never called her after coming back; eventually she became a realtor and a Republican state senator from San Angelo.)

This was all intolerably square to me; it was painfully difficult for me to imagine that I was part of this place and time, that I had to endure coexistence with these peers.

I was all but completely in a stupor when a local watercolor landscape artist named Doriss Bagget got up to announce the awards in art, which he had been invited to judge.

He looked the part of a Bohemian—shaggy hair and a huge, Dali-esque moustache, khakis, a black turtleneck under a rumpled cordoroy coat with patches on the elbows. He was, at least, an unknown quantity, and looked enough like a Jules Feiffer character that his appearance alone made me tune in for a moment.

He held up a large oil painting in a gilded frame that must have cost a hundred collars. A horse, saddled but without a rider, stood in a pasture looking quite without expression toward the viewer.

This was the winning student entry in the contest, and Bagget said he was proud to award first prize to Amanda Vincent for her work "My Horse" and that he was especially proud that her art "shows no sign of the decadent taint of communism. This is good old healthy American realism."

I grinned; I thought he was joking, satirizing local critics, and I perked up. A hipster! A kindred spirit! He was going to gore somebody's ox here, and I was gleeful to witness it!

"I know many of you are probably aware of what went on this past year at our own museum. For years they've been ignoring Dallas artists because they know that our paintings and drawings won't create brainstorms that weaken people's ability to reason."

He delivered this line completely dead-pan, and I snickered out loud to let him know somebody out there understood irony. Not a one of the officials seated behind him was smiling. I looked about me and realized that a cloud of torpor hovered over the student body so thick and gray that Bagget could have confessed to diddling his six-year-old neice without creating a stir.

Maybe he heard my snicker. He smiled.

"You look at some of this modern stuff like Picasso's and you wonder if he's been chewing too many poppies from his garden."

Now he got some titters. Two teachers behind him smiled at that and nodded. Baggett took the stir in the crowd as encouragement. "They've got a work down there on display right now by some woman named Pereira that ought to be called 'Fried Egg by Moonlight.'"

Now the laughter was widespread: now everyone knew that this fellow was or could be funny, and they were ready to be entertained. Modern art was an easy target, a guaranteed thigh-slapper. And now I saw that I'd been terribly wrong about him. It was hard to believe that one artist would attack others this way, but he made several more jokes about modern art. It was my first time to hear the old saw about monkeys with crayons making a painting that sold for a million dollars, and then, when he'd gotten the full, sympathetic attention of the crowd, he must have thought he'd bought the right to preach.

"It would be nice if we could just laugh this stuff off the walls of all the museums," he said, "but the sad truth is it's really dangerous. That Pereira and her fried-egg painting is a member of twenty communist-front organizations. We American artists have got to hold fast to conservative principles of painting and to oppose these sensationalists, revolutionists and innovators of insidious isms."

If that had been all he said I wouldn't have felt such a strong compulsion to speak, Aunt Vicky, but this Bagget couldn't leave us with merely his opinion.

"If you students want to do your country a service, hear me out: every time your museum or your library puts up a show by these people, you let them know that you don't want your taxes to be used to support such garbage! That's your museum, and if you don't want the art of communists hanging on the walls, you should tell them how you feel!"

Surely Mr. Devere, our civics teacher, will say something? I thought. After all, he was sitting right behind Bagget and was listening with what appeared to be strained courtesy. Everyone seemed aware that Bagget was using this occasion inappropriately to air his political views, but since they were of the unimpeachably patriotic sort, he would be allowed to go unchallenged, just as he would had he chosen to lead us in a short but impromptu prayer.

Well, I can't tell you I caused a riot, Aunt Vicky, or that what I did got me a standing ovation. Baggett received a round of moderate applause when he stepped aside from the microphone, and Miss Browning moved over, leaned up to it, and said, more to be polite I believe than to corroborate his remarks, "Thank you, Mr. Bagget, for taking the time to teach us about the fascinating world of art."

I knew at that second that I could let this pass and simply stroll out of the assembly and home; that is, I could if I didn't know that I shouldn't. When people say they "made" themselves do something, it means work, and that's what I had to do: shout at my legs to straighten, tug at my body to stand, heave-ho like a Volga boatman with all of my will to create a very conspicuous visual image of a single person standing in a sea of his peers in the middle of many rows of bleachers. I had to let the backs of my knees rest against the bench I'd been sitting on to still their quavering.

I forced my arm and hand into the air. This was a completely unprecedented act in and of itself: no student in my memory had ever volunteered an unscheduled comment from the convention floor, you might say, particularly when it was obvious that within ten seconds we would be dismissed. I said, "Miss Browning? Miss Browning? May I say something?"

She looked puzzled and surprised, and a few of the faculty heads turned up.

She said, "Yes, James?" with a small frown: after handling Bagget's unexpected digression, who knew what she was in for now?

I was trembling all over and I could feel the collective attention of 250 students on me, students who had been gathering their satchels and lunch pails and violins and shrugging into their sweaters and coats as they itched and squirmed on the verge of being dismissed, students now surprised and annoyed to see a classmate not known for making himself conspicuous now deliberately retarding the end of the assembly for some weird reason. I pretended that you were sitting back behind me waiting and listening.

What I said wasn't earthshaking. "I just wanted to say to Mr. Bagget that, you know, freedom of speech and of all other kinds of expression is a really important part of our American heritage. I mean, even President Eisenhower dedicated the Museum of Modern Art in New York City, and he said in a speech at the opening of it that art is one of the pillars of liberty. When you have controversy, it means that you live in a healthy society. So it's not a good idea to tell people not to see or read or hear something, even if you don't care for it. People need to be able to make up their own minds. At least, that's what I think." I sat down, more to hide than to put a period on my speech.

"Thank you, James," said Mrs. Browning, as if I'd announced the time and place for a benefit car wash.

Everyone began filing out. I lumbered along in the teeming herd milling at the exits, staring straight ahead, aware by an internal antenna that people were putting a tad wider gap than usual between themselves and me.

I can tell you there were long-term consequences, short-term results. You sat on my shoulder as a conscience for the next several years, even as it became easier (because our whole generation turned to the task) to join the sit-ins at lunch counters and to march against the war in Vietnam.

As for the short-term results: three jocks were walking behind me as we shuffled to wedge through the gym door that day, and one said, "Hey, weirdo! You gonna be a pervert artist?"

I turned and, flexing my leftover muscles, said, cleverly, "No, I'm gonna hump your mother." The next day a new male teacher I didn't know approached me in the hall and said, "Good going," and walked away. I was sorry that my speech didn't get me invited to any parties, but I did get a note from the smartest person in our class (a girl, naturally) saying that she'd thought the very same thing and was really glad somebody had to guts to say it. I wrote her back and told her I'd learned to do that from an excellent teacher.